MW00614641

WATER FINDS A WAY

WATER FINDS A WAY

For information, address DELPHINIUM BOOKS, INC.,
1250 4th Avenue, 5th Floor
Santa Monica, California 90401
Library of Congress Cataloguing-in-Publication Data is
available on request.
ISBN 978-1-953002-41-9

Jacket design by Isaac Peterson
Jacket painting: John Lynch

WATER FINDS A WAY

a novel

Meghan Perry

Delphinium Books

For Logan and Liam;
may you find your way.

Prologue
1992

When Angel climbed the stairs to number 37B, Blake knew to take her clothes off in a hurry. She would fold them neatly atop the dresser beside her stuffed bear and schoolbooks and wait in her room that overlooked the old, dead mills, hair hanging black and loose the way he liked it, lips slick with strawberry balm. Most days, he hardly looked at her. She was a dependable toy. Shoving her face into the polka-dot sheets, he would grunt some ugly words, then stomp out to drop his pills in her mother's waiting hand. On those days, Blake got her homework done. She wrote out her compositions in her marble notebook and cooked *caldo verde* while her mother floated away on an opium river. On other days, when a deal had gone bad or some prettier girl had failed to pay him worship, Angel Salazar took his time with her. On those days, Blake wailed atonement into the sweaty clamp of his palm, and afterward, her brain felt too banged up for math problems or cooking. She would walk to the park and slump upon the rusted swings, creaking back and forth as the secret, tender parts of her body throbbed with the lesson of his keys and cigarettes.

It happened weeks after one of Angel's patient days, the May before Blake turned seventeen. She pissed on a drugstore stick and cracked apart a little at the seams. Once before, she had scraped up the money and brought it down to the basement on Ashmore Street with its stained subway tiles and its blinds drawn tight against the world. Afterward, she had gone home and bled, her departed father's rosary wound so tight around her wrist that the beads left tiny bruises. Since then, she had sent all those beads and prayers clattering three flights down to the Dumpster. But the deep red smell of the basement had leeched into her dreams, so, that spring, Blake fled north to a pair of old, long-waiting people and the refuge of a cold, unfurling sea.

1.

Present Day

Blake left the car on the edge of the road and took the driveway on foot. It was a rutted vestige of a driveway that spelled death to city cars in mud season. The wind carried curls of woodsmoke and a pervasive current of salt, and she walked with her head bent against it, hands stuffed in the pockets of her big coat, the black rope of her braid smacking at her back. Patches of late spring snow still clung to the shaded slope where blueberries once grew. A dark fringe of evergreens shivered icy dew as she passed beneath them. The land was familiar still. She remembered the lichen-splotched knuckles of granite that poked up from the hill like a tease to clumsy feet. When she reached the house, a silvered skeleton of a farmhouse with a sagging roof and boarded windows up top, she allowed herself to pause briefly and acknowledge its emptiness. Then she beat her way through a gauntlet of thorns that clawed her coat. Beneath her boots, rusting disks of beer cans broke apart in the weeds. The loiterers and revelers had all gone. There were only ruins.

Her ruins now. Her single inheritance.

In the rear yard, she found the shell of a rotted-out skiff where her grandmother had once planted marigolds—great buttons of tangerine and gold that bloomed all the way to first frost. She blinked away the memory. The birdbath had toppled and cracked in two. Beside the shed, her grandfather's wooden lobster traps sat decaying like a pile of old rib cages. She pressed past these relics, her eyes hard and determined, her heart an unrelenting drum.

The apple tree stood at the edge of the yard. It was a gnarled relic now whose tattered limbs still sported a few black, shriveled fruits. She knelt beneath it and pressed her fingers to the scarred bark, announcing herself. Then she worked them down to the base of the trunk and searched. Though weeds had engulfed the tiny slate marker, its etched initials had endured twenty-seven winters. She traced them once with a ragged fingernail, then lifted the stone clear, and with her knife, commenced to carve at the soil. The job proved difficult, the earth still winter-bound and reluctant there in the shade. She shucked off the coat and blotted sweat from her temples, set her teeth.

The urn she found first—a tiny vessel for a tiny purpose. She lifted it out and set it among the slick roots. Her heart shuddered once, then settled. She continued to dig until the blade struck the lockbox. Its weight as she pulled it to her lap reassured her, and when she thumbed the numbers and popped the rusted clasps, she found inside, still wrapped in plastic, the big nickel-plated Smith & Wesson. Six .357 Magnum rounds popped from the cylinder into her hand. She jangled them like loose change, reloaded them, hoisted the barrel. She pressed it to her cheek until she felt the metal strike her teeth.

The wind came softly there below the hill. It washed over her broad shoulders and sighed away across the tidal marsh. She drew slow breaths, her finger bent around the trigger, the damp of the ground bleeding through her jeans. A squirrel skittered through nearby bushes and stopped to peer with its beady eyes. At last, she lowered the gun and zipped it inside her coat.

Her first test. She had passed.

She reburied the urn and the empty box. When she was satisfied that the place looked no different, she stood and smacked the mud from her knees and retraced her steps past the old front porch. She glanced again at the boarded door with its sun-bleached sign, the broken chair pushed against the railing where she once sat picking out distant stars. Silently, she sheathed the knife that hung muddy in her hand and trudged back down the hill, leaving the house and all its tethered ghosts behind her.

The village stood six miles east, a tangle of weathered buildings overlooking a shabby wharf. Long ago, her grandfather had kept a boat there. He would sell his lobsters on the pier with a handful of other wind-chiseled men who had since passed into whatever afterlife they imagined to exist beyond the vast smear of ocean and sky. A quarter century had slapped another layer of gray on the town, but mostly, she found it as she had left it. She drove the main street, dodging debris that had rattled loose from fishermen's trucks, noting the shuttered windows and flapping screens, the paint that persistent fog had peeled away. There was a restaurant now, a place named Coasters with a tattered awning and salt-streaked windows. It abutted the squat, brick hardware store and the pharmacy that still called itself an apothecary. After that, business trickled off quickly in a smattering of machine shops and warehouses that screamed their failure from gaping doors and shattered glass panes. If Raker Harbor had been a hard place then, it was a harder place now, but Blake was well-adapted to hard places.

She swung west onto the Post Road and followed graded dirt past a handful of capes and sagging trailers until the land opened up once more onto the marsh. There, perched on the ragged edge of things, she found number 54, a faded red saltbox with a tacked-on porch set back from the road. A detached garage dwarfed the house, its front festooned in teal and orange buoys. In the yard, a wooden lobster boat squatted on a trailer, blue tarp flapping from its transom like a naughty skirt. Blake coaxed the Kia up the gravel drive and saw that a rust-chewed pickup sat beside the house, driver's door ajar.

She swapped the revolver for her Merits and climbed out.

The yard was tidy for a Maine yard, with evidence of garden beds visible in spots where the snow had receded. A dozen metal wind spinners whirled along the walkway. She gave the front door three hard raps, then stepped back and lit a cigarette. Listening. A great V of geese honked past overhead and vanished into a pastel portal of clouds. Tugging the cuffs of her coat down over her wrists to hide them, she stood alert to the soft creaking of the spinners, the pat-pat of meltwater leaking from a clogged gutter. Then she spotted the purple crocuses poking up from a seam beneath the porch. Fragile and stubborn, perfect. The surprise of their beauty caused something in her brain to scramble. She gazed at them, eyes fogging with moist heat. When the lock finally scraped back on the door, she jumped and stamped out her cigarette.

The woman who peered out at her stood engulfed in a man's enormous John Deere hoodie. Deep shadows cut her fine-boned face, which was dominated by thickly lashed eyes. Clutching the doorframe, she attempted to wiggle one child-size foot into a comically white sneaker. It took a moment for her exhausted features to betray the faint alarm to which Blake had grown accustomed when introducing herself to strangers.

"May I help you?"

"You Honora Hayes? I emailed you about the apartment. Name's Blake Renato."

The woman's foot dropped back to the floor with an unnatural heaviness. "*You're* Blake Renato?" One hand flitted to a tiny gold cross at her throat. "But I thought . . . you were a man. I mean, I just assumed, from your name . . ."

Blake stood rigid on the stoop. She watched the woman's eyes move over her the way everyone's eyes did, taking in her drab clothes and men's work boots, her olive skin and the scar that ran the length of her jaw, her absurd height, good for nothing but drawing attention she did not seek. Blake stuck out her hand, surprised when the woman received it in both of her own. A self-conscious smile dispelled some of the shadows in her face and revealed a woman much younger—and prettier—than Blake had first assumed.

"Forgive me! Of course you're a woman. How silly of me! Yes, I'm Honora. Just *Nora*, actually. Please."

She spoke with a soft voice that neglected its *r*'s and suggested a penchant for booze or pills or whatever else turned a person's speech languid before 6 p.m. Blake knew of a buffet of things.

"You want to see the space? Just give me a second. I'm a bit of a mess today."

Blake waited while the woman located a hiking pole she had propped just inside the door. When she stepped out upon the porch, she tested her balance against the steel shaft. Her face reddened when she spotted the open pickup.

"Well," she sighed. "There's the proof."

As she veered to shut the truck door, Blake saw that she did not so much limp as defer to the pole to pick out steady ground. Her sneakers made soft scuffs on the grit of the driveway. Blake found something inexplicably lonely about the sound.

"It's just you here?"

"At the moment. My daughter's back at school. A junior at UVA." Nora's smile faded. "She took a leave during fall semester, after my husband's accident."

Accident? Blake wondered but didn't ask.

Nora gestured toward the mothballed Beals boat looming like a dark monument in the yard. "That was Ed's pride and joy. But I think . . . I think it killed him."

The shadows returned to her face, lent it a quiet woundedness.

"He was hauling traps one morning last August and vanished. Marine Patrol thinks he went overboard. His heart, maybe. I don't know. It's usually their hearts, isn't it?"

Turning from Blake, she shook a ring of keys from her pocket and wedged one of them into the tarnished knob of the garage door.

"They never found him?"

"Poor Glory—my daughter—was out there all autumn looking." Nora shook her head. "I'm glad she didn't find him. You ever see a drowned body?"

Blake watched the key twist in the lock and muttered no.

"Count yourself lucky, then."

Inside the garage, a brigade of fluorescent lights flickered on with a buzz that made Blake's stomach tighten. The space reeked of oil and rust and projects unfinished. She gazed at a wall of plank shelves that sagged under the weight of Hamilton Marine paint and sinking line, big blocky tackle boxes and engine parts. A black Ford Ranger in an even sorrier state of repair than the one in the driveway occupied the first of the enormous bays. In another, a dinged-up speedboat listed starboard onto stained concrete. Blake made note of the gun safe, the game cooler, the pink Huffy bike with purple streamers collecting dust in the corner. Then she followed Nora up a narrow flight of stairs and waited as another key turned.

The finished loft boasted three big windows and a nineties-era kitchenette. A pair of Quaker rockers stood sentry beside a pool table that might have been salvaged from a bar, judging by its stains and scars. Several mismatched braided rugs broke up the expanse of the buckling laminate floor. In one corner, beneath a sun-bleached poster of Hopper's *Nighthawks*, stood a double bed made up with a new duvet whose somber colors reflected the presumption that the tenant would be male. The tacked-on bathroom was tiny, but it would hardly be the worst place she had been required to shower or shit. Blake walked the wide space end-to-end, her big boots making noise and tracking mud.

"Five hundred a month, you said?"

"Cash, if you have it. I hope I mentioned that in my email?"

Blake turned her gaze from the tidy bed and focused it on Nora Hayes, holding it there until a flush rose in the woman's cheeks.

"Check is fine, too," Nora added hurriedly. "It's just that things have been tight since Ed passed, and I'm trying to put something away for Glory. I waitress four days up to the restaurant now, but things are slow this time of year."

Without comment, Blake produced a leather wallet, counted out five crisp hundreds. Nora appeared to shrink farther beneath the hoodie as she accepted the bills and folded them into the pocket of her jeans.

"You're from Massachusetts?" Fatigue bled into her voice.

"That's right."

"What is it you do?"

"Ex-military. I'm between jobs." Blake unzipped her coat and set her cigarettes on the counter. "Okay to smoke in here?"

"I'd prefer you didn't. Our fire department is all volunteers."

Blake's eyes swept the ceiling. "I don't see a smoke detector. And I doubt that thing you've got passing for a heating unit up there is up to code. That propane?" She locked her hands before her, unable to curb the frost in her voice. "How about that door, there? Does it have a fireguard?"

Nora's face lost what remained of its color, telling Blake what she needed to know about the lobsterman's widow.

"You haven't had tenants before, have you?" She tried to soften her tone, but the words came out tight, almost strained.

"Just my mother-in-law, before she broke her hip." Reaching for the hiking pole she had propped against the sill, Nora tucked a limp strand of hair behind one delicate ear. "The space was just going to waste, so I figured why not rent it?"

She dodged Blake's stare, plucked an invisible speck of lint from the curtain. "You didn't say what brings you to Raker Harbor. In your email, I mean."

"Did I need to?"

"I only wondered how long you might be staying."

Now Blake turned her back and peered down at the muddy yard with its empty lobster boat and its lonely spinners that turned and turned. She took a sharp breath and released the fog of it onto the windowpane.

"Just tell me if you need me gone."

She had packed her whole life into three duffel bags, and after Nora clacked away with her pole, Blake carried them up from the car. The heaviest contained her books. She arranged them on the pool table, alphabetically by author, enjoying the look of them there, gathered like a vigilant regiment of old friends. Next, she folded her clothes into the pressboard dresser, taking care to remove their discount store tags. When this was done, she stuck the revolver in a box of sponges below the sink, then set about taking an inventory of the dusty dishes and glasses, the half-dozen cooking pots rimed with char. Inside the fridge, she found two cans of Coke and a sixer of Coors. She poured the beers down the sink and rinsed out the bottles, leaving them to dry in a glistening line atop the counter. Then she cracked a can of Coke and dropped into one of the rockers to pick apart the remains of a gas station sandwich.

The wind turned angry as darkness fell. It shook the windows and teased the cheap voile curtains. Blake watched them sway, her head tipped back against the chair, her fingers, stained still with dirt, curled around the worn, oaken arms. Solitude pooled around her like the waters of a warm bath, and she stretched out her long legs to bask in it. Gradually, her thoughts slipped their mooring, drifted back to the apple tree and the old couple and a distant summer when she first experienced a love that did not slap or bruise or crackle like some five-buck firework. It was a love she had not known what to do with. A love she had cast away.

She stood with a jolt. When regret took hold like this, Dawn Evers had advised, she must *breathe and redirect her thoughts*. She found the phone that she was still learning how to use and opened Dawn's last email. *Status report, Alvares?*

Made it north, Blake typed back, big fingers clumsy on the tiny, glowing keys. *The house is still standing. Needs work, though. Have rented an apartment. Will find a job soon. I'll be fine.*

She hit send, hoping she was right. Had no idea what fine was, really, absent the confines of steel doors and cinderblock, the predictable course of windowless corridors and scuffed tile.

The last light had winked off in the house across the drive, so she walked down to the garage, feet bare on the cold concrete. There, she propped the hood of the Ford Ranger and assessed the maze beneath, surprised to discover no missing caps or severed hoses. The alternator looked new, and the belt was in decent shape. The wiring showed no obvious deterioration. Someone had worked on the vehicle recently. The husband, maybe, before the accident. She thought of his bones tossing beneath the sea and eased shut the hood, then walked the shelves of gear, touching tools and other hardware in an effort to recall their purpose. Her memory was good. Toward one corner stood a metal desk framed in corkboard. Pinned to it, she found several photographs of the dead lobsterman and his penny-haired daughter—a sturdy girl with her mother's cheekbones and her father's reckless smile. They stood on the boat whose transom bore Glory's name, posed with various oddities they had hauled up in their traps. Beneath this collage hung a single picture of Nora Hayes. She squatted on a beach, supporting a chubby toddler by his sandy hands. Her sunlit face, fuller then, contained an old-Hollywood beauty with its large eyes and full, arched lips. Blake got the impression she was staring at a phantom. She turned from the smiling young mother and continued her exploration.

The bike she saved for last. Cobwebs wreathed the rusted spokes of the tires. Blake squatted before it and ran her fingers through the dusty streamers, pressed them to her cheek. A moment passed in which she felt herself drawn to the edge of something windy and dangerous. Then she pulled back and retreated up the stairs to the loft, where she dutifully locked herself in for the night.

In the gray light before dawn, her grandfather woke her, calling gently as she uncoiled from dreamless sleep. He was careful never to touch her, just waited there, a lanky silhouette, beside the bed until she pushed herself up on one elbow and gave him a nod. While he thumped downstairs to help her grandmother pack sandwiches, Blake pulled on layers of pilled fleece and a pair of elastic-waisted jeans. They talked little on the ride to town. He smoked Winston Golds with the window down, and she watched the house lights blink on across the marsh, chapped hands folded lightly across her swelling abdomen. The rubber waders hid her well. She always pulled them on before they trooped down to the wharf past the other lobstermen who watched them over the rising steam of their coffees.

Early on, he let her row the skiff to the mooring, but as fall arrived and she grew bigger, he took over the oars and pulled them swiftly through the dark water. When they reached the Edna Star, Blake hauled herself aboard and tied off the painter while he coaxed the big diesel engine to rumbling life. Then they stood side by side in the cockpit and motored into break of day, the silence between them sacred as prayer. He had taught her how to navigate, and sometimes, he let her steer the boat out past the ruin of the lighthouse and the stubby pine isles that dotted the horizon at that hour like so many dark stars. She liked the solid feel of the brass wheel under her grip, the subtle kick of the throttle. She liked the old man beside her, too, and the peace that washed over his haggard features the farther they motored from shore. Sometimes, that same peace lapped against her until she let it in. If she was lucky, it lingered all day while they toggled from buoy to buoy, he hauling up the traps on the old, groaning winch, she changing out the bait sacks and inspecting the catch. She had learned how to measure the lobsters with the metal gauge she kept clipped to her waist, how to check the females for eggs and carve a notch in their tail, if she found them. Her grandfather was adamant; eggers were to be protected. When he said this, his gaze lit upon her with rare warmth.

On land, his speech came labored, but on the boat, his words tumbled out in full sentences, and Blake collected them carefully as she might insects in a net, savoring their cadence, their salty wisdom. He spoke mostly of fishing and the natural world, never of the war that had left him with a limp, and never of Blake's troubled mother, who had fled the peninsula at seventeen and left him with a heartbroken wife. Blake did not ask about those things, aware she was the product of a coupling they had not condoned, and that her presence in their home was a piercing reminder of another's absence. For these reasons, she did not ask for more than the favor of their roof. Yet, by mid-autumn, her grandfather had built her a crib, and her grandmother had knit her a wardrobe of tiny jumpers. They had driven her to her first appointment in Machias, where they waited in a lobby full of swollen bellies and screaming babies while Blake was led in, stiff and terrified, to be examined. And afterward, when her eyes refused to quit streaming, they took her for ice cream, the three of them pressed together on the front seat of the Ford, scraping at plastic dishes as they studied the shadowy printout she laid upon the dash. Blake loved them for these things. It frightened her how fast and how desperately she loved them. And it frightened her, too, that she loved the little smudge on the image—a smudge put into her by a hateful man. On land, the fear could stop her breath. But when she stood on the boat, with the water rolling beneath her and the big diesel engine's rumble in her bones, her breath came freely. There, on a deck strewn with fish guts and cigarettes, Blake's heart found a brave, new rhythm. It belonged to her grandfather. It belonged to his ocean. . .

The wind died in the night, and she woke to a stillness that made her jump. She peeled her face from the pillow and tasted a residue of salt, but when she rose, her body felt strong again and ready. Dropping to the floor, she worked through a routine of push-ups and sit-ups. Twenty years in a prison cell had ingrained some unbreakable habits. Then she ran to the shower and let its cold water pummel her shoulders, bracing herself for the day and the things she must do. When she stepped out into the raw brilliance of the morning, she discovered that Nora's pickup was gone. A note fluttered from the wiper of the Kia:

Working til 3. Need anything, call cell. Cooking lasagna tonite if u r interested.

Blake crumpled the note. She made a sweep of the house and found the side door unlocked. Her hand rested a long moment on the knob before she let it drop and trooped around to the rear yard. There, she discovered a small greenhouse filled with tender plants, a fenced-in plot where she imagined summer vegetables grew. There was a garden shed, too, a little place prim as a dollhouse with white shutters and a Bible verse stenciled on a placard: *The LORD will guide you always; he will satisfy your needs in a sun-scorched land and will strengthen your frame. You will be like a well-watered garden, like a spring whose waters never fail.* Blake took all of this in and then climbed into her car and drove to town. She dangled an arm out the window and let her hair blow loose. Behind the mirrored glasses, her eyes searched for a glimpse of the sea through gaps in the passing trees. She could feel its nearness, the cold throb of it, and her heart beat faster at the knowledge.

Stopping at the hardware store first, she purchased a roll of duct tape, bleach, and a smoke detector. Then she explored the apothecary, with its dusty postcards and deep-discount Easter candy, and picked up a local paper with a Classified section. She carried the paper to the restaurant, where a shrill brass bell announced her entrance. A handful of gray-haired diners turned in unison to take her measure.

Blake chose a corner booth by the window. She propped her elbows upon a surface still tacky with breakfast syrup and waited for a trio of grizzled men in heavy flannel and Xtratuf boots to swivel back toward their plates at the counter. The squeak of the kitchen doors distracted them. Blake blinked as Nora Hayes emerged, toting a pot of coffee. Her hair sat in an elegant pile atop her head, trickling honey-hued curls down her slender neck. A generous amount of powder had muted the shadows in her face, and her snug sweater and jeans ensemble revealed a ballerina's figure, all long lines and delicate curves. She flashed a smile at the fishermen before she made her way toward Blake. Only the care with which she planted one sneakered foot before the other suggested anything amiss with her gait.

"You got my note, I guess."

"I got it," Blake said.

"And?"

Blake shrugged. "Not a huge fan of lasagna."

"Oh." The little gold cross at Nora's throat caught the sunlight through the window as she reached to fill Blake's mug. She smelled of buttermilk waffles and shampoo, of mornings cloaked in the comfort of routine. "I hope everything was all right last night. I heard that awful wind. If you need some extra blankets—"

Blake pushed the laminated menu back at her. "What's decent here?"

"I like the blueberry pancakes. But if you want something spicier—"

"Spicier?" Blake arched an eyebrow at her.

"I just meant . . . some people find the food here a little bland."

"Uh-huh." She snapped open the newspaper. "Pancakes sound fine. You can hold the hot sauce."

Nora fidgeted with the coffeepot. "I'm sorry, I didn't mean . . ."

Blake waved away the apology, bored of the assumptions her father's dark eyes and skin tone inspired from strangers. She stabbed a finger at the Classifieds. "I'm looking for a job. Know anyone who's hiring?"

"What kind of job?"

"On a boat." She glanced toward the fishermen at the counter. "Maybe one of them needs help?"

Nora set down the coffeepot and crossed her arms beneath her small breasts. "I don't think so. Those old soakers are mostly retired." Her frown bore an edge of pity. "Do you know anything about lobster fishing?"

"I know it's not rocket science to stand on someone's stern, stuffing bait sacks."

"You've done it before?"

"A long time ago." Blake lowered a hand over the steam rising from the mug. "You know anyone else who runs a boat?"

"I know plenty of people—but none who are going to hire a woman who just showed up to town yesterday."

Blake met the striking amber of Nora's gaze, found it empty of hostility but full of a curiosity for which she had no patience.

"Pancakes," she said. "And no hot sauce."

When Nora had returned to the kitchen, Blake tore a corner from the paper placemat and squinted out the window at the wharf. A half-dozen battered pickups occupied the lot, several piled high with lobster traps. She sighed and commenced scrawling a grocery list. Dawn—and AA—had taught her the necessity of lists, of tackling each day, each task, in careful steps. Midway through the word *tomato*, the cop strode in. Her eyes flickered up, fell on the steel cuffs fastened at his waist. Blue ink bled across the list as her spine pulled taut. The cop paid her no attention. At the counter, he shook hands with the three old lobstermen and accepted a to-go cup from Nora, whose face tightened at the sight of him.

"Leland Savard been in here lately?" he inquired.

"Ain't seen him," grunted the largest of the fishermen. "Check up to Brewster's? Know he likes watchin' that sister of his curl herself around a pole."

This evoked a chorus of wheezing chuckles from the huddle. "Ain't the only thing she's curled herself around, is it, Chuck?"

Nora bent her face to the silverware she was rolling into paper napkins. A flush crawled up her delicate neck.

"It true the brother OD'ed last week?" another of them asked.

"Won't deny it," replied the cop. "Can't say much more about it than that."

"World's down another asshole junkie," grunted the big man in buffalo plaid. "That's what *I* can say."

A fork clattered to the floor. Nora vanished briefly behind the counter to retrieve it.

"Leland's girl hasn't been in school these past four days," said the cop. "Either the funeral was in Mexico, or she's got a hell of a case of the flu."

"She's gonna have a case of worse'n that once she sprouts," sneered Buffalo Plaid.

Blake listened with her fist curled around the pen. Then she heard Nora's voice ring out clear and sharp from the silverware tub.

"Watch your mouth in here, Harley Cann, or you can get your coffee someplace else."

The fishermen hunched back over their plates. The cop, a square-faced man with an emerging paunch, dragged a hand over his blond buzz cut and cleared his throat.

"Apologies, Nora. I didn't mean to get these old guys all stirred up. But if you see Leland or his little girl, let 'em know she needs to get back up to Regional, all right?"

Nora nodded. A pile of dirty plates cradled to her chest, she retreated behind the doors of the kitchen. After she had gone, the cop clapped the man named Harley on the shoulder.

"Go easy on her, huh? Looks like the poor gal needs a vacation."

"Needs her man, more like. Ain't right what happened to Ed."

"No," agreed the cop. "But that's fishing."

"Yeah, that's fishin'."

Blake held herself rigid in the booth, eyes fixed on her smeared shopping list until she felt the cop pass by her table. When the bell announced his exit, she pulled several bills from her wallet and pinned them beneath the salt shaker, hurrying out before Nora re-emerged from the kitchen. She had lost her appetite.

The nearest grocery was a glorified liquor store with a dubious produce aisle and end caps loaded with two-for-one diabetes specials. She managed to find milk and eggs, peanut butter and protein bars, enough green stuff to imitate a salad. At the checkout, she waited behind a young mother hell-bent on haggling over the price of Virginia Slims with the cashier. When the woman's tiny daughter veered around to peer at Blake, she broke into a gap-toothed grin.

"You look like Maleficent!" announced the green-eyed, pigtailed creature, whose lips were stained lollipop pink.

Blake shifted her feet and looked away. She suspected that being likened to a Disney villain might be the closest thing to a compliment a woman of her age and stature could hope to receive. The girl's mother, meanwhile, resembled a redneck Cinderella, all beach-blonde hair and twinkling rhinestones. As she thrust a French-tipped nail in the cashier's face, Pigtails slipped a pack of gum off the adjacent rack and into the pocket of her ratty pink coat. She caught Blake's black glare and returned it with the cool indifference of a nine-year-old felon. Then her mother caught her by the arm and dragged her out of the store, leaving behind a cart full of breadsticks and Bacardi.

"Friggin' Savards," muttered the cashier, slapping the drawer shut. He jerked his fuzzy jaw at Blake. "You want paper or plastic?"

2.

She remembered the breakwater at Moran Point and turned off there. Bumped over a rut-road sprinkled with gated entries to castle-size summer estates that would remain buttoned up tight until Memorial Day. Her grandfather had kept a gang of traps in the adjacent cove, and Blake remembered looking up from the deck at those tall mansions full of glass, wondering what a person had to do to afford so many windows. *Business or brain surgery*, the old man grunted. *Or get elected to fuckin' Congress.*

In summer, cars populated the turnaround at the point, but today, the gravel horseshoe lay vacant. Blake fished her knapsack from the back seat she had emptied of groceries and scrambled up atop the enormous boulders that stretched like a ragged spine into the spangled bay. The sea air welcomed her with a powerful sigh. She flung out her arms for balance and stumbled along in booted feet, numb-fingered and smiling. Free. As she made a game of hopping from boulder to boulder, she let out a whoop, straddling crevasses full of snared garbage and dirty snow. Out in the channel, a bell buoy clanged furiously in the flood tide, matching her haphazard footwork. When she reached the farthest boulder, she stood with the roar of the wind in her ears and the hiss of the ocean below her boots. Far out on the horizon, the phantom shape of a passing tanker rose and vanished. Blake drank in the expanse of rolling blue and thought of how easily all that water could swallow a person. How easily a person could allow herself to be swallowed. She had known her grandfather would do it that way when the time came. When cancer took his wife and sank its fangs into him, too, he would take the boat out as far as it would carry him and erase himself. She never asked how he pulled it off the day they brought her into the deputy warden's office to tell her—the same way they brought her in the year before to learn about her mother's overdose. She just sat silent in the metal chair, her cuffed wrists heavy in her lap, and watched the CO's thin-lipped mouth move. And when they told her about the inheritance, how it had been placed in a trust pending her release, she hung her head. The fight had left her. The anger and resistance that had earned her five separate stints in solitary deserted her all at once. In its place bloomed a regret that she would cradle for the remainder of her sentence. A regret that even now drooped its soft petals inside her heart. It was her singular compass, the needle that had pointed her back to this distant, windy place.

She lowered herself to the cold granite and watched the tide. Her mind floated to a room with no windows and a pock-faced corrections officer whose eyes still followed her in dreams, and she tugged it back sharply like an errant kite. Eventually, she remembered the knapsack and produced from its front pouch a dull bronze sobriety token. *To thine own self be true.* Her fingers read the familiar engraving, the Roman numeral X stamped at its center. That the last ten years of her life could be boiled down to such an insignificant achievement brought a sting to her eyes. And yet it was all she possessed as an offering—the sole proof she could produce that the kindness of two old people had not been entirely lost on her, that she had not forgotten herself completely in the tempest of years that followed her departure from this place.

She touched the coin to her lips, then tossed it with all her might, watched it arc and vanish into the sea with a glint so fleeting she might have imagined it.

Chilled and stiff, she returned to the Hayes property after dark. As she trudged up the steps to the garage apartment, she nearly tripped on the to-go box that had been left by the door. She carried it inside and peeled open the lid, found a stack of blueberry pancakes and several packets of syrup. She ate all four pancakes standing at the sink, watching the TV light flicker in the house across the way. At last, she licked the sweetness from her fingers and went down to cross the driveway muck and rap lightly on the side door. Through its curtained window, she made out a living room cluttered with an ironing board and heaps of magazines and laundry. The glow of the wide-screen flickered across Nora's sleeping body on the couch, hair a heap on the armrest, one thin white arm dangling from the cushions. It was the sleep of the exhausted—or the drugged—and when three more raps elicited no movement, Blake cracked the door and slipped her hand through until she found the lock on the opposite knob. She twisted until she heard it click. Then she eased the door shut and returned to the garage, where her boots stood awaiting their duct tape patching.

The next day was Sunday, and the clouds piled up fast—big, wooly, winged beasts that raked the treetops and growled threats. The rain caught Blake three miles into a jog along the Post Road and forced her to turn around, sputtering and swearing, her sweatpants waterlogged, sneakers chafing. Two vehicles trundled past. One had the courtesy to veer; the other splattered her in road grit and exhaust. Blake scowled into the retreating taillights. She was not in the shape she had been when she left the military, a seven-minute-mile kind of shape, but thanks to much devoted circling of the prison rec yard track, she could still cover distance when she found the need. She powered through the deluge until Nora's brown truck came squeaking to a halt in the shoulder ahead.

"Get yourself in here, Blake."

The cab smelled like drugstore perfume and hazelnut coffee. Nora cleared a pile of mail from the seat to make room for Blake, who dripped puddles onto the worn leather.

"You coming from church?" Blake guessed, eyeing Nora's dress as she attempted to towel off her face with the bottom of her sweatshirt.

Nora reached behind the seat and produced a yellowed roll of paper towels. "I play organ over at St. Cat's. The stone church out by Frye Cove. New members always welcome."

"Uh-huh."

Blake tore off a generous wad of towel and blew her nose. She looked at the rose quartz crucifix dangling from the rearview, then at Nora, whose mascara had smudged in the rain.

"Thanks for the pancakes."

"You paid for them. Why'd you take off anyway? Did I offend you that badly?"

"What?"

"The whole . . . *spicier* thing."

"Oh." Blake wrung out her black ponytail on the floorboards. "No. For the record, I like hot sauce. Just not on pancakes."

Nora's face relaxed, though she continued to grip the steering wheel tightly in her small hands, her back pulled very straight so she could see the blur of the road through the flailing wipers. A Christian rock station played softly over the speakers. After a moment, she switched it off, flicked Blake a glance.

"I did some thinking. I might know someone who needs a sternman—I mean, stern*woman*."

The pile of mail Nora had slung up on the dash slid back and forth as she navigated the worst pits in the road. She drove a bit like she walked, as though she did not entirely trust herself.

"He's young. A couple years older than my daughter. He's had a hard time finding reliable help. Anyway, if you're serious about it, he might be open to giving you a chance."

Blake held a hand toward the warm breath of the air vent. "All right."

She saw Nora's gaze snag on her scarred wrist before darting back to the road.

"His name is Leland Savard."

"The one that cop was looking for yesterday?"

"That was nonsense." Nora's quiet voice took on an edge. "Jerry knows Lee just lost his brother, that he's probably had no way of getting Quinn to school. He just likes to shoot the you-know-what with those seniors."

"The you-know-what," repeated Blake under her breath, wondering if the widow had uttered a single four-letter word in her life.

They splashed up the muddy drive toward the house, which sat dark against a line of wind-bent trees. The rain was busy chiseling down the last nubs of the snowbanks. Blake found it a dreary scene to watch through the streaming windshield.

"You got to fix those gutters." She pointed toward the warped, cascading trays.

"I've got to fix a lot of things."

"Don't you have any help?"

"My brother, Gordy, up to Lubec. I hate to ask, though. He's done so much for me already." Nora killed the motor and slumped a little in the seat. "Were you ever married, Blake?"

"No."

"In love, then?"

Blake balled the soggy paper towel in her hands and shook her head. She felt Nora watching her but could not quite bring herself to push the door open into the rain.

"If not, then, you don't know what it's like to wake up feeling like half of a person," Nora sighed. "To have given away half of yourself and lost it. And when your whole self wasn't very strong to begin with . . ."

Her voice drifted off as she fell to twisting the little gold band that sat loosely on her ring finger. The printed violets on her dress drooped.

Blake listened to the rain pummel the hood. Her muscles threatened to cramp in the chill that seeped into the cab. She retrieved the Burpee Seed Catalog that had tumbled to the wet floor and bled ink, set it on a dry section of seat between them.

"I saw your garden out back," she ventured. "You got any extra space where I could drop a few tomato plants? Maybe some basil and peppers come late May?"

The inquiry shook Nora from her momentary fog. "Space? Why, that's all I've got, Blake. Of course you can put in some plants. Any kind you like."

The brightening of her eyes was the first suggestion of real joy Blake had witnessed in her face. She looked away, the paper towel now a hard marble in one fist.

"Good. Fine. Now, tell me where I can find this Leland guy."

The Savard place was not so much a home as a compound.

To reach it, Blake had to navigate a half-flooded gravel trail through a tunnel of ragged spruce and widowmakers. Broken bottles and *Beware of Dog* signs lined the way. Abruptly, the gauntlet opened onto a clearing the size of a football field. The cabin proper hunkered on the perimeter of the trees like something the forest had belched out and might soon reclaim. Low-slung and asymmetrical, its back end was propped up by cinderblocks, while the front sported two duct-taped windows like stitched-up eyes. A pair of decrepit single-wide trailers, dropped at haphazard angles, kept it company. At the center of it all loomed a flagpole, where a tattered Gadsden flag whipped yellow streamers in the gale. The rest of the open space was littered with a predictable assortment of defunct autos and decaying machinery, the exception being a tower of neatly stacked, vinyl-coated lobster traps, each of which contained a triple-striped, lime-green buoy. As she stepped from the car, Blake half expected a pack of pit bulls to come lunging from the shadows. Instead, a child's hooded figure pushed out the door of the cabin and strutted toward her in bare, filthy feet.

"What do you want?" demanded the shrill little voice.

As its owner pushed back the hood to better glare at her, Blake realized that it was Pigtails from the grocery store. Her gaze drifted from the small, hostile face sprinkled with freckles to the six-inch switchblade protruding from one pale fist.

"I'm looking for Leland Savard. He home?"

"Who's fuckin' askin'?"

"My name's Blake. Nora Hayes sent me."

The girl lowered the blade, swiped at her nose with her sleeve. "Nora? For real? Did she send any of them oatmeal cookies?"

"What? No." Blake held up her empty hands. She could

see the girl shivering in her splattered tights and baggy sweatshirt. "Is your name Quinn?"

A jerk of a nod.

"Leland's your father? Do you think I can talk to him?"

Quinn eyed her once more, then shrugged. "You can try. He's been sleepin' one off most of the day. Lemme check he ain't naked."

Before Blake could respond, the tiny mud sprite scampered back to the cabin and sent the door screeching wide on its hinges. Her voice carried far into the trees.

"*Papa! Réveille-toi! Il y a une femme ici pour te parler!*"

Blake mounted the rotted steps, wondering how the child's feet were not full of splinters. She caught the door before it swung shut, peered into a smoky gloom that made her eyes sting and her throat seal shut. A table scattered with empties hogged most of the kitchen space. In the living room beyond it sat a defeated-looking couch piled with kid's junk, a wide-screen that sported a long crack. Across the plank floor, two dozen pieces of construction paper were laid out like squares of a checkerboard. They comprised a fragmented mural of fantastical, crayon creatures. Quinn hopped between them on muddy feet, in a hurry to reach the kitchen, the apparent source of the smoke. With a dish rag, she flung open the door of the oven and tugged out a pan of charred cookies.

"Fuckin' hell!" She coughed into the gush of black vapor. The pan clattered to the floor. She yelped as it grazed her toes.

Blake sent the pictures flying as she leapt from the doorway. Kicking the oven shut, she snatched the cloth from the girl's hand and hoisted the pan and its blackened contents into the sink. She was pivoting to examine the child's toes when a figure crashed out from a back bedroom, flapping a T-shirt at the smoke.

"Goddamn it, Quinnie! What'd I say about usin' that oven?"

Leland Savard stopped short at the sight of Blake. His hand shot to his hip but found only the waistband of an ill-fitting pair of jeans. He wore no shirt since he had repurposed the stained garment as a fan. One glance showed Blake he possessed the lean, powerful body of a man who had grown up hauling fifty-pound pots most of the year. She made note of a sleepless, stubbled face and a set of deep-set eyes so bloodshot, she could not discern their color.

"You the law?" he grunted.

"You'd be screwed if I was."

At these words, Quinn sprang to her father and flung her arms around his waist.

"Nora sent her! That's what the giant said. Her name's Blake, and she knows Ms. Nora!"

For the second time in a span of five minutes, the mention of Nora Hayes appeared to sap some of the hostility from a hard face. Leland gave Blake the once-over, then turned to yank open the back slider and usher out the smoke. As he did, Blake caught sight of his back—a broad tapestry of familiar, penny-size scars that elicited a sick curling in her stomach. She looked away, watched Quinn scale the countertop to switch on the hood fan. The drawings in the living room scattered from the incoming breeze, and Blake pinned one beneath her boot as it came skittering into the kitchen. A unicorn with blue teeth and three heads leered up at her.

"You gonna tell me what you're doin' here, lady?"

Leland dragged out a chair from the table and collapsed into it. He gave each of the bottles there a quick shake. On cue, Quinn popped over and handed him a fresh Bud from the fridge.

It took Blake some effort to unclench her teeth. "Nora

said you might need help on your boat. Someone to stern for you."

"So what?"

"So, I know the work."

He barked a laugh and rocked back in the chair, dragged a hand through greasy hair the color of old acorns—the same color as Quinn's.

"Like my luck ain't bad enough! Now I'm supposed to invite some Amazon on my boat."

"What's a Amazon?" asked Quinn, who floated, wide-eyed, by his shoulder.

"A woman who doesn't take any crap from men," Blake replied before Leland Savard could offer his own definition.

Quinn pounced onto the couch with a warrior's cry. "I'm a Amazon! I beat up Tony Bouchard 'cause he was givin' me crap!"

"That don't make you an Amazon," growled Leland.

"It does, too! He was talkin' shit about Uncle Jonny!"

The muscles in the young man's powerful torso tightened. He took three long swigs of beer and thumped the bottle on the table.

"Go to your room, Quinnie."

"But, Papa—!"

"*Vas-y!*"

Peeling herself off the cushions, the girl cast Blake a look of such green-eyed woe that Blake briefly forgot she had pulled a knife on her in the yard. When she had disappeared down the hall, Leland jerked himself straight in the chair and fixed Blake with a more focused scowl.

"Listen, lady—whatever you are. I just buried my brother. I ain't in the mood to fuck around."

"Just to get drunk and let your daughter burn your house down, then?"

His square block of a jaw twitched. "Who the hell do you think you are?"

Blake had her fists balled in her pockets now. She took a step toward the table, kept her voice quiet and tight.

"I'm someone who knows about burying relatives and crawling down a bottle. For the record, it's a dead end." She shot a glance down the dim hall. "But I came here to talk about a job. Judging by all those traps you've got just sitting out there in the mud, you could use a pair of hands."

The air in the kitchen had cleared some. Big, fresh gusts swept in from the slider and spattered the floor with cold rain. As he sat glaring at her over the bottle, Leland appeared oblivious to the chill in the room, though Blake saw the gooseflesh rise on his bare shoulders. A Norse compass tattoo branded his left biceps. The greater definition of muscle on that side told her that he was a lefty, like her grandfather. That he had spent years feathering the throttle with his right hand and gaffing buoys and wrangling line with his left.

"My big brother was a Marine," he said, voice so quiet she barely made it out over the whine of the fan. "He got shot up by rag heads and kicked in the nuts by the VA, and all anyone's gonna remember 'bout him's that he did a line too many in some rat piss motel room."

Tipping back the bottle once more, he drained it in four swigs. Then he set it to rest among the others, arranging them like a rack of pool balls.

"He was the best of us Savards, just so you know. Nora mention *that*?"

When he rose, a stench of sweat and grease rolled off his skin. He stood an inch shorter than Blake, but even hungover, there was an electric readiness to his body that made him seem larger. Blake had known men like this. She stood ready.

"How do you know Nora?" he demanded. "You don't look like no Jesus freak."

"I rent her garage apartment."

His eyes went over her again. "You Mexican?"

"Brazilian. Half, if that makes any goddamned difference on a lobster boat."

"Don't know shit about Brazilians. That'd be a new one for this harbor."

Blake held his stare until he walked to the stove and punched off the fan. He found a pack of cigarettes on the counter and fired one up, stood looking out the kitchen window at his stack of idle traps.

"Where's Quinn's mother?" Blake asked.

Leland exhaled a long cloud of smoke. "Left me for fentanyl."

"I saw her with a blonde woman at the grocery."

He pivoted sharply. "You some kind of predator, stalkin' my kid?"

"This isn't exactly a metropolis. There another place to buy groceries besides Kinnon's?"

Turning away, he flicked ashes into the sink with the pile of charred cookies. "That was my sister. Nicky."

Blake fit the pieces together, decided not to mention the stolen pack of gum.

"So, about the job."

Leland spread his hands on either side of the sink and hung his head like he was about to vomit. His shoulders seized, but to her relief, nothing spewed from his mouth but more smoke.

"*Marde*. You gotta be the first person ever beggin' to work for *me*."

"I'm not begging."

"Whatever." He coughed, a bad sound. "I'd have to try

you out. Never hired no *Brazilian*. No woman, neither. I'll be the laughin' stock over to the Broken Oar." A sudden grin split his face. "Who am I kiddin'? Already am."

He dropped the butt in the sink, where it died with a hiss. "This snot's s'posed to clear out tomorrow. You meet me over here at five, we'll see if you're any good at stackin.'"

When he yanked open the fridge and dug out another beer, Blake interpreted this as the end of the conversation. She picked up the picture of the tri-headed unicorn, set it on the counter, walked back out into the blowing drizzle. Every muscle in her body felt knotted up. She sucked in gulps of fresh air as she walked to the car in long, twitching strides. Even as she moved, she felt the girl watching her. At the Kia, she glanced back to see her waif's figure push from the doorway.

"Bye, Amazon!" she called, sending up a sloppy wave.

She was still standing there as Blake drove away.

3.

In the evening, after Quinn had curled herself into a catlike ball and fallen asleep to the jabbering of Nickelodeon characters, Leland carried her into the tiny bedroom off the kitchen. He covered her in the faded unicorn quilt, fumbled the butterfly clips free of her tangled hair, and set them on the nightstand cluttered with trading cards and beach junk— her life's little treasures. By day, her face adopted a pinched, impatient look that had begun to worry him, but in sleep, it relaxed again into a smooth blanket of freckles. He touched her cheek gently with two calloused fingers, his heart quiet and heavy. The rain had ceased. In the stillness between her soft breaths, he could hear the bleating of the foghorn from Raker Light. The sound had been a comfort to him as a boy, when he lay trying to sleep in this same narrow bed. It had served as a reminder that the sea would always be there waiting for him, no matter which of his kin lost bets or blood or teeth before morning. One of them was always losing something. That was just the law of averages with Savards.

When he heard brakes squeak in the yard, he pulled the door shut on his sleeping daughter and walked out to deal with the mess in the kitchen. He was fisting wet glops of the spoiled cookies into the trash can when his sister came in the only way she knew how. Teetering and loud.

"What the hell stinks?" she scowled, yanking out one earbud.

"Fuckin' oven."

Her bag spilled cosmetics and pills onto the cluttered table. She shrugged off her coat, flashing a tangle of cheap necklaces and a surplus of cleavage.

"I need you to bring Quinn to school tomorrow," he said. "Gonna get the rest of my traps put in."

"The mournin' period's over, huh?"

"I hired someone."

"Hope he ain't another junkie. You're two-for-zero on that count."

Leland ran the tap to scalding. He scoured the sink and did not answer. After he had set the pan to dry in the rack, he wiped his hands on his jeans and gathered up Quinn's drawings.

"I still owe forty on the boat. Gonna lose her if I can't turn things around this season."

"You could sell her. Ain't like she's some lucky charm or nothin.'"

"And do what? Flip burgers? Truck long haul? I ain't cut for that shit, Nicky."

"Ain't cut for *much*, far as I can see." She flopped into a chair and chased an upper with a gulp of Mountain Dew. Her lips left a bright fuchsia smudge on the can. "You gonna go talk to Dad about Jonny, or you hopin' I'll do it?"

Leland cracked open a beer and drained half of it, avoiding her eyes. "Last time I went down there, he told me to piss off."

"That's 'cause you didn't bring money. Always got to bring money to put on his account, or he won't say shit to you." She picked at an acrylic fingernail and sighed. "He always did like Jonny best. Probably get himself thrown into the hole again when he hears how it happened."

"He's already heard."

"You know what I mean. 'Bout his dope bein' spiked by the McDowells."

"That's just rumors, Nicky. And he ain't hearin' that from me."

"I think you're chickenshit scared of that Swift Harbor crowd."

"Think it, then."

He joined her at the table, helped himself to one of her cigarettes. For a while, they smoked together in silence, watching Sponge-Bob gyrate across the muted screen in the living room. Nicole was pushing thirty, but she enjoyed cartoons as much as his nine-year-old daughter. Sometimes Leland wished she would stick to animated company. The real-life kind she kept made his teeth ache.

"You're a sorry sight, you know it, baby bro?"

He tipped back the bottle, finished it. "Jonny always said you got the looks, and he got the brains."

"Still tryin' to figure out what it is *you* got—aside from a potent pecker."

"Hope you ain't talkin' that way in front of Quinn."

Her lips curled. "You think that girl ain't figured out how she came into this world? That her daddy slipped up at *fifteen?*" She looked about the room and sobered some. "I already miss that crazy son-of-a-bitch Jonny, you know it?"

Leland nodded, didn't trust his voice.

His sister tipped her head back in the chair and exhaled smoke at the water-stained ceiling. "Quinn seems to be takin' it okay."

"She's breakin' noses and talkin' 'bout how he's probably up in Heaven, flirtin' with her mama," Leland frowned. "Wouldn't call that *okay.*"

"Well, *que faire?* Get her a shrink?" Nicole sniffed. "We're all a bunch of fuckups."

He stubbed out the cigarette and stuffed his feet into their mud-caked boots. "Not her," he muttered. "Never Quinnie."

His sister just blinked at him from the table, twirling a tendril of bleached hair. "Delusion. I think that's the gene *you* got, baby bro."

Outside, the night dripped with the cold of a grudging spring. Leland shoved through it, his lungs shuddering, temples throbbing. The motion light flicked on, and some big, clumsy creature went crashing into the sodden woods beyond. Leland got a running start. When he reached his brother's trailer, he kicked in the aluminum door and threw on the lights. His hand landed first upon a glass ashtray and sent it hurdling into the opposite wall, where it left a fist-size dent. Next, he flung a chair into the kitchenette, knocking the faucet crooked and bringing down a tower of moldy plates. The place still smelled of leather and smoke and foreign deserts. The odor only grew stronger as he tore loose the VA calendar and the poster of a young Megan Fox, smashed the hurricane lamp, and overturned the card table. When he wrenched the mattress from its frame, a nine-millimeter thumped to the floor. The sight of it quieted him. He picked it up, ejected the clip and the chambered round. Dropping to his knees amid the shattered glass, he sank his teeth into his arm to stifle his scream.

The wind through the broken door sent a deck of playing cards skittering across the trailer. In the distance, the foghorn droned gently as he wept.

Quinn shook him awake in the dark. He was sprawled on the floor of the living room, filthy with dried blood and tears and whiskey. One boot was missing, though thankfully, nothing else.

"Papa, she's here."

His groping hand landed on her cold, bare ankle.

"*Qui?*"

"Blake, the Amazon. She's waitin' in the yard."

A bottle went clattering across the floor as he shoved himself to a sitting position. In the dim light from the TV console, he saw Quinn's pajama-ed figure stoop to pick it up. His head rang with a thousand bells.

"Fuck," he groaned. "Fuck, fuck, fuck."

"Fuck, fuck, fuck," Quinn parroted cheerfully as she hopped to switch on a lamp. "That okay, Papa? That too much brightness?"

Leland staggered to his feet, rubbed his throbbing eyes, begged for coffee.

"Yes, sirrrr!" she sang out, and waltzed away to the kitchen, tattered nightshirt flapping against her skinny, urchin's legs.

While she went about banging cabinets, Leland limped to the bathroom and shocked himself awake with a brief, frigid blast under the showerhead. He saw that Quinn had laid out his toothbrush and razor, so he took the hint and made hasty use of both. By the time he swallowed two aspirin and located a clean set of clothes, every light in the house was blazing, Taylor Swift screeched from the radio, and an aroma of burnt Folgers usurped the lingering stench of blackened cookies.

He found Quinn standing out in the flood-lit yard, her legs now swallowed by a pair of his old trawler boots as she chatted up the swarthy giant to whom she had delivered a steaming mug of coffee. Blake leaned against the frame of her decrepit car, dressed in the same men's clothes she had worn yesterday. She had twisted her hair into a thick, black knot at the back of her head and hidden the rest of it under a Red Sox cap.

"Guess Sleeping Beauty's up," she remarked when Leland trudged down the steps.

His daughter giggled. "Can I help, Papa?"

"No. You got school. Go wake up Aunt Nicky."

While Quinn pouted, Leland thrust out a hand to the woman who was drinking his coffee. "Never got your last name."

"Renato." Her grip was brief and strong. She jerked her square chin at the stack of traps looming behind him. "How many you got?"

"Three hundred soakin' off shore. Hundred down to the wharf. This here's the final three."

"That's not so bad."

"We'll see what your back says when we're done today."

Blake's eyes turned to chips of obsidian. "What're you paying anyhow?"

"Fifteen off the bottom."

"That's shit."

"Yeah, well, I ain't even hired you yet. All I know, you'll break a nail and call it quits."

The stillness of her hard features unsettled him, so he turned away and gave his eavesdropping daughter a tap on the bum. "*Vas-y, ma puce!*"

For the next two hours, as pink light crawled over the treetops, Leland and Blake tackled the trap pile. Posed upon the precarious stack, Leland would lower down one of the fifty-pound traps, and Blake would receive it in her gloved hands and cram it into the open bed of his Silverado. He barked directions, but the woman did not appear to need many. She swung easily on and off the pickup, tetrising the big yellow cages and helping him to secure them with bungee cords into an efficient, four-level, winged arrangement. They managed to stack twenty-four at a time like that. When they had loaded the back of the truck to its maximum sag point, he had Blake pump the accelerator while he gave a hard shove from behind to coax the overburdened wheels up off their makeshift plywood ramp in the mud and onto the more stable gravel of the drive.

Within the first hour of their labor, Leland discovered that Blake Renato was strong as a horse, smoked like a chimney, and did not care for small talk—three qualities that suited him just fine, as it took most of the morning for his head to clear and his own limbs to feel solid again.

At seven, Nicole emerged from her trailer, a liter of Mountain Dew in one hand, Quinn's battered school bag in the other. She took a long look at Blake, who returned the favor, then threw back her blonde head and howled.

"Now I seen it all, Leland! *Ai-ai-ai!*"

Thankfully, Quinn tugged her aunt toward the car, shutting her up. Leland noticed the fuchsia pop of his daughter's lips and hollered at her to wipe it off before she climbed inside.

"Fuckin' Nicky," he muttered, ignoring Blake's inscrutable look as he heaved another trap into the bed.

Leland kept the country station on during the ten-minute ride to town. By the fourth trip, they were playing repeats. If Blake had an opinion on music, she kept it to herself, alternately smoking and chewing on protein bars as she watched the scenery pass. The day had bloomed bright, calm, and cold, and there was plenty of action down at the wharf as the harbor's dozen other lobstermen vied for a tie-up by the trap hoist to stack their sterns. While waiting their turn, Leland and Blake piled his traps in a vacant space by the bait house. Before long, the typical crew of loafers shuffled across the street from Coasters to get a better look at his new helper.

"New girlfriend, Savard?" hollered Chuck Stone over a Styrofoam cup of joe. "Didn't know you liked the exotic type."

Leland ground his teeth, aware of a running bet between Chuck and some other old- timers regarding how long it would take him to lose the *All In* and hop onto the government dole. As far as humiliation went, stacking traps alongside a swarthy female hardly took the prize that spring—though if she turned out to be a dud on deck, he might have to find himself another harbor to fish from. He and Blake finished unloading his truck, mouths drawn into matching, taut lines of toleration for one another.

Just shy of noon, they loaded on the last group of traps. When they pulled up to the fishermen's lot, which had emptied out some, Leland found Nora Hayes waiting beside his stack, a plastic bag of takeout cradled in her arms. His heart ticked up a little, the way it always did when he sighted her. As she ambled toward his truck, he saw that she was having one of her better days. Her fine eyes looked bright and clear, and she walked without stumbling.

"I thought you two might be hungry," she said, passing the bag through his open window. "You've been at it all morning."

She shook her head at the money Blake dug from her wallet. "Lee, I know you like the club. Blake, I just guessed. There's some . . . um . . . hot sauce in the bag."

Blake's mouth twitched. It was the closest thing to a smile Leland had seen the woman crack all day. He nodded at Nora, uncomfortable with the charity but well acquainted with the hurt his rejection of it would provoke.

"Quinnie back in school?"

He nodded, poking at some French fries.

"I lit a candle for your brother at St. Cat's. If there's anything else I can do—"

"You done plenty already." He doused the emotion in his voice with the remains of his coffee.

Reaching through the window, Nora rested her small hand on his arm. He noticed how thin and fragile her fingers had become, wondered what her daughter would think when she saw her, all whittled down this way. Then he felt Blake watching them through her mirrored glasses and gave an awkward cough.

"You heard from Mornin' Glory?"

"She's burning the midnight oil preparing for the MCAT. Lord knows, I can't help her with any of that." Nora smiled in a way that brought out faint creases at the corners of her eyes. "She'll be home in four weeks, Lee. Just four more weeks."

He hoped she did not see the color that rose in his cheeks, though he was pretty sure Blake did. Those dark, sullen eyes of hers did not seem to miss much. Beside him, she sampled one of the donut-size onion rings Nora had piled into the Styrofoam tray.

"Thanks for the food," she grunted between chews.

"Sure thing."

Arms wrapped around her thin frame, Nora picked her way back across the street to the restaurant. Leland held his breath until she disappeared safely behind its painted door, then let it out in a stronger gust than he'd intended. As Blake punched her straw free of its paper wrapper, she shot him a look.

"You got a thing for the daughter, don't you?"

"Shit. Mornin' Glory'd sooner chew glass than date me. Her words, by the way."

Blake's lips drew back, revealing a ridge of large, mostly even teeth. "I like her already."

After lunch, they rowed out to his boat. He had neglected the gasoline for the outboard on the skiff, and in the newly arrived afternoon chop, he had to lean hard on the oars. The flood tide beat against the rickety vessel, licking his forearms with frigid spray. By the time they reached the *All In*, he wanted a drink more than he wanted to load on traps. Jonny had left a quart of Fireball in the forward cuddy, but Leland refrained from reaching for it as he gave Blake the nickel tour. A red-hulled, thirty-seven-foot Novi, the vessel—and her debts—had become his after his father got into the trouble in Swift Harbor ten years earlier—a gun-toting, boat-burning trouble that had landed him thirty-to-life in Maine's supermax. He left this history out of the introduction.

Blake's expression never changed as he showed her the hauler and the saltwater tank, the bilge pump and safety gear and the panel of mostly outdated electronics.

"What kind of engine does she have?"

"Deere, 550 horse."

She arched a black eyebrow. "What's she do, thirty wide-open?"

His mouth dropped. "Close enough. Novies ain't built for speed. Displacement hull and all."

"But they're seaworthy. You can stack 'em high."

Blake still wore the mirrored glasses that hid her eyes, but Leland sensed a momentary softening in her. She ran her hand along the wash rail and looked about appreciatively at the broad deck spattered in dried fish blood and bird shit.

"Where'd you say you were from?" he asked.

"I've lived a bunch of places."

"Where'd you learn about boats, then?"

She cupped her long hand around the lighter, firing up

cigarette number thirteen. "I learned right here. I worked stern for my grandfather, Jesse Teale."

Leland jolted. "Teale? Like the Teale from that old, empty farm up to Harlow's Crossin'?"

"That's right."

"My old man used to talk about him. Crazy bastard. Recluse. POW in Korea."

"He wasn't crazy."

"Hardly talked, so the story goes. Took his boat out one day and blew himself to smithereens. 'Nough ordinance on that thing to take out a whole town, my old man said. Pieces were washin' up for miles—"

One swift lunge landed Blake inches from his face. Her words poured out on a stream of bitter smoke.

"Shut up about him. He was the best man I ever knew."

"Take it you ain't known too many."

He stared into the mirrored discs of her glasses, as repulsed by his own haggard reflection as he was by the closeness of a woman who looked capable of kicking his ass. She smelled like a man—sweat, smoke, and diesel fumes. Uncurling his hands from their ready fists, he asked, "How'd you get that scar?"

She stepped away from him, stomped out her cigarette good and hard on the deck. "Fuck you. I'm here to bait your traps and hose your deck."

"Never said you were hired."

"Then, you can find another sternman. Looked like there was a whole *line* of them just waiting back there to work for you."

They glared at one another across the narrow space as the boat jounced in the tide. Finally, he stuffed his hands in his pockets and turned into the cockpit.

"We're burnin' daylight," he said. "Let's go."

They did not speak another word to each other after that, beyond the grunted exchanges requisite to the functioning of a lobster boat. At the pier, they loaded on a crate of salted herring and the first gang of fifty traps. He was forced to loan Blake his brother's Grundéns since she lacked a pair of her own. The perfect fit struck him as a bit uncanny. Then, when he had fueled up, they lumbered out into the afternoon swells, the bow pitched high, the heavy transom dragging. Leland knew it was a poor time of day to be motoring out, but with spring breathing down his neck, he had to haul ass to mark his territory. When he reached the first set of coordinates he had punched into the nav, it was close to two o'clock, and he felt the toll of the day begin to pull on him. He joined Blake at the rail, watching closely as she baited and secured the sacks for the first string. Her fingers were quick and efficient. He issued a nod of grudging approval before he nudged her clear of the line and set the pair of traps flying off the stern.

"Whatever you do," he said, "watch your feet."

She acknowledged the warning by spitting her gum out over the rail.

She was no Jonny, but she would have to do.

The sun was spilling a gaudy palette of colors over the western hills as he returned the *All In* to her mooring. Blake beat him to the skiff and took up the oars, and he offered no protest, secretly thankful he had been spared this last physical hurdle. She rowed with a vengeance, her teeth flashing every so often as she pulled. Only when she finally shoved up her shades did he see that she had not been impervious to the taxing day. Her eyes had sunk a little deeper in their sockets, and the skin beneath her nose was red and chapped from constant running in the salty cold. It took her a moment to pull herself onto the pier. She ignored the hand he tossed out.

Back at the cabin, Quinn came bounding out to greet

them. She wore one of his old sweatshirts like a dress and had her hair done up in a dizzying maze of braids that screamed Nicole's handiwork. When she hugged him, it was all he could manage to hoist her sharp-boned weight in his arms and kiss one peanut-butter-smeared cheek.

"I made 'em, Papa! I made the cookies right this time! Blake, you want some?"

"No. Thanks."

She had made a beeline to her Kia, which Quinn had decorated with dandelions. Blake plucked several of the wilted weeds from the windshield before dragging open the door.

"See you tomorrow?" Leland grunted.

"Fine." She dropped into the driver's seat, shutting the door on Quinn's singsong farewell.

4.

That first week, Blake's body became a walking symphony of pain. Lifting her arms provoked a screech of violins. Bending over elicited a crash of symbols. Even blowing her nose brought about an unpleasant blast of brass. She could not recall such misery, even back in Basic, and to discover herself middle-aged and suddenly so full of cacophony gave her a jolt. At night, she stood in the shower, forearms braced against the far wall, and waited for the hot water to tune down the noise inside her. She gulped ibuprofen with her microwaved dinners, then stretched out flat on the bed, only to repeat the hot water ritual in the black-and-blue hour before the sun rose.

I found a job, she informed Dawn, glad, at least, that she could report this news. *I am now someone's sternman.*

She did not describe the someone, thinking it best to paint an optimistic picture to the old prison shrink.

Blake's consolation amid this initial stretch of sore days derived from the fact that her twenty-something captain looked little better than she for the wear. Most mornings, he staggered from the cabin like a man on wooden legs. Little Quinn had to carry out his coffee and lunch, which he routinely forgot in his blundering state of half-wakefulness. Blake guessed from his reeking breath that he drank most of his dinners. The thought kept her stiff and alert on the bench seat beside him as they drove to town through the pre-dawn gloom. Sometimes, she found herself wondering about Quinn and what transpired in that smoky cabin on the afternoons after she drove away. She was quick to cut herself off from this contemplation, though. She worked for Leland Savard; that was all. What he did off the boat was his own business—just as what she did was hers.

Blake had come north, after all, to be left alone. Even on nights when the pain made it difficult to think, let alone move, the hours belonged only to her. She owed them to no one. That freedom never lost its luster, was itself a sweetness that washed away the salt and stench of a difficult day with a difficult man. Lying naked in the dark of the loft with her headphones shoved in, she floated on a tremulous current of near-contentment. She wished to remain there always, in that unremembering place brought on by physical exhaustion and Debussy. It was a beautiful and private realm that she refused to surrender to the occasional knock at her door or buzz of her phone. *How's it going?* Nora Hayes always wanted to know.

I paid your rent, Blake thought. *Please leave me the fuck alone.*

And if, occasionally, she glimpsed the lights of the saltbox across the way and wondered about its emaciated, soft-spoken occupant, it was only with the fleeting, morbid curiosity of a woman well versed in the arts of self-delusion and destruction. Blake derived no pleasure from the suffering of others. If anything, she was more sensitive to it than the average forty-something human. She simply had no room to let it in. Having managed at last to stamp out the many disparate fires in her own heart, she now presided over the tepid ashes, frightened by nothing so much as the prospect of a spark that might rekindle the inferno. She knew herself. Corrections had made sure that she knew. They held up the mirror until she had been forced to stare deep into it. There had been AA and SA and group therapy, rehabilitation in all its state-approved forms. Meditation and support circles, and on Thursdays, ebony-skinned Dawn Evers and her full-voiced, tough-love banterings that chiseled through Blake's indifference like a diamond file. They won. They made her see. And now her reward for participating was devotion to a safe and sterile loneliness. She did not long for company, male or female. The experiences of her early life had forever squelched the appeal of male anatomy, and two decades in state prison had left her weary of the female body's mechanics. Should the impulse seize her, which it infrequently did, she knew how to take care of herself. But there was no elation in it. No release. Just a seizing of muscles, and afterward, a long stillness that stretched like a gray horizon. A stillness she accepted as the cost of survival.

So, she was thankful that she departed in the morning before any lamps were switched on in the Hayes house—and equally glad, when she hauled herself from the car in late afternoon, to find that Nora's truck had not yet returned to the driveway. Sometimes, she would stand a minute watching the wind spinners turn, the grass blush green in the late-day sun. She would gaze at the irises and lilies that had begun to push through the soil, even stoop to pluck a deadhead off one of the early pansies that sat on a pot beside Nora's porch. But always, she turned and tromped up the plywood stairs to her precious rented piece of privacy. Up there, she would gratefully lock herself into her freedom with her books and her cigarettes and her grandfather's gun. And when she felt so moved, she might lift one of the windows and let in the evening breeze.

It was on one of those open-window evenings that her plan for distance shattered. A cry of pain carried through the shuddering of the blinds and reached her in the rocker, where the ruminations of Emily Dickinson spilled into her lap. The book flapped off her leg as she was pulled from a poetic malaise into searing wakefulness that shot blood through her sore limbs. At first, she wondered if she had imagined the sound. She had imagined far worse in her fitful dream world. Then through the twilight came a muffled tide of sobbing.

Blake descended from the loft to find Nora in a heap upon the concrete stoop of the side entry. Grocery bags lay around her, a sprawl of produce and yogurt cups and ruined eggs. Against her chest, she cradled her right wrist like something that did not quite belong to her but which she had picked up and was now too frightened to put down again.

"Jesus," Blake said, scooping her up like she might a child. The tiny widow weighed about as much. As usual, the door was unlocked, so Blake carried her inside and set her on the couch, where she saw that the wrist was badly sprained if not broken, the swelling already fierce and ugly. A smudge of blood painted one of Nora's cheeks. Blake touched her thumb to it, found it derived from a gash high on her forehead, near the hairline.

"You see me okay?"

It took Nora a minute to summon a nod. "I'm f-fine. P-please. I'm fine, Blake. Thank you."

"You're not fine. You're in shock, if you're anything."

Nora's small teeth chattered. "I'll c-c-call G-Gordy. He'll know what t-to do."

"Your brother in Lubec? That's an hour from here."

Blake squatted before her. She tried to pin the whiskey

gaze, but Nora's eyes refused to meet hers. "Where's the nearest ER? Machias?"

A squeak of fear escaped through Nora's sobs. She commenced rocking back and forth on the plaid couch. Still decked in her restaurant apron, smudged with tartar sauce and ketchup, she smelled like a deep fryer.

"No," she moaned. "No, no, no."

Blake lowered her hands atop Nora's quaking knees to keep her from rattling right off the cushions. "Look at me," she commanded. "Where do you keep your Band-Aids?"

"B . . . Bathroom."

"Don't move."

Blake strode through the living room adorned with coastal artwork, ruffled curtains, and family portraits. All the trimmings of a proper life. A short hall carried her past an office in which a large easel stood dark against a bay window, a modest bedroom whose chunky pine furniture left little room for maneuvering. In the adjacent bath, she flipped open the medicine cabinet and found herself staring at a shocking gallery of prescription bottles. Her heart dropped. Seizing the package of bandages on the top shelf, she slapped the cabinet shut and was turning to leave when she spotted the syringe. It lay at the bottom of the trash can, half concealed by wadded tissues. On heavy feet, she plodded back to the living room.

"Get up," she said. "I'm taking you to the ER."

The new briskness in her voice startled Nora quiet. She rose as if tugged up by a string, still clutching her wrist. "You don't have to—"

"Yes, I do. Let's go."

Blake yanked open a Band-Aid, pushed back Nora's hair to apply it to the cut. The roughness of her hands made Nora flinch.

"Get your cards or whatever and wait in my car. I'll get the keys."

"The groceries—"

"Forget the fucking groceries!"

The ride would take twenty-five minutes. Blake remembered. She kept the needle right on the speed limit and did her best to avoid the worst pits in the road for Nora's sake. Every so often, when they hit a rut, a soft cry of pain escaped her passenger, who had fallen into subdued silence as the last light deserted the sky. Blake felt tired and inexplicably furious, and she kept her eyes locked ahead of her on the narrow road. It wove past farmhouses, dark and empty, bleached For Sale signs creaking on rusted hooks, an occasional filling station or antiques shop that had managed to maintain a pulse through tourist traffic. The moon reeled up over the hills, voluptuous and bright, spilling wan light over the fallow fields and waking marshes. It spilled over Nora, too, where she rested against the seat, eyes gazing vacantly, jaw rigid with pain.

Blake unclenched her teeth. "If you're using, they'll know. You should just be honest about it. Get some help."

Nora's face turned toward her slowly. "What?"

"The dope. Pills. Whatever the fuck you're taking."

Fresh pools formed in Nora's stricken eyes. "You think I'm a junkie?"

"Don't bullshit me, all right? That bathroom's better stocked than a CVS, and I saw the needle in the trash."

With a small gulp, Nora sank back against the seat. "That's for Copaxone. It's a medication for MS."

Blake veered around the tattered remains of a raccoon. "MS?"

"Multiple sclerosis. I have to inject meds every other day to keep my immune system from destroying my nervous system." Nora's voice wobbled. "If you're wondering about all

52

the pills, they're for the dizziness and the headaches and to keep me from wetting the bed at night. All right?"

Blake's breath escaped in a soft hiss. She groped about for the canister of tissues in the cupholder and held out a wad to Nora, who ignored them and turned her face away.

"My mother was an addict," Blake muttered. "I see needles, and I just assume. I'm sorry."

"Why should you be sorry?" Exhaustion shredded Nora's voice. "It's probably what everyone thinks of me who doesn't know. Poor Nora, the widow, numbing all the pain with dope. I'd hardly be the first around here."

She pulled herself straighter in the seat then. "It's not that bad," she said quickly. "I'm a pin cushion, sure. And some days I feel like I'm losing my mind. But it's a test. God's just testing me."

Blake glanced at her. Though still damp with tears, Nora's face had recomposed itself. In its taut lines, Blake saw resolution.

"I'm glad you have a faith like that," she heard herself say.

The car hit a bump. Nora flinched. "Don't you believe in anything?"

"No."

"Because of your mother?"

"Her. A bunch of other things. It doesn't matter."

"Of course it matters." Nora pulled her wounded wrist against her heart. "You must feel very . . . alone."

Now it was Blake's turn to flinch. "Listen. I'm driving you to the damned ER, and I hate hospitals, all right? So, let's just listen to some music or something. You want the Jesus station?"

She punched on the radio, and Nora said no more as they shuttled through the trees and on toward the first lights of Machias.

The last time she had an accident, they made Nora's husband step out, then asked her if she felt safe at home. The question so humiliated her that she had burst into tears, which prompted a further battery of well-intentioned questions. Her responses eventually earned her an injection of sedatives and an overnight stay. A psychiatrist came to talk to her and wrote a prescription for antidepressants. She knew she had embarrassed Eddie. The whole next day, he had trouble looking at her, just as he had trouble looking the handful of other times she had lost control of herself in a public place— mostly after they buried Benji, then again, when her mother died. So part of her felt glad he was not here tonight, though it frightened her a little to sit alone on the curtained-off bed with all the bleeps and murmurs that swirled around her. She thought of texting her daughter, then frowned at herself for that fleeting consideration.

No reason to upset Morning Glory. She had done more than enough of that already.

Atop a steel bedside cart lay the clipboard of paperwork Blake had filled out for her. Never had Nora envisioned dictating to anyone unaffiliated with the medical field the details of her past surgeries and childbirths, abnormalities of her internal organs, family histories of depression and suicide. Yet, there it all was in Blake's tight, mechanical print. Now a stranger knew everything. It turned Nora cold with shame. She should have called Gordy. He could have answered all of the questions from memory. But he also could have barked at the nurses, demanded ice chips, fed them to her through his fat fingers like he did when she was sixteen and her appendix ruptured. He had not looked away when the nurse opened her gown to examine the sutures. For better or for worse, Gordy had never ceased looking away from her.

She shivered atop the table and sent new pain daggering through her wrist. Closing her eyes, she called up a verse from Jeremiah: *Heal me, Lord, and I will be healed; save me and I will be saved.* She thought of St. Cat's, with its cool, sea stone walls and stained-glass saints, and she imagined that the pain subsided.

The ordeal took three hours, between her intake and the application of the splint. The doctor, a balding Indian with bloodshot eyes but steady fingers, informed her that she had sustained a distal radius fracture. After it grew clear to her that she would be out of work for at least six weeks, the rest of his instructions floated past her like bubbles on a fast creek. She grasped at the ones she could. In several days, once the swelling had receded, she would need to see an orthopedist for a plaster cast. She would also need to follow up with her neurologist, as the failure of coordination that had led to her fall was suggestive of new lesions on her brain. The nurse gave her four enormous tablets of ibuprofen and a book-length stack of paperwork. Then she was cleared to shuffle out to the waiting room in a daze of disappointment and fatigue.

Blake shot to her feet in a way that made Nora think her eyes had been glued a long time upon the intake doors. Several patients looked up from their phones and magazines to watch the giant with the wild, dark hair stride toward her. Nora's lips quivered at the sight of her hard, tired face.

"I'm so sorry, Blake. It's nearly ten, my God."

"You're all right?"

"Yes. Well, I mean, it's broken, but—"

"Let's get out of here, huh? You hungry? That McDonald's should still be open."

Before Nora could respond, Blake had taken her paperwork and purse and looped her arm through Nora's uninjured one. The steadiness of that arm felt better than anything the hospital had been able to provide her, so, bleary-eyed and spent, she let Blake guide her out through the sliding doors and into the chilly, spring night.

They ordered shakes and chicken sandwiches and ate them in silence as they rode back to Raker. Blake drove with a stiff-jawed alertness that characterized most of her activities. Nora guessed that she had picked that up in the military, just as she had probably picked up the scars and her general aloofness. It made her uneasy. Anyone empty of faith worried Nora—and Blake's prior revelation that she had never been married or in love hardly assuaged her concerns that her tenant was something of a lost soul. People like that could be unpredictable. Daughter of an addict? One more tally in the worry box. Still, Blake Renato paid her rent in cash and had survived two weeks on Leland Savard's lobster boat. Although the first might not qualify as a miracle, the second almost certainly did.

After Nora had eaten, she fought a war with her eyelids. She did not want to fall asleep in the woman's car—not after Blake had waited three hours for her in that dingy waiting room.

"What did you do in the military?" she asked.

"Nothing exciting."

"Is that code for something you can't tell me?"

Blake popped the lid off her shake and sucked out the bottom dregs. "That's code for I refueled a lot of tanks and helicopters."

"Did you like it?"

"It was a job."

"Why'd you enlist?"

"Is this Twenty Questions?"

"I'm just trying to stay awake." Nora adjusted the sling,

which bit into her shoulder. "I can't imagine joining the Army. I married Ed when I was seventeen. I think maybe that's the bravest thing I've ever done."

"That sounds more impulsive than brave," Blake said.

"If you'd known Ed back then, you might think it was at least a little brave." Nora smiled wistfully. "He was ten years older than me and played drums for this awful band that called itself The Keepahs. They played for tourists off the back of the guitarist's lobster boat. Ever heard 'Sweet Caroline' with a Down East accent?"

Blake sniffed. "All right," she agreed. "I guess you *were* a little brave."

Drunk on fatigue, Nora called up the tune. "And when I huht, huhtin' runs off my shoulders. How can I huht when holdin' you?"

"That's pretty good." Blake grinned. "Were you the backup singer?"

Nora's laugh earned her a jolt of pain. She fell quiet after that, watching the stars whip past through the leafing trees. Her thoughts began to melt into one another like pats of butter, and when they pulled up at the house, Blake had to nudge her awake and guide her up the steps past the spoiled groceries.

Inside, Blake went about flicking on lights as Nora felt her way to her bedroom. She leaned against the dresser and used one foot to pry the shoe off the other. For a while, she found herself staring blankly at the dizzying pattern of her wedding quilt, unable to summon the energy to move. The room felt inexplicably unfamiliar, a place of hazards she must now navigate with one fewer working limbs. Then Blake appeared in the doorway with a toothbrush slathered in white paste.

"Brush," she ordered. "Then we'll figure out what to do about your clothes."

Nora complied, grateful for instructions on what suddenly felt like an overwhelming number of complex tasks. She avoided looking at herself in the mirror, stood still as Blake worked her sweater up over her head, then patiently maneuvered the bulk of her splint through the sleeve. Next, she unfastened Nora's jeans and shimmied them carefully off her hips as Nora, blushing, held her cotton panties in place with her good hand. She saw Blake's eyes travel the constellation of marks on her stomach and thighs left by the needles, some of them salt-grain-size depressions, others, more recent, pinkish welts like bee stings. No one but Ed and her daughter had ever seen these. But Blake worked quickly and said nothing, and after she had helped Nora into the velour robe she had collected from the back of the bathroom door, she appeared anxious to leave.

"You're all right here?" she said, backing through the doorway. "You need anything?"

Nora shook her head. "Thank you, Blake."

"Yeah. Sure. Feel better."

Then, she was gone, and Nora stood alone in the bedroom with its soft-glowing lamp and hand-hooked rug and bureau still full of her deceased husband's clothes. It was familiar again. Drawing down the shade, she knelt beside the bed and pressed her face into the quilt, inhaled the scent of twenty-four wedded years compressed into those tightly stitched cotton squares. Her prayers came long and labored that night, and they began and ended with the name of Blake Renato.

5.

In the evenings, she chose the rocker by the woodstove to nurse him, his warm, gurgling weight nestled against her ribs. Her grandmother had shown her how to maneuver him for a proper latch, sat up patiently those first long nights helping her to guide his tiny, baffled mouth to her nipple. At first, the pain made Blake flinch away from him, but she learned to relax into the dull throb of his suckling, her body at last a thing she could give willingly, tenderly. Smiling, she watched her son's papery eyelids flutter as one shriveled bird claw of a hand curled itself around her finger. He was the most peculiar and incredible thing she had ever laid eyes upon, and when she traced the small perfection of an ear or the dusky feathers of his hair, she saw a creation all her own, a miracle that transpired entirely of her own volition.

Her grandmother fixed a salve of sandalwood and rose. When Blake finished nursing, she dabbed the ointment on each of the dozen, dime-size craters that scored Blake's chest, her fingertips gentle and consoling, her eyes wet with questions she never asked. No remedy could erase the topography of the past from Blake's skin, but in those moments by the stove, she believed in the healing magic of the old woman's fingers, in the possibility of caressing all the pain smooth.

By day, she carried her son bundled in a sling as she rambled across the snowy expanse of winter afternoons that stretched long *shadows over their heads and poured cold down her boots. She would walk the empty country road with his weight pulling on her shoulders and return to the house delirious with fatigue and the dazed joy of new motherhood. Sometimes, her grandfather would surprise her by scooping him into one gnarled arm and growling some unintelligible melody. Then she would collapse into the recliner to dream dreams permeated with the warm smells of her grandmother's cooking. It was an almost perfect time. Even in January's droning bleakness, she never missed the city with its noises and its hurry. Nor did she miss the mother who had ceased loving her, either by side effect or necessity. The mother who had nudged her toward Angel, muttering, "Keep quiet and do what he says." The mother who had never bothered looking for her. Sometimes, a memory of the woman would visit Blake as she cradled her son and leave her temporarily breathless with wounded rage. It was more than a daughter's rage now. It was a mother's, inexorably entwined with her love for her son.*

She never told her grandparents how all of it had happened. How did a person tell a thing like that? The truth was a dagger, so Blake kept it sheathed. She turned her mind to the future and pinned her hopes there in that shadowless place. Mornings, while the baby slept, she helped her grandfather repair his pots and paint his buoys.

"I want to be a lobster fisher," she announced one day as the snow fell.

He glanced at her through the smoke of his cigarette. "Sternman of yours is kinda young, don'tcha think?"

But she knew that he was pleased. The knowledge put a light in her heart.

When she came in later from his trap shed, fingers stiff with cold, full breasts aching, she found her grandmother by the woodstove. She smiled tenderly at Blake in her man's overalls and her fraying, dark braids, and patted the stack of folded diapers in her own lap.

"The lad must have worn himself out last night. Ain't heard a peep."

Blake smiled back into the sagging visage of milky blue eyes and wrinkles. It was the last time she would see a face clearly again for many years. She climbed the stairs to the bedroom, lifted her son's small shape from the crib before she registered his stillness. His head sagged back against her arm. Then she saw the blueness of his lips, the dull, dark slits of his eyes. She put her finger in his slack mouth and let out a scream that she did not recognize as her own human noise. It was the sound of a final thread snapping. The sound of a soul going dark.

Her scream yanked her from sleep, sent her stumbling from bed with the pillow clutched to her chest. She blinked about at the burning lights of the loft and saw that the clock on the oven read ten minutes to four. Swiping at her cheeks, she remembered Nora and her fall, the groceries she had forgotten in their bags beside the stoop. She pulled on her fishing clothes and forged out into the darkness with her cell phone light to salvage what she could. Some of the produce was still good. She gathered up the canned goods and the foil bags of health foods and slipped inside the house to set the items on the counter. The bulb on the stove hood provided sufficient light to examine the pantry shelves and stack the recovered groceries in the appropriate places. The residue of the dream clung to her like a cobweb. She attempted to shuck it off as she worked. In the refrigerator, she discovered a chaos to which she felt compelled to put order. She weeded out several expired cheeses and a brown head of lettuce, organized soft drink cans and yogurt. Behind the orange juice, she discovered the rack of syringes and peered at them with morbid interest, then slapped the door shut and was turning to leave when she caught sight of Nora's small profile in the hall. Both of them jumped.

"Blake?"

She lifted her empty hands, then dropped them, locked them before her, embarrassed. "I was just putting away your groceries. I thought you were sleeping."

"I heard the door."

Nora switched on the overhead light. The bones of her face pressed sharply against her skin. She looked delicate as a child in the robe. Blake recalled the milk-pale body beneath, the angry injection marks, and the startling trellis of her ribs.

She cleared her throat. "Want some coffee? I can make some before I head out."

"You don't have to do that."

Nora felt her way to one of the chairs at the small table, which was piled high with catalogs and bills. She turned some of the envelopes face down.

"You never told me how it's going with Leland."

"It's going."

"How bad is he, Blake?"

"If he hasn't pickled his liver yet, he'll manage it by thirty." She flipped open an oak cabinet. "Where do you keep your mugs?"

Nora shook her head. "It breaks my heart. He and Morning Glory were so close as kids." She sighed, turning over more envelopes. "He was a gentle boy, really. He just . . . lost his way after his father got in trouble. All three of those Savard kids did."

"What'd his father do?"

"Drank and poached and beat his children." Nora's shoulders stiffened. "The thing they finally put him away for, though, was murder."

The mug Blake had located in an upper cabinet clattered from the shelf. She managed to catch it just before it smashed against the counter.

"He turned into a monster," Nora whispered. "I never understood why. I just know he's unforgivable, that man."

Blake stood very still by the sink, the mug clutched between her hands, nausea roiling in her stomach. Then the clock chimed four-thirty in the hall, and she shook herself.

"I had to throw out the eggs and all those TV dinners you got. Want me to swing by Kinnon's this afternoon and get some more?"

"No, thank you. I can go myself. I'm not an invalid."

"You're a righty who broke her dominant wrist. That's at least *half* invalid."

Nora pulled herself up from the chair. In her bare feet, she stood a full foot shorter than Blake, but her hand, when it caught Blake's arm, proved firm and determined.

"I can't be even half," she said. "Do you understand? I've got to try every day to be a whole person, no matter what parts of me are broken."

"That doesn't mean you don't need help—"

"They say I'm probably going to end up in a wheelchair." Lips trembling, Nora peered up into Blake's hard face. "I'm going to need help just getting in and out of bed because that's the burden God has given me. But it's not going to happen until my daughter is through with college and med school. I promised myself that—to be strong. So, if you want to help me, Blake, please, help me be strong, all right?"

The coffee had finished percolating. In the absence of its gurgling, the silence of the house poured between them. Blake took a step backward from Nora's solemn gaze and knocked her hip against the counter. Her heart beat strangely fast.

"What makes you think I know how to do that?" she

snapped, snatching the colander from the machine. "I'm sorry you're sick. I think it's more proof God's just a sack of shit."

She ignored Nora's flinch and filled the mug, thumped it on the counter. "Here's my help. Take it or leave it."

The wind came up early and made for misery. Bleary-eyed and stiff-limbed, Blake propped herself at the rail and endured assaults of cold spray as Leland gaffed his buoys and landed his traps. She was glad for the work, for a purpose that kept her hands and mind busy, but in the intervals between sets, when Leland drove the boat miles through the mounting swell, her thoughts veered back to the frail widow with her fridge full of syringes and her table piled with bills. It angered her, to lose control of her thoughts this way. She smoked through half a pack of cigarettes and glared moodily into the chop as the boat pitched and heaved.

"Don't you think this is getting a bit ugly?" she shouted at her sullen captain.

A gush of green water poured over the gunwale. Leland just threw her a surly look beneath the frayed brim of his cap. "Scared, Amazon?"

"I'm not in the mood for a swim."

"We ain't even close to swimmin'."

As if to prove the point, he bore down on the throttle, sent the nose of the *All In* pitching up into the face of another swell. Blake gripped the frame of the cockpit and clenched her teeth. She watched the depth sounder wink and the cord of the VHF mic swing. She liked keeping an eye on the gauges, her trust in the coarse young lobsterman about as threadbare as the jeans he wore beneath his Grudens. Today marked the third day Blake had caught alcohol on his breath before noon. She had seen the bottle he kept stashed with some other junk in one of the forward compartments, the pulls he snuck when he thought she was not looking. She suspected there were pills, too.

There were always pills.

On the bulkhead, he kept a single photograph of his daughter taped in plastic. Quinn looked to be about three in the picture, with round cheeks and champagne hair that had yet to darken. She sat on the lap of a woman who had been raggedly cropped from the image.

"You kill yourself out here, who takes care of Quinn?" she asked.

Leland rolled his broad shoulders, soggy cigarette clamped between his teeth. "Thought we agreed no small talk."

Blake grimaced as the bow took a hard hit of spray. "Nora had an accident last night."

This earned her a sideways glance. "What kind of accident?"

"Fell and broke her wrist."

He gave the brass wheel a spin, sent them plunging again. "Fuckin' MS."

"So, you know?"

"'Course I know. It's the whole reason Mornin' Glory wants to go to med school 'til she's forty." The radio spit a burst of static. He punched it off and squinted at the coordinates on the Garmin. "She's gonna lose it when she finds out her mom hurt herself again."

Blake caught a blast of his bourbon-tinged breath and frowned. On the dash, the coordinates ticked, ticked, ticked.

"You know anything about gutters?" she asked.

"I know they're a pain in the ass. Why?"

"That house of theirs needs work. Might think about helping them out a little, fixing a few things. Sure the daughter would appreciate the gesture."

When he said nothing, she pressed on. "Tomorrow,

maybe. Weather's supposed to be good. You come over and work on those gutters after we're done out here. They'd be all fixed before she got home."

Leland laid off the throttle. Through the chop, Blake spotted his next string of buoys bobbing like bloated limes off the starboard bow.

"I can't tomorrow," he growled. "You get a day off. I got business downstate."

"What kind of business?"

"The kind that ain't yours," he said.

6.

Quinn surprised Leland in the bathroom, where he had gotten lost briefly in the foggy horror of his reflection. She pranced in wearing one of Nicole's sequined T-shirts, which she had gathered in a bunch at her waist, tie-dye leggings torn, tennis shoes dragging muddy laces. He grimaced. Only a matter of time before the school sent another social worker to sniff around and dig up more dirt for their Savards-Are-the-Scourge-of-the-Peninsula file, which dated back to his own bruise-mottled boyhood.

"You goin' to see Grandpa Jake?" Quinn asked as she perched atop the john to watch him finish with the razor. "Can I come?"

"No way. That place ain't for little girls." His hand shook slightly. The razor dragged away a crescent of skin along his jaw. "*Tabarnak!*"

His daughter handed him a wad of toilet paper. "You ain't much good at that, Papa."

"Nope."

"You worried about Grandpa?"

"He's the kind of man you got to worry about, Quinnie."

"Like you."

He turned from the sink to peer at her, wiped the sparkling evidence of rouge from her cheek. His mouth felt lined with cotton, and blood roared through his temples like a pack of derby cars.

"You ain't gotta worry about me, *comprends*, Quinnie?"

"You got your shirt on wrong."

Leland glanced down at the crooked row of buttons and sighed. He let Quinn rework them into an even line with her skinny fingers, sharp face pinched in concentration. He knew he was going to be sick, but he tried to wrestle down the sensation until she hopped off the can.

"Teacher's makin' us do a report about a country," she chirped. "I picked Brazil. Think the Amazon'll help me?"

"*Marde*, I dunno, Quinnie."

He stood up and inspected himself in the mirror, knowing already that his red eyes and chapped nose would earn him an extra frisking at the prison, regardless of whether he made it through the metal detectors without a chorus of beeping. The prospect of freezing his ass off on deck with Blake Renato suddenly struck him as less abhorrent than it had the previous three weeks.

Out in the main room, his sister's heels paced the linoleum as she jabbered on her cell.

"Go on," he told Quinn. "Don't give Nicky no more excuses for speedin'."

"She can't help it," replied his daughter, all green-eyed solemnity. "It's the lead she's got stuck in her foot."

When she went out, he shut the door and dropped in front of the toilet again, heaved until his eyes streamed and his shoulders ached. He waited until he heard the tires of Nicky's Rav crunch down the gravel lane. Then he picked himself up and prepared himself for the journey down to Warren.

The visit room reeked of nervous sweat and anger, and every time Leland entered it, he experienced a kind of buckling dread that accompanied premonitions of his own world reduced to four walls, steel doors, and bulletproof glass. His personal scrapes with the law had acquainted him with handcuffs and piss-stained holding cells, but those stints had been of the local, short-lived, teach-the-trailer-trash-a-lesson variety. It was not until his father landed here in state prison that Leland got a full look at the thirty-to-life kind of purgatory. That look scared the shit out of him. He never felt quite so worthless as he did inside this particular room—and he was not even the one wearing the inmate duds and Crocs. It took him days to drink off that feeling. Today, it worked its way particularly deep as he sat waiting for his father at the table assigned by the Visit Officer.

Years ago, he had made the mistake of bringing Quinn and her mother along. He had been eager to prove to his cynical old man that he had succeeded at putting a ring on Anna Jarnot's finger and clothes on his daughter's back—two feats Jacob Savard had accused him of being too young and stupid to pull off. Anna, guessing his motive, had resisted the visit from the start, and Quinn, who had just begun to toddle, refused to cooperate by sitting in her mother's lap. When she squirmed loose, Leland jumped up to corral her, and two spooked COs advanced in his direction, barking reprimands. Anna lunged at them, spitting threats, and in the end, the three of them had been strong-armed out of there while Leland's father sat calmly at the table, sneering at the whole scene like he had written the script for it. After that, Leland came only with Nicole or Jonny. His older siblings possessed more talent at deflecting Jacob's snide remarks and deadpan gaze and, for that matter, the general horror of the place. But today, Leland had come alone. His stomach remained a sea of white caps well past the time the officers led his father in.

Fifty-five years old, Jacob Savard stood six-three,

dark-bearded and barrel-chested, with all the swaggering confidence of a pirate king. The sight of him standing still, waiting for the coffee-skinned, five-nine corrections officer to uncuff him, might have struck Leland as comical had it not frightened him a little. Childhood experience had taught him how fast his father could move, how quickly he could morph from a quiet, smirking giant into an F5 tornado with iron fists. Leland owed his first (and last) broken bones to the force of nature that was Jacob, having spent the first fifteen years of his life atoning for the sin of his mother's flight from the family just months after his birth. Not until Quinn came along did he understand the absurdity of blaming an infant for the faults of its mother. But by that time, his father was awaiting trial for murder. There seemed little point to addressing the lesser of the man's evils.

They did not shake hands. Instead, his father dropped into the opposite chair and regarded him with eyes cold and dark as saltwater mussels.

"I put a hundred on your account," Leland said. "Just so you know."

His father's face still bore the wind-chapped quality of a man who had spent his life on the water. Its expression proved difficult to read beneath the beard, but Leland sensed the contempt radiating off him long before he decided to speak.

"Why'd it take you so long to get your ass down here?" he wanted to know.

"Had to take care of things on the boat. You know what it's like this time of year. You don't stake your territory, you lose—"

"Don't tell me about fishin'." The cords of his father's neck jumped. "Don't tell me anythin' except how you plan to honor your brother."

Leland kept his big hands flattened atop the table. It took

all of his effort to keep them there. He looked away from his father's eyes, their chill penetrating to his marrow.

"I bought a stone. A good one. He's got a spot up to Sagamore with Aunt Lis—"

"I mean *honor* him," repeated Jacob.

The painted cinderblock wall beyond his father's head proved a more inviting place to fix his eyes, so Leland kept them there, aware Jacob was not waiting for words, but for the sag of his head, the acknowledgment that he understood and accepted the responsibility to carry out a vendetta. It was not that Leland had arrived unprepared for this pressure from his father—the noise of flapping mouths always made it, somehow, within the walls of the Maine State Prison and directly to his old man; rather, his body was not responding to it the way he imagined it would. Instead of its usual inward collapse, its biological compulsion to consent, he felt the greasy stirrings of a rage he had kept tamped down for the entirety of his adulthood. A rage that scared him almost as much as his father did.

"I don't know what you've heard," he said through his teeth. "But there ain't no truth to it. Jonny just . . . made a mistake. It was an accident."

"Even you ain't dumb enough to believe that."

Leland pinned his right hand atop his left, which was getting twitchy. The air felt too thin, the chair too confining. "I got Quinn to take care of. I got a boat and a new sternman—"

"A dyke Mexican," his father sneered. "Nicky told me. Ain't you progressive."

He finally met his father's eyes. "I'm fishin'. That's more than you're doin', ain't it?"

Jacob creaked forward in the plastic chair, a subtle movement that still managed to convey the horsepower he packed beneath those baggy clothes.

"Your brother was a warrior. He did things you would have pissed your pants just thinkin' about. And here you are, a grown-ass man, still pissin' your pants."

"I'm not—"

"*Calisse!* Think of the favors he done you. Hell, you never would've had the opportunity to stick your prick in the Jarnot girl if he hadn't buttered her up for you first. And this is how you thank him, sittin' on your ass 'stead of doin' your duty."

Slowly, Leland unfolded himself from the chair. His father rose at the same time and barked at the CO before Leland could signal.

"Get me outta here, huh? We're done."

They stood glaring at one another until the door clicked open and a different burly officer in a brush cut moved in to re-cuff his father and escort him from the room. Sweat prickled on Leland's scalp as he followed his own escort down a garishly lit corridor and out to the lobby. There, he retrieved his wallet, phone, and keys from the quarter-operated locker and shoved out into the relief of fresh air. By the time he reached the truck, his phone lit up with seven missed call alerts and three voice mails. His already hammering heart performed a cartwheel when he recognized the number of Quinn's elementary school. Before he had the chance to check the message, Nicole sent him the last of what proved a tirade of texts that had begun half an hour earlier.

Get the fuck back here. Q's done it again

punched her gym teacher suspended for 2 days principal's ripshit

had 2 pick her up. U plan on payin me for this shit??

im gonna lose my job!!!

u there?

hello?

Leland sent his fist into the hood of the cab, where it left a mark to join the half-dozen others put there by his kin. He waited for the rage to split him apart like so many continents, for old fault lines to simmer red and gap wide. But all that happened was that his knuckles began to throb, his eyes to pool. Flinging the phone on the seat, he took a squealing left out of the prison parking lot and sped north toward his next reason to drink.

Nicole came flying at his truck before he even had it in park, breasts bouncing inside a zebra print sweater that crawled up toward her navel and exposed the top of a new and alarming tattoo.

"She's not *my* kid, Leland! I can't swoop in whenever she loses her shit and that pansy-ass principal wants her out! I was s'posed to be at work an hour ago—"

Her noise sailed past him like a breeze. Armed with a case of PBR and liter of Jack Daniel's, he strode toward the cabin and kicked open the door she'd left hanging ajar. Quinn let out a startled yelp. She stood in the kitchen in her drooping ponytail and too-big sequined shirt. A bout of early crying had left her face looking blotchy and bee-stung. When she saw his expression, she backed up, a spiral-ringed notebook hugged to her chest.

"I'm sorry, Papa . . . I'm—"

The case of beer landed with a thump on the table, scattering the artwork she had assembled there. He had already opened the whiskey, so he tilted the bottle to his lips and took three desperate swallows. Quinn began to sniffle. She retreated farther into the shadows.

The warmth of the liquor buzzing through Leland only made the prison stench rise more sharply from his clothes, his daughter's fear of him more depressing. It wasn't supposed to work this way.

"The hell's gotten into you, girl? You want the state to come take you away?"

"The teacher was makin' fun! He was sayin' junkies are what's wrong with our state, that it would be better if they all OD-ed. He was—"

Leland sent the bottle hurdling at the TV, where it knocked the screen dead. Hands pressed to her ears, Quinn cowered behind the couch and began to sob in earnest. Leland pulled her up by one scrawny arm and pushed her onto the cushions. Like a cornered rabbit, she tried to scramble away from him. The fear in her face only made him angrier. He dropped down on one knee and pinned her legs under one hand.

"Look at me! People talk shit. You can't go punchin' all of 'em. You won't have no knuckles left."

"But Uncle Jonny—"

"Uncle Jonny had problems! I got problems, too! You wanna hit someone, hit me, not your fuckin' teacher. You're so angry, girl, then hit me, huh? *Vas-y!*"

Face crumpling, Quinn shrank into the cushions. She shook her head, but he leaned into her, blood roaring as he shouted madly, "Hit me! Do it! Do i—"

Her fist caught him just under the left eye, a sharp-boned missile that packed enough power to knock his head sideways. She cried out as she did it. Leland rocked back on his heels, a little stunned. The pain drove home the reality of the thing he had just made her do. Meanwhile, Quinn twisted off the couch and bolted for the slider, fled in bare feet down the mossy step into the woods. The sequins of her shirt caught the sunlight like sparks as she bounded away through the trees.

She knew the deer path well and did not slow her pace, even as her feet struck roots and acorns and her leggings snagged on tufts of bark and tangles of wild berry vines. Through her tears, the forest morphed into a deep green watercolor. Twice she tumbled, spattering Aunt Nicky's sparkly rainbow shirt in mud, but she picked herself up and pushed on until the woods opened up onto the tidal marsh. There, the gold-brushed expanse of cordgrass greeted her like a familiar smile. She halted to wipe her eyes and gaze in appreciation at a pair of slender white cranes posed on the bank of the tidal creek, elegant as statues as they stalked minnows and eels. This had always been Quinn's invisible place, a landscape into which she could disappear when necessary, let her anger and sadness leech into the creek and be ferried off to the sea.

Today, the rank odor of low tide stormed her nostrils as she waded out through the marsh grass, crunching periodically upon the bleached skeletons of crabs and other sea life that lay snagged among the long blades. In late summer, heather bloomed here in abundance. She once helped Aunt Nicky harvest lush bouquets of it to fasten with Papa's lobster bands and sell on the roadside. When she wasn't drunk or hopped on Quinn's ADHD medicine, her aunt was all right. But now Aunt Nicky wanted nothing to do with her, and Papa was on the brink of another bender, and even this place of moving water and lifting wings could not fully console her.

Lately, it seemed that all Quinn did was make people angry. Papa was right; she was angry, too, though she did not know exactly why. Nor did punching him make her feel any better. Her arm ached from the effort, and her heart ached, too, because his face as he had yelled at her to do it belonged to a man she did not recognize—a man who looked like he could hurt her. Though he had spanked her a few times, and occasionally, he played too rough, Papa had never harmed her. The thought that the man she'd left back in the cabin might made Quinn start to cry again.

Crouched on the cold clay of the bank, she poked at snails,

big browns and creamy whites with stripes, and a few tiny and gold as fake teeth. With a stick, she scratched her name in the pungent muck and took her time to perfect a long, squiggly tail on the *Q*. Sometimes, when she came here with Papa, they played tic-tac-toe this way. Once, they had even unearthed a whole collection of pottery shards caught like jagged teeth in the bank. They spent an afternoon trying to fit them together like pieces of a puzzle, and she still kept them in a shoebox underneath her bed in case she ever found the rest of them. That was the papa she loved best, the quiet, clever adventurer who could make games from anything they stumbled across on their walks and rambles. The papa she once heard Uncle Jonny refer to as a pussy—before Papa showed him how a pussy could punch.

A chilly May breeze licked the bank, but down below the ragged lip, it was not so bad. The soft suck of briny mud helped to soothe her injured feet, and after a while, she waded into the shin-deep water and let them go completely numb. Posed there as still as the birds, she watched afternoon shadows crawl across the marsh until she grew too cold and hungry to commune any longer with nature. With a soft sigh, she made the turn for Jonny's trailer.

She would sleep there for the night, she decided. Just to be safe.

7

Blake spent her day off in Machias, perusing preowned lots until she spotted a beige 2002 Sierra that looked like it hadn't gone completely through the mill. She spared the salesman his pitch, laid down her terms, and started to walk off the lot twice before the disheartened old Mainer threw up his hands and accepted her offer on a trade for the Rio. Emboldened by this small victory, she set off down the coast to tackle her next set of errands.

The salesclerk at Ritter's Marine Supply didn't know quite what to make of her. His eyes followed Blake from aisle to aisle as she collected muck boots and oil gear, narrowed as she paused by the corkboard up front to scan a smattering of lobster boat listings.

"Doubt there's anything there that'd interest you," he remarked.

Blake slung her pile of purchases onto the counter and gave him the dead-eyed stare she'd reserved for newbies in her cellblock who made the mistake of pegging her for lonely. The kind of stare that she could inhabit with all seventy-three inches and one hundred eighty-two pounds of her body. The effort drained her. Afterward, she trudged out, convinced she'd overpaid for everything—including the truck.

Agitated, she drifted down to Roque Bluffs State Park, where she perched on a ledge overlooking the cobbled, near-empty beach and watched winking shapes of boats trundle by on Englishman Bay. The distance calmed her some. Though the wind still carried a bite, the sun smiled warmly on her back, so she camped there awhile and read through a *National Geographic*, glancing up from time to time when a pedestrian crunched by leading a bundled child or a panting mutt. All it took was watching an elderly woman pick her way along the shoreline with trek poles to send Blake's mind pinwheeling back to Nora Hayes. Avoiding her since their exchange in the kitchen had done little good. She did not understand Nora's illness, nor the kind of help she might find acceptable, which seemed only to confirm that remaining indifferent to the affairs of the lobsterman's widow was the logical course of action. Blake owed her nothing but five hundred dollars a month—and that was all she planned to deliver.

Flopping back upon the stones, she tracked the path of a bald eagle as it wheeled against a backdrop of blue so intense, it hurt her eyes even through the glasses. The smells of waking earth surrounded her, and for several minutes, the beauty of Blake's resting place overwhelmed her senses. She folded her hands behind her head and envisioned shucking off the weight of her sore body, allowing herself to be carried away like a milkweed seed upon the breeze. How wonderful it would be never to confront her hard face in another mirror, to be rid of her hollow womb, her scarred, useless breasts, her cold, viscous heart. Her first years in prison, she had been consumed by the piercing desire to exit her body for good. Twice, she made earnest attempts. The second involved driving a contraband file into her femoral artery—a blundering and ultimately unsuccessful effort that earned her even more unwanted attention from Corrections. That was how she had first met Dawn Evers, handcuffed to a hospital bed with a pint of some stranger's blood freshly pumped into her veins.

"Aww, baby. You done fighting yourself yet? Aren't you close

to done? There's hurt spilling out of your ears, baby, but I still see you fighting. When you get tired, you let Dawn know. She's got eighteen better plans for you than this sad-ass hospital's got."

Blake opened her eyes on another eagle, traced its powerful ascent into the first of the afternoon clouds. She thought of Dawn, bald from chemo that first time, later a bold experimenter with African American wigs, the personalities of which would grow to be the topic of a running joke between them. Often, she wondered why the old prison shrink had put up with her after the first two dozen occasions when Blake confronted her outreach with outrage.

Vái te foder? Really, baby? You think I haven't been told to go fuck myself in twenty different languages? And Dawn had proceeded to drily rattle off the proof. You want to shock me, baby, tell me you love me. That sounds prettier in Portuguese, I bet.

It did.

Blake sat up and dug out her phone, snapped a picture of the cobalt bay ruffled white. She sent it to the now retired Dawn with the subject line: *Today's Therapy.* Then she stood and stretched and hiked back to her truck and drove home to Raker Harbor.

Next morning, only the sequins spared Quinn Savard from becoming a hood ornament. When she sprang into Blake's headlights, big-eyed as a startled doe, it was the sparkle of her T-shirt that Blake saw first. She stomped on the brake, sent her lunch bag and pile of new gear crashing into the dashboard. For a moment, the girl stood frozen six feet from the pickup's grille, a shivering phantom bleached white in the high beams. Only when Blake shoved open the driver's door did the small face twitch with any sign of recognition. Crossing her skinny arms over her shimmering chest, Quinn met Blake's sharp rebuke with a hung head.

"Papa ain't fishin' today. He's real sick."

As Blake took in more of the girl's appearance, alarm replaced her anger. Mud caked her bare feet and leggings, and her hair drooped in two, filthy clumps over her tensed shoulders. Her eyes looked suspiciously puffy.

"What do you mean *sick*?"

Quinn shrugged, stared at her feet. "You know."

It took Blake great effort to refrain from sputtering oaths as she moved toward the cabin. Inside, the overhead light in the kitchen gave her a sufficient view of things. Chairs lay overturned, joining dozens of cans and bottles that littered the linoleum. In the living room, the smashed TV lay on its side amid a glittering sea of glass from the missile that had caused the damage. Worst was the smell: a too-familiar mingling of piss and vomit. The muscles of Blake's back pulled tight. Her hands curled into fists inside her sweatshirt pockets. When she glanced back at the door, she saw Quinn leaning against its frame, the shame on her face the crowning horror of the whole scene.

Blake strode down the back hall, pushing open doors until she found the room containing the lobsterman. He lay face down and naked across a frameless double bed whose covers sat in a grotesque tangle upon the floor. Blake was thankful for the low light, though she could sense the general filth of the room, smell the dirty sheets and soiled clothes, the curtains that hung heavy and yellow with smoke. She groped for the nearest article of clothing, a flannel shirt, and tossed it over his hips, then gave his shoulder a hard nudge with her knuckles.

"Leland! Wake up, damn it!"

Were it not for the heavy sound of his breath expelled against the mattress, she might have worried he had finally done himself in. She let her fist strike the hot skin of his biceps with greater force.

"Wake up!"

His eyelids fluttered briefly. He gave a short groan before dropping back into his senseless stupor.

Blake contemplated a third blow, then turned and left the room in fear her gag reflex would trump her fury. In the kitchen, she found Quinn cradling a roll of paper towels like a doll. The sight was like a knife's twist. Blake snatched the towels away, slammed the chairs back into their place at the table.

"Don't you clean this up! It's his mess. Let him see what he's done."

Rage, old and dangerous, scratched its claws in Blake's throat. She made herself draw five slow breaths the way Dawn had taught her. Then she squatted before the girl, started to reach for her shoulders, thought better of it.

"Did he hurt you?" she asked more quietly. "You can tell me."

Quinn sniffled. "I hurt *him*. He told me to punch him, and I did."

Blake just stared as the girl held up her bruised little knuckles as proof. Slowly, she reached for her cigarettes and lit one, sucking the smoke into her lungs with quiet desperation.

"Can you go stay with your aunt until school time? Doesn't she live in that trailer, there?"

The girl's tears cleared trails down her dirt-smudged face. "I can't go to school. I'm suspended 'til Monday."

"What?"

"And Aunt Nicky's gonna lose her job if she misses another day. I heard her say it. She said she's gonna be broke, and the State's gonna come and take me away from Papa 'cause he's such a fuckup . . ."

With a choked sob, Quinn flung her arms around Blake and clung to her.

"Help me, Amazon! Can't I just stay with you for the day?"

"Stay where?" Blake did not know where to put her hand besides atop the girl's snarled hair. Even this simple act left her paralyzed. Her cigarette turned to ash in the other hand as her body went rigid. "I live above a *garage*. And I'm not a babysitter."

Quinn pulled back, her nose wrinkled in indignation. "I don't need a *babysitter*. I just need . . . a big friend."

Blake peered down at her, nerves raw from the stench of the cabin and the tears that had leaked through her shirt. Her heart was doing the odd tripping thing it did sometimes when she smoked too much, except she'd had only one cigarette that morning. *You're not my problem*, she wanted to scream. *I can't make you my problem*. Instead, she kicked away some cans and picked up one of Quinn's rogue crayons. On the back of one of her drawings, Blake scrawled a note to Leland or the sister or whoever else might think to come looking for a raggedy, suspended third grader. She threw in a few choice words and signed off with her phone number.

Quinn was already halfway to the truck before Blake caught up with her, toting a pair of kid's sneakers she had grabbed from beside the door.

"You got some explaining to do," she said as the girl scampered up into the passenger's seat. "Why are you suspended?"

Quinn shrugged and reached for the radio dial, but Blake intercepted her small fingers.

"You're gonna tell me the truth, or no music."

The girl slumped into the seat and sulked. In close quarters, Blake realized she smelled like a tidal marsh. She had lacked the presence of mind to ask her to change her clothes. The thought of returning to that godawful cabin made her stomach turn, so she kept her foot on the accelerator and barreled out through the tunnel of trees toward the Post Road. She had no idea where she was going. She simply drove and smoked, physical speed and nicotine the two addictions she had never managed to kick despite the best efforts of Dawn Evers and the Massachusetts Department of Corrections.

"I hit Mr. Yunker," Quinn confessed, five minutes into Blake's stony silence. "He was talkin' shit about junkies, and he knew all about Jonny."

Blake kept her eyes fastened to the road.

"You can't hit people. Not even if they ask you to, all right?"

Quinn just stared out the window at the sprinkle of lights from the fishermen's cottages across the marsh.

"You can't steal stuff, either. Even a lousy pack of gum. You'll end up in jail if you do that kind of stuff."

"I'm not scared of jail," sniffed Quinn. "Half the Savards are in there."

"You'd be scared if you were locked in a cell with a total stranger who got to watch you piss and shit. If you only got to go outside for an hour a day and always had guards yelling at you to hurry the fuck up—"

"That's just movie stuff."

"It is *not*," Blake snapped, her mouth going dry as she felt the green slats of the girl's eyes turn toward her. "My friend wasted twenty years of her life in prison because she screwed up big."

"What'd she do?"

"Never mind what she did. Just keep your nose clean."

Quinn gave her nose a puzzled swipe with the back of her hand.

They rumbled along in silence as Blake tried to cobble together a plan. They were headed south toward town, so she decided she would find them both some breakfast at the general store. When Quinn's fingers crept back to the radio dial, Blake let her scroll to the country station. She left her experimenting with the other dated controls while she tramped into Moody's. Several fishermen loitered by the register, cradling paper cups of coffee pumped from the big stainless vat at the counter. They watched her ponder the narrow aisles, pulling packages of mini-muffins and chocolate milk, a box of colored pencils, a coloring book. She felt flustered and clueless, had so carefully suppressed memories of her own girlhood that she struggled to recall any of its amusements. Candy necklaces? Puzzle books? Bubble wands?

"Colorin' book for your captain?" quipped Harley Cann as she reached the counter. "Looks 'bout his readin' level."

Blake was glad Quinn had stayed in the truck. She pushed some money at white-whiskered Chester Moody, who offered more soberly, "Oughta know that boat's cursed, ma'am. What with how them last two sternmen ended up."

With a shrug, Blake collected the items from the counter, then waited for the men to shuffle aside so she could pass. It took a moment, but eventually they made way, and she hurried through the gauntlet of smoky flannel and salt-stained boots into the first timid light of the morning.

They ate parked out by the breakwater on Wind Cove. Blake wished to spare the girl from becoming the next piece of general store gossip and thus avoided the wharf. The sun came up slowly, and with it, birds arrived by the dozens. Quinn pushed down the window and tossed bits of her muffins to the squalling flock of enormous gulls who swooped and squabbled over the crumbs.

"You think I want my new truck painted in poop?" growled Blake.

"Poop washes off. And this ain't really *new*, is it?"

Blake frowned. The radio thumped with the twangy beats of artists she did not know, but Quinn could sing along to almost all of them in a voice so sweet and clear, it seemed shoplifted right out of a choir girl's throat. Blake picked up two bars of reception in the lot. She found Dawn's reply to yesterday's picture sitting in her otherwise empty in-box.

True to form, the shrink's email consisted of a single pointed line:

You finding any peace yet, or are you just taking pictures?

Blake clicked off the phone. She doubted Dawn would consider babysitting the borderline juvenile delinquent daughter of her alcoholic captain a step in the right direction of well-being. She picked at a callus on her left hand, watching Quinn empty her foil packet of muffins on the assembly of avian beggars. When the girl ran out of enticements, she turned to Blake, mouth ringed with chocolate milk.

"I can wash your truck if you want. Papa lets me wash his."

"Well, that's something," muttered Blake. "Maybe I can put you to *work*."

By the time they reached the Hayes place, the morning had lost some of its raw edge. Quinn was still singing, and Blake felt a bit steadier. As she parked the truck by the giant garage, the girl sprang from the cab and bounded toward the house before Blake could call out to her. Nora must have heard the truck. She appeared almost immediately at the door, wrapped in the same bathrobe Blake had helped her into the night of her accident. The force of Quinn's hug caused her to stumble backward, but she caught the doorframe to steady herself and promptly looped her good arm around the girl, all the while lifting startled eyes toward Blake.

"Goodness, Quinnie! Shouldn't you be at school?"

"I'm suspended," declared Quinn, with considerably more gusto than earlier. "The Amazon says I can help her today!"

"The Ama—" Nora flushed when she realized who the girl meant. She stood, briefly speechless, lifting a lock of Quinn's filthy hair in her fingers.

"Her father's sick," Blake said. "I thought she could help with a few projects over here. Maybe get started on that garden?"

"I'm a good planter!" piped up Quinn. She noticed Nora's wrist, then. "You get hurt again, Ms. Nora? You got to be more careful on your clumsy feet!"

Nora's face gave way to a smile of perplexed sadness.

"You're right, Quinnie. I really do."

She looked at Blake, who hovered awkwardly on the stoop. "Why don't you both come in? I think the garden is a great idea, but we'll need a plan. And Quinnie, no proper gardener *starts* the day with a dirty face. Go down to the bathroom and scrub up. I'll find you some clean clothes from Morning Glory's room."

The quiet authority Nora's voice adopted both surprised and relieved Blake. As the girl marched obediently down the hall, Nora turned and pinned her with a questioning stare.

"I . . . I couldn't just leave her there. The place is trashed. He was completely out of it."

Nora nodded slowly. Then she reached for Blake's arm and gave it a gentle squeeze. Her eyes shone a bright, clear amber as they caught the light from the kitchen window.

"You did the right thing bringing her here. Let me get dressed. We'll get it sorted."

Thirty minutes later, the three of them crowded Nora's little kitchen table, a piece of chart paper spread before them.

Quinn, her face a freshly scrubbed pink, wore one of Glory's old track sweatshirts, rolled up half a dozen times in the sleeves. It appeared that Nora also had dipped into her daughter's wardrobe. Beneath a loose brown sweater she'd donned a pair of sweatpants with the *Down East Tritons* logo emblazoned across the ass. Blake bit down on a smirk at the sight of the prim little woman dressed like a teen slob. She suspected Nora had run out of outfits easily navigated with one hand.

"Blake, you draw us a nice neat rectangle," Nora directed, handing her a pencil and ruler. "And Quinnie, I want you to read these seed packets, here. First, find our zone on that little map. Which one are we?"

"5b!"

"That's right. Now, which of these are safe to plant in early May?"

Quinn sifted through the packets, eyes narrowed in concentration and an obvious desire to please. "Broccoli, carrots . . . spinach . . . peas . . . kale. Ugh! *Kale!* Who eats that shit?"

Blake smothered another smirk, but Nora's face remained solemn behind the pair of tortoise-rimmed readers she had pulled on to inspect their progress.

"Language, Quinnie."

"Sorry."

Next, Nora asked Blake to create a grid in the rectangle. Quinn used her new colored pencils to color-code each section of the garden according to which crop they would plant there. For a rule breaker, the girl showed exceptional talent at staying in the lines. Blake noticed that she even texturized each of the boxes to further differentiate them. When she'd finished, Nora instructed her to spell out the names of each of their crops at the bottom of the paper.

Blake's gaze flickered to the widow. "Were you a teacher?"

Nora shrugged. "Just Sunday school. A long time ago."

"Bet those kids learned their Jesus."

This made Quinn choke on the orange juice she was sipping. It trickled from her nose as she gave way to sputtering giggles. Nora frowned at Blake. Then one corner of her mouth pulled shyly upward.

"They did, as a matter of fact. I guess I was pretty good at it."

"Why'd you quit?"

The smile faded. "Oh, I don't know. Benji . . ."

Blake remembered the picture of the little boy in the garage, a boy Nora never mentioned. A grim suspicion squeezed her heart. She diverted her eyes to the chart paper, where Quinn was grappling with a creative spelling of *broccoli*.

"*C*, not *k*," Blake said. Then to Nora, "What genius decided it was smart to suspend a third grader who can't even spell basic vegetables?"

"The principal's a pussy," offered Quinn. "Aunt Nicky says so."

Nora pursed her lips. "No more swearing, young lady. Dirty words will poison the plants."

"Will not."

"Will too," Blake surprised herself by jumping in. "I've killed a whole bunch from cussing. That's why you got to yell at me if you hear me doing it, okay?"

The girl frowned at her. "I thought Amazons could do whatever they want."

"Within reason," Blake said with a wink.

Outside, the sun had succeeded in chasing off the chill. When Nora stepped into it, she experienced a brief dizziness that had less to do with her erratic nervous system than it did with the joy of beginning another garden. Each year, this little plot behind the house became her special project, a sacred place of quiet summer afternoons spent on her knees amid pungent stalks and buzzing bees, weeding, pruning, harvesting. While her daughter and husband had the ocean, Nora had the earth itself. Nowhere was she more at peace than with her hands in the soil and the sun on her back. But every year, the labor became more difficult. The complaints of her body grew louder, and at unpredictable times, her limbs betrayed her, simply refusing to perform in the way she needed them. The past several springs, she had relied on her husband to haul in the compost and break up the soil. And this year, with her broken wrist, she had all but given up on the project. Now, as she watched Blake and Quinn retrieve the steel rake and spade and hoe from the shed, her fingers slipped to the cross at her throat.

She recognized a blessing when she received one.

With the trek pole, she picked her way along the rectangle of the garden plot as Blake and the girl endeavored to break up the soil. Quinn danced around with the hoe while Blake, a veritable giant beside her, worked with long, practiced strokes, the thick cord of her braid swinging across her shoulders. The sunlight brought out the rogue threads of silver in it, though the energy with which she applied herself to the task belonged to a woman half her age. Nora felt a twinge of jealousy, quickly supplanted by guilt.

"I wish I could help with this part," she said.

"We don't need help!" sang out Quinn. "Blake and I are Amazons!"

"Hoe a little faster, Amazon," grunted Blake.

A pile of compost sat at the far corner of the yard. The next step consisted of ferrying it to the plot with the ancient wheelbarrow. Blake stationed Quinn at the pile to help shovel on the load, but soon the two of them were racing each other across the lawn, Blake pushing the barrel and Quinn loping alongside in her muddy Keds, all loose limbs and laughter. Nora watched them beneath the brim of her straw hat, Leland Savard's wayward little girl and the swarthy, ex-military atheist, and she thought, if it was an incongruous pair, it was, at least, a productive one. They had the pile transferred and mixed in under an hour.

When they'd finished, Blake paused to strip off her sweatshirt. Beneath it, she wore a sleeveless T-shirt that revealed the impressive musculature of her shoulders and arms. Nora saw at once why the woman had no trouble working on a lobster boat. The crude tattoo of a dagger consumed by flowered vines ran inside the length of her left biceps. Quinn spotted it at the same time Nora did.

"What's *that?*" the girl murmured, spellbound.

Blake folded her arms, a gesture so quick, it ended all discussion.

As she caught herself staring, Nora retreated inside to prepare them a snack. Her face felt sunburnt, though she had worn the hat all morning. She chopped recklessly at some strawberries, unable to quell the uneasiness Blake's appearance had touched off. She knew better than to judge people this way—and yet, when she carried the plate of snacks out to the back patio, she could scarcely bring herself to look in Blake's direction, afraid she might glimpse the inked weapon again. Her tenant and the girl were seated on opposite sides of the weathered picnic table, studying a bright green caterpillar that inched along its surface.

"Do Amazons eat bugs?" Quinn inquired.

"We're not that uncivilized."

"Ms. Nora, do you know Blake's from Brazil?"

"Not *from*," Blake corrected her. "My father emigrated from there."

"Why?"

"He was poor." Blake paused to light a cigarette. Her face had darkened.

"Can you talk Brazilian?"

"Portuguese. And I haven't 'talked it' in a long time."

"Why?"

Blake exhaled smoke through her nostrils, shifting uncomfortably. "My father died when I was your age. My mother didn't speak it, so she didn't like when I did."

Hearing the edge in her voice, Nora nudged the plate of fruit in front of the girl, a well-received distraction. Then she plucked up the caterpillar and carried it to an azalea bush at the corner of the patio.

"That's a cabbage looper," Blake remarked. "It'll feast on anything we plant here."

"Live and let live." Nora shrugged.

"Live and let destroy, you mean."

Her dark eyes had turned impenetrable again. She rose from the bench with such suddenness that Nora flinched. Walking to the bush, she ripped off the leaf containing the tiny denizen. A chill washed over Nora as she envisioned Blake crushing the caterpillar between her powerful fingers. Instead, she stalked away across the field, leaf in hand, and did not stop until she had reached the distant wood line. Even from a distance, Nora saw the care with which Blake bent to deposit the creature in the brush. She released her breath, unconscious until then that she had been holding it. Beside her, she heard Quinn do the same.

"She ain't as scary as she looks," concluded the girl, popping a strawberry into her mouth.

Nora touched her necklace again. "Most people aren't."

They spent the rest of the morning planting. Nora tapped the seeds into Quinn's palm, and Blake, squatting in the dirt, directed her on the spacing and depth. In this way, they moved as a little trio down their established rows, each contributing what she was able. Quinn took her job seriously. When she accidentally dropped a seed, she insisted on conducting a search and rescue mission for it, which usually culminated in Blake guiding her hand in the right direction. But Blake was patient with the girl—exceptionally so—and the stoniness that came over her at snack time soon dissolved once more. When they had finished, and Quinn had stuck labeled Popsicle sticks into each of the rows, Blake offered her an approving nod.

"*Bom trabhalo.* That means good work."

"That's kinda like French!" Quinn beamed. "*Bon travail!*"

Though her own role in the garden-making had not been particularly strenuous, by noon, Nora felt a front of exhaustion pushing in. Her wrist ached badly, and her hips were hardening up like cement.

"I'm going to take a little break," she told Quinn and Blake as they worked on patching the garden hose. "You two help yourself to some lunch when you're through."

It was after three when she awoke on the couch. Someone had covered her with an afghan, and her hair clung to her neck in a sweaty clump. She sat up to discover Quinn seated cross-legged on one of the kitchen chairs, absorbed in creating an elaborate colored-pencil collage of various flowers and insects.

"I call it *live and let live*," announced the girl when Nora shuffled over to examine it.

Nora lay her hand atop the child's thin shoulder, remembering her own daughter at nine, too impatient for coloring books and art projects—a copper-haired fury who ran with the boys, and who, when injured, sought the comfort of her father. Nora had spent the greater part of her life terrified for Morning Glory, envisioning broken bones and knocked-out teeth and all manner of horrific accidents. Only in her later adolescence had she mellowed, ceased bristling at Nora's suggestions that she select clothing that matched, wear her hair in something other than a snarled ponytail, spend some time cultivating skills unrelated to harvesting lobster. She had grown tall beside her father, keen in the wheelhouse, but too bright to make their lonely coast her world. For this last, Nora never ceased to be grateful. She would not see her anchored to this place now. More specifically, she would not see Morning Glory anchored to *her*. But there were moments, like this one in the kitchen with Quinn, when Nora ached to turn back time and embrace that stubborn, headstrong girl just as she was. And be embraced in return.

Perhaps, she had earned her daughter's aloofness. The loss of Benji had injected a crippling fear into Nora's heart, along with a cold stake of self-doubt. By the time she was diagnosed with MS a year after his death, she had difficulty differentiating between physical and psychological symptoms, and every day of motherhood grew to feel like an exhausting (and unconvincing) performance of masking her own suffering. She knew her weakness had appalled Glory, that it was part of the reason she had chosen a school six hundred miles away. That in itself had been difficult to bear. But when, after Ed's accident, her daughter rejected Nora's every effort to console her, she felt more inadequate than ever as a mother.

Now, as she took up a comb and worked it gently through Quinn's hair, she made herself focus only upon the rhythm of these strokes, the softness of the girl's tangles. She could still give of herself in this simple way, at least. Like a contented cat, Quinn stilled under her touch. The two of them remained quiet, let the droning of the old refrigerator fill the space between their breathing.

"Where's Blake?" Nora asked at last.

"Workin' on her truck." Quinn peeked up at her through the bangs Nora had combed straight. "She's angry at Papa. I heard her yellin' at him on the phone. What's AA?"

Nora lowered the comb. "It's a group that helps people who drink too much."

"Blake said he has to go to AA or she'll quit him." The girl's eyes puddled. "I don't want her to quit. Everybody quits Papa."

Nora closed her arms around the girl, wincing as her wrist issued sharp complaint. That was how Blake found them a moment later when she stomped in from the driveway, her own arms black to the elbows with engine grease, jeans sporting a new rip up the thigh.

"You're up! Mind if I use your sink?"

She stopped short when she saw Quinn's face. "What's this? Amazons don't cry."

Quinn wiped her nose on her sleeve before Nora could find her a tissue.

Long wisps of hair had pulled free of Blake's braid, and her face bore a camouflage of grease and dirt. Even across the distance of the kitchen, Nora could smell the oil, sweat, and cigarettes on her skin. Revulsion mingled with a sentiment more complicated.

"Your papa's coming for you soon as he gets your place cleaned up."

Blake turned her back to run the tap. Her boots had tracked commas of mud across the kitchen linoleum. Nora looked at the mess, said nothing. Another wave of fatigue lapped against her, but she fought it off and walked to the refrigerator to assess its contents.

"I think we might have enough time to make some cookies."

"Oatmeal chocolate chip?" inquired Quinn. "Hell, yes!"

"Hey!" Blake whipped around from the sink so fast that they both jumped. "Don't poison the cookies with that mouth!"

Nora caught her wink before she bent her head back toward the steaming tap.

Quinn gave a sheepish grin. "Guess maybe that's been the matter with mine all along."

When Blake heard tires crunch in the driveway, she assumed it was Leland's truck. She had an ambitious chunk of cookie jammed into her glass of milk when a stout, middle-aged man in a cheap sport coat strode through the door. He carted a giant blue binder in one thick hand. At first glance, Blake mistook him for a presumptive salesman. Only when she glimpsed his eyes, guarded by a pair of shaggy copper brows, did she realize they were the same distinctive amber as Nora's.

"Hope I'm not interrupting," remarked the visitor when he sighted them huddled at the table.

Nora shot to her feet as though she had been zapped with an electrical current. Blake caught her chair before it toppled, felt Nora's hand fall briefly on her shoulder as she checked her balance.

"Goodness, Gordy! I didn't know you were coming down here."

The man's gaze snapped to the splint, which Nora tried to hide behind one hip.

"What's that? Jesus Christ. You fall again?"

Quinn's mouth dropped open, but Blake sent her a look in time to check her exclamation. Meanwhile, Nora crossed the room on careful feet and pecked her guest on his fleshy cheek. Side by side, they stood nearly the same height, though Nora seemed a mere wisp against his considerable girth.

"It's nothing, Gordy. You worry too much about me."

"Well, *someone's* got to." He caught hold of her injured arm and examined the splint. "Nothing, huh? You break it? How?"

She pulled away from him, then reached immediately for the support of the counter. "I just tripped bringing in the groceries. But I—"

"When do you go for your next scan? July?" He grimaced as he passed a hand over his thinning crop of hair. "I told you that you needed to move that up. Every time I come down here, something else is wrong with you."

The words clattered like stones across the quiet kitchen. Blake felt a tightening in her stomach as she watched Nora's gentle schoolmarm air desert her. She clutched her splinted wrist to her chest as though she had just remembered it pained her, small shoulders sagging.

"Will you join us?" she said. "You've met Quinn Savard—"

"Didn't know Savards were still welcome here." He frowned.

Quinn let out a sharp hiss of breath. Blake dropped a hand to the girl's knee, glancing between the visitor and Nora, whose face had gone ashen.

"Gordy, please..." She tried to clear the sudden hoarseness from her voice. "This is Blake Renato. She's renting the garage apartment. Blake, this is my brother, Gordon Wright."

"Twin brother," amended Gordon.

His attention shifted to Blake, lingered in the usual places. She regretted not pulling her sweatshirt back on. Her forgotten cookie had dissolved in the milk glass. At last, Quinn fished it out with sticky fingers.

"You didn't tell me you were renting the apartment," Gordon said to his sister. "Full of surprises today, aren't you?"

"Let me get you a plate."

Gordon dragged a chair from the living room and

dropped it opposite Blake. It landed like the thud of a gavel. He possessed the soft, delicate features of a woman, with full lips and long, rusty lashes. Though he sported multiple rings on his thick fingers—among them a chunky sapphire commemorating his graduation from some college—none was a wedding band. He thumped the binder in the space where Nora was about to lower his plate, forcing her to balance it on one corner of the table. The cover bore the label of a legal firm in Bangor.

"You a lawyer?" Blake asked.

"Do I look like a lawyer?" His smirk revealed a row of small, corrected teeth. "My interests are more entrepreneurial, actually. I'm in the rental business. Tourists and philandering spouses pay my bills."

Nora made a small sound in the back of her throat. She lowered herself into the chair beside Blake and nudged a napkin at Quinn, who had propped her flour-caked elbows on the table.

"And what's it *you* do, exactly?"

Gordon had renewed his visual study of Blake, who kept her arms tightly folded.

"I work stern for Quinn's father."

"Smelly work." He snapped off a piece of cookie. "Midlife crisis?"

"Blake's up from Massachusetts," Nora offered quickly. "She's ex-military."

Quinn swiveled in her chair, eyes lit with renewed awe. "Like Uncle Jonny! Did you kill lots of rag heads, too?"

"There's lots of jobs in the military besides killing," Blake said.

Gordon just pushed half a cookie into his mouth and tapped a finger against the binder to get his sister's attention.

"I came down here because you need to sign this

paperwork. Mason says he sent you pdfs but you never returned them." His voice adopted a slow, patronizing tone. "Have you checked your email?"

"I've been busy, Gordy."

"I didn't know waiting tables was a twenty-four-hour job."

"The printer—"

"Let me guess. It's broken. Like the dryer and the lawnmower and almost every other damned thing around here."

Nora rubbed at an invisible spot on the table, lips pressed into a flat line.

"It's times like these I worry about you living alone," Gordon said, a shade more softly.

Blake spoke up. "She's not alone. I live right across the way there."

A rap at the door interrupted Gordon's grim stare. Quinn sprang from her chair so fast that she upset her glass. Milk pooled across the table before Gordon could lift the binder clear. As he lurched up with an oath, Nora received the brunt of the flood down her sweater. Blake was racing for the paper towels when Leland Savard appeared in the doorway. He looked like a man who had been dragged out of his own grave, eyes sunken and laced with red, hair a disheveled mop heavy with grease. When Quinn threw herself at him, he flinched and dropped a hand atop her head with a dazed expression. Then he caught sight of Gordon. The slack lines of his face pulled taut.

"What a party!" snorted Nora's brother as he used a wad of napkins to wipe the binder clean. "Your charity has always impressed me, Honora."

Milk continued to drip from the table into her lap. She sat strangely still in the chair, lips parted as she took in Leland's appearance. Then she picked up the empty glass and set it carefully back upon the table.

In the ensuing silence, Blake curled her fingers tightly into her palms and watched Quinn attach herself to her father like a floury barnacle. Above the girl's head, Leland gave Gordon the middle finger, then turned and stalked out, tugging his daughter with him. Blake pursued him into the late afternoon sunlight, palms throbbing where her nails had dug in.

"What the hell was that? We just took care of your daughter the whole afternoon, and you're just gonna walk out without a word?"

Leland wrenched open the passenger's door and ushered the uncertain Quinn inside.

"Thanks," he grunted, pushing the door shut behind her.

He would not meet her eyes, so Blake stepped in front of him as he attempted to round the hood to the driver's side. She dropped her voice in hopes Quinn would not hear.

"You're a real asshole, you know that?"

When his eyes met hers, the hopelessness in them sent a jolt through her. "That s'posed to be some epiphany?"

"I meant what I said. I won't work for you if you keep drinking."

"I heard you."

"And?"

"And I don't take orders. From you or anyone else."

Blake fought to keep her voice steady. "You've got a little girl. Doesn't that mean anything? You're all she's got—"

Their shoulders collided as he brushed past her. She flinched, glimpsed Quinn's anxious face through the windshield, and turned away from it. When she caught herself walking toward the house, she halted and made a sharp turn for the garage. Behind her, Leland's truck tore up gravel as he roared out of the driveway.

Stomping up the steps, she locked her door and slammed shut the windows. She climbed into the rocker, pulled her knees to her chest, and waited for her heart to quit banging. Hands clasped fiercely upon the armrests, she rocked until her thoughts ran empty and her mind coiled itself back into the tight, safe place where she intended to keep it for the rest of the night. But as dusk spilled over the marsh, Blake slipped into dreams rich with the smell of turned earth and the hope of a thousand fragile seeds that she, Nora, and Quinn had offered into it.

8

On Sunday, Nora rose at dawn to dress for church. Right away, she knew her body was still punishing her for the effort of gardening. Simply manipulating the buttons on the front of her pinstripe dress took more effort than usual. She tried to be patient with herself. Yet, every time she missed a loophole, she heard Gordy's voice in her ear, insisting that she see her neurologist—that this was just another sign she had entered a more progressive phase of her illness and could no longer be trusted to live on her own. His visit had left her shaken and sleepless. He was pressing for power of attorney. She knew her husband would oppose her brother exerting any control over her finances. The way Gordon had stepped in to cover the half of Morning Glory's tuition that her merit scholarship did not had just about shredded Ed's pride. But Ed was gone, and now Nora felt she had no other option but to trust Gordon's superior financial acumen—particularly when her medical bills would rapidly deplete the meager sum she had received in life insurance.

This kind of math always gave her a headache. She sat down on the bed and peeked under her left sleeve at the thumb-size bruise Gordon's grip had left on her forearm. She knew she exasperated him. They had only recently buried their father, who had lingered an entire decade in assisted living, so Nora understood the burden she could become to her brother. It was the reason her cry of pain had died in her throat when he grabbed hold of her, the reason she had let him guide her left hand across the signature lines of paperwork authorizing his access to her husband's bank account. Closing her eyes, she summoned the energy to stand once more and finish her makeup.

She would feel better at the stone church. She always did.

Though Jody Poole had taken over as the organist, Nora planned to arrive early, when the great slate-floored sanctuary lay cool and quiet, and she could sit in peace among the polished wooden pews that smelled of dusty hymnals and the inevitable damp of the coast. So much weighed upon her heart that morning that she nearly forgot the tiny Lego dinosaur she had dug out of the living room closet the night before. Tucking it in her coat pocket with her car keys and her prayer book, she pressed out into the fog-bound morning.

A light burned in the lower level of the garage. As Nora felt her way toward the pickup, she paused to peer inside the dirty glass pane of the garage door. Inside, she made out Blake's long profile bent over the old Toro lawn tractor. Cigarette clamped in her teeth, she worked steadily with the wrench, removing lug nuts, dismantling the rugged frame.

Nora's hand grazed the doorknob, then she withdrew it. She would take it up with God, the puzzlement she felt about this stranger.

St. Catherine's stood on a dramatic elbow of rock overlooking open ocean. Built a century earlier, when rural Maine had already begun hemorrhaging industry and young people, this rugged house of worship had borne witness to countless tempests of sea and soul. Nora had been both baptized and married at its altar, but not until she had buried a child in the shaded plot beyond its walls had she grown especially purposeful in her pilgrimages here. Sometimes, she came simply to sit among the headstones and listen to the tide scrape the rocks beyond the seawall. At others, she brought her easel and paints and waited for a higher power to direct her hand across the palette. The ever-present fist of fear that had clutched at her since Benji died loosened its grip a little in this place. So she came faithfully and with an open heart to gaze upon the stained-glass saints and offer gratitude, even on the days when her body most betrayed her, rendering the walk from parking lot to pew a treacherous odyssey.

Today, Clyde Mortensen's truck was the only other vehicle parked in the lot at this early hour. A big-boned boom box of a fellow, Clyde had served as Morning Glory's indefatigable American history teacher. After losing his wife several years earlier, he had become a regular attendee at St. Cat's, even volunteering with Nora at food drives and bean suppers. Sometimes, he came to the restaurant to sit and pick her brain about books or politics, but they shared different opinions on both, so the conversations never proved particularly long or uplifting. Still, he had been solicitous since Ed's accident. Nora recognized that a similar, unspoken need drew them to the church before services. She was not sorry to see his truck— though it did make her regret that she had been reduced to wearing a ten-year-old dress on account of its loose, splint-friendly sleeves.

Before entering the sanctuary, she picked her way along a stony detour to the cemetery. Fog draped itself more thickly there. Even with the help of her walking pole, she felt as though she were wading through a river of clouds that might collapse and tug her under at any moment. Using the dark pillars of trees as signposts, she located the cluster of headstones that bore the name *Hayes*, and there, willed herself to her stiff knees. The effort left her dizzy. She braced herself against the damp moss with her good hand.

Her husband's stone still bore the wreath of plastic flowers she had bracketed there for winter. In a few weeks, she would replace it with impatiens. But Benji's little stone had never worn flowers. Instead, she had assembled there a company of the Lego figurines that had been his favorites. Had he lived, he now would be a freshman in college, likely long past interest in playing with such toys. But Nora could no more picture her brown-eyed, freckle-faced five-year-old a grown man than she could have pictured Glory an aspiring medical school student when she had been Quinn's age. Part of her felt thankful for her own lack of imagination. It was hard enough just to hang on to her good memories. She prayed that whatever other havoc MS wreaked on her mental faculties, it would never bleach away those precious images of her son.

"You know, I'm starting to think Ed might get jealous that you don't bring him any toys."

Startled, Nora twisted around to see Clyde standing a few paces behind her, hands plunged in the pockets of his baggy trousers. He wore the tweed sport coat that comprised his customary attire up at the U in Machias, where he now taught night classes in political science.

Nora dredged up a smile. "The kinds of toys Ed liked are too big to bring here, Clyde."

"I'll bet! Need some help there?"

Before she could answer, he caught her arm and hoisted her up from the ground. The dew had left dark stains on her skirt that she attempted in vain to brush away.

"What'd you do to yourself, Nora? Hope that's not a gardening injury."

"Oh, no! Nothing that exciting."

Blushing, she re-secured her grip on the pole. Clyde knew about her illness, but only because Morning Glory had mortified her by writing her junior research paper on the historical treatment of people who suffered from the disease, tacking on a personal preface about living with a "family member" who had been diagnosed. Her daughter had been too proud of the piece for Nora to voice her objection to this part of it, though it took weeks to shake off her sense of betrayal at Glory's candor. Nora had known nothing yet of true betrayal, however.

"I was thinking snapdragons at MaryAnn's stone this year," Clyde was saying. "Since we've got a sunny plot. I'm open to suggestions from the green thumb, though."

"Snapdragons sound nice," Nora murmured.

Together, they made slow progress through the fog. She stumbled once on a root. After that, Clyde took the pole and gave her his arm, which she accepted gratefully. Sometimes, surrender felt good. He smelled faintly of sawdust, for he kept a woodworking studio in the neighboring harbor and had swapped out teaching summer school for selling homemade Adirondack chairs to summer people. Nora had bought a set from him long ago, big, solid, reliable pieces that required little but a good hosing down each spring.

"And when will we be seeing that young scholar of yours?" he inquired.

"She comes home Thursday! I doubt I'll get her into church, though."

"Well, you got her into college. Can't have it all, you know."

She supposed not.

"Will she be fishing this summer?"

"Thank goodness, no. Dr. Ainsworth has agreed to let her shadow him for a few months. It will be a wonderful experience for her."

Clyde nodded. "Wish I could have interested my two dolts in opportunities like that. All they ever wanted to do was party and flirt with girls. A wonder either of them amounted to anything!"

Nora chuckled. Both of his boys had cleared out of Maine a

decade ago. She wondered if their absence had punched a hole in him as Glory's had her.

The sea remained invisible through the fog, but the deep bass of its thrashing suggested some system out in the Gulf of Maine had riled it up. Nora shivered. Despite the fact she no longer had to worry about Morning Glory motoring out alone in such conditions, big surf always made her uneasy. After it had swallowed her husband, the ocean's heaving presence had become a thing she forced herself to tolerate, like a lover who had lost his charm. She had not made her peace with it. Perhaps she never would.

At the steps, Clyde let go of her. They lingered on the granite threshold as fog grazed their cheeks with cool fingers. Clyde removed his glasses and wiped at them with his checkered pocket square—a carryover from the classroom persona he had taken great pains to cultivate.

"Kit Sheldon's giving a talk at the U next month," he announced. "That anything you'd be interested in?"

Nora had yet to make it through a Kit Sheldon novel, with their violent, self-destructive characters and careening plotlines. She preferred the kind of quiet, sweet stories for which the rest of the world seemed to have lost an appetite. But today, she found something comforting about Clyde's deeply creased face, with its drooping gray moustache and mild blue eyes. She thought she might stomach another attempt at *Midnight at Mount Husky*.

"Yes," she said. "I'd be interested."

"Excellent! We'll make an evening of it, eh?"

They walked in side by side, then, and took their places in separate pews. Nora sat through the entire sermon without hearing a word.

The lawn tractor gave Blake a run for her money. The fuel line was clogged, the spark plug was shot, and the blade belt had cracked in two places. The first issue proved a quick fix, but the remaining two required a trip to the hardware store, which she undertook just as the sun began to burn through the fog. She needed the project. Leland had failed to take the boat out since their spat, and she had not yet mustered the heart to return to the old farm at Harlow's Crossing. Something inside her had rattled loose over the course of the day she had spent with Quinn and Nora. Now she felt herself scrambling to fit it back into place, shore up the walls. She was glad Nora had been avoiding her since Gordon Wright's visit. The sight of her at that kitchen table, wilted and pale and soaked in spilled milk, still made Blake want to drive her knuckles into something.

When she returned from town, Leland's dilapidated Chevy sat in the empty space left by Nora's truck. Blake did a quick double-take and discovered him two stories up on a dubious-looking aluminum ladder, banging away at the gutters. At the sound of her truck, Quinn came bounding around from the back of the house, a jumbo wand of bubbles trailing in one hand. A costume gown of tattered blue gauze floated about her, its hemline spattered in mud.

"I'm Elsa!" she declared as Blake unfolded herself from the cab. "I was just singin' to the plants. Papa says it helps 'em grow."

"He did, huh?"

Blake shaded her eyes to peer up at the young lobsterman. He had already stripped to the waist, despite the fact the thermometer had not pushed past sixty. When he caught her looking, his hammer clattered down into the bushes.

"Damn it!"

"Ten cents!" called out Quinn.

Blake hoisted an eyebrow at the girl.

"I'm chargin' him a swear tax." Quinn proudly jangled some coins she had stuck in the pocket of the princess gown.

"Like I ain't broke enough," muttered Leland, tramping down the ladder. "*Marde.*"

"French still counts!" Quinn chirped.

Leland had shaved, a small improvement. Around his neck hung a set of dog tags Blake supposed to have belonged to his dead brother. A surreptitious sniff in his direction yielded no obvious traces of alcohol. She watched him dig two dimes from his jeans pocket and plant them in his daughter's waiting hand. Then he jerked his chin at the hardware store bag.

"You quittin' me to become a handyman?"

"Not yet." Blake held his eyes. "Just fixing the mower."

"Good luck. Glory rode that around like the fuckin' Lone Ranger."

"Ten cents!" reminded Quinn.

Grimacing, he dredged up a quarter. "That's a credit toward my next one." Then to Blake, "If you're so handy, why ain't *you* up on this ladder?"

"I don't do heights."

He poked his daughter's shoulder.

"Make a note, *ma puce*. Amazons are *afraid of heights!* We found her weakness."

This flash of humor transformed his haggard face. It shocked Blake how much younger, almost boyish, it made him appear. He possessed the kind of smile she imagined girls probably noticed—sudden, bright, and reckless. A lightning bolt out of blue sky.

"Oughta challenge her to a tree-climbin' contest," he told Quinn.

Blake fished a dime from her wallet and flipped it at the girl.

"That's for the one I'm *thinking* about your papa," she said, turning for the garage.

It took all of two minutes before Quinn poked her nose

inside the bay. Like a muddy shadow, she lingered in the doorway, watching Blake lay out parts.

"You need help?" she asked.

What Blake needed was concentration, but she flagged the girl over, recognizing the futility of any attempt to ignore her. Together, they knelt on the cool concrete, Blake talking her through each step as she removed the desiccated snake of the old belt and worked the new one around the elaborate series of pulleys in the blade deck. The whole process took less than ten minutes—though it did earn Blake twenty cents in fines. Afterward, she replaced the spark plug and directed Quinn to feed the machine some gasoline.

The tractor started up with an encouraging shudder. Blake steered it out onto the lawn, where a quick manipulation of gear settings revealed that the old mower still had plenty of cutting power left. As Quinn galloped a celebratory lap around the yard, Blake followed at a distance, pleased by the clean swath of fragrant, green carpet she created. A victory of crisp, shorn blades. She lifted her cap and let out a whoop, which the girl mimicked as she leapt over flower beds on bare, filthy feet.

"Crazy Amazons!" Leland shouted from the ladder, hurling down an armful of leaf confetti in their wake.

When Nora nosed her truck up the drive at noon, she found Blake zipping around on the mower in her dark braids and a backwards ball cap, cigarette burning as always. Quinn twirled about in a maze of bubbles while Leland balanced on a ladder, sweeping great clumps of pine needles and dead leaves from her gutters. It took her a moment to process the sight of these three individuals laboring on her lonely property. She idled in the pickup, her good hand wrapped around the wheel, the other drifting to her bewildered heart.

Then Quinn appeared at the door, pink-cheeked and panting.

"Come see how pretty we're makin' it for Mornin' Glory, Ms. Nora!"

Nora allowed herself to be tugged gently across the lawn toward a wonderland of bubbles. Someone had raked out her garden beds and weeded the walkway and even fixed one of the wind spinners—the large spherical one that Ed had gifted her on their twentieth anniversary, broken since the prior summer. When she failed to summon any words, Quinn peered up worriedly into her face.

"What's the matter. Ain't you happy?"

"Oh, yes. I'm happy, sweetheart. I guess . . . I just don't know what to do with all of it."

"All of what?"

"The happiness."

Aware that Leland and Blake had paused their work to come greet her, she attempted to blink the sheen from her eyes. Their two blurred figures lingered a moment in her peripheral vision until Blake finally strode forward and picked up the prayer book that had tumbled from her arm. She tucked it gently into the pocket of Nora's coat. The surprise of this simple gesture brought Nora back to her senses. She looked up and saw the creases at the corners of her tenant's dark eyes, the ghost of a smile on her lips.

"Hell of a sermon today?" Blake asked.

Nora caught hold of her rough fingers and squeezed them once.

"Ten cents," whispered Quinn, sending up more bubbles.

The glow of the afternoon he had spent at the Hayes place faded the instant Leland reached the Savard compound. A caravan of mud-splattered vehicles clogged the yard before his cabin—

beaters plastered with military stickers and pickups jacked on mudding tires and rigged with twin American and Confederate flags. At the sight, Quinn shot up in the seat beside him, where she had been picking apart a bouquet of irises Nora had cut for her.

"It's the vet-necks!" she exclaimed—Jonny's slang for the motley crew of ex-military and hillbilly pals he fell in with after his medical discharge from the Marines.

The assembly of dominantly camo-clad, heavy-booted men had convened in camp chairs around the firepit, where his sister, decked in her tightest camisole and cut-off jeans, was busy distributing cans from two enormous cases of Coors. Leland could smell the pot and pent-up anger from the distance of his truck. He cracked his knuckles grimly against the steering wheel.

"Go inside, Quinnie."

But she bounced out and skipped ahead toward the entanglement of roughnecks who greeted her with boisterous cheers and several whistles that made Leland's back stiffen. His own reception in the circle was not so warm. Mac Douglas and Troy Ahearn, two infamous deer poachers closer to his age, rose slowly to demonstrate their steroid-enhanced strength through brief handshakes.

"Finally, the party can start."

"What party?"

"Jonny's party," grunted Troy, thrusting a can of beer at his chest. "Two whole months since the world lost the best goddamned shot and card cheat there ever was."

A rumble of assent swept the circle. Quinn scrambled into Nicole's lap, where she clutched her bouquet of drooping flowers and surveyed the circle through eyes gone suddenly wary. At the toast to her uncle, the earlier light deserted her face. Its pinched solemnity pained Leland, who stood gripping the unopened beer and slapping at mosquitoes. Memories of that morning, of Blake's gruff nod of approval and Nora's grateful embrace and Quinn's elated bubble dance, collided hard with the scene before him of men who dressed and spoke and drank like his beloved big brother—and who, yet, would never fill the space.

A throb began in his temples and worked its way down into the fissured core of him. Within minutes, he had cracked open the Coors and delivered his own rambling toast. After an hour, he lost track of how many empties he had flattened into tin discs and chucked like ninja stars into the fire. There, he watched them curl and blacken like his own thoughts, Quinn's thin face fading to a pale blur across the flames. Not even the knowledge of her green-eyed vigilance could restrain him from popping another tab or accepting the pungent joint that was passed around the circle—though he shook his head at the little blue pills. Most weekends of his adolescence had been spent performing some variation of this ritual with these men, who had never quite qualified as *his* friends on account of the ten-year age gap. The fact that none of them were fishermen put further distance between them. These were men who measured their dicks by the amount of messed-up shit they had seen and done overseas and not by the lives they had built—or failed to—after returning from it; men who were just calling an end to their nightly benders as Leland climbed aboard his boat to work a twelve-hour day. But Jonny had dubbed them brothers, and accordingly, Leland had learned to accept them as crude patches to the holes torn in the Savard clan.

It was Willis Dawes, an orange-bearded ex-Marine with a lumberjack's physique, who finally flung the question at Leland.

"True about the dope? Them asshole McDowells over at Swift Harbor spiked it?"

"Just a rumor," Leland said.

"Got some proof they didn't?"

He looked down at his hands, still black with dirt from Nora's gutters. He thought of her kaleidoscoping wind spinners, and of Morning Glory, who would return in just days, trim, tanned, and taken.

"Go watch TV," he heard his sister slur at Quinn.

"It's broken."

"Go watch mine, then."

Willis climbed to his feet and hurled another stick of kindling into the blaze.

"So, you don't plan on doin' shit, then?"

"Do what? Poke that fuckin' bee's nest, and I'll start a harbor war."

Leland flattened another can against his knee and felt the disgust of the vet-neck brotherhood leeching toward him with the pot smoke.

"I make my livin' out there," he went on. "Last thing I need's my gear cut out or my boat sunk 'fore I even finish payin' her off. Let alone start the MP breathin' down my neck."

"Sounds like chickenshit talk to me," Willis said.

As Leland stood up, he felt the ground tilt like a dory beneath him. The sun had sunk behind the tree line, abandoning the clearing to cold night shadow.

"How many of you buy your dope over in Swift?" he asked. "Any of you ever gotten spiked product?"

"We ain't Savards, man. Could be the McDowells saw their chance with Jonny. Hell, think of all the shit they've talked over at the Oar. Never had to throw a punch. Easier to pay off one of Maynard's men, slip somethin' in, take him down quiet."

Leland whacked at a mosquito, left a bright smudge of blood on his wrist.

"Maybe Jonny should've had the sense to buy somewhere else, then."

The words dragged in a silence around the firepit. Troy and Mac paused with their beer cans halfway to their mouths. Nicole looked away from him and swiped at her cheeks. Only Willis stepped closer. His eyes contained the darkness of Afghani caves, of madrassa ruins and nights in distant deserts strewn with IEDs. The darkness of unspoken deeds. Leland had watched the same darkness hollow out his brother until no drink or drug sufficed to fill the void. He was beginning to understand that darkness. Though he had never peered down the scope of an M16 or marched through puddles of human gore, at its essence, horror was horror and pain was pain. Once the splinter was in you, it worked its way deep and bled its poison. As he looked at Willis, it was not the man's trunk-size tattooed arms that scared him, but the reflection of his own untethered rage.

"Jonny always worried you'd end up a pussy," Willis said.

"He shoulda worried about other things."

When Leland smashed his fist into the hooked nose, he felt the snap of cartilage all the way down to his armpit. It was a brief and gratifying pain. Despite the eruption of blood down his beard, Willis countered with a swift left cross that caught Leland in the ear as he made a clumsy dodge. Chairs and cans clattered to the dirt as the other drinkers lurched to their feet.

Leland maintained his footing. He had come of age swinging at the world. He was no stranger to landing a punch— or absorbing one. Yet it had been a while since he'd faced off with another man of Willis's size. Nicole, empty of faith in him, staggered across the circle, wedge heels crunching on cans. She made a weak grab at the sleeve of his opponent, but Willis shook her off like he might a tiny, yapping dog. Firelight jumped in his eyes as he kicked a chair clear of the space between himself and Leland.

"C'mon, little lobsterman! Let's see what you got!"

Leland lunged and landed a glancing blow to the bloody beard before a fist like an iron mallet caught him in the pit of his ribs. It sent his breath daggering out. With it came the acid contents of his stomach. He groped for the support of one of the lawn chairs, brought it over as he dropped to his knees, eyes streaming. For a full minute, his lungs sagged like two plastic bags in his chest, refusing to re-inflate. Then a kick in the shoulder sent his head into the dirt. As the earth spun, a shrill scream penetrated the ringing in his ears. The whisper of a gauze skirt grazed his cheek. Suddenly, Leland saw Quinn standing over him, her pocketknife brandished in one trembling fist.

"Leave him alone! All you shitheads just back the fuck up!"

Her high voice sliced across the circle, provoking a chorus of rough laughter.

Leland caught hold of her shin and pulled her behind him. Above him, Willis loomed, blood draining from his nose down into his grinning teeth. He looked like a Viking ready to conclude a blood rite, earn his ticket to Valhalla right there in the firelight.

"Saved by a little girl!" he smirked. "'Least *she's* got some of Jonny in her." He pitched a wad of bloody spit into the flames and jerked his chin at the grim faces gathered around him. "Let's leave this little warrior to patch up her papa. He's ruined the taste of my beer."

Quinn surged forward, but Nicole managed to grab hold of her and wrest the knife from her hand. His daughter fought hard, pitching her fists into his sister's thighs until Nicole released her with a slurred oath. As she bolted toward the house, the pieces of her tattered gown floated out behind her like iridescent wings.

Though he recovered his breath, Leland found himself seized by another violent fit of vomiting. That was how the men left him—on his knees amid a debris of beer cans and cigarettes, covered in mosquitoes and the contents of his own stomach. Weeping boozy tears of embarrassment, his sister stumbled away to her trailer. When he finally picked himself up, he pointed himself in the opposite direction, trampling Quinn's abandoned bouquet of irises as he went.

In the bathtub, Quinn piled herself high with suds and braced for Papa to come staggering in. She did not bother snatching the curtain around herself when the door finally banged open. He didn't look at her, just knelt in front of the toilet and threw up a little. Afterward, he flushed and flipped down the lid, sat hunched upon it with his back to her, big shoulders quaking.

"You mad at me?" She tried to make her voice sound plucky, but it squeaked out on the edge of a sob.

She had screwed up again. She knew it.

Papa said nothing. An ugly welt had risen along his right cheekbone. Eventually, he bent to retrieve the puddle of her Elsa dress from the floor. He held it balled between his two big hands and hung his head. Quinn could feel the hurt oozing out of him the way it did when his silences stretched out long as kite tails. She wrung out the washcloth and lowered it over her chest, picked at the dirt caught under her fingernails. The fan rattled clumsily in the ceiling. She was glad for its clatter. Sometimes Papa's silence hurt too much to stand.

"I know you ain't a pussy," she muttered. "I know you ain't, Papa."

He made a noise like a cough and buried his face in the ball of her dress. She eyed him cautiously. She did not know what spiked dope was, and she was too afraid to ask, so she sank a little deeper into the cooling bathwater.

"I think you were real brave climbing that ladder today. Even Blake wouldn't do that."

Gradually, his shoulders ceased their jerking. He rose and

pulled her pink towel from the bar and held it open with his head turned. When she stepped into it, he tousled her hair with the top edge like he used to do when she was little and Mama was too sick to give her a bath. She stood there, dripping suds, while he held her close.

"Don't tell Blake about none of this, okay, Quinnie? Please?"

Something in her heart twisted like a tiny screw. The last secret Papa had asked her to keep—the one about Aunt Nicky and Ed Hayes—had just about eaten her up. Still, she nodded dutifully, sick at the thought of what Blake might do if she found out about Papa's latest fall from grace.

Later, before bed, she dug out the little jade cross Ms. Nora had given her back when Mama died. It bore a chip on one edge from where she'd flung it at the wall after Jonny's death. Now she ran a contrite finger over the jagged wound before tucking the cross beneath her pillow. Maybe it would work like the Tooth Fairy, and she would wake up to discover her wish come true: Papa would be happy again, like he had been that morning, grinning at her from atop that big ladder.

Maybe.

9.

Blake sensed the danger in her captain that next week, a tension riding beneath his surface that breached at random moments, such as when he failed to gaff a buoy or could not get one of his rusty lighters to work. He snapped at the men on the wharf and nearly came to blows with Jonas Agnew, the lobster dealer, when he announced a ten-cent reduction in purchase price. Unlike the passing flares of temper or mischief Blake had witnessed in the past, this ill-humor seemed to have settled in for the long haul. She felt fairly certain he was back on the bottle, especially when Quinn failed to come out to greet her for the third afternoon in a row. But in the absence of concrete proof—he refrained from drinking on the boat, at least—Blake continued to show up to work.

In truth, she required a rhythm to her days that could most easily be achieved by laboring on Leland's stern, regardless of his mood. And part of her had begun to wake each morning in hopes of seeing Quinn, whose unbridled joy that past Sunday had left a curious afterglow around the Hayes property. At the very least, it had played a role in supplanting Blake's image of Nora as the ashen-faced receptacle of her brother's derision with that of a woman with shining eyes and sun-pinked cheeks who had spent the better part of that afternoon puttering in her garden and laughing at Quinn's improvisational dances.

The change in Nora astounded Blake. Each afternoon, when she returned from the wharf, she discovered the tiny woman out in her yard, tugging at weeds with her good hand or poking around at various plants that appeared to proliferate the instant they felt the first true warmth of spring sun. Seated on a wheeled plastic cart in her floppy straw hat, she seemed lost entirely to another world as she labored. And when Blake called out a shy greeting, Nora would break into her radiant, straight-toothed smile and rise to offer her some clipping of whatever flower happened to be in bloom. Blake carried these gifts up to her apartment and pressed them carefully between the covers of her heaviest hardbacks. Somehow she could not bear to watch them wilt in a vase.

On Tuesday, Nora showed Blake her new cast.

"You aren't gonna ask me to sign it, are you?"

Nora laughed in a way that engaged her whole body, as if she had slipped free of some great mooring chain and could now give herself over to whatever current of humor pulled at her.

"Lord, no, Blake! But maybe I could get Quinnie to decorate it, you think?"

And on Wednesday, Blake returned to find the window boxes of the garage stuffed with pansies and sweet alyssum, an enormous crate of strawberries sitting on her stoop.

"Oh, those are just little thank-yous," Nora explained when Blake tracked her down around back, attempting to drag the hose out to their vegetable garden. "Anyway, it's practically a sin not to eat fresh berries when they're in season."

"A sin, huh?"

Even smudged with dirt, Nora's face was open and lovely. Blake experienced the fleeting wish to frame it with her hands and preserve its beauty the same way she attempted to preserve the gift of her garden clippings. Instead, she looked away and took hold of the hose, which had snagged around a tree stump.

"Let me, Flower Queen."

"Flower Queen?"

Blake flushed. "If I'm the Amazon, you've got to be something," she muttered.

"Oh!" Nora laughed. "Well, I suppose I can live with that."

She wanted to know about Blake's day, what kind of landing she and Leland had made, whether the seals had returned to the rocks off Sully's Island. Then the slam of a car door carried from the driveway and interrupted their conversation. Nora let out a gasp as she turned toward the sound. Her hand flew to her heart. Only when Blake pivoted to steady her did she catch sight of the young woman who had entered the yard: unruly auburn hair and a broad, high-boned face lit by a crooked smile Blake recognized from household pictures. As Nora pulled free and stumbled toward her daughter, something sharp turned in the pit of Blake's stomach.

Morning Glory Hayes cut a striking figure in a fluttering sundress the color of a tropical sea. In her heeled sandals, she stood a whole head taller than her mother, whom she enclosed in her bronzed arms with a soft exclamation of "Surprise!" The two women stood locked in their embrace so long that Blake's gaze fell to the grass, where Nora's hat had sailed in her rush to reach the girl. As Blake retrieved it, she noticed a slender young Asian man round the hedge of azaleas. He wore a polo shirt tucked crisply into khaki pants, and his black hair was molded back in a way that gave him an inescapably metropolitan appearance. One of his brown leather shoes snagged on the hose, nearly bringing him down in a stylish heap upon the lawn. At the sight of him, Nora released her daughter and promptly seized him in a hug. Then she pulled back and allowed both young people to examine her cast, shaking her head gently at their frowning inquiries, all the while grasping her daughter's arm as though to confirm the realness of her presence.

"I wasn't expecting you until tomorrow!" Nora kept repeating. "Oh, this is wonderful. I'm so glad to see you both, safe and sound!"

The girl noticed Blake first. In long, deliberate strides, she crossed the lawn, her heels stabbing at the tender grass.

"You must be Blake. Mom's guardian angel."

Blake was uncertain whether it was the epithet itself or the wryness with which the girl delivered it that made her uneasy. She returned the brisk handshake, noting the coolness of her hands, the filed squares of her fingernails. Her eyes were a hazelnut brown, slightly darker than her mother's, and though she was small-boned like Nora, she exuded a bold athleticism that fell in stark contrast to her mother's delicate frame. Blake saw at once why Leland Savard was smitten—and also, as her eyes strayed toward the well-groomed young man beyond them, why he had laughed off his chances with her.

Morning Glory introduced the visitor as Alan Zhang, a fellow pre-med at UVA and the son of a pair of cardiologists from New York. He had accompanied her on the long ride back to Maine, where he planned to spend several days before flying back to the city to begin an internship in the lab of New York Presbyterian.

"Alan doesn't get this far *nawth* very often," Glory said, and grinned, elbowing him in the ribs. "I thought I'd drag him up here and cram some lobster down his throat before he spends the summer with his eyes glued to a microscope."

Something in Nora's flushed face made Blake think she might not have been expecting the boyfriend, a suspicion confirmed when Nora announced, "Oh, he's always welcome.

I can make up the guest bedroom in a wink." She glanced at Blake. "Won't you join us for dinner?"

Shaking her head quickly, Blake thrust out the hat she had inadvertently crushed between her hands, its chiffon ribbon stained from her fingers.

"Had a long day. You all catch up."

She felt the girl's eyes follow her as she strode away toward the garage, where she reminded herself that four walls and solitude were a blessing.

Leland found out Morning Glory was home through his sternwoman. As usual, Glory had not bothered to call or text him, leaving it to chance for their paths to collide—which they usually did at the least opportune moments. The prior winter, he discovered she had returned for holiday break only when he nearly ran her over with his snowplow. Exercise nut that she was, she had decided to go jogging in a blizzard. Then, last spring, she had driven over to announce her homecoming just as Jonny was shooting up at the kitchen table. The time that took the prize, however, was May of her freshman year, when she happened to be zipping up Route One at the same time a state trooper had him bent face down against the hood of his truck, his hands twisted behind his back—all for blowing .01 over the limit. She never let him live that one down, not even after he spent half of last autumn helping her search for her missing father. The girl had him pinned to the board of her memory with every Latin label for loser that existed.

So when Blake let the news of her return slip halfway through a rainy string out by Porcupine Island, it hardly improved his sour mood.

"The boyfriend with her?" he couldn't help inquiring.

"The future cardiologist? Yep."

"Figures."

He suspected Alan Zhang was one of the reasons Morning Glory had never called him after Jonny OD-ed. Instead, she sent a card full of elegant expressions of sympathy he had needed a dictionary to unpack. She might as well have sent him a punch in the gut.

"Guess I'll hear from *you* if she passed the MCAT, too," he said. "I ain't *educated* enough to warrant updates no more."

Blake plucked a clump of seaweed from the gunwale. "You ever think about college?"

"Ha! Never finished high school. After my old man went away, it was work or collect stamps." He eyed her bitterly through the rain. "Sure you've heard about that by now—the long, proud Savard tradition of keepin' cells warm."

His sternwoman just reached inside the trap and tugged loose the old bait sack. Her lack of reaction to most things he said occasionally made him wonder if she was hard of hearing. He raised his voice over the engine's growl.

"It don't bother you? My father blew a hole through a guy's guts, and the last two people who worked on this boat are six feet under?"

She lobbed a flopping sculpin overboard. "That why Gordon Wright doesn't care for Savards?"

Leland blinked. "Gordon Wright's got a whole list of reasons."

When he failed to do so, Blake retrieved the three lobsters from the pot. One was a V-notched female, which she tossed overboard. One came up short against the gauge. The third, a keeper, she placed in the saltwater tank. Then she swapped in a fresh sack and shoved the trap down the rail.

"What your father and brother did has nothing to do with you," she said.

"It has *everything* to do with me. I'm the one who's s'posed to keep it goin', pay back the McDowell shitheads who killed Jonny."

Finally, he had her attention.

"What are you talking about, Leland?"

He took a step back from her hard, dark eyes, startled by his own anger, by how close he had just come to striking her unflinching face. "The McDowells sold Jonny bad dope. Everyone's sayin' it. And now they're waitin' for me to do somethin' about it."

Too sudden for him to dodge, she caught him by the front of his slicker.

"You got *Quinn*," she said, the flash of her teeth revealing the absence of the same bicuspid that his father had knocked from his own mouth when he was thirteen. "So you better make sure you worry about your *daughter* before you worry about avenging anyone who's dead or locked up."

Cold rain fell in the narrow space between them. If she saw the tears that pushed into his eyes, she offered no sign of it. She gave him a shake, bringing her face so close that the clouds of their breath collided.

"You're too fucking young to talk like you don't have choices. That's a load of shit, and I won't listen to it!"

Releasing him, she gave the bait tote a kick that sent it careening into the gunwale. Several pale, dull-eyed herring spilled out. At the stern, she yanked off her hood and lifted her face to the sky, eyes pressed shut. Rain plastered her hair to her scalp and sluiced down the steep slopes of her cheeks, the scarred ridge of her jaw. She was not a beautiful woman by any stretch, but as the tension washed from her features, Leland was overcome by the sense he was no longer looking at his gruff-voiced sternwoman but at someone else entirely. The profound stillness of her quieted the clawed beast that had taken up residence inside him since his trip to the prison.

He sank to his knees in the slurry and felt the tide roll under the boat, the deep idle of the diesel as it banged away. For an instant, he was twelve again, on the receiving end of the gaff pole that his father brought down across his back once, twice, a dozen times, for the crime of baiting the traps too slowly. Arms folded across his face, he had absorbed the abuse until his T-shirt hung in bloody shreds, and he lay curled and sobbing against the transom.

"I'm nothin', don't you get it?" he said—to Blake, to the open water. "Ain't about choices. It's my fuckin' blood."

Blake pivoted. He thought she might deliver him a kick in the teeth, and he would have welcomed it just then, a jolt of physical pain to briefly eclipse the other kind that would not quit him. But she halted before him, dripping seawater and rain. Silently, she removed her rubber gloves and raised the sleeves of her slicker and flannel undergarments. She extended her wrists. Up close, Leland made out a set of faint, pale scars, most prominent on the outer sides nearest the bone.

"Do you know what these are?" she asked.

He kept his eyes fastened to the scars. He had sported chafe marks in the same place once, though they disappeared by the time of his OUI hearing. These were worse, evidence of a past he had never thought to ask her about beyond determining her relation to the infamous Jesse Teale. Now his pulse ticked up.

"You're a long way from nothing," Blake said. "I know exactly what *nothing* is. I spent the last twenty years of my life as *nothing*."

Still, he could not look at her face. He knelt with the chill of the rain working its way down his neck, trickling toward his collarbones.

"What'd you do?" he heard himself ask.

"I killed a man." Her voice shrank to a rasp. "He was a

125

cruel son-of-a-bitch, a drug dealer who hurt children. Who hurt me. So I stuck a knife in him."

For once, he found himself speechless. He thought of Quinn dancing ahead of her on the grass last Sunday, of the awestruck way his little daughter looked up to this quiet, terrifying woman. This *killer*. His gaze fell to the knife fastened to Blake's hip.

"I shouldn't have done it," she continued. "It wasn't for me to do. But I made the mistake, and I paid for it."

"Why're you tellin' me this?"

She watched him with her steady, dark eyes, her hands with their exposed wrists hanging limp at her sides.

"Because I want you to know how full of it you are when you act like you have nothing. You have the whole goddamned world, Leland."

She gestured into the grayness that surrounded them, shifting her weight in her big boots. The rain drummed away at the deck. When he said nothing, she cleared her throat.

"There's another reason, too. I was planning to ask to apprentice under you. Put in my hours toward licensure. My name will be on that paperwork—my real one, I mean."

His startled eyes refocused on hers. "Your *real one?*"

"It's Alvares. Blake Alvares." She paused, curled and uncurled her long fingers. "I go by the other because I know what a name can be to a person trying to make a clean start. I know perfectly well. So I'd ask, Leland . . . I'd ask that you keep it to yourself."

His heart banged. It was an unfamiliar feeling, to hold someone's livelihood in his hands this way—even if that someone was a convicted felon. As she pulled down her sleeves, his eyes skidded once again to the knife. She saw. Her hand moved slowly to her hip and withdrew the blade, extended it to him hilt-first.

He looked at it a moment, then shook his head and climbed to his feet.

"Keep it. You wanted to gut me, I guess you'd have done it already."

They held each other's eyes a moment. Then she nodded and stuck the knife back in the sheath. They lingered on the wind-lashed deck, miles from anywhere, coming to new terms with one another.

"For what it's worth," he said, "I'll sign your paperwork. But there's a long waitlist for a lobster fishin' license in our zone. You'll probably be waitin' years. Maybe a decade."

Her smile peeled slowly across her face. The melancholy of it doused the last flicker of uneasiness inside him. When she put out her hand, he took it.

"I'm good at waiting," she said.

At night, Nora listened to her daughter make love to Alan Zhang in the bedroom above. She did not mean to hear, but lately, she slept so poorly that it was inevitable that she awoke to the slightest thump or creak. The rain had ceased, so there was no other natural sound to which she could divert her attention. Pillow crushed atop her chest, she stared up at the ceiling and recalled when those muffled sounds of pleasure had been her own, when her body had still excited rather than frightened her husband. Part of him had left her long before that August day when his boat was found turning circles on its own. He had broken his vow, and the truth of that was etched in her heart. Still, she had continued to slip on her lace underwear, slather herself in scented lotion, take pains with her hair. He had loved her once. She held on to that. Some people, Nora knew, were never even *that* lucky.

But it was hard to think she might never be touched again. Hard, because at forty-one, that part of her had not yet been snuffed out by MS—even if the sight of her own body in the bathroom mirror brought stinging tears of disappointment to her eyes. She doubted even Clyde Mortensen would find much appeal in her small, sunken breasts and bony hips, the pin cushions of her abdomen and thighs. Still, her heart skipped at the thought of climbing into his Ford, even if it was just to attend some tedious book talk. Recalling the firmness of his arm beneath hers, the fresh-cut pine odor of his clothes, she allowed herself to drift for a time into fantasies of his mouth against her neck and the weight of his big, knobby hands traveling her hips. And as her mind began to whirl, confusing imagination and memory, she found herself pressed against the back seat of a quaking pickup, her lip snagged in strong teeth, her body arched in pleasure. She sank her nails deep into a heaving, muscular back, heard the sea pounding through the open window, tasted the salt of it as her mouth gapped wide to unleash a breathless cry. But when she opened her eyes, it was not Ed's face that loomed over her but Jacob Savard's. For an instant, she clung to him in desire mingled with terror. Then she shot up in bed, her body sweat-soaked and spent, her underwear too damp. Upstairs, the sounds had ceased. She wondered if she had truly cried out and clamped a hand over her mouth to contain her mortified gasp. Crouched there in her ruined sheets, knees drawn tight to her trembling chest, Nora listened to the silence until it swallowed her.

The next morning—a morning that Glory had been dreading, Alan's last—she found her mother at the kitchen table, bent over her Bible. Neat plates of strawberry pancakes waited under plastic wrap on the kitchen counter, and a pile of clean laundry sat folded in a basket by the stairs. Glory recognized the laundry as her own. She and Alan had hauled it in by the bagful several days before.

"I told you I would do that," she said, nodding at the basket.

Her mother glanced up, eyes already red with fatigue behind the readers.

"It wasn't any trouble, Morning Glory."

Despite the blue veins that stood out on the backs of her hands like the roots of trees pushing up from thin soil, her mother appeared almost childlike seated there, her face clear of makeup, her hair neatly plaited. Thus far, MS had wrought its cruelest work on her interior, sparing the exterior. But Glory knew it was a matter of time—and maybe not much. She had read every article and study she could get her hands on, bracing herself.

"I hope Alan enjoyed his visit," her mother offered politely.

Glory nodded and made a note to strip the guest room sheets before her mother could remark upon their lack of use. Ignoring the pot of Folgers on the counter, she set to work preparing two cups of Starbucks instant coffee. Her father had always complained that her mother liked her coffee weak. Glory had no reason to believe she had changed.

"How are you feeling, Mom? I mean, *really?*"

Her mother eased her arm back into its sling and gave her the same careful smile she had perfected since her father died. "God's looking out for me. I know He is."

Glory sampled the black contents of her mug. She found it hard to look at her mother when she spoke this way.

"You're lucky that Blake found you when you fell. I keep thinking about that. If she hadn't—"

"I'm sure I could have called Gordy. Or Jody Poole or Roger, from up the road." Her mother shrugged, rising to pluck at the dead leaves of a potted violet. "Tell me, when do you start with Dr. Ainsworth?"

"Tuesday."

The deflection irritated Glory, but she knew that pushing further on the topic of health would only cause her mother to retreat into silence. She would attend her appointments and take her medications, but when it came to thinking of the future, she was content to stick her head in the sand of religion. Though Glory had never been fond of her uncle Gordon— her father had dubbed him "the meddling midget"—his recent emails to her expressing frustration with her mother's shortsightedness had resonated to a troubling degree. In his latest one, he had floated the idea of moving her to Lubec, where he could keep a closer eye on her. Glory didn't know whether the idea repulsed or relieved her.

"Maybe you could stop by and see Lee when you get back from Bangor," Nora said, interrupting these thoughts. "It would mean a lot to him."

When Glory said nothing, her mother persisted. "He was over here last Sunday clearing the gutters and raking the beds."

"Maybe he was high."

"Don't be nasty. You forget how good he was to you after your father's accident. He didn't sleep for three days searching for him. He helped you pull Ed's traps, fixed the hauler—"

"All right!" Glory thumped the mug on the counter. "I don't need a goddamned recap."

"Please, don't swear."

The shower had stopped upstairs. In the absence of its whirring, Glory could hear a flock of chickadees cheeping outside the window. Her mother's bleeding heart for all winged creatures drew thousands of ravenous birds to their feeders—and come summer, to the garden, where they devastated the crops she spent all spring nurturing. Often, the futility of her mother's endeavors made Glory want to scream. Now she folded her arms and narrowed her eyes at the prim little woman painstakingly collecting fallen petals in her good hand.

"How much are you charging Blake to live in our garage, Mom?"

"That's not your concern."

"Gordon thinks you're probably not charging enough. Did you do any research on what apartments go for around here?"

Her mother failed to hide her wince as she carried the petals to the garbage can.

"I told you not to worry about it."

"For Christ's sake. It's just you and me now, Mom. I've got to know about these things. I've got to—"

"No, you don't! You don't have to know everything, Morning Glory."

Rarely did her mother's voice achieve such volume.

"Dad didn't treat me like a kid," she countered. "And he definitely didn't turn to Jesus to solve all his problems."

"And look how it turned out for him," whispered her mother.

It was too early for an argument—especially one Alan might overhear—so Glory abandoned the coffee and pushed out into the rain-damp yard. Heavy clouds still sulked over the marsh, but the air felt softer that morning. A blush of pink to the west brought hope of a partial clearing. Her father had taught her how to watch the sky, make determinations of when to set out and when to call it a day without having to wait for some crackled instruction over the VHF. She would never be able to think of weather without thinking of her father. Some days, her need for him swelled into something so enormous and unruly that she feared her ribs would crack open.

He had not been perfect. She knew this. It made no difference.

As she kicked her way along the gravel drive, anger subsided into desolation. She had known coming home would be difficult, but not until this morning, when Alan packed his bags, did she realize how very much she dreaded the prospect of being left alone here with her mother. She and Honora Hayes were such opposites that her father had often joked he had dragged Glory up in one of his traps as an infant. At times, Glory wished that were the case. It would be easier to love her mother if she did not have to square with the reality that their shared DNA might one day render her as frail and steeped in denial.

She mounted the rickety stepladder to her father's boat. There, she planted her two feet firmly on deck and filled her lungs with the residual stink of rotted fish and salt. It felt strange to look out onto a carpet of green grass instead of an ocean. Stranger still to think the boat might never again make the familiar trip out past Raker Light into the distant smear of dawn. Her decision not to fish that summer had been the most difficult one she had ever made. Summers had always been synonymous with rising in the dark to haul lobster traps on the boat that bore her name. It was a popular joke among the local fishermen that her father had gotten the christening of boats and women backwards. But he had always insisted that he had known exactly what he was doing; he wanted a daughter as strong as the vessel he trusted his life upon, and she grew up determined to prove to him he had gotten one.

Now she stood in the cockpit and wrapped one hand around the tarnished brass wheel. With the other, she touched the salt-stiff pennant of her university, which he had nailed to the roof the day before she left to begin her freshman year. Back then, she worried she had hurt him by turning down all the Maine scholarships to take off for a university six hundred miles away. But once he realized UVA had the best pre-med program of any of the places to which she'd applied, he would not hear of her attending a different school. And each summer when she returned, they fell into rhythm alongside one another so quickly that she realized her fears had been foolish. They would always share the ocean. As long as she lived, it would be the place to which she would return to speak to him. The place she knew herself best.

So, later that day, after she had pulled loose from the comfort of Alan's embrace at the airport, she drove back to the coast and took the turn out along Wind Cove toward the breakwater. The sun had nosed free of the clouds in time to make a dazzling exit. Hoping to relish the vision alone, she was more than a little irritated to find Blake Renato's truck parked in the turnoff.

She idled, teeth clenched, fingers wrapped tight around the wheel. For years, she had returned to this place of special memories when she needed to think. She and Benji used to fly kites here, bright, clumsy, homemade creations that their father had helped them engineer and send off to the wind. And it had been a favorite family spot to view the New Year's Eve fireworks. When she was twelve, Leland had walked her out along these rocks and lifted her mouth to his, quickly and shyly—her first kiss, and the last, for years to come.

The past autumn, she'd made the hike out here at least once a week just to sit and listen to the bell buoy clang and cry where no one would see or hear her. In a thick fog, a person could walk all the way to the breakwater's end and enjoy the sensation that they were walking off the edge of the world. Today, though, there was perfect visibility. When she climbed from her Prius, she could see the dark shape of her mother's tenant seated on the rocks of the far point.

A cool breeze sailed out of the north and breached the zipper of her fleece pullover. Glory hopscotched across the gaps between the big boulders until she stood behind the stranger, startling her so badly that she dropped the book she had propped on her knees.

"*All the Light We Cannot See*," Glory observed. "Heard that was good—if you're the fiction-reading type."

Blake shot to her feet, maneuvering fast for a large woman. She looked about with alarm.

"What happened?" she asked in the gruff, smoky voice Glory recalled from their initial meeting. "Is something wrong with your mother?"

"What? No." Glory blinked. "Well, I guess it depends on what you mean by *wrong*."

Blake just stared at her.

"I'm kidding. Mom's fine. I just come out here when I need space. This is my spot."

"I must have missed the name-plate."

Blake possessed one of those unsmiling, vaguely terrifying faces that Glory associated with the people in the military who did things they could not talk about. That her mother had no qualms about letting such a person reside on their property made Glory wonder if her mind had truly begun to skid.

"What brought *you* out here?" she asked, voice bold with a confidence she did not feel.

Blake tucked the book inside the front pocket of her sweatshirt and lit a cigarette. "I come here to read. I like the water."

"You don't get enough of it on Lee's boat?"

"I'll never get enough of it."

The woman appeared to have no intention of vacating the rock, so Glory crossed her arms against the breeze and held her ground. Blake's intrusion here felt like her mother's fault. Lately, many things did.

"Mom dragged you to church yet?"

Blake shrugged. "Don't need a church. I've got this."

"That's how I feel. She still thinks my soul is in peril."

Smoke streamed from Blake's nostrils. She frowned toward the darkening seam of sea and sky. "Your mother's been kind to me."

"Kindness isn't her problem. It's everything else."

The bell buoy clanged in cold punctuation of this remark. Blake just stood in silence, finishing her cigarette. All the while, she watched the sea. Before Glory could muster the courage to ask her how long she intended to stay, Blake flicked the butt away and commenced her journey back down the line of boulders.

"Enjoy your *spot*," she tossed over her shoulder.

Fists plunged into her pockets, Glory watched until she reached the parking lot. When she turned again to face the incoming tide, she realized she was trembling. It was almost six o'clock. Her mother would be expecting her for dinner, but after their morning exchange, she had no intention of showing up. A whole summer's worth of evenings remained in which she would be expected to fold her hands and murmur grace and carry on like the emptiness of the third chair at the table had always existed.

Dropping to the cool granite, she stretched out on her stomach so that she could prop her chin on her folded hands and gaze into the rolling distance.

I'm home now, Daddy. Please, help me get through this.

The tide tumbled wearily over the rocks below her. Beyond, the sun had bled all its fierceness into the sea.

In the twilight, Blake almost missed Nora's hunkered shape on the porch step. She parked and walked warily around to the edge of the yard to say good night.

"Will you sit with me a minute, Blake?"

"Haven't showered yet. Don't think I'm the company you want."

"I was married to a fisherman. You think I care what you smell like?"

Nora's voice carried the same sleepy lilt it had at their first meeting. As Blake came up the walk, she saw the glass of white wine propped beside her. A heavy sweater lay knotted over her small shoulders, and in her lap, she clutched her cell phone. Blake seated herself a deliberate distance away and inhaled the fragrance of distant lilacs.

"Would you like some wine?" Nora asked absently, eyes fixed on the darkened road beyond.

"I don't drink."

"That's good. I shouldn't, either. Not with the meds."

As though to spite herself, she picked up the glass and took a big gulp, then rested her head against the porch beam, as though the burden of holding it up were too much.

"I measure it out," she explained. "Five ounces, right in my measuring cup. I try to be so careful. So careful with everything . . ."

She glanced down at her phone. The glow of the empty screen briefly illuminated her face. Blake glimpsed the strain in her features, the old sadness. She stretched her sore legs down the steps and said offhandedly, "Saw your daughter out on the breakwater just now."

"You did?" Nora perked up. "She wasn't answering me. I thought . . . What was she doing out on the breakwater?"

"I don't know."

Blake lit a cigarette. She rested her elbows on the step behind her and peered up at the first stars that winked on above the marsh. She wondered if her grandparents had sat on their own porch, worrying in a similar way about her after she took off and joined the Army. At first, she had called, a few times. Their conversations, punctuated by long silences, proved too painful. After that, she sent them postcards, but within a year, she quit writing altogether, unable to muster lines enough to fill even a three-by-four square. She had tangled her life into such a tight knot of hurts that she lacked both the words and the desire to explain it. Years later, Dawn described this as just one symptom of *depression*—the inability to reach out to the people who cared most, the long retreat into crushing silence. By the time Blake learned how to properly identify her feelings, to peel back the black sheet of self-loathing and hopelessness, her grandparents were gone, and she still owed the state a decade of her life. Justice, she supposed, had been served to her. But what justice had there been for those two old people upon whom she had turned her back? Blake had grown exhausted of the word *justice*. It was a word that bent in the wind. Dawn suggested she focus on a new term. *Forgiveness.* But even at forty-four, Blake felt herself circling around the idea, never quite able to touch it.

Beside her, the wineglass clinked against the step.

"My daughter scares me to death," Nora confided. "How's that for foolish? She's lived away so many months, but when she's here, all I can think about are the terrible things that might happen to her."

Blake blinked, banished an image of her dead baby in her arms. He would be older than the girl, she realized. Older than Leland. Had he lived, would her heart be twisted up in a pretzel of fear the way Nora's was? She didn't know, so she smoked some more. Then, finally, she asked the question that had festered inside her since she sighted the photo of the little boy in the garage.

"What happened to your son? Benji."

Nora pressed herself a little closer to the porch rail.

"We had a trampoline—one of those great big ones, out

in the yard there. He and Glory, they could jump half the day away on that thing." She sniffed. "He went out there on his own one afternoon. I was in the garden. He must have landed on the frame. When I found him, his neck was just . . ." She lifted her hands, as though still trying to support what had been broken.

Blake fastened her eyes upon the pinpoint of a satellite floating across the sky and followed it until her vision swamped. She blinked fiercely until the evidence was gone. It might have happened at any time, she realized, the sudden, unfathomable loss of that in which she had invested her whole heart. How foolish she'd been at seventeen never to think of that, the utter fragility of her joy. Instead, she'd blithely trusted in its permanence. It seemed that the woman beside her had made the same mistake.

"I thought it would be different," Nora murmured. "When Morning Glory came back this time, I thought she wouldn't resent me so much."

"Resent you for what?"

"Everything."

Now Blake sensed Nora was sinking back into a place from which she had only recently emerged. She almost heard the clink of the rusty mooring chain tightening around her and dragging her deep. It stirred in Blake a strange desperation to tug her loose.

"I'm sure she just misses her father. That's not on you."

Nora's shoulders sagged. She drained the wine from her glass and stared off into the yard. "I wish it had been me who fell off that boat. I wish it every day."

Blake held the smoke in her lungs a long moment before releasing it in a slow stream.

"Why would you ever wish a thing like that?"

Nora shrugged. Her voice was alarmingly matter-of-fact.

"Because she needs him more." She glanced at Blake then. "I'm sorry. I shouldn't have made you sit here and listen to me."

"I'm here now."

"I'm sorry."

"Stop saying that!"

Blake brushed ashes from her pantleg and refocused her attention on the bed of irises beneath the porch. In the twilight, their pale, bearded heads appeared to glow like the white flames of a hundred candles. How could a woman who created such beauty wish herself gone?

"Maybe you can help me with something," she tossed out.

"Anything, Blake."

"If I were to start a flower garden—just a simple one— what would you recommend for plants? The best bets for some color, I mean."

The inquiry appeared to have its intended effect. Nora sat up straighter on the step, pushed aside the empty glass.

"Do you need a space for a bed? I told you, you're welcome to—"

"Not a space," Blake interrupted. "This is just . . . hypothetical."

"Oh!" Nora dropped her head back against the beam once more. "Well, it would depend on how much sunlight you had, and if there was protection from critters. Deer will eat most anything—but hostas and daylilies especially."

"Let's assume mostly sun, and protection."

"Well, then. Hydrangeas do pretty well. They come in a variety of colors and bloom all summer. I'm partial to roses— they have breeds now that are pretty resistant to disease, and they'll bloom right through the first frost. Yellow are my favorite. Black-eyed Susans can be spectacular come August. And butterfly bush—that's what I've got over there by that fence. Late summer, you should see all the monarchs! The air is just full . . ."

The falling dusk concealed the faint smile that pulled at Blake's lips. She smoked and listened as Nora's voice picked up a breathless energy.

". . . Marigolds are always a safe bet. They *stink*, so nothing wants to eat them. And have you ever seen a fully mature hibiscus? Their blooms are the size of dinner plates, and . . ."

Already, the garden was taking shape in Blake's mind. She saw the backyard plot that she would clear of junk, right there on the hill above the apple tree. She envisioned a tidy wire fence and some stepping stones, perhaps even an improvised version of a wind spinner. Water from the well, a string or two of solar lights, a bench where she might sit and gaze upon it all.

"You know," she said, interrupting Nora's explanation of coreopsis, "you really are the Flower Queen. You get a degree in this or something?"

Nora chuckled. "There's no degree, Blake. Just hands in the dirt, you know?"

"Hands in the dirt. Yeah. I get that."

And then she reached for Nora's hand, which lay upon the step between them. She placed it palm upward in her own and uncurled each delicate finger, dragged her thumb along the frayed crease of her lifeline.

"Are you going to read my fortune?" Amusement lit Nora's quiet voice.

Blake spoke around the stub of the cigarette she had clamped in her teeth. "I don't believe in that crap."

"What, then? There has to be something. Every good person believes in *something*."

The cool metal of Nora's wedding band pressed against Blake's callused palm. Gently, she folded Nora's fingers closed again. Held them fast. Her throat felt suddenly hot and thick.

"Don't ever say you wish it had been you on that boat. Don't think it, either. All right?"

After a moment, Nora took back her hand and settled it upon her lap with her casted one. She turned her face upward to the spray of stars above the marsh. "All right."

They sat awhile longer, until the breeze carried off the last of Blake's cigarette smoke. Then she rose and walked back up to her apartment above the garage, where she opened all her windows onto the night.

10.

Since the television now crowned the junk heap out in the yard, Leland and Quinn spent dinners listening to the radio or playing the old board games she had dug out of the debris of Jonny's trailer. Most were missing pieces, so Quinn improvised with bottle caps and slips of cardboard she had cut from cereal boxes and decorated with markers. That evening, preoccupied by thoughts of the murderer he had hired to work his stern, as well as by the bills that were accumulating on the countertop, Leland soon found himself beat for the third round in a row of Checkers.

"You're not even tryin'!" accused Quinn. "Guess you want the loser's punishment. Nail paint!"

"Shit, no. You ain't touchin' me with that stuff."

"Ten cents, please. And I'm willin' to settle for toenails."

He fished a dime from his pocket and narrowed his eyes at her. "Anythin' but pink."

Naturally, that was how Morning Glory Hayes found him, one dirty-soled foot propped on a chair as Quinn slathered turquoise lacquer all over his big toe. When the door cracked open and a head of copper hair poked in, he jumped and sent a streak of blue polish across his foot.

"Glory!" squealed Quinn, dropping the brush as she caught sight of the visitor.

Morning Glory caught his daughter by her arms and gave her a spin. "Jeez Louise, Quinnie! You're almost as tall as me!"

"Forty-six inches!" Quinn proclaimed proudly.

"What happened to your hair? You're getting movie star highlights."

"Nicky's brilliant idea," grunted Leland from the table.

Morning Glory flashed him a lopsided grin. Her hair had gotten long since autumn, and the bones of her face jutted a little. With all the makeup, it was difficult to discern vestiges of the mischievous tomboy who had lit his childhood with a thousand small joys. He needed to believe part of her was still in there.

"Nice toes. The turquoise really compliments all those calluses."

He dropped his foot from the chair. "Ever think of callin' first?"

"And miss *this?*" She winked at Quinn, who looked on with delight. "Let me guess, he asked for hot pink, but you were all out."

Quinn burst into snorting giggles. She tugged on Glory's hand. "Hey, you a doctor yet, or you gotta take more classes?"

"I've got to take a *lot* more classes!" Glory collapsed dramatically into a chair, managing somehow not to topple it. "But I get to shadow Dr. Ainsworth this summer. He's going to show me how to do all kinds of cool stuff."

"Like give shots?"

"Not just that." Glory picked up the nail brush and wiggled it at Leland. "You need a touch-up?"

He coughed and reached for his lighter. "Quinnie, go brush your teeth. It's bedtime."

"Since when do I got a bedtime?" she scowled.

Leland ignored the eyebrow Glory arched at him. "*S'il te plaît, ma puce.*"

"You owe me," Quinn retorted in the haughtiest voice he had heard her summon yet.

She took her time collecting her supplies from the table,

then huffed off down the hall, where Leland felt certain she took up her usual listening position at her bedroom door. She had reached the age when he had begun wishing for thicker walls and doors that actually locked.

"You know, if you quit smoking those things now, it would take your lungs fifteen years to recover," Glory remarked as he lit up.

"Were you gonna bother tellin' me you were home, or does a man gotta use chopsticks to get your attention these days?"

Her jaw twitched. "Don't be ignorant. I didn't come over here for that."

"What'd you come for, then? The pretty view?"

She glanced about the room. After Blake made him give the place a thorough scrub-down several weeks ago, he'd made some effort to keep it neat. Quinn's pictures now formed a tidy collage on the wall where the TV had once stood. On the coffee table, he had arranged her art supplies in a series of mason jars and cigar boxes. The counters were scrubbed, and the couch cushions were flipped to their cleaner sides— though there was no masking the cigarette scars on the armrests and carpet, nor the fist-size hole Jonny had punched in the lampshade. The curtains bore the orange stains of Quinn's kid-size, cheese puff fingers, and the wood furniture sported its share of nicks and scratches. Still, he had managed to keep the lights on without filing for state assistance. Some days, that struck him as nothing short of a miracle.

"Your sister figure out how to use a vacuum?" Glory asked, face darkening briefly.

"Give me a *little* credit, Mornin' Glory."

She frowned at the two cans of soda he retrieved from the fridge. "The one time I was hoping you'd offer me a beer."

"My timin' with you's always been shit."

A sardonic grin rendered her face once more familiar. He watched as she popped the tab on the Pepsi and slurped the foam from the rim like she used to do when they were kids. Some of it stuck to her nose. When she wrapped her hands around the perspiring can, he caught sight of a new ring—a pair of tiny sterling hands cupping an emerald heart. A set of burly mitts closed hard around his own.

"You ain't fishin' at all this summer?"

"I'll be working five days at the clinic. Even if I could manage to get some gear in, I couldn't haul enough to turn a profit." She doused the rasp in her voice with more soda. "Money's tight. I saw some of Mom's hospital bills."

"Fuckin' doctors."

She sent him a look over the rim of her can. "Yeah. Fuckin' *doctors*."

"You gonna give up your license, then?"

"Not yet. If I bombed the MCAT, I might have to slum it as a lobsterman."

"You've never bombed nothin', Mornin' Glory."

They fell silent. She picked at a smudge of teal polish that had hardened on the tabletop.

"My mother said you cleaned her gutters the other day. Is she starting to hallucinate?"

He flushed. "That was Blake's idea."

Glory tilted forward in her chair, bright eyes betraying a glimmer of the insatiable curiosity that had led to countless childhood adventures.

"What's her story anyway? That woman kind of scares the crap out of me."

Leland caught a whiff of her jasmine shampoo. Even back before she ever paid any attention to her appearance, he remembered her hair smelling good. Now it was a scent that visited him occasionally in dreams from which he woke awash in longing. He frowned down at his hands. For four months, he had waited to sit and talk to her like this, to drink in her smell and her smile and recommit all her curls and curves and freckles to memory. But now that he had her full attention, he found himself curiously mute. His sternwoman's confidence in him was not a thing he could simply toss away, even if revealing the story of her past might earn him a few points in Glory's book.

"She works on your boat," Glory prodded. "You've got to know *something* about her."

He suspected then that her curiosity about Blake Renato was the real reason she had come to see him. The stranger living above her garage interested her more than he did. That figured.

"She's Brazilian," he muttered.

She blew out her breath. "Wow. Thanks for that, Sherlock."

Suddenly, it hurt to look at her. Some foolish part of him had believed that after that autumn, when she had stood in his yard and cried her grief over her father into his chest, she might come home and decide she cared for him, that no New York–born pre-med could ever share the same bond with her that the two of them had forged growing up one boat apart on their windy hangnail of a peninsula. A part of him had even hoped she might finally have forgiven him for Anna and the long, reeling rebellion he had staged in the wake of his father's crime. But Nicole had been right. He got the delusion gene.

Rising, he went to run the tap aimlessly over Quinn's dinner plate.

"You want me to go?" Glory asked. Her voice fell flat across the kitchen.

"Do whatever you want. Ain't that what you always do?"

She let her chair scrape back, looked at him once. "It's nice to see you sober, Savard. Even if you're still an asshole."

The door echoed the final slap of her words.

The following Sunday, Blake drove out to the old farm at Harlow's Crossing. She parked the truck beside the silent house and pulled a tarp, shovel, and hedge clippers from the bed. She was not yet ready to twist the key in the front door lock and meander through dusty rooms, so instead she tramped through the knee-high weeds to the rear yard. Absent the snow, it appeared as dreary as it had upon her last visit, though a few of her grandmother's roses had come back along the rear porch, offering a surprise button of color here and there through the overgrowth. Blake pinned one of the blossoms between her fingers and stooped to inhale its dewy fragrance. Thought of Nora. Then she turned her attention to the sweep of wilderness she intended to convert into a garden.

Though a frown of fog lingered over the marsh beyond, Blake knew from the thin hue of gray overhead that there would be sun by midmorning. A favorable omen. She measured off an eighteen-by-eighteen square of level land and marked the corners with fieldstones. Then she set to work clearing a decade of debris, dragging away branches and rusted cans, uprooting wild rhubarb and raspberry and an army of enormous dandelions so entrenched, she resorted to hacking at the sausage-thick roots with her shovel. It was satisfying work. When she paused to catch her breath and lean her weight against the spade, she felt brushed by something that was not quite joy but more like the tickle of hopefulness that preceded it. Her hands were no strangers to dirt. On the back end of her sentence in state prison, she had enrolled in a horticulture course, joined a crew of fellow inmates who had been deemed sufficiently rehabilitated to be trusted in the maintenance of the cafeteria garden. Little of what Nora had rattled off to her that recent evening on the porch had been news to her, but she had enjoyed hearing her pronounce the names in her soft, Down East accent. *Foh-sithia. Buttah-fly bush.*

At times, Nora's voice seeped into Blake's sore places like a salve. At others, it touched off a disquietude that lingered for hours. It was becoming more difficult to simply mount a flight of stairs and escape the goings-on in the Hayes household. Through open windows at night came the clatter of plates and murmur of voices, an undulating soundtrack of familial life to whose occasional strained crescendos Blake could not render herself deaf. To her relief, Gordon Wright made no further visits, though she picked out his name from time to time when the voices grew elevated. After one particular argument, which occurred out at the firepit behind the garage, Blake had glimpsed Nora sitting alone beside the chair her daughter had vacated, her face in her hands, the firelight dancing across her defeated frame. It had taken Blake great effort to turn her back on that scene.

But today, she did her best to brush all of that away. She stood on soil that belonged to her—the first piece of land she had ever owned—and though she believed she did not deserve that privilege, her possession of it fortified her nonetheless. It seemed a proper first step to make something grow here, a small means of proving herself a worthy steward of a place that had been built and cared for by better people than she. Thus, she worked tirelessly through that morning and into the afternoon, even as the sun scorched her shoulders and her T-shirt grew so plastered in sweat that she stripped it off.

After she had cleared a plot and done her best to break up the ground, she sat in the sprawling shade of a burly oak and scrawled a supply list. As her pen lolled across the page of her notebook, she listened to the scampering of squirrels in the undergrowth, the distant squalling of gulls in the marsh, and her heart beat slow and steady against these sounds. Though an ache of loss had taken up permanent residence there, no longer did it hold tyrannical reign. She rested her hand atop the quiet rhythm, wishing always for this calm, for these still waters inside her. When she was satisfied with her list, she dug out her phone and tapped a quick email to Dawn.

I've broken ground on a garden. Hope you would be proud. Working toward a lobsterfishing license. Need to log 1,000 hours in 24 months. Hope my captain can stay sober that long.

She deleted this last line, envisioning Dawn's soft cluck of worry.

In other news, I'm staying clean. It's easier than I thought. I keep busy. I read. And I think I've made a friend.

She also deleted this line, then put it back in. She was not certain what qualified as a friend—or if she truly wanted one. But it seemed like a reassuring thing to tell Dawn. Blake suspected the old prison shrink would consider it progress.

Blake had made no friends in prison.

I'm going to fix the house, make it nice again. It won't be easy. One day at a time, right?

She pressed send before she let herself further scrutinize these claims. Then she rose and walked to the apple tree, whose branches sported a frail struggle of green. Standing there in her sports bra and filthy jeans, she touched the timid leaves and gazed down at the stone whose face had already become re-engulfed by weeds.

"I love you," she whispered.

She had not spoken the words in twenty-seven years and was surprised by how easily they floated from her lips, hovering there like cobwebs in the grass. By how true they remained, even now.

Gathering the tools from the yard, she tossed them back in the truck and set out on the next phase of her mission.

*　　*　　*

June brought rain and new seedlings—and mud for miles. When she was not attempting to mop it from the restaurant floor, Nora was kindly requesting that customers use the thick mats the manager had flung out at the entrance. He had allowed her to return part-time to play hostess and pour coffee now that a trickle of the Wind Cove summer people had begun to find their way in. Nora felt as grateful for a purpose as she did a paycheck. While she enjoyed the quiet of her home, the opportunity to retreat to her couch whenever fatigue overcame her, she knew it was good for her to be out among people again—even if it did require a certain amount of pretending. On days when her legs played their concrete joke, it took exceptional effort to force herself across the small space between the counter and the booths. She established a map in her head of which corners she could grab hold of quickly, which stools and chairs she might rest her hip against and use as a counterbalance. Gradually, she developed one-handed skill at many tasks and made ample use of her right elbow as a nook for toting menus and stacked cups.

In the early mornings, the old-timers shuffled in to work crossword puzzles and nurse cups of coffee. Nora always had an easy time talking with the seniors. They did not seem to notice nor mind that she moved more slowly than Bert, the other full-time waitress who had just entered her seventh decade. She nodded with enthusiasm at rambling stories about grandchildren, offered frowns of sympathy to tales of declining health and unhelpful state institutions, laughed convincingly at jokes she had heard a half-dozen times. They appreciated the company and tipped well by Maine standards, and she was always a little sorry to see them leave.

Afternoons proved more challenging. While she liked watching the fishing boats return to the harbor and always kept an eye out for Leland and Blake, her energy waned exponentially around two o'clock, when she would resort to perching on one of the counter stools as she helped Bert scrub down menus or refill condiments dispensers. If anyone suspected she was ill, no one ever ventured to ask about it. She was grateful for that old-Mainer stoicism, the good sense that most people possessed not to pry into another's personal affairs. Still, there were moments when she could not deny to herself that even this scaled-back work sapped her strength twice as much as it had a year ago. On days when she fumbled and broke a plate or failed to make it to the bathroom before soaking her Poise pad, it took all the resolve she could summon to shuck off the blanket of gloom that was always hovering just above her shoulders, ready to engulf her in its heavy, binding wool.

Gordon had insisted that she move up her MRI, and on the allotted day, he drove her to the appointment in Machias. Though the procedure was familiar by now, she still flinched at the injection of the gadolinium, and her heart refused to cease pounding as she lay stripped of her wedding ring and cross necklace inside the whirring, clacking scanner. Afterward, she shook so badly that she had difficulty getting dressed. She tucked the necklace in the pocket of her jeans and kept her jaw clenched for much of the ride home, listening to Gordon bark at one of his associates over his cell phone. When he finally hung up, his mood had fouled. He drove so fast that Nora found herself gripping the seat with her good hand.

"When will you have the results?" he wanted to know.

"I don't know, Gordy. They make me come into the office for that."

He turned up the air conditioner, despite the fact she was already shivering sealed inside his frigid Buick.

"You given any more thought to my proposition?"

He meant selling her house and moving to Lubec—an idea he had sprung on her only last week, when she had called to invite him to Morning Glory's birthday gathering.

"I could never leave my home, Gordy. Ed and I built the place, for godsake. And to give up all my gardens, my plants . . ." She shook her head harder. "I can't even think about it."

"Well, your daughter can."

Her brother hit the brakes hard at the stoplight. Nora felt all of her freshly dyed insides lurch forward.

"You spoke to Glory about this?"

"Come on, Honora. She's a smart gal. She's worried about you. Sure she doesn't want to take off for her senior year worried you're going to fall and hurt yourself again."

Nora sat silent, clutching the belt that had pulled tight across her chest. She found it hard to breathe with it cutting into her this way. Yet, the instant she popped it free of the latch, Gordon yanked it back across her body and clicked it tight.

"Are you losing your mind?"

"No!" She turned her face to the window to hide startled tears. "Gordy, how could you bring that up to my daughter? How could you?"

The obsidian arrowhead that hung from his rearview swung like a jagged pendulum as he made a screeching turn off the highway.

"Did it ever occur to you that staying in that house is selfish? That if you have another accident—a worse one—it's going to cause your daughter and me a lot more trouble than getting you relocated now, before that house goes to ruin and you're in a wheelchair?"

She bit the insides of her cheeks, thinking of Gordon's spare condo with its postage stamp of a yard and its windows overlooking the string of drab, low-slung apartment buildings he managed. She could not believe her daughter would approve of selling the home in which she had been raised, where Benji's crayon scrawlings still graced the back walls of certain closets, and all four of their handprints lined the concrete of the back patio.

Part of her wished to scream at her brother, voice every accusation of heartlessness she had been holding back since Ed died, when he had stepped in so brusquely to manage her life. She had to remind herself how good he had been after their mother's stroke, relocating their bewildered father, shifting funds to cover first a funeral, then long-term residential care. Then there had been the quiet panic of funding the balance of Glory's tuition—panic Gordon had squelched with a single check. Nora would never be able to repay him. And so she stayed silent the rest of the ride.

By the time he delivered her home, all of her muscles ached from bracing against the bumps and ruts of the road. Hugging herself, she walked out to the vegetable garden she had started with Quinn and Blake. There, she thinned some of the plants, which had shot up tall as a result of the recent rain, then gave in to spiraling fatigue and sank down on a patch of dry grass to watch the clouds cycle by. A terrible heaviness pressed upon her. She ripped off the strip of tape from the site of the contrast injection and lay down, pressed her cheek to the comfort of the tender, fragrant blades. Fingers woven into the cool tufts, she fell asleep to the drone of bees and the distant calling of tidal birds.

"Mom! Can you hear me? Mama!"

Her daughter's frantic shouts jolted her awake. Morning Glory hovered over her, outfitted in clinic scrubs, her thick hair pulled back in a professional bun. Eyes wide, she grasped Nora's good wrist in her fingers.

"Mom? Did you fall?"

Nora sat up so fast, she felt briefly dizzy. She pulled back from her daughter and blinked away the residue of some pleasant dream whose details she could not remember.

"No, no! I just fell asleep. It was so lovely out here ..."

But when she cast her eyes toward the sky, she saw that it had grown overcast, and the pleasant warmth that had earlier lulled her into slumber had deserted the yard. Her clothes had absorbed the dampness of the spring earth and taken on a chill. She swept the grass from her blouse and stood stiffly. The residual alarm in her daughter's face called back the earlier conversation with Gordon. All at once, Nora feared she might be sick.

"Mom?"

"I'm fine. Please, Morning Glory. I'm fine."

Her eyes moved past her daughter and caught sight of Blake's tall figure at the edge of the yard. Still dressed in her filthy boat clothes, she appeared to have come running at the sound of Glory's cries. Embarrassment washed through Nora like cold, dirty water.

"I just took a nap!" she snapped at both of them.

Arms crossed against a wild, gusty anger, she started for the house. But as she yanked the slider open, she stopped short at the sight of several banker's boxes that stood on the table. They brimmed with medical texts and various instruments and equipment.

Glory stepped inside behind her.

"Ainsworth's cleaning his office," she explained. "He let me have a bunch of his old stuff."

"So you decided my kitchen table was where you would dump it?"

Nora did not recognize the harshness of her own voice. She pulled the bottle of chardonnay from the fridge and splashed it into the measuring cup. Through the window, she watched Blake retreat into the garage, black hair streaming from her frayed braid.

"This is going to save me a lot of money on training equipment, Mom. This stethoscope kind of sucks, but everything else—"

Nora turned from the sink. She studied her daughter's face, which appeared hazy in the low light without her glasses. She tried to find something familiar about it, but it seemed, in that moment, to belong to a different young woman. A total stranger, in fact.

"Come to church with me this Sunday," she interrupted. "Will you do that for me, Morning Glory? Just once?"

Her daughter let out a hiss of breath. "I'm going to Bangor on Sunday with Kate."

"You can go to Bangor anytime."

Morning Glory stacked the boxes roughly. Hoisting them in her arms, she stomped toward the stairs. "You say enough prayers for the both of us, don't you think?"

11.

On Friday, Aunt Nicky had to work a double at Brewster's, so after some Grade A pestering, Quinn finally got her father to agree to let her join him and Blake on the boat. He warned her she would have to be gentle with the catch. It was molting season, the time of year when the lobsters hid out under rocks to shed their old shells. When they began to emerge, hungry for the bait in his traps, they were not as tough and tossable as they normally were. Quinn promised to be careful, too excited even to eat breakfast. She had not gotten to talk to Blake for weeks. Papa had arranged it so they now met up at the pier in the mornings, and he always had some excuse for why they could not go and see Ms. Nora (Quinn guessed that he'd messed things up with Morning Glory again). So when they arrived at the wharf that morning, Quinn dove from the still-moving truck to run and greet the dark-haired giant who stood waiting for them by her pickup.

"Amazon!" she cried, enclosing her smoky waist in a tight hug. "Did our seeds sprout? Are the plants real big? How many do you think—"

A sharp, French rebuke from Papa made Quinn jump. Her arms fell slack just in time for him to yank her away from Blake. Confused, she looked back and forth between her father and his sternwoman. Blake appeared as startled as her, though she recovered quickly. Sticking her cigarette back between her teeth, she took a step away.

"They're coming up real good," she told Quinn quietly. "Nora's taking nice care of them. Maybe you and your papa can come by sometime and see."

Quinn watched her father shrug and settle his cap a little lower over his face. He seemed twitchy and wouldn't meet Blake's eyes.

"Papa's two weeks sober," Quinn announced, hoping this piece of information might dispel the awkwardness. She knew the number because her father kept track on a piece of paper he had taped to the fridge—the only paper in the whole house she was not allowed to color upon.

"How about that," Blake said. "Your papa's stronger than he thinks."

Her father just grunted as he hauled the cooler out of their truck bed. "We're wastin' time. There's bugs to catch."

"Buggzz," trilled Quinn, reaching for Blake's hand.

But Blake stepped carefully around her and walked ahead of them down the ramp toward the skiffs. Quinn had no idea why she and Papa were acting so strange. She watched his face as he helped her into the skiff and fastened the mildew-spotted life jacket around her, yet found no answer before he stepped over the seat to give the cord on the outboard a swift yank.

On the boat, things got a little better. Papa let Quinn stand atop an empty bucket and help him steer the *All In* out through the channel. She liked the feeling of his big, rough hands wrapped around hers on the wheel. When she glanced at his face, he gave her a smile that showed his chipped tooth and made his eyes crinkle—in other words, a *real* smile, the kind that had become an endangered species ever since Jonny died. Once they were clear of the bell buoy, he hit the throttle. She laughed as the nose of the boat tipped up and they went bumping out into open sea. When she glanced back at the deck, she saw Blake watching them from her post by the sorting box. Something about her shadowed eyes looked sad, but Quinn forgot about it as soon as Papa switched on the radio and Old Dominion came thumping through the speakers.

As they motored toward their first sets, Papa sipped from his thermos and rattled off names of islands and rocky points that Quinn already knew by heart. She had spent a good part of the prior summer knocking around his deck on days when Uncle Jonny was too sick to drag his ass out of bed before five o'clock. Those had been some of her favorite days. Papa had acted like a kid on the water back then, singing along to the radio, telling jokes, performing "lucky lobster" dances by pinching his hands together and hopping from foot to foot. In between, he had shown her how to bait the traps and sort through all the junk other than lobsters that they hauled up inside them. But all of that came to an end after Morning Glory's father went missing. Suddenly, she was not allowed on the boat anymore. It had hurt her feelings. She thought she had made a pretty good sternwoman.

Yet when they reached Papa's first string that morning, and Quinn saw the way Blake could hoist the fifty-pound traps, change out the bait sacks in mere seconds, and send the cages hurtling off the stern, all the while hopscotching over the lines, she realized why her father had agreed to let Blake apprentice. He and the Amazon had mastered a working rhythm that required few words. Quinn had rarely witnessed her father labor as steadily as he did with Blake there alongside him at the rail. As she watched them, Quinn got the feeling that Blake was holding her father to task. Whatever strangeness had transpired between them that morning seemed to evaporate as they harvested the lobsters. With a series of signals and nods, they plowed through the first gang of traps and trundled on toward his second.

The trouble did not begin until Papa sighted the ruby buoys out by a shoal known locally as the Dragon. Quinn recognized them right away as McDowell buoys. Her heart gave a little shudder at the sight of them bobbing so close to her father's sets. Tim McDowell was the son of the man her grandpa had killed—in self-defense, Papa always insisted— and he and his four brothers ruled the roost in the neighboring village of Swift Harbor. A couple of them were bad into dope. The rest were just generally terrifying. She had heard Uncle Jonny talk about the things that the McDowell boys did to little girls. Ever since that fireside education, Quinn had steered well clear of McDowell offspring in the regional elementary. But Papa's face did something scary when he saw those buoys. His eyes went dark, and his lips pulled tight against his teeth. Quinn's stomach lurched when she saw him give the wheel a brisk spin starboard and pull the *All In* broadside to the jouncing, blood-red spheres.

"What're we doing?" Blake peered up from the cigarette she was trying to light. "Those aren't yours."

"Damned right they ain't."

He seized the gaff pole and snagged the buoy, pulled it, streaming, up onto the rail without looping the line through the winch.

"Hey, Quinnie! Want a souvenir?"

She watched him brandish the buck knife from his hip and saw through the line. When he tossed it her direction, she had sense enough to throw out her arms and receive the dripping Styrofoam missile. She stood, holding it in her two hands like a grenade, something she was afraid to drop but eager to be rid of.

Papa once told her that a lobster pot that had lost its buoy was known as a ghost trap. The term made her shiver. Here he was, making *ghosts*. That could not be good luck.

Blake's eyes snagged on her hers. She stomped out the cigarette she had just lit.

"Cut it out," she told Papa. "That's illegal."

"Right up your alley, then, *n'est-ce pas?*"

He was already busy toggling the boat toward the next buoy. Blake crossed her arms, face stony beneath the shade of her cap brim. Together, she and Quinn watched him slice free another buoy. This one, he tossed at Blake, but since she made no attempt to catch it, it struck her chest and hit the deck, rolled aft into the bait tote.

"Leland. Stop it!"

He ignored her.

"Here's a history lesson," he said, working the wheel with one hand. "The assholes who set these traps are drug-dealin' motherfuckers whose territory starts three whole miles *that* way."

He gestured with the knife. The blade threw back a mean glint of sunlight. "Only one reason they're droppin' traps this far north."

"What's that?" Blake demanded.

"To rub it the fuck in."

The boat grunted and chortled its way to the next buoy. Quinn sat down hard atop the bucket and wiggled out of her life jacket. The sun had come up high, and she was sweating in her many layers. Plus, watching Papa break the law and anger Blake made her armpits sticky. Hunkered there with the McDowell buoy propped in her lap like a severed head, she listened to the two of them argue.

"Is this how we're going to spend our day?"

"Don't worry. I'll still sign your log sheet."

"That's not the point! You've got to set an example—"

"*You're* talkin' about settin' an example? *You?*"

"Don't you dare!" Blake's voice cracked. "I paid for my mistakes. I don't need to pay for yours."

"I ain't askin' you to."

"I'm on your fucking boat!"

"Then why don't you go for a nice, cold swim!"

Quinn pressed her hands to her ears. Fortunately, Papa soon ran out of McDowell buoys to cut and bumped into his own. As he looped the line through the whirling steel plates of the hauler, Blake rejoined him at the rail and received the trap he sent clattering rudely in her direction. The half-dozen cut buoys rolled about the spackled deck like accidents waiting to happen. While Blake and Papa exchanged further jabs at the gunwale, Quinn sprang up to clear the debris.

Mid-stride, she felt a sharp yank on her ankle. She crashed to the deck and flew straight off the stern faster than she could shout.

Whoosh!

The impact of water knocked her breath out. She threw out her arms, but already, the trap that weighed as much as she did was tugging her down, down, down toward the ocean bottom. She could not free her ankle. Something was wrong with it. Panicked, her mouth formed a scream. Saltwater poured in.

Papa! Help!

As she failed in the roaring murk, salt scorched her lungs. Her heart became a swollen fist, knocking uselessly at her ribs. She kicked and choked. Fireworks exploded across her vision. Then, almost mercifully, the water crushed her in its arms.

Blake caught the flash of color out of the corner of her eye—a smudge of sunbeam yellow that vanished off the stern just as she spun toward it. She blinked at the empty bucket and Quinn's life jacket lying beside it.

"LELAND!"

He pivoted from the wheel, registered the emptiness, threw the throttle in reverse.

"Fuck!"

Blake hit the water, knife in her teeth, overclothes a pile on the stern. The cold was shocking, briefly paralyzing. Still, she dove deep, following the trap line, a wobbling thread of beige that led down into the frigid gloom. She knew Leland had snared the buoy and hooked the line into the hauler when a constellation of bubbles shook loose from it.

Quinnie.

She saw the girl's hair first, undulating like seaweed in the murk. Her lips were open, her arms floating out like wings as her body was dragged slowly upward with the trap. Blake spotted the hitch around her ankle and seized the line, sawed through the warp. The trap dropped free, and she managed to catch hold of the rising line with one arm as the other encircled Quinn. With the last of her oxygen, she kicked furiously upward toward the muted light of the surface.

Leland heard Blake emerge with an otherworldly gasp. As her shoulders breached the surface, he saw his daughter's lifeless head sagged against one of them. He leapt to the stern and caught hold of the cold, limp body Blake passed up to him. His knees gave way as he laid her upon the deck.

"Oh, Christ, *ma puce!*"

He split open her sweatshirt and commenced frantic chest compressions. She felt no larger beneath him than a doll, nor more animate. His eyes stung so with tears that he lost all sight of what he was doing, his arms working automatically in motions of thirty. He did not see Blake drag herself over the stern. Yet suddenly, she was there beside him, his daughter's head stabilized between her knees, her face bent over Quinn's to administer the two safety breaths he was incapable of giving amid his panicked sobs.

"Again!" she shouted at him after each set. "Again!"

Leland pumped and pumped. Blake bent and breathed. In that interminable span of seconds, he saw himself from above, a helpless, weeping human instrument hunched over the child he had failed to protect—the only scrap of good he had ever brought into the world now lost to his negligence. He found himself sucked into a crushing vacuum of despair even as he went on throwing his weight against those tiny ribs. So black and engulfing did it prove that he failed to register the warm surge of seawater and bile that came pouring over his hands, nor the first, feeble cough or shuddering wheeze expelled by the blue-tinged lips. It took Blake knocking away his arms to realize that the body beneath him was moving, the pale chest heaving of its own volition.

"Quinnie? *Ma puce?* Quinnie?"

Someone had poured fire down Quinn's throat. It blazed through her chest and brought up surges of puke. She flopped to one side, felt herself hoisted into someone's lap as stars peppered her vision. The sunlight was too bright. It knifed at her as she coughed and choked and coughed some more. When she finally managed to slit her eyes, she saw Papa's blurry face contorted by snot and tears. He was rocking her back and forth, one of his heavy hands fastened over her heart. He wept so hard that she could not make out his words. Her attempt to speak came out as a gurgle.

Papa.

Then she felt someone's cool fingertips upon her forehead. Blake's dark eyes peered into hers. She did not look like any kind of Amazon just then. Fear creased every feature of her face, from her broad mouth to her long, black brows.

"Quinn? Can you hear us? Can you breathe okay?"

She nodded once and heard Blake murmur something to Papa, who pulled her more tightly against him and kissed her fiercely on the forehead.

"Quinnie," he whispered. "I need to get you back home, okay?"

His arms could not seem to let go of her, though. He shook as though some motor inside him had gone berserk. Blake reached for her gently and pried her loose. She bundled her into the foil blanket from the first aid kit, then carried her inside the cockpit, where she sat with Quinn cradled in her lap while Papa picked up the radio. His words were muffled over the sudden rev of the engine, but Quinn caught the word *ambulance* and burrowed deeper into Blake's lap. The shivering Amazon held her tight.

As Papa raced for port, the radio erupted with crackling. He shouted more indecipherable words into the receiver. Fear and sleepiness overtook Quinn all at once. Blake's cold fingers stroked her cheek each time she started to drift off against the cushion of her breast.

"Stay with us," she whispered. "*Por favor, amazona pequena. Por favor.*"

It had turned into too lovely a day to hide inside and surrender to aches and pains, so when Nora returned from her morning shift at the restaurant, she stationed herself in the yard, which now burst with so much green, it stung her eyes. Her daughter would not return until evening. The relief Nora found in this afternoon solitude made her feel a little guilty. For a while, she sat by the roses and attempted to make headway in *Midnight at Mount Husky*. But she quickly found herself bristling at the graphic description of a crime committed by crossbow, and soon, she had swapped the novel for her garden trowel, wondering what excuse she might muster for Clyde in several weeks if he were to question her about the intricacies of the plot.

The distant wailing of sirens brought her briefly still in the dirt. Seldom was the peace of her peninsula disturbed by so much noise. The insistent crescendo called forward an image of the ambulance that had raced out to her home all those Septembers ago, lights whirling as if there were still time to make a difference. Both the urgent cacophony of their arrival and the solemn silence of their departure were forever etched in her memory. She shook her head, slightly frantic. She could not allow her mind to go galloping off like this—not when her brother already thought she was slipping, and her daughter watched her like she might break into a million pieces.

So instead she focused on digging dandelions and wondering how she might manage to celebrate Morning Glory's twenty-first birthday in the absence of her husband. Part of her worried that even a small party might somehow anger her daughter. Every decision she made seemed to be the wrong one in Glory's eyes. Ed probably would have taken her out to the Oar for her first legal drink or maybe even driven her down to Boston for a Red Sox game. Nora's mind drifted more in the direction of a garden party. She still possessed her mother's yellowing book of recipes for dainty teacakes and appetizers. Perhaps Blake could help her haul out the gelato maker and string some lights. With his fondness for cocktails, Clyde could concoct a special drink in Glory's honor. And if she played her cards right, she might recruit Jody Poole and her husband for an appearance with their string band. As these ideas came together, Nora grew steadier. She would draw up a menu that evening and speak to Clyde on Sunday. If she could get invitations out in the next week . . .

In this manner, an hour flew by. Only when she ventured inside for water and caught a glimpse of her beet-red reflection in the living room mirror did she grow aware of the sun's power. In a hunt for sunscreen, she allowed herself a glance at her cell phone. She started when she saw seven missed calls.

Mom. The breathless opening of Morning Glory's voice mail message made Nora's heart stop. *Please pick up. Quinn got dragged overboard. Lee and Blake brought her back with CPR, but she's having some trouble breathing. I'm on my way to the hospital. Let me know when you get this . . .*

The voice mail was twenty minutes old. For a moment, Nora stood in her silent kitchen, the phone clutched to her chest as a scream formed in her throat. Initial horror still had her paralyzed when she heard Blake's truck barrel up the drive. She watched it lurch to a halt, Blake stumble from the driver's seat. Her clothing clung to her skin, and her hair was a black, sodden mess across her shoulders. But it was her face, blanched paper-white, that made Nora's hand fly to her mouth. She ran to the porch, but Blake was already tripping toward the garage and either ignored or did not hear Nora's shout. Flinging the door wide, she vanished up the stairs in a clunking thunder of boots.

Nora flinched as the swinging door banged against the side of the garage. The broad faces of the pansies shuddered in their window box. Cold with dread, she made herself cross the driveway and tackle the perilous wooden steps to the loft apartment.

"Blake?"

When her knock went unanswered, she twisted the knob and found it unlocked. At first glance, the apartment appeared empty. Nora's eyes swept over the spartan space, taking in the immaculate countertop, the tightly made bed, the tidy display of books on the pool table. Beyond the ashtray on the kitchen table, there were few signs that the place was occupied. She hesitated, wondering if it were possible she had imagined Blake's flight up into this room. Then she spotted her on the floor in the far corner, legs drawn up to her chest, arms folded over her head in the attitude of an airline passenger bracing for impact. She made no sound at all, but as Nora ventured toward her, she noticed the violent way she was shaking.

"Blake?"

Her tenant condensed herself into an even tighter ball—a feat, given her size.

"Leave me alone. Please . . ."

Nora's heart thumped too loudly for her to register this command. With some effort, she lowered herself to the cool laminate beside Blake and reached timidly for one of her sopping sleeves. Blake instantly went rigid. She tugged her sleeves down over her hands, as though she wished to vanish into the briny flannel.

Nora's phone buzzed with a text message: *They have her stable. Think she'll be OK. Where r u?*

She let out her breath. Blake continued to shudder uncontrollably. Gently, Nora wrapped her arms around her sodden form, wincing at the chill of the sea against her sun-scorched skin. She said nothing at first, just sat there and held the giant, trembling woman while her mind made various fragmented attempts at prayer for Leland and his little girl. Whole minutes passed before she felt Blake's body begin to relax. Meanwhile, the phone buzzed and buzzed. She ignored it until Blake finally unfolded herself.

"Is she okay?" she asked raggedly, nodding toward the phone. "Is Quinnie okay?"

Nora picked it up and read the messages aloud. "They're keeping her overnight, just to be sure."

Blake's face appeared so spent that Nora did not have the heart to ask her what happened. She already knew of the myriad dangers posed by fishing boats and had little trouble imagining how a young girl might fall prey to them. Instead, she caught a piece of Blake's damp, salty hair and tucked it behind one ear, her fingers grazing the long scar on her jaw. Blake kept still, her hands locked together at her waist, her long legs sprawled before her. She stared ahead at the wall in a kind of grim trance.

"I thought she was dead. I thought . . . I held a dead child in my arms. I couldn't."

"Oh, Blake."

When the woman finally looked at her, Nora saw in her eyes something fathomless and terrible and so familiar that her own throat thickened with grief. She took Blake's hand and gripped it between her own, waiting for her to say more. But Blake just tipped her head back against the wall and pressed her eyes shut. Her chest rose and fell in shudders.

"I'm tired," she whispered. "I'm so tired, Nora."

The words hung in the air like dust motes. Nora lowered her head to Blake's hard shoulder. It felt strangely necessary to be pressed together there in that corner as the fragile pieces of the world slowly glued themselves back together. Quinn would be okay. Today, at least, they would all be okay. A powerful gratitude overcame her.

"I'll pray for you. I always pray for you, Blake. Even if you think no one's listening."

Blake's teeth chattered faintly. "Save your prayers for Quinnie," she said.

The ambulance ride was almost as terrifying as getting dragged off the boat. Strapped to a gurney with an oxygen mask fastened to her face and a blood pressure cuff squeezing holy hell out of her arm, Quinn tried to be brave. Papa held her hand and spoke soothing words in French. Seeing the fresh tears peel down his cheeks inspired her to stifle her own as a medic jabbed her arm with a needle and sent a stinging warmth through her veins. *Amazons don't cry.* She remembered this creed, though she was pretty sure Blake had been sniffling on the ride back to the harbor, as she held Quinn bundled in her lap.

At the hospital, they took X-rays of her lungs and also her ankle, which had begun to hurt pretty badly as soon as she regained feeling in her extremities. Her ankle was just sprained, which meant she would not get to have a cast like Ms. Nora. But the doctor said he saw fluid in her lungs on the X-rays, so she would need to stay the night. The disinfectant smell of the hospital made Quinn anxious. Even after they put her in a bed with a heated blanket and brought her apple juice, she felt twitchy until they let Papa back in to sit with her. His face looked worse than it did when he was hungover, but he mustered a smile as he pulled his chair up close. He even let her play with Jonny's dog tags, which fell from the open collar of his shirt.

"You wanna drink, dontcha?" she said when his silence began to feel too heavy.

It hurt to talk. The words came out all raspy. Papa looked at her, startled.

"Quinnie, I ain't ever gonna drink again. Not ever. Do you hear me?"

He picked up one of her fingers and dragged it across his heart, and Quinn nodded because she wanted very badly to believe it.

A few minutes later, Aunt Nicky teetered in wearing

rhinestone sandals and a skirt that came straight off the juniors rack at Walmart. As she bent to kiss Quinn's cheek, her breath exuded a sweet hint of booze.

"No more fuckin' fishin', huh?"

She wedged a gift shop teddy bear into Quinn's armpit and inadvertently disconnected one of the cables attached to her arm. The machine by the bed started to bleep and brought a nurse running. Papa's face darkened in annoyance. He often said you could not take Aunt Nicky anywhere. Apparently, that included the Down East Community Hospital.

"You know, there's easier ways to kill your daughter than draggin' her out on a goddamned fishin' boat," her aunt told Papa.

"I been out with him lots of times," Quinn croaked. "It ain't his fault."

"Please, honey. It's *always* his fault."

Quinn decided her swear tax must finally be working because Papa bit down on whatever he was about to say. Slumping back in the chair, he just fidgeted with the dog tags until Aunt Nicky finished fussing over her and announced she had to get to work.

Spending a whole night in this strange room felt like an eternity. Fortunately, they were going to let Papa stay, too, even though there was no bed for him to sleep in. He chuckled at her concern about that, said he had slept in worse places than a hospital room chair. She figured he meant the drunk tank at the jail.

"Papa," she whispered, trying hard not to scratch at the sticky pads on her chest. "Did you *have* to cut those buoys?"

His head dipped. He pinched the bridge of his nose and said nothing.

"Ain't the McDowells gonna—"

"Shhh." Rocking forward in the chair, he tucked the

blanket more snugly around her and tried to arrange his face back into a smile. "Just rest, now, okay? Don't you worry about nothin.'"

The talking had drained her, and the monotonous bleeping of the machine slowly droned out the uneasy rambling of her thoughts. The last thing she remembered was Papa's hand stroking her hair before she let herself sink again into the safety of Blake's lap.

Por favor, amazona pequena. Por favor.

Morning Glory entered in scrubs and sneakers, and it was not until Leland raised his bleary eyes to her face that he understood why this most recent visitor was extending to him a cup of Dunkin' Donuts coffee. He started to his feet, but she dropped a hand to his shoulder and kept it there even after he sank back down into the worn vinyl.

"Everything in that gift shop is crap, so I brought her these."

Glory held up a bag containing a dozen chocolate Munchkins. Quinn's favorites. He nodded, not quite trusting his voice. Earlier, in a state of sheer distress, he had texted her without real hope of an immediate response. Her presence here now threatened to knock loose his last brick of composure.

"How is she?"

"Worn out. They're watchin' her for pulma-somethin' or other."

"Pulmonary edema." Morning Glory nodded and squeezed his shoulder once before dropping her hand. "She'll be okay, Lee."

He watched her drag a chair to Quinn's bed and gently touch her ankle, which was propped upon an ice pack and sported a vicious rope burn. Her mouth warped. She quickly buried this small tick of emotion and turned toward him with searching eyes.

"She wasn't wearing a life jacket?"

"She slipped it off without me seein'."

"Jesus, Lee."

He looked away, needing no reminders of his negligence. As it was, he would never send another trap off the rail without envisioning his daughter's body dragged off with it.

"I can't take her out there again," he whispered.

Morning Glory shook her head. "You'll break her heart."

"Better than killin' her."

The chiming of the monitor filled the silence that opened between them. As she slept, Quinn's little face struck him as frighteningly pale beneath the oxygen tube, her eyelids blue-veined paper, her freckles scattered like tiny mistakes across her nose and cheeks. He recalled holding her as an infant, fearful of the fragile, howling thing he had brought by accident into the world, believing she had cost him everything. But she was his fault, through and through, a reflection into which he was forever forced to peer, whether or not it hurt. Without Quinn, he realized, he was a stranger to himself. And his love for her had proven his only mooring against the darker tides that pulled at him. Now, for the first time, he saw with perfect clarity that if he were forced to choose between the child in the bed and the woman who sat beside him, he would choose Quinn—that he *had* chosen her nine years and counting, even though it meant his heart would never be whole. For what he felt for Morning Glory refused to be sunk on bricks at the rugged bottom of his consciousness. It tugged upward, ceaselessly, demanding a place on the glittering surface.

Her phone buzzed, making them both jump.

"Mom's with Blake," she said, frowning at the screen. "Guess she's a little shaken."

Shame swept through Leland. Blake Alvares, the felon whom he had not let his daughter embrace on the pier, had later delivered to Quinn the very breath that revived her. He dropped his head in his hands and ground his palms into his burning eye sockets.

"She pulled Quinn out," he heard himself say. "It wasn't me. It was Blake. If she hadn't moved so fast . . ."

Glory watched him with those bright, discerning eyes that had a knack for peeling back all his secrets.

"You trust her, then?"

"Shit, Glory. Whatever bill this place throws at me ain't gonna be nothin' compared to what I owe that woman."

Her eyes dropped to the dog tags that hung against his chest. "We all have debts, I guess. I owe you—"

"No, you don't," he sniffed. "You'd have done the same for me, so just leave it. We ain't talkin' about that."

He gulped the coffee, hopeful it would wash out the strain of these words and revive him. His gaze roved over her dusty pink scrubs. "You look the part, you know it?"

Her mouth twitched. "Well, no one gave me any shit about coming in here."

"You remember when you performed surgery on that old wharf cat? What'd you call him? Heathcliff?" He grinned. "Used your mom's tweezers to pry that industrial staple from his paw while I got the pleasure of restrainin' him."

She smothered a laugh. "I probably shouldn't lead with that in my med school interviews."

"Why not? I thought it was one of your finer moments—and mine. Still got the battle scars."

Lifting his sleeve, he revealed the needle-thin marks left by the frantic claws of their feline patient. A decade old, they were barely visible through the hair of his forearm.

Glory passed a finger over his skin, a touch as light as the brush of a butterfly wing. "Feels like a lifetime ago," she said.

He refocused his gaze upon his daughter's sleeping face. "Yeah," he muttered. "'Cause it was."

The kitchen blazed warmly with lights, the stove's enticing aromas of garlic and oregano gradually restoring to Blake some semblance of an appetite. From the table, where she sat freshly showered and bundled in clean clothes, she watched Nora fumble the big, stainless spaghetti pot from a lower cabinet.

"I can help," she offered, though her body resisted her initial attempt to unfold it from the chair.

"Don't you move. You saved a little girl's life. I can manage dinner, for heaven's sake."

Hearing the fiber of determination in Nora's voice, Blake swallowed her protest with a sip of the herbal tea the widow had insisted on making for her. Every molecule of her body felt bruised. She could scarcely muster the energy to lift the steaming mug. Now and then, her thoughts would slide to Quinn's limp weight in her arms, the girl's bloodshot eyes as they fixed on her during the ride back to port. In these moments, Blake's breath would hitch, and her body would give a visceral shudder. She felt glad for Nora's turned back and her clumsy noises at the stove. In truth, she had never found these mundane, domestic sounds quite so comforting.

The back slider stood open onto the humid twilight. A soft breeze shuttled in the deep, verdant fragrance of cut grass and coming rain. Now and then, the distant sky flickered with lightning, but Nora made such a ruckus in her cupboards that the accompanying rumble remained undetectable. Blake's eyes moved up her slender back to the pale length of her neck, searching for the delicate wink of the gold chain that normally rested there.

"What happened to your necklace?"

"Oh, that. They made me take it off for my scan."

Blake watched her rummage through an impressive collection of spoons. "What's the scan for?"

"To see if I have more lesions on my brain."

Nora's voice adopted the same matter-of-fact tone it had the night she announced that it should have been her who fell off the boat. She kept her back turned as she poked at the pasta sauce. More lightning rippled across the marsh and splashed across their garden out back. In the wash of light, Blake glimpsed the knee-high rows of adolescent plants.

"And if you do have more lesions?" she ventured.

"Then the neurologist decides if I've entered a more advanced stage." Nora pivoted before Blake managed to suppress her frown. "It just means the symptoms don't come and go as much," she said quickly. "They mostly stay. It's not... There's other medicines..."

A glob of sauce dripped from the spoon onto the floor. Nora bent very carefully and wiped it up with a paper towel. It was impossible to disguise the toll even this simple task took upon her, however. When she rose, she reached for the counter and leaned against it a moment.

Blake diverted her eyes to a dog-eared paperback that sat at the edge of the table.

"You a Kit Sheldon fan?"

"Good lord, no!" Nora let out a little laugh. "The world is full of enough thieves and murderers. I don't need to *read* about them."

Blake's insides cooled like the murky green liquid in the mug.

"What's the book for, then?"

"Well." Nora pulled the wine from the fridge and dutifully measured out five ounces. "I've got a date, Blake. A book talk, but I think it counts. Unfortunately, I couldn't pick the author."

She left the sauce to simmer and came to sit at the table, smiling shyly. "Do you think it's wicked?"

"Do I think *what's* wicked?"

"Going on a date. I mean, it hasn't even been a year yet since Ed . . ."

"I don't think it's wicked at all," Blake said, struck by the loveliness of Nora's face across the soft glow of the hurricane lamp, her eyes wide and bright, hair all humidity-teased curls. Clearing her throat, she picked up the book and thumbed through the pages. "Wanna know how it ends?"

"You've read it?"

"Sheldon was pretty popular in my block." She caught herself. "In the military," she clarified. "Anyway, Art Anderson finally tracks down the climbing guide who left his girlfriend behind on that ridge in the storm. He drags him all the way back up to the summit and nails his hand to a rock with a tent spike—"

"Stop! Stop it." Nora's hands flew to her temples. "That's awful. Who could write something like that?"

The genuine horror in her eyes made something inside Blake shrink. She set the book cover down upon the table.

"How are you going to make it through a book talk if you can't even stand hearing the ending? It happens to be a pretty good revenge story."

Frowning, Nora wrapped her thin fingers around the stem of her glass. "'Avenge not yourselves, but rather give place unto wrath: for it is written, Vengeance is mine; I will repay, saith the Lord.' Romans 12:19, Blake."

The first deep boom of thunder sounded through the

slider. The ensuing shudder of the earth reverberated through Blake's bones. She pushed up from the chair and walked to the screen to welcome the cool breath of the storm on her pulsing face. Locking her arms around her ribs, she gazed toward the jagged silhouettes of dancing trees and felt her past rise up around her like black water, closer now than it had come in a long time. Her breath grew ragged at the memory.

They caught her in the alley behind Kappy's, cracked her ribs as they tackled her to the gum-spackled curb and wrenched her hands behind her back. While they shouted her rights, she kicked and thrashed and spit, but when she discovered she had, in fact, succeeded in killing Angel Salazar, she gave up the fight. She had flung the knife in the Merrimack, but she wore his blood like an apron. Later, at the trial, the DA would present her spattered Spinners T-shirt as one piece of a collage of evidence that she was the coldest form of human filth Lowell's working class had ever belched into its streets. By then, she would almost agree with him. But on the humid summer evening that she found Angel— six months out from her Army discharge and five into a bender of cocaine and vodka—she had briefly believed she was doing the world a favor. The kind of favor a person in a uniform could not always do.

She had returned to town to see her mother, break an eight-year silence. But the bloody-eyed, wasted woman who cracked the door of their old apartment had no idea who she was—nor any desire to find out. "Fuck off," she coughed, letting the door fall shut on its heavy chain. In a way, Blake had been waiting for this final rejection, this excuse to toss her life away. So, on the night of August 2, 1998, as she sat propped beneath a tree in Armory Park, sick and sad with nowhere else to go but the sorry VA hospital that had already washed its hands of her, she had been contemplating her own death. No one else's. Certainly not Angel Salazar's.

It was the girl she saw first, dark and slim and trailing in the wake of a man Blake could smell before seeing. That stench of cheap cologne on expensive clothes raised the hair on her neck and wrenched all of her muscles tight, collapsing years into seconds. He never saw her there beneath the tree, sheltered from the wan ooze of the streetlight. But she saw him. And more than him, she saw the girl whose throat he turned to ensnare in his grip—a pretty child, not more than twelve, with loose black hair that swung out as he shook her, growling Spanish abuse. Within Blake's bruised brain tossed images of torn sheets and seared skin. Her ears filled with a child's scream. When Angel twisted toward the tree, her body moved before she registered the raw terror in her throat, the shrill, wounded wail as her own.

She ran at him blindly, knocked him to the cracked pavement with one gusty swing. For an instant, he lay, stunned, uncomprehending. One hand floated to his bloodied nose. Then, as she lurched into the light that fell between him and girl, his lips peeled back in ugly recognition. Blake sent her boot flying into that scowl. He flopped sideways and crawled for the shelter of a vacant bench. Meanwhile, she felt herself tugged backward. The girl had taken hold of her wrist and was shaking her head as she mouthed frantic words. Blake heard none of them above the howling in her ears, a gale force dirge that electrified her limbs. Her eyes latched upon the girl's cheekbone, where a long scar ran like a crooked seam. The frightened child shrank from her outstretched fingers and left Blake just time enough to dodge the switchblade that came glinting toward her neck. It grazed her jaw instead, then escaped its owner's slick grip and clattered to the asphalt. Their bodies dove as one, entwined briefly in a final, sickening struggle. Blake's fingers reached the knife first. They closed upon it with singular purpose . . .

Later, the prosecutor would argue that what ensued in the park had been a result of her malicious provocation—

the gruesome slaying of an innocent man in the presence of his young daughter. Marbella Salazar would testify that a deranged woman had disrupted their evening walk, tearfully deny any altercation between her father and herself, insist her cuts and bruises were results of soccer injuries. And Blake would stare into her curled hands, cold with silent knowledge, unable, once she took the stand, to speak of her own childhood and the ways Angel had darkened it. Not that the truth would have mattered. It was too complicated a patchwork of horrors for any stranger to comprehend. She had confided none of it to the brisk young public defender who had done his best to plumb her life for details that might render her more sympathetic. Her son was a sacred secret. She would give no more of herself away. It did not matter to her what the jury decided anyway. Her life had ended in Maine years before. Where she spent the rest of it made no difference.

In the end, only the girl's admission that Angel had been first to strike with the knife spared Blake a murder conviction and a life in prison. The shaken jury found her guilty of voluntary manslaughter instead. But a killer was a killer was a killer. She knew to the eyes of the world—and the eyes of her grandparents, who surprised her by appearing in the courtroom, grizzled and hunched, on the day of her sentencing—that a killer was what she had become. What she had made herself. Eighteen to twenty years in a cell would make her nothing different.

And now, two decades later, Blake could still recall clearly how she had seized upon a hatred she had whittled down, fine and sharp, since she had buried her son. A hatred she had dragged again and again across a whetstone of grief until the edges glittered. It had not mattered, in the end, that it was a hatred of herself, that she might as easily have plunged that knife into her own breast. In the end, hers was not a story of revenge, though Kit Sheldon probably could have written it convincingly as such. It was merely a story of *death*—the death of her baby, the death of herself, the death of a man who had stolen her childhood.

Until today, Blake's life had been a canyon carved ragged and wide by death's river. But that afternoon, she had halted death in its barreling track and resuscitated Quinn Savard. It had astonished her that her own hands had brought this about. Yet as she held on to the girl on that excruciating ride back to port, unquestionably, it was *life* she cradled in her arms. Breath and heartbeat, gooseflesh and green eyes.

Still, a killer was a killer was a killer . . .

"Blake?"

She lurched at Nora's touch. Her back hit the slider door, where she flinched against an assault of lightning. Rain blew in through the screen and sprinkled Nora's fluttering tunic with dark drops.

"You all right, Blake? Dinner's ready. I think we ought to close this door."

For a moment, Blake stood frozen against it, terrified by Nora's nearness, by all the soft smells of her and her accidental beauty there in the stormlight. Equally frightening was her gentleness, her inability to stomach the plot of a crime novel, her refusal to lock doors or question the forces working against her fragile existence. Blake knew that if Nora saw her, *truly* saw her, she would not tolerate her presence at her table or anywhere near the periphery of her life. Blake was getting reckless, losing sight of the solitary existence she had come here to pursue, that she *must* pursue. The remainder of her life sentence.

She yanked the slider shut. "Where's your necklace?"

Nora blinked and reached into her jeans pocket.

"I've been carrying it around because I can't work the clasp with this cast."

Blake took it from her and made a spinning gesture with her finger. Silently, obediently, Nora turned and allowed her to fasten it around her neck.

"Next time, make them help you put it back on. You'll lose it, otherwise. All right?"

Nora just smiled. She led Blake to the table, where she took her hand and said grace.

12.

Nes got around school quick: Quinn Savard had come
back from the dead, and the Mexican dyke who worked
on her father's boat had saved her. All week, Ms. Toussaint's
third grade classroom buzzed with rumors. Quinn might not
have minded so much had they not gotten all contorted by
certain other students in her class, primarily ferret-eyed Eric
McDowell.

"It true she gave you mouth-to-mouth?" he hissed as she
copied down spelling words in her blue book. "Know what
that means? You'll turn into a dyke, too!"

Quinn's fist itched to make a permanent impression on
his broad, flat face, but she had promised Papa she would keep
out of trouble for the rest of the school year. She only had
to make it through another week. Still, it felt like a tall order
when she was surrounded by trash-talking idiots. Her pencil
scratched a hole through her paper. When it came time for
reading, she spent the entire story time envisioning how it
would feel to knock out Eric's buck teeth and wear them as a
necklace like Jonny's dog tags, two clattering ivory charms to
rub together whenever it pleased her.

She did not actually know what a dyke was beyond a girl
who liked another girl. How the actual *fucking* happened was
a bit beyond her, since the crash course on mating that Aunt
Nicky had provided her, using a banana and a bagel, did not
cover those specifics. In truth, anything that involved naked

people sickened Quinn a little, especially since the day last spring when she had barged into Nicky's trailer and found her straddling Morning Glory's father. Papa had spanked her hard for that, made her cross her heart she would never say a word to anyone. Quinn herself would have preferred to forget the whole thing, except that her mind had this stubborn trick of remembering all the stuff she wanted to delete from it. Stuff like Papa getting sick-drunk and Jonny sticking himself with needles.

On the plus side, things between her and Papa had improved since she came home from the hospital. True to his word, he didn't drink. And he finally took her to see Ms. Nora's garden the next Sunday. While he stood on the front porch talking to Morning Glory, Nora accompanied her around back and walked her along the rows of plants, pointing out the differences between the leaves and flowers.

"They grew so fast," she said, smiling at Quinn. "It was your magic touch."

"And Blake's," Quinn pointed out. "Where is she anyway?"

"I don't know, sweetheart. She takes off most Sundays. Goes driving, I guess."

Quinn found it hard to conceal her disappointment. Besides the quick visit Blake had made to the cabin the day she came home from the hospital, Quinn had not seen her father's sternwoman.

"Can I trust you with a secret?" asked Ms. Nora, bending to look at her.

She still wore her pretty church dress with the sunflowers. The neckline gapped a little, giving Quinn a peek of her breasts. A lace bra harnessed them to her chest like two small scoops of vanilla ice cream. Quinn hoped hers turned out like that, then wondered if she was a dyke for thinking about it.

"What kind of secret?" she asked a bit uneasily.

"Morning Glory's birthday party is next Saturday. We're going to hold it right here. I was wondering if you might want to sing a song for her? I could get Mr. Poole to loan us his karaoke machine."

"You mean, like a *real* singer?"

"Yes, honey. Exactly."

This news almost made up for the fact that Blake was nowhere to be found. Quinn spent the rest of that afternoon scrolling through her repertoire of country songs and practicing with an empty toilet paper roll before the bedroom mirror until Papa showed up at her door to grin at her.

"That's the one," he announced through the smoke of his cigarette. "That 'Bluebird' one. I like that."

"It's got a swear in it, though."

"Sure Nora will forgive you just one. Now, come and eat 'fore the pizza's cold."

"You *made* pizza?"

"I might be just a lousy lobsterman, Quinnie, but I'm capable of slappin' sauce and cheese on a circle of dough."

She could not remember the last time Papa had made a meal that did not come directly out of a box. When she padded into the kitchen, it smelled so good, she almost thought he had cheated and run up to the Quik Mart.

"What're you gonna do for Mornin' Glory's birthday?" she asked as he presented her with a plate of cheesy goodness.

"Gonna be payin' that hospital bill 'til I'm fifty, so I'll have to make somethin'."

"You're good at that," she said. "You can make just about anythin', Papa."

"'Cept a girlfriend," he said, and grinned.

She laughed at that. If he ever managed it, Quinn suspected his creation would have auburn hair and a med school degree. "Hey, Papa," she asked. "Is Blake a dyke?"

He spit out his bite of pizza like it had scalded his mouth. "Why in Christ are you askin' me that?"

"Eric McDowell said she is. That she probably turned me."

"You stay the fuck away from him!"

Her father's face had turned stormy. She regretted asking him the question—even more so when he continued to peer at her as though she had turned purple.

"She's never touched you, has she?"

"Not besides kissin' me back to life."

"Jesus, that ain't what she did!" He pushed his plate away so hard, their glasses shook. "What else are people sayin'?"

"Nothin'." She picked apart the crust, confused by his anger and worried by the way he'd started cracking his knuckles. "I just wondered if maybe . . . that was the reason you didn't let me hug her that day."

His gray eyes flickered strangely. "What?"

"Forget it, Papa."

But she knew she had ruined dinner because, after that, he hardly touched his pizza. He kept doing the cracking thing with his knuckles, staring at the tabletop like there was some hidden message embedded in its fake grain. Quinn finally cleared the dishes and got ready for bed. When she came out to kiss him good night, he was still sitting there in a way that made her nervous he might stalk over to Aunt Nicky's trailer after she had gone to bed and raid her liquor cabinet. Then, as she turned for her bedroom, he called out to her.

"Quinnie!"

The tightness in her belly eased as he flipped her two quarters. "Keep the change, *ma puce*. I snuck a few today when you weren't listenin'."

Blake spent the day at the farm, planting lilies and hydrangeas, daisies and lavender and coneflowers. Over the past several weeks, she had hauled in a truckload of compost and manure and engineered a six-foot wire fence around her plot. She had divided the garden into quadrants with crushed stone paths, designed a small circular sitting area at the center, rigged up an arbor at the entryway consisting of bowed birch saplings she hitched together with some of the old man's pot warp. At each corner of her fence, she fastened one of his buoys, which she hoped would double as décor and animal deterrent when they scraped along the wire in the breeze. Now she planted with abandon, digging holes and filling them, patting the earth firmly around the root balls, whispering encouragement to her new leafy wards. It was the most rewarding step yet in a month-long process. As she stood back that afternoon to admire her work, slapping at mosquitoes and swiping at sweat, she grinned at the birds who watched her from the bushes.

"Not bad for a human, huh?"

She had yet to step inside the house. That evening, however, she did walk up onto the back porch and survey her work from afar. The beauty of it pleased her. Still, something was missing. As she stood finishing her cigarette, she worried that she knew what it was. She lifted her eyes to the marsh, had learned from studying a map of the township that if she were to follow that creek far enough northeast, it would carry her to the flats beyond Raker Harbor—that her property and the Hayes property were, in fact, connected through that sinuous network of tidal creeks. So, in some way, she would never be free of that place, even when she managed to get the house fixed and no longer needed to rent the garage apartment. She would always look out the back windows and see the marsh, just as, when she looked in the mirror, she would always see the body that had been fucked and beaten and burned, a body that she had worked tirelessly to render as hard and impenetrable as possible, doubling up her sports bras, buckling leather belts over her jeans. She had no use for the soft places of herself. They had given her nothing but trouble.

And Blake was through with trouble—trouble she could control, at least. She hoped that saving Quinn Savard's life was the last great trial this place would hurl at her. Because even this extra-toughened body of hers was a little worn out.

Tonight, she got as far as the front door of the farmhouse. Key brandished in one hand, she fitted it into the lock, then pulled it out without twisting and returned to her truck.

She had some more time, she thought. Just a little more.

That Wednesday, Morning Glory met Gordon for lunch at the greasy little diner in Jenksport. He proposed the rendezvous as a way of honoring her birthday since he would be unable to attend whatever embarrassing event her mother had planned for that Saturday. Though Glory guessed he had another motive for footing the bill, she accepted the invitation, preferring to discuss the inevitable topic of her mother's health in person as opposed to doing so through email. So, when she dropped into the booth across from him at noon sharp, she did not feel very hungry.

As usual, Gordon wore business attire he had pulled off the rack at the Salvage & Surplus though he could afford to drive to the city and purchase it at a brand name retailer. His thinning hair was slicked back with pomade, and his collar hung open to reveal a triangle of graying chest hair. Glory had always found it difficult to reconcile the fact that he and her mother had shared a womb. Beyond the color of their eyes and a penchant for dropping their *r*'s, they were as alike as a hornet and a butterfly.

"Hey, there," he said, looking her over in her scrubs. "How's business at Oceanview? Getting any tourist accidents yet?"

"Mostly just allergies and stomach bugs."

"Well, there's a business you couldn't pay me to go into."

He pushed an envelope across the table, damp with the perspiration of his water glass.

"To commemorate your twenty-first," he said. "Go out and get hammered, get it out of your system."

"It's already out of my system." She glanced at the fifty he had slipped into the card. "Thanks, though."

She ordered a Diet Coke and a salad and picked at it half-heartedly as she watched a lobster boat jounce by in the bay. Her father had once warned her never to give Gordon the satisfaction of paying for a meal. *The man keeps score. You don't want to land in his debt.* He never disclosed the circumstances of how *he* had landed in debt with Gordon years ago, but he had made it clear to Glory and her mother that he would take any manner of extra work before he ever found himself in that position again.

"Have you talked sense into your mother yet?" Gordon wanted to know.

"Define 'sense.'"

"If you want her moved before you head back to school, you need to start talking now."

"Who said I want her moved?"

Gordon poked at the brownish wedge of lemon that floated in his water glass. "You know your mother isn't going to make the right choices on her own. When's she ever done that?"

She forced herself to swallow a bite of lettuce. "She's not *incompetent.*"

"Not yet. But she could use some guidance on her investments to avoid having a lien on that house—if she keeps it." He placed his elbows on the table and folded his thick hands in the fashion of a chief executive. "I need power of attorney, Morning Glory. Unless you'd rather trust your mother's fate to some stranger."

Glory hoped the soda might settle her stomach. She sipped it slowly. "What would that mean exactly? Power of attorney?"

"It would mean I could manage her finances more easily. Help her extend the life of what little savings she has. It's *very little*, Morning Glory."

"Would that mean she could stay in her house?"

He blew his nose loudly into a paper napkin and frowned. "You really think she can keep that place up by herself?"

"She could get help. Blake's been doing a bunch for her. They seem to be friends."

Gordon showed her his mouth of capped teeth. "Blake the Drifter, huh? Your mother's always had interesting taste in friends. Don't forget she used to run around with Jake Savard before she met your father."

The soda was not helping her stomach. Glory nudged it to the corner of the paper placemat, which featured an elaborate diagram of how to take apart a boiled lobster. Tourists seemed to require extensive instructions on this topic.

"Mom thinks Jake's the Devil now, so I guess her tastes have changed."

Her mother's past was no mystery to her. Her father used to enjoy telling stories of what a hot ticket Nora Wright, Down East Regional Homecoming Queen, had been. She had seen pictures of her mother posed atop her father's truck with her big, early nineties hair and the kind of bikini most women could not pull off without a year on a liquid diet. And Glory could still remember the spark in those amber eyes, the way her mother had once filled the house with the music of her piano and chased her and Benji around the yard with the garden hose, laughing whenever one—or all three of them—

landed in a mud puddle. But Benji's accident, followed within a year by the MS diagnosis, had proved to be the one-two punch that had knocked her mother into the strange, sad, religious version of herself that Glory had at first feared, then tried to fix, then ultimately grown to resent. When Gordon spoke of her mother's failures, however, Glory could scarcely resist lashing out at him.

"She's been happier with Blake around." Glory realized the truth of these words as she spoke them. "And she hasn't spent a day yet laid up in her bedroom like she used to."

"Yeah?" Gordon signaled for the check. "And what do either of you know about this *Blake* character anyway? Could be she sees exactly what a sad, vulnerable woman your mother is. Might be just waiting for the chance to take advantage of her."

He pushed a manila folder toward her as she slid from the booth.

"Here's more information on power of attorney. I suggest you review that with her when you both have clear heads. You never know when she might have one of her relapses."

With a sigh, Glory collected the folder and walked out. Gordon was right about one thing, she realized: She needed to find out more about Blake Renato.

At three o'clock that Saturday, Leland turned the boat for port. Glory's party began at seven, and he still had to put the finishing touches on her present. Nora had let slip that the boyfriend was hung up in New York, which meant he might have an opportunity to show Morning Glory he could clean up okay if he set his mind to it. All day long, he had been jumpy. When Blake appeared in the cockpit—something she rarely did—he gave a start and knocked the radio receiver from its cradle.

"I've got 'em all banded," she announced, thumbing her lighter. "We'll make a good landing today."

Leland had never encountered a woman who smoked as much as Blake Alvares. But beyond her habit of calling out every idiotic thing he did (and said), the cigarettes had thus far proven the worst of her vices. After she had gone in the water after Quinn, it had grown increasingly difficult for him to find fault with her. That day, he had glimpsed a very different woman from the gruff, cold, borderline-hostile giant with whom he usually shared deck space.

"You gettin' all gussied up for tonight, Blake?"

She exhaled a hiss of smoke. "Nora didn't tell me it was a dress-up thing."

"Probably gonna be hard to choose from all those froofy dresses you got, huh?"

She sent her fist into his biceps with a flash of teeth so brief, he was not sure it counted as a smile.

"By the way, I'm givin' you a raise. Twenty off the top. Keep me honest."

"I'd say you didn't have to do that, but since you were paying me shit to begin with . . ."

"I'm sorry about that." He punched off the distraction of the radio and tightened his hand on the throttle. "Every dumbass thing I ever said to you I'm sorry for, too, just for the record. Can't promise I won't say more, though."

"Fair enough."

Leland found he did not mind her presence there beside him as she finished her cigarette. She seemed to want nothing more than to share the view—and his company, such as it was. So few people had ever shown such an inclination that it took him several minutes to appreciate the gesture. By then, the rugged U of the harbor had come into view, and she returned to the deck to finish hosing it down.

She was correct. They made an *excellent* landing that day, particularly for mid-June when the water was still taking its time to warm up and the lobsters were taking *their* sweet time to migrate to muddy ground closer to shore. He cut Blake her share in cash and signed her log sheet, then headed home, heart already knocking double-time with anticipation of that evening.

At the cabin, he found his sister swigging her sixth Mike's Hard Strawberry Lemonade as she twirled Quinn's hair around her super-size curling iron. Her cosmetics tote, a container of toolbox proportions, lay open on the table, and her face, flushed from a combination of alcohol and hairdressing exertion, took on an Oscar-worthy exasperation when he halted before her.

"I got to listen to this damned 'Bluebird' song one more time, I'm gonna slit my wrists," she declared, pausing to swap out the bottle for a joint.

"Jesus, Nicky. You tryin' to get my girl high?"

He stomped to the window and shoved it farther open. Quinn just grinned up at him from her chair, where she sat wearing a plastic trash bag like a salon smock.

"Don't worry, Papa. I ain't inhalin'." She cocked her head at him quizzically until Nicole yanked it straight again. "Ain'tcha gonna shower?"

"Yeah, I'm gonna *shower*." He tossed his empty lunch box on the counter and propped his hands on his hips. "Nicky, I don't want her lookin' like a tramp. You go light on them powders."

"Fine thanks I get," snorted his sister. "I ain't even invited to this thing."

"I think we both know why you didn't get no invitation."

She sneered at him. "Won't Dad have a good yuck when

he hears *you're* goin' to a Hayes party! Like you've got a shot in hell with that coppertop."

Quinn rolled her eyes at him before his sister gave her head another fierce yank. He retreated to the bathroom before he said something he regretted.

In the kitchen, Quinn suffered through ten more minutes of agony with the curling iron before Aunt Nicky finally declared her hair too damned pin-straight to curl. She wanted to ask why her aunt always had to be so mean to Papa and lord her five years over him like it was fifty, but she kept quiet because Nicky had agreed to let her play with her "top stash" of makeup. When one of the boyfriends rumbled up suddenly in his mudding truck, Quinn found herself left alone with the giant box of treasures. She carried it to her bedroom and set it carefully before the mirror. Once she had picked out all the blunts—a part of the "stash" Aunt Nicky had not warned her about—Quinn enjoyed exploring the trove of berry-bright glosses and shimmering talc. There was something womanly and forbidden about them, and she relished mixing up the powders with the big, tickly brush and sweeping them across her eyelids like a CMT star. She practiced her song some more sitting cross-legged on the bed just like Miranda Lambert in the birdcage in her music video. Then she pulled on her green sundress—the one Nicky said made her eyes *pop*—and strapped on the one pair of sandals she had not yet managed to spoil by traipsing through the spring mud.

When she went to check on Papa, she discovered him standing at the bureau in his bedroom, frowning over a greeting card he had laid open across its surface. She watched him quietly, aware his hand had trouble forming proper letters, that something starting with *d* that she could not pronounce made it so that his handwriting came out sloppier than hers.

He had to concentrate when he was writing anything more complicated than his name—and Quinn suspected that whatever he was writing in that card qualified as complicated. Her mouth gaped open a little at the sight of him. He had put on new khaki trousers and a pale blue collared shirt that he had actually *tucked in* and secured with a belt. His hair was too long to qualify as *neat*, but he had made an effort with the comb, and he had shaved so that his dark brows stood out above his storm-gray eyes. Quinn thought he was very handsome, despite the fact that Grandpa Jake had knocked some of the symmetry out of his face and peppered his back with so many cigarette burns that it looked like he had suffered from a strange form of chicken pox.

He caught her eyes in the mirror. "You spyin' on me?"

"You look like a prince, Papa."

His cheeks reddened. "*Merci, ma puce.* You're my princess, *n'est-ce pas?*"

He stuck the card in the envelope and came to stand before her, swept his thumb across each of her cheeks. Then he took her chin in his hand and tilted it toward him.

"You look like your mama."

There was a flicker of sadness in his eyes, so she grasped his hand and tugged him out of that room she had always found a little too small and into the familiar smokiness of the kitchen.

His present consisted of a bookcase he had fashioned out of old lobster traps. It contained three wire shelves, and its frame was reinforced by wooden slats. He had even created two mini buoys out of Styrofoam to-go cups, which he had painted the same colors as the Hayes buoys.

"I want one of these!" she cried as she watched him load it into the bed of the pickup.

"Just about broke my fingers fittin' these hinges." He rolled his eyes, but she could tell that he was pleased with his work.

The Hayes house was lit up like Christmas. A bunch of people were already milling around the yard when Papa pulled up in the side lot. Quinn saw that someone had constructed an actual plywood *stage* in the front yard. An older man was busy hooking up enormous speakers atop it. Farther out in the yard, long folding tables covered in bright, fluttering plastic bore trays of treats and coolers of drinks. Galaxies of balloons were tethered to the fence. Even Papa appeared shocked.

"Didn't know Nora had it in her," he muttered as he hauled his present from the truck bed.

They walked together up the long drive, dragonflies darting every which way in the twilight. Ms. Nora found them first. She floated down the walk looking like she had stepped out of a fancy painting, her hair pinned up elegantly, her eyes dramatic with makeup. Tiny crystal teardrops winked in her earlobes, and her dress, something vintage that bore the color of a robin's egg, complimented her tiny waist. When she pulled Quinn against her, she smelled like an acre of roses.

"Oh, Leland!" she gasped, spotting the present. "What have you made?"

"Just somethin' for her books." Papa hugged it awkwardly against him. "You want me to put it somewhere?"

"By the porch. That's the present table. And Quinnie! You're an absolute vision!"

Ms. Nora looked so happy that she seemed about to burst into tears like she had that day she caught them cleaning her gutters. The happiness spilled over onto Quinn like warm ink. She grinned ear to ear, then let out a gasp when she glimpsed Blake's figure emerge from the garage. Ms. Nora and Papa turned to stare in unison.

Blake crossed the lawn in a pair of studded black jeans and a crimson chiffon blouse whose bell sleeves fluttered like wings from her wrists. Even more shocking than her clothes was her hair. Quinn had never seen it hang loose before. It was long and lovely and full of gentle, dark waves that tumbled across her shoulders as she walked. When she saw the three of them staring, she halted and crossed her arms over her chest as though she had caught a sudden chill.

"What?" she snapped. "It was the only damned blouse in my size at the S&S."

"You're so pretty!" exclaimed Quinn.

Ms. Nora stepped forward and discreetly broke off the price tag that still dangled from one sleeve.

"Quinn's right, Blake. You look lovely. But my goodness, you're not wearing any shoes!"

"They didn't have any fancy ones in a women's 11," the Amazon grumbled. "I swear that store was made for midgets— no offense, Nora."

Ms. Nora just grinned. "You all enjoy yourselves. I've got to go make sure Clyde's getting along okay with that equipment. Lee, Glory's around back with some friends from Regional if you want to say hi."

She left them then, walking carefully in her pointy ballerina shoes across the yard crowded with guests. Quinn saw how Blake's eyes followed her, like Nora was something she had yet to commit to memory and the test was in five minutes.

"Think scarlet's your color," Papa said.

Blake turned and speared him with her dark gaze. "Never knew *khaki* was *yours*."

She squatted on the balls of her feet before Quinn so they were almost equal height.

"You're still limping," she observed. "Your ankle still hurt?"

"Only a little." This was the first time Quinn had been able to speak to her rescuer up close. Her words tumbled out shyly. "I owe you big, Amazon. You're the bravest person I know."

Blake's brow furrowed. "It wasn't brave, Quinnie. I didn't even think about it."

"Still."

She wrapped her arms around Blake's neck. This time, Papa did not say a word or yank her back. It took a moment, but Blake seemed finally to remember what a hug was and folded Quinn in her chiffon-sheathed arms. Though not the crushing embrace she'd anticipated from a woman so strong, it was full of a smoky gentleness that made Quinn feel warm all over. Afterward, she could not read the look that passed between Blake and Papa, but his eyes were soft. He nodded once before walking on toward the backyard, hands shoved in the pockets of his slacks, where he always put them when he was nervous.

Blake smiled at her. "Want to help me with the ice cream?"

"Hel—eck, yes!"

"Good. Let's go see what kind of mess we can make."

The grass bent quietly beneath Leland's stiff shoes. He could hear Morning Glory's laughter before he rounded the corner of the house. Posed atop the picnic table, she was surrounded by a group of young people with whom they had both once ridden the bus up to Regional. Some sort of sugar-rimmed pink martini teetered in one hand as she used the other to admire an engagement ring that plump Kate Bouchard had extended for inspection. The straps of her fluttering dress were the kind that sagged off the shoulder. Leland's gaze passed over her in a quick, guilty sweep, landing on one slender foot from which a heeled sandal dangled like a tease. He envisioned himself kneeling before her and fitting it back on her foot, then knew for certain he had watched too many of Quinn's sappy cartoons.

He walked toward her, fearing that if he withdrew his hands from his pockets, they would land upon her tanned shoulders and wind up in that cascade of unruly copper hair. So he kept them anchored in his trousers, like that other stubborn part of his anatomy that had already come to life. When she lifted her head and called out to him, the best he could muster was an awkward nod.

"Wow!" She grinned. "Got a court date, Savard?"

The remark evoked snickers from the cluster of young guests.

Some of the drink splashed over the side of her glass as she slid from the table. She paused to lick it from her hand, laughing at herself. Leland guessed it was not her first cocktail of the evening.

"Heard about your little girl!" exclaimed Kate. "Is she okay?"

"Quinnie!" Glory burst out before he could respond. "Is she here, Lee?"

"Yeah—"

In a gust of ruffled cotton and sweet booze, she swept past him, trailed by her cluster of equally tipsy friends, who tottered in heels and platforms unintended for grass. He did not know what to do but follow like a clumsy shadow. Already, the pull of the beverage cooler was coming at him strong. He did not want his daughter to see him like this—she would read his face in an instant. So instead, he let the girls surround Quinn like a flock of clucking hens and made himself join a group of men busy demonstrating their lack of talent at cornhole.

Among talk of rising fuel costs and new legislation pertaining to right whale protection, Leland felt safer, a whole lawn apart from the cloud of colorful dresses and pink martinis.

Several of the men with whom he tossed faded beanbags had been close friends of Ed Hayes, career lobstermen whose beefs with big government and local conservation agencies outranked any lingering ill will they harbored toward his loose cannon father and the trouble from Swift Harbor he had brought down on Raker a decade prior. They were cordial enough to ask his opinions, and Leland gave them. Still, their voices contained a suggestion of weary tolerance, for he was a generation younger than the spriest among them, one of a dwindling population under thirty on their peninsula who had not yet fled for cities or a sunnier coast. Had Leland not been born predisposed to loneliness, it was an inevitable affliction to pick up in Raker once a person passed eighteen and proclaimed no plan to *get the hell out of nowhere.* But the fact was, he had never seen a need to get out. What was so wrong with nowhere, he wondered—provided he had someone to share it with? In his heart, he knew he belonged right here on the jagged eastern edge of the continent. He loved it despite its ghosts and grudges, its punishing seasons and inherent isolation. Yet Morning Glory saw his loyalty to their home as a failure, his desire for a life here with his daughter and, one day, a wife, as naïve and simplistic. He wished like hell he could get over the wound of that. But more, he wished she would quit dangling his mistakes in his face as if they were the results of where he had chosen to anchor his heart. As if she could not see that she had been shaped by this place as much he had. As if she had never loved it here.

The brooding dragged him deeper. Thankfully, the encroaching darkness helped to mask his mood. Clyde Mortensen, the man who had flunked Leland in freshman history, had finally gotten the sound equipment running. As more cars crowded the field beyond the garage, the twangy beats of Country Top 40 rolled across the lawn and inspired clusters of dancing that speared him with longing. He wished to place his hands on a pair of warm hips and sway with his face pressed into a heap of fragrant hair. Instead, he drifted among the guests, keeping an eye on Quinn, who proved as popular among the revelers as the birthday girl herself. She twirled about among the older girls, a natural socialite. Her mother's gene. A few children her age scampered among the adults between devouring desserts. Leland credited the impressive turnout to Nora's church network, as well as the fierce allegiance of her late husband's friends. Though he knew better than anyone that Ed Hayes had possessed his flaws, he could not deny that the man had been a figurehead of their community—a man who was remembered long after Leland's own living father had been forgotten.

Amid the merriment, only Blake appeared to feel as out of place as he did. When Nora was not attempting to introduce her to people, she loomed, cross-armed, behind the refreshments tables or busied herself with collecting trash and hauling plates back to the house. Leland ambled over when he sighted her alone out by the *Morning Glory*, which Nora had spotlighted and draped in the American flag in honor of the upcoming Independence Day. It was quieter in that distant corner of the yard. Leland guessed that Blake had desired a moment of solitude as much as he did, for her face darkened at his approach.

"No dancin'?" he asked.

"That's not my scene."

"No dance parties in prison, I take it."

Blake turned away from him and ran her hand along the transom of the boat.

"I want one like this," she said. "I like wooden boats. I don't care how much work they are."

"You'd care if you owned one, I bet." He touched a finger to the flaking paint. "What would you name it?"

"I don't know." Her voice was soft, pensive. "Maybe *Amazon.*"

"Think Quinn's already got dibs on that one."

She glanced at him. "Quinn still wants to fish?"

"Think a little thing like almost dyin's gonna change that girl's mind? She's more stubborn than a pack of mules."

"Just like her papa."

Blake took a seat on the ladder, her feet black with dirt and plastered with blades of cut grass. In the silence, they both resorted to smoking. The boat afforded a good vantage point to observe the party. Leland could pick out Morning Glory amid the strings of lights, her head thrown back in laughter at some provocation from one of her friends. He could also see Nora Hayes, who was swaying to a slow tune with the sport-coated giraffe of the high school history teacher. If Blake harbored particular thoughts about the scene before them, she kept them to herself as she sat with the night breeze lifting her hair and scattering her smoke. Leland rested his back against the old lobster boat and peered up at the collage of distant stars.

"You got anybody anywhere?" he asked. "Family or somethin'?"

"No." She said it so quietly, he barely heard her over the music. "I've made my peace with that."

"How does anyone make peace with that?"

Her face readopted a stoniness that told him he had pressed too far. "I haven't seen Morning Glory dancing with anyone," she remarked.

"If she wanted to, she would."

"Maybe nobody's asked her."

He glanced quickly at Blake, but she was staring straight ahead.

Finally, she said, "It's probably hard for her, going away and coming home. Back and forth like that. You know her better than I do."

He forced a shrug. "I used to."

They smoked some more, listening to the distant laughter and the music that lapped against them, not quite engulfing them.

"You're her friend, is all I'm saying. Everyone needs friends, Leland."

"Everyone but you?"

Though he did not ask it unkindly, Blake's eyes flashed toward him in a way that made him grateful for Glory's sudden emergence in the side yard. She staggered a little in her heels, which she promptly wrenched off and tossed up inside the boat. Somehow, she managed not to spill her beer in the process.

"What're you two chimneys doing out here?" she asked, fanning at their smoke. "Lee, your kid's about to sing. I told her we'd be in the bleachers."

She started clumsily up the ladder, nearly trampling Blake in the process. Leland threw out his arms, in fear she would topple right off, but she conquered the climb and settled herself triumphantly upon the gunwale, beckoning to him with a coy finger that succeeded in jump-starting his foolish heart. He scrambled up beside her, then noticed his sternwoman lingering below.

"Come on up, Alvares!"

Blake looked at him sharply, but Glory failed to catch the gaff, busy downing the rest of her beer.

Silently, Blake climbed up beside him, leaving plenty of distance between them. She focused her eyes ahead on the stage, where Clyde was escorting Nora and Quinn up the steps to the microphone. It was obvious Nora was tipsy. Some of her hair had come loose from its pins, and she relied on Clyde and the nine-year-old for balance. As she took hold of the microphone, Leland felt Glory stiffen beside him.

"Dear Jesus," she muttered. "Don't let her talk."

But Nora composed herself. When she spoke, her soft voice came off only faintly slurred.

"Thank you so much for coming tonight. I can't tell you all how much it means that you've joined us in celebrating my beautiful daughter, who, God save me, turned *twenty-one* today!"

A cheer went up among the guests. As they twisted about looking for the birthday girl, Leland understood why Morning Glory had chosen this moment to join them in the privacy of the boat. He jabbed her in the ribs, and she smacked him. It took Quinn pointing her out from the stage for Nora to realize where she was. The expression on her face suggested she could not see them clearly.

"Morning Glory," she resumed, "you're my heart. I'm so, so proud of you, and I know your daddy in heaven is, too."

Her voice faltered. Beside him, Glory's breath hitched. Her hands tightened around her beer can.

"Please, don't," she whispered.

"And because I love you so much, honey, I have decided *not* to sing to you."

The crowd murmured with amusement.

"Instead, I've found Raker's finest emerging vocalist to treat everyone to a song. Ladies and gentlemen, please give it up for Miss Quinn Savard!"

As Quinn took hold of the microphone, perfectly poised and smiling, it was Leland's turn to catch his breath. Swaying delicately on her skinny colt legs, she gave her sprayed hair one flirtatious flip, a move pulled straight out of Nicole's playbook. His hand found his mouth and stayed there in an attempt to hide its vacillating expressions of awe and terror. He had heard his daughter sing plenty along to the radio. But now, amplified by the microphone, which projected it upward toward the stars, her voice took on an ethereal quality that sent a shiver throughout his body. She even effected a perfect country twang.

"Jeez, Lee." Morning Glory seized his arm. "She's a *natural.*"

Knuckles pressed to his teeth, he fought to blink back the heat that rose behind his eyes. His daughter, the little girl who broke noses and exasperated teachers, *was* a natural. He had not ruined her. Not yet.

By the time the song finished, he had bitten bloody marks in his fingers. Quinn waved and bowed grandly to the eruption of applause. Beside him, Morning Glory let out a whistle that nearly knocked him off the gunwale. Only Blake remained perfectly still. She sat with her hands folded in her lap, her eyes fastened on the stage as though she were still hearing music that the rest of them could not. Then Leland saw the single tear that escaped down her cheek. He watched it disappear off her scarred jaw, then he forced himself to look away, unsettled by that fleeting trickle and the peculiar impulse he felt to brush its residue from her cheek.

"You've got to get her signed up for *America's Got Talent,*" Glory murmured beside him. "Seriously, Lee!"

Before he could summon a reply, Blake leapt from the gunwale. She landed light as a cat in the grass below. Without so much as a word or glance back at them, she disappeared into the tangle of dark silhouettes on the front lawn.

A certain urgency rose in him, then—a need to prevent all that he felt and desired from one day being reduced to a single tear on his middle-aged face. He turned to Glory, took the cool smoothness of her shoulders in his hands, and kissed her.

Nora excused herself, stumbling toward the bathroom with an urgency she hoped everyone else—particularly Clyde—was too tipsy to notice. The fact she made it to the toilet without spoiling her dress proved one more, small miracle of the evening. Clyde's signature birthday cocktail packed a punch. As she washed her hands, she made a vow not to ruin the evening by losing control of herself. Quickly, she rubbed at her smudged makeup, attempted to re-pin her hair, then gave up and shook it all loose. She touched her necklace once—a habit she had adopted whenever she glanced in a mirror. A way of checking herself. When she emerged, she discovered Blake at the kitchen sink, scouring a serving platter.

"Goodness, Blake! Didn't I tell you not to clean anything? Go out and enjoy the party."

"I already enjoyed it."

Her tenant's voice sounded suspiciously husky. She kept her back turned, scraping with the sponge as though her life depended on it. The long sleeves of her blouse dragged in the dishwater and dripped suds as she transferred the platter to the dry rack and reached for another dirty plate.

Now that she had made it through her speech and wept herself hoarse at Quinn's song, Nora felt the energy rushing out of her like the air in a punctured tire. She paused by the counter and spread her hand across its cool, solid surface. The relative quiet of the kitchen proved a welcome respite from all the noise outside.

"Blake? Put the plate down, please. I want to ask you something."

Her tenant took her time switching off the tap. As she pivoted from the sink, her face looked hesitant, even a touch fearful. She wiped her hands on the front of her jeans and waited for Nora to speak.

"What?" she asked finally.

At that moment, Nora could have selected from dozens of questions she harbored about the woman standing before her. Yet something in the rigid set of Blake's shoulders, like she was bracing for a blow, caused Nora to retreat from personal inquiries. She looked up into the hard face whose deep-set eyes appeared red around the rims, and her voice curled like a frost-nipped leaf in her throat.

"Never mind," she said, turning toward the door.

"Nora!"

She jumped, felt her earrings bump against her cheeks. "Hmmm?"

Blake held her in that fathomless, dark stare, hands clenched at her sides. "Just ask me."

Outside, the music changed. Several cheers went up at the cornhole game, which had become something of an Olympic sport this many rounds in. Nora listened to laughter and the rustle of ice in the coolers and the voices of Ed's friends arguing good-naturedly about baseball. All of these sounds made her happy. At the same time, she found herself miles removed from them, a moon orbiting a familiar but intangible planet. She didn't mind the distance. It was a lovely thing to float apart from it all just then.

She walked toward Blake, limping slightly in her painful shoes. As she kicked them off, she saw how horribly swollen her feet were, and knew that Blake saw, too. But Blake had seen worse parts of her, so she smiled and held out her good hand.

"Will you dance with me?"

Blake blinked. "I don't dance."

"Everybody dances."

Nora picked up Blake's hand and positioned it on her waist, then took hold of the other one, an awkward, one-handed arrangement of limbs. For an instant, her dance partner remained anchored to the linoleum, as unbudgeable as a redwood. Her features tightened with a reluctance that bordered on terror. Then Nora gently pressed her weight forward against her hand, and Blake shuffled backward, following her lead. It was nothing fancy, just an old-fashioned two-step that fit well with the slow music drifting in through the screens.

Nora smiled. "Didn't you ever do this in junior high?"

"No."

"Let me guess. You were the skip-the-dance-to-study type?"

Blake peered down at her, frowning, her body still rigid as a steel pike. "I was the too-damned-ugly-and-tall type. What boy do you think wanted to dance with *me* anyway?"

"Oh, Blake! Those silly boys didn't know what they were missing!"

"Sure they did. Me tripping all over their feet like I'm tripping over yours."

"I hardly feel it."

Blake's mouth twitched. She gave Nora a sudden spin. Nora teetered, uncertain whether it was the drink or the MS or simply the surprise of the movement that left her dizzy. Blake caught her by the waist.

"You okay?"

"Yes, just give me a heads-up on the twirling."

"I think you're a little drunk."

"I think you're right." Nora laughed.

"No measuring cup tonight?"

"Not tonight, Blake. Everything is out the window tonight."

Carefully, Blake re-wove her long fingers through Nora's. The lines in her face had dissolved. She finally appeared to feel the music. "That was a nice speech you gave."

"She probably wasn't even listening."

"I happen to know she was. She's lucky to have a mother like you. Twirl okay?"

Nora nodded. Blake executed it with more grace this time, using her left arm to steady Nora. Their bare feet made soft sticking sounds on the linoleum. A fly buzzed lazily about the overhead light.

"Quinnie took my breath away," murmured Nora.

"Mine, too." Blake fell quiet a moment, watching her. "You look real happy tonight, Nora."

"Why shouldn't I be? My daughter is home, and I'm still walking on my own two feet. Well, *mostly*." She closed her eyes and smiled, swaying softly. "And I danced with a man tonight. It felt so good, Blake. Just to dance, to be held. That's probably selfish."

"I don't think there's anything selfish about that," Blake said.

They stopped talking then, moving back and forth to the floating chords, their toes touching from time to time. Blake's smoky, soapy smell enveloped Nora. When the song ended, she found that her cheek rested against Blake's chest, that Blake had looped her arm around her in a steadying half-embrace. That was how Morning Glory found them when she came crashing in, her dress rumpled, her face smeared with tears. She halted at the sight of them.

"Mom?"

Nora blinked hard, like someone had just thrown on a vicious, blinding light. She pulled away from Blake.

"Glory, my lord. What's wrong?"

Morning Glory stared between her and Blake, her eyes a

little wild. Her sharp-heeled shoes dangled from one hand. Abruptly, she hurled them into the corner, where they collided loudly with the coat rack.

"What's *wrong*? Lee's out of his mind, and you're in here, drunk and . . . and slow-dancing with a woman."

Heat flared in Nora's face. She tried to catch her daughter's hand, but Glory jerked away from her, staggering.

"What did Leland do?"

It was Blake's stiff voice that interrupted the brief, crackling silence.

For an instant, Glory looked as though she wished to strike one or both of them. Instead, she dragged the heels of her palms under her eyes in an attempt to check the flood of mascara that had pooled there. Shaking her head, she swept past them to the bathroom and slammed the door so hard, Nora could feel the rattle of hinges in her bones. She wrapped her arms around herself, as if that could somehow fend off her embarrassment and hurt. Blake dragged out a chair, which Nora vaguely understood was intended for her. Before she could will her body into it, however, Blake marched out and sent the screen door swinging.

Nora brought her hand to her mouth to stifle a cry, but all that came out was a ragged whisper.

"Don't go."

The night vibrated with so many noises that Blake felt tossed through it on a rippling current of delirium. The people she passed were simply faces suspended in darkness. Her eyes roved across twinkling lights and murmuring shapes in search of Leland. She told herself she was on a mission to find her captain, but really, she knew she was fleeing the kitchen and the warmth of Nora's cheek against her breastbone—a feeling so good, she feared she would go on yearning recklessly for it as she had once yearned for lines of white powder and bottles of cheap booze. She wanted to scrub off the whole night the way she daily scrubbed off the reek of the boat, slap herself until the memory of their dance dislodged from her brain. But then a small, sticky hand caught hold of hers.

"Blake! I saw you up on the boat! Did you like my song?"

Quinn's eyes danced brightly in the glow of the solar lights. Her cheeks were smeared with chocolate icing. The storm of Blake's thoughts came to a lurching halt when she looked down at that face.

"I—I thought you were a star," she stammered. "I've never heard anything more beautiful, little Amazon."

Beaming, Quinn held up a packet of what looked like long pencils.

"Ms. Nora bought me sparklers! Can you help me light 'em?"

At that moment, Blake wanted only to escape this human entanglement and retreat to her four walls, where, if she could not entirely block out the sound, at least she could enjoy a refuge from the lights and eyes and the looming sight of the Hayes house. She felt like an imposter here, an errant seed that had blown into a beautiful garden only to wreak havoc. But there was tiny Quinn, gazing up at her exactly like she belonged. She felt herself nod and allowed the girl to lead her toward the empty field behind the house.

Blake had never lit a sparkler. Amusements of that kind had not been a part of her childhood, though she'd occasionally watched children streak across the neighborhood park with their crackling wands, screeching with a delight she could only imagine. Now she pulled one of the slender sticks from the box and let out a yelp when she touched the flame of her lighter to the tip, sending off a racket of sparks. With a squeal, Quinn took hold of the handle and bolted across the meadow with her awkward limp. She proceeded to draw great waves and loop the loops across the darkness.

"Blake, you light one! You gotta help decorate the night!"

Following her lead, Blake swept the flare like a streaming torch across the black smear of June sky. She called out to Quinn and drew her name in a glittering script that turned to smoke. The girl laughed and made a sloppy attempt to write *Blake* before her sparkler sputtered out. Blake lit her another. As she watched the girl dance across the smoky distance like a fairy trailing light, yet another coil in her heart gave way. She did not know what was happening to her, only that, suddenly, she, too, was running across the damp grass, twirling, wild and breathless amid the rain of sparks.

They danced around and around one another. Blake did not recognize the sound of her own laughter any more than she recognized the constellations that spun above her. Only gradually did she grow aware of Nora's silhouette standing on the patio, watching them. And then, moments later, her streak of sparks lit up Leland's face, which appeared all at once out of the darkness. Blake saw the defeat in it, a sorrow as familiar to her as the scars on her wrists. But his hands were empty, so into one of them, she placed a sparkler, and into the other, she placed her own, pulling him into their twinkling spiral, turning and turning until she saw nothing but light.

13.

Glory awoke with a world-class headache and regret so strong, it overpowered the aftertaste of raspberry sherbet martini. The clock read eleven, so she knew her mother would be at church, but even this casual thought of the woman made her stomach flip-flop dangerously. She lay curled on her side, pillow crushed to her chest, her mind cycling haphazardly through a collage of images from the night before—Quinn Savard swaying like a little skirted elf atop the stage, Leland's plaintive gray eyes looming above hers after he'd kissed her, her mother leaning against Blake Renato in the kitchen the same trusting way in which she had once leaned against her father. It all confused Glory so terribly that she wanted to retreat like a mollusk into the shell of her comforter and remain there until it was time to return to school.

Eventually, she got up to search for Tylenol. In the bathroom, she perused the sprawling pharmacy of her mother's medicines, turning some of the orange bottles on the shelves and reading the familiar labels. When she came across one that bore her father's name, she stilled. It was Lisinopril, his blood pressure medicine. She twisted off the cap and tapped out the remaining tablets in her hand, counted eleven. A quiver of grief ran through her. She flushed the pills but somehow could not bring herself to discard the bottle. Instead, she stuck it in the top drawer of her bureau with other childish artifacts of the past that she had yet to find the courage to purge, then fled to the kitchen. A pot of coffee waited there, much stronger than her mother's usual brew. And on the counter, a tower of clean plates and platters waited to be put away. She shimmied them back into the cabinets and, afterward, ventured onto the porch with a mug of coffee and her phone, hoping for some sunny solitude in which to return Alan's birthday call. But with a jolt of displeasure, she discovered Blake stooped before one of the lily beds, plucking out party litter, which she stuffed into a bulging black trash bag. She was dressed in her usual drab work clothes. A pair of mirrored shades masked her eyes.

"Hey!" Glory shouted, wincing at the volume of her own voice. "I'll pick up the rest of that. Just leave it."

Blake ignored her, extricating napkins and plastic cups until she appeared satisfied that the bed was cleared. Then she hauled the bag to the porch and set it down with a thunk beside Glory's bare feet.

"I put your presents in the garage."

"Thanks." Glory could not pin exactly what about the woman made her nervous, but her pulse picked up at her nearness. "How much longer are you staying here?" she blurted out. "In the garage, I mean?"

Blake wiggled a cigarette from her pack. "Does it matter?"

"Not much heat up there in the winter. Lots of drafts."

"I told your mother when she wants me gone, I'll go."

The coolness of the woman's reply made Glory's head throb more powerfully. "I think my mother's too polite to admit something like that."

Blake stuck the cigarette in her teeth and lit it. She peered up at her a long moment through the mirrored glasses.

"You're breaking her heart, Morning Glory."

The words caught her like a punch. "And you're going to make her sicker, smoking around her like that," she snapped.

"Smoke makes MS worse, just so you know. I'm sure Mom would never tell you *that*, either."

Blake flicked at her ashes. Slowly, she shook her head and retreated down the path to her truck. Only after it had disappeared up the Post Road did Glory let out a big breath and abandon her spot in the sun to wander into the cool dimness of the garage, a place she had avoided on account of their tenant's presence. Now she paused to reacquaint herself with its familiar smells, its shelves stuffed with rusting memories. Her father's Ranger sat precisely where Harley Cann had delivered it several days after the accident. Gordon had pressured her to sell it—along with the boat—but auctioning off the two pieces of equipment in which her father had spent the majority of his life felt akin to burning him in effigy. Now, however, it was impossible not to recognize that the truck and the boat were the only two pieces of property that held any value beyond the house. If Glory could sell them, how much time might that buy her mother? A year? It sounded pitiful, but a year was better than nothing.

The pile of presents sat in the defunct speedboat in the second bay. Glory counted an array of envelopes—all likely donations to her medical school fund. A dozen wrapped gifts lay there, too. Her eyes glided over their shapes to the trap wire bookcase. She knew who made it even before she picked up the card that had been taped crudely atop it.

To the future Doctor Hayes,

Something to keep your books looking pretty. Happy birthday.

Love,

Lee and Quinnie

Glory knelt beside the bookcase, ran her fingers over the hinges she knew he had soldered himself, the imitation Styrofoam buoys he had slathered in paint. For all his faults,

Leland had always possessed an artistic side, though Glory knew he had never viewed it as a valuable part of himself. His father and siblings had all but taunted the creative inclination right out of him by the time he hit puberty. It angered her that he felt greater loyalty to a lineage of losers than he did to himself. It saddened her, too.

When her mother returned, just after noon, her stiff, crawling gait told Glory how much pain she was in. Watching her pick her way along the walk with the trek pole, Bible folded against her body with the casted arm, proved excruciating, so Glory beat her to the door and grasped her arm to assist her inside to the kitchen. There, Nora half collapsed into the chair, fanning herself with the holy book and smiling in the apologetic way she did whenever she had to accept someone's assistance.

"Hot day," she breathed.

Glory poured her a glass of lemonade and lowered it before her a bit contritely.

"Thank you for the party, Mama. It was amazing. I mean it."

Her mother nodded faintly, eyes fixed on the ovals of her fingernails, which she never bothered painting on account of all her gardening. "There's something for you on my dresser. Go get it, please."

Her voice sounded the kind of tired that preceded a day-long collapse, so Glory quickly retrieved the wrapped package from her mother's room and returned to the kitchen table. Peeling back the foil paper, she discovered a Littman Classic stethoscope, complete with royal blue tubing.

"Mom, this is . . . *really* nice. How did you afford this?"

Her mother waved off the question. "I had to consult with Ainsworth. I wanted you to have a good one."

Glory wrapped her arms around her mother's neck. Part

of her wanted to give in to the childish impulse to cry, lose herself briefly in the illusion that this tiny, gentle woman could make the world okay again. There had been a time, very, very long ago, when she had believed in such miracles. A time before she lost her baby brother on a perfectly sunny September afternoon. Ever since, the realities of life had been drawn too sharply into focus for Glory to entertain a desire to blur or obscure them. She needed to see the world clearly, even when it hurt. Even when it made her want to tear it all down and scream.

So, as she sat sipping lemonade with her mother on this quiet Sunday in June, it took great effort not to ask about Blake Renato. Instead, she brought forward the folder Gordon had shared with her regarding power of attorney. Her mother listened in silence to her argument, her calm, frank laying out of the facts. In mid-August, she would depart for another year. While her mother knew many people, she lived alone. The flares of her disease were increasingly unpredictable, and what would happen if she injured herself more seriously? If she did not want to move, she needed to find the means of procuring more regular assistance.

"You can't rely on Blake," she pointed out. "When she leaves, you'll be alone here."

Her mother lifted her shadowed eyes briefly, the look in them unreadable.

"You want me to sign these papers, then?"

"I just want you to think about it, Mom. You know I don't *love* Gordon. I'm just . . . scared for you."

Her mother's fingers found the cross at her throat. Glory remembered when her father had given it to her, the first Christmas after Benji's death, when her mother had just begun to surface from a pool of grief so vast and profound that neither of them had really recognized her.

"If you believe that's what I should do, Glory, then I'll do it. I won't be your chain. That's the last thing I ever wished to be."

Glory clenched her teeth. "That sounds a bit melodramatic, Mom."

"Is that what you think I am? Melodramatic?"

"No, Mama!" Glory shook her head, added more softly, "I'm sorry I said that."

Her mother rose slowly, used her good hand to push herself up from the table. Her face appeared as exhausted as her voice sounded. "I'm going to lie down for a little while."

As Morning Glory watched her retreat down the hall, one hand thrown out to the wall for balance, she worried that Blake was right. She *was* breaking her mother's heart. But how could Glory protect her without wounding her? She dropped her face into her hands. They still smelled like the brine from Leland's lobster trap shelf. She closed her eyes and let herself ache for the sea.

Late that afternoon, after a five-mile jog failed to improve her spirits, Glory drove over to the Savard place. She did not wish to put off the inevitable confrontation with Leland any longer than possible. When she pulled up, she found him crouched in the back of his sagging pickup, heaving armfuls of ruby buoys off the side of the bed. The sight sent a chill through her.

"What's all that?" she asked, stepping from the car.

He shot her a cold glance. His left cheek bore a faint mark where her knuckles had landed. It had been a sloppy drunk's punch, but it got her point across. A bit too well, perhaps.

"Did a little ocean cleanup this morning."

"*McDowell* buoys? Why, Lee? You're asking to get your boat sunk."

"These were all over Raker territory, practically on *top* of my strings! You think that's an accident?"

His foul mood seeped toward her like a red tide.

"Are you trying to end up like your dad?"

It was not at all what she had come to say, but she was so stricken by the scene before her that she forgot about the birthday present he had made her.

Leland turned on her so fiercely, she flinched.

"Those motherfuckers might've killed my brother. And *now* they're makin' a play on my turf. You think I'm just gonna sit around and let it happen?"

"You're going to start another harbor war."

"They already started one!"

"Who? The McDowells or your redneck friends? You're smarter than them, Lee. Really, you are."

In lieu of responding, he swung down from the truck and began herding the buoys toward the woodpile with a series of rough kicks. Glory kept stride beside him, thankful Quinn was nowhere in sight to witness this confrontation.

"What're you going to do with all these?"

"Target practice."

She grabbed his arm, but he shook her off. Hard.

"Lee, would you stop a minute! Listen, I'm sorry about hitting you."

He paused just long enough to touch his face and sneer. "This? I'm embarrassed to say I taught you how to swing."

Though she smelled no alcohol on him, his words and gestures bore the kind of sharp edges that made her uneasy. "Like I said, I'm sorry. It was wrong. That's what I came to say." Although she really did come to say more.

She turned and walked slowly back to her car, had her hand on the door when he spun around once more.

"Did you even see what I made you? Or was it not good enough for you, *princess?*"

The rawness of these words made her flinch. "What did you call me?"

"Ain't nothin' wrong with your hearin', girl."

Stooping, she gathered a fistful of mud and flung it at him as hard as she could. It struck him in the shoulder and exploded in brown clots down the front of his shirt.

"Nothing wrong with my aim, either!"

All at once, the hard lines of his face broke apart. He leapt from the stack of kindling and seized a fistful of earth, clocked her in the ass. Before she knew what she was doing, she was gathering more mud and sprinting away from him as he advanced with two more dirt balls. They skipped and ducked across the yard, the way they used to do as kids, hurling Franglish taunts, pausing for shelter behind old hunks of machinery as they packed together new missiles. The exchange carried on ten minutes before he caught her behind Jonny's trailer. There, they both went crashing into some empty barrels that had stood for months, collecting pine needles and rain.

Even as she fought him, he managed to catch both wrists in his powerful hands and pin her to the damp earth. Mud plastered his skin like war paint, making his gray eyes stand out like two pale gems from his rugged face. As he bent over her, his brother's dog tags spilled out of his open shirt collar and smacked her in the chin. She thought he was going to try to kiss her again, and she did not know whether to deploy her knee or simply give in and plot future revenge. Instead, he just gazed down at her, loosening his grip on her wrists without quite letting go.

"Say you're licked."

"I'll never be licked."

His grin revealed the dirt that had embedded itself between his crooked teeth. "Keep tellin' yourself that, Mornin' Glory."

The ground had absorbed the shape of her body. When he let go of her, she lay there, gazing up at the violet-tinted sky beyond the trees. Leland sat beside her, flicked a mosquito from her knee. She could feel the radiating animal heat of his body as she had felt it the prior night on the boat and did not know why it comforted her today when it had frightened her then.

"Come on, I love your gift," she said finally. "It's beautiful, Lee. Too beautiful for books maybe."

He nodded once, staring off into the shaggy curtain of evergreens. The flap of a torn trailer screen rasped above them. As she studied him, Glory noticed threads of premature gray had begun to work their way into his sideburns. Briefly, she felt she was looking at a much older man, one whose hurts and dreams were no longer familiar to her. It pricked her with unexpected sadness, so she sat up and made a fuss of digging the mud from her fingernails.

"You ever miss fishin'?" he asked quietly.

She kept her face bent and shrugged. It hurt too much to admit how keenly she felt the absence of her father and their summer ritual. "Of course I do." She deliberated over her next words. "Is she any good, your new sternwoman?"

"Probably better than me."

Glory waited until he was looking at her directly again before she said, "I need to know more, Lee. There's just something about her . . ."

The way his big shoulders stiffened confirmed her suspicion he was holding something back. "Blake's had a bad life. Ain't nothin' so strange about that."

"I'm worried about Mom," she persisted. "She's let that woman close. I can't let her get hurt—"

Leland rose and shoved back the salt-stiff mop of his hair. "*Calisse*, Mornin' Glory. Blake just wants a fresh start. Who the hell's never wanted one of those?"

"A fresh start from *what?*"

Shadow poured across his face as he peered down at her. He shook his head slowly. "*You* got one, didn't you? Got to go away and reinvent yourself?"

"*Reinvent?*" she sputtered.

"You know what I mean."

"I finished high school, Lee. I got a scholarship."

"And I didn't. That's what you're sayin'."

"You could have finished. I don't need to tell you that. I used to hope . . ."

"Hope *what?*"

But she knew that if she said it, she could never unsay it, that he would never let her forget it. So she bit her lip and looked away from him. And after a moment, he turned and strode away through the muck, returned to his pile of stolen buoys and brewing trouble.

The lock turned reluctantly. As Blake laid her weight against the door, it clattered inward onto the dusty gloom. At once, the smell of death hit her—mice, most likely, and anything else that might have found its way in during the twelve years the house had stood vacant. She took a tentative step inside, testing the creak of floorboards, eyes adjusting to the angle of murky light that fell through the lower windows. Mold spackled the walls in alarming patterns. A wintery chill lingered in the foyer. She looked once at the narrow staircase leading up to the bedrooms, then walked past it into the old living room. The oak rocker stood there, still, and the enameled card table where they had played checkers and Scrabble and blackjack. So much remained as she remembered it, except that the cot by the stove had not been there before. Her grandmother must have slept her final nights there. Perhaps her grandfather, too. A single quilt lay folded atop it, and Blake recognized its worn star pattern. She studied the shapes of her grandfather's wood carvings of loons and eiders upon the mantle, the braided rugs and tarnished tea set and cabinet full of ornate glass bottles. Knickknacks of another lifetime.

She touched the curtains tangled with cobwebs and sent spiders skittering. Then she lifted her face to the ceiling, where strips of paint had pulled free and dangled like so many pale, withered leaves. She wondered if the house was salvageable— if the bones would prove solid enough to withstand the plans she had for them. She knew she would have to climb to the second level to gain a better idea, but she worried what would happen to her if she passed her old room and found it made up and waiting. If she discovered the empty crib and the drawer full of tiny suits and the blanket knit with sea stars. The photographs her grandfather had taken on his cumbersome Canon. So instead, she walked into the kitchen and stared into the empty cabinets, caressed the dusty red kettle that perched on the stove like a sleeping rooster. She wondered what thoughts had turned in her grandfather's head the last morning he had stood in this room, in the moment he had returned the kettle to the burner and switched it off for the final time. Perhaps there had been no thoughts at all save for the one thing he had decided to do, that culminating mission on a boat loaded with explosives. An ending that he could control. It was the easiest thing to believe, so Blake tried to.

He had left her a simple note, passed to her by Corrections some weeks after the news arrived. She had not kept it, committed the words to memory instead, so that she could discard that last thing he had touched and spare herself the pain of a tangible artifact.

All is left to you. No great fortune, but an option, if you need one. Water always finds a way back to the sea, and maybe you will, too. Left some gear in the shed if you ever feel called again to fishing. The ocean don't give a damn about your past. Remember that, and our love . . .

Blake walked to the back window, which framed a view of her garden. She pulled out a chair by the table there and sat looking out at her work. Would they have been pleased? Would it have made up for deserting them after all they had done? Her eyes welled. She lay her dirt-creased hands, palms up, upon the table, and considered all the uses to which she had put them. Mapped into them were memories of the softness of her baby's hair, the greasy warmth of Angel's blood, the chill of cinderblocks that had formed her world for half of her life. And now, too, they contained the memory of Nora's delicate hand, the light pressure of her palm against her own as they had danced. Already she knew that if she lived fifty more years, she would recall that hand as vividly as she could recall the velvet arc of her son's ear or the pop of the knife she had driven into the man she had killed.

Help me, she wrote to Dawn, later, after she had locked up the house and seated herself among the flowers. *I'm going to break apart. I cracked the door, and now I can't keep myself from filling up.*

The response proved brief as ever.

Baby, you've been empty too long. You keep that door wide open.

Though Nora never made it through *Midnight at Mount Husky*, she found herself anticipating Saturday's rendezvous with Clyde Mortensen with a mixture of giddiness and unease. The giddiness derived from a hunger for touch that had blazed in her since Glory's party. No amount of prayer or throwing herself into the work of the restaurant had sufficed to tamp down the swelling need. Even when she knelt in her garden and attempted to absorb nature's calm, her heart railed against the cage of her ribs, demanding, demanding. She found it difficult to look customers in the eye, felt grateful for Morning Glory's preoccupied distance. The one person she did ache to talk to appeared set on avoiding her. All week, Blake had departed for the wharf before Nora awoke. She did not return again until dusk had fallen, and Nora, besieged by the fatigue she recognized as the harbinger of another bad flare-up, had retreated to the couch. There she lay with the TV switched to mute, thinking too often of their dance in the kitchen, caught in a confusion of embarrassment and longing as she recalled Blake's hand on her hip and the collision of their toes atop the linoleum. Always, her mind stuck on the moment when the song had ended and Blake's arms had closed around her. At first, she tried to tell herself she had imagined it—but Glory's searing words in her ears had dispelled that possibility. And though she had been tipsy, Nora also knew she had not imagined Blake's heartbeat against her cheek. It had been there, steady as a clock.

Perhaps that dance was just one more sign she was losing her mind, allowing nostalgia for her husband to bring her teetering into the arms of a strange woman. Clearly, that had been her daughter's take on things. Why else would she bring up giving Gordon power of attorney the day after Nora had thrown her the nicest party of her life? That wound still smarted. Over the years, she had endured various episodes of Glory's anger. They had begun to tick off her like balls of sleet, the sting brief. Strangely, it was the things her daughter said in moments of measured intimacy between them that lodged in her like shrapnel, refusing to heal.

Nora's uneasiness was hardly assuaged by a voice mail she received Friday morning, while rolling silverware at Coasters. Her neurologist wished to see her on July third.

She pushed the ominous message from her mind. She wanted one weekend—one *real date*—before she had to contend with the news that her body had possibly entered a new phase of self-destruction, and that new, more powerful drugs would be required to trick it into submission. Surely, one date was not too much to ask.

So, on Saturday, though she woke with a headache and two hips that felt as though they had been pounded by mallets, Nora combed out her hair until it shone and put on a lavender dress she had not worn in years. The neckline plunged a bit low for her liking, but she could think of no other occasion for which she might reserve it. She cinched the belt tight in hopes of accentuating what few curves her body had retained, pressed a set of pearl earrings through her earlobes, and allowed herself several sips of wine before walking out to wait on the porch for Clyde's truck.

It was a tame evening, the very last in June. Fat bees droned lazily about her lilacs, whose sweetness trickled across the newly softened, summer air. Morning Glory had gone grocery shopping in Machias (the more local food selections did not live up to her organic standards), so Nora sat alone on the step, contemplating the chemtrails that streaked the pinkening sky. Fatigue and excitement tangled inside her, and her hands trembled lightly in her lap. At the sound of a pickup jouncing down the Post Road, she struggled to her feet, but she soon saw that it belonged to Blake. Nora stood against the railing, purse clasped to her waist, as her tenant swung down from the cab. A cigarette glowed between her teeth as she strode around to the rear bed and dragged down a lobster trap. In the process of carting it to the garage, she spotted Nora and halted, the cumbersome trap braced against one hip, one broken strap of her Grudéns sagging off the shoulder of her bait-spattered T-shirt.

"You meeting the President?" she called out.

Nora blushed, aware of the breeze that pressed her skirt against her thighs and swept her hair off her bare collarbones. "I've got a date."

"That's right!"

The trap gave a quiet creak as Blake eased it to the ground. She came up the path in the loose-limbed stride fishermen adopted after ten hours on a boat. "You look real nice, Flower Queen."

"Thank you . . . Amazon."

Blake stopped beside one of the gerbera daisies Nora had recently splurged upon at the local nursery. With care, she snapped off one perfect, sunny blossom and carried it to the step where Nora stood. Her wind-chapped face adopted a ceremonial solemnity as she extended the freshly plucked offering.

"He's a fool if he doesn't kiss you," she said.

Nora dropped her eyes to the slender stem she'd taken between her fingers. "Well . . . I hope he does."

"He will. I'll lay ten bucks on it."

A honey bee lighted upon the blossom. Nora kept still as the tiny creature conducted its brief exploration. "Where've you been all week, Blake?"

"Fishing."

"After dark?"

Blake blew smoke out the side of her mouth, then bent to stub out her cigarette on her boot heel. "Can't spend every free minute up in that apartment."

Nora tried not to flinch. Of course this woman had things to do, a life that consisted of more than filling the strange void Nora had come to feel in her absence. She set the daisy on the porch rail, relieved when she spotted a pair of headlights weave around the turn on the road beyond.

"Well, *boa sorte!*" Blake called out, as she retreated quickly down the path of flagstones. "That's good luck."

"*Boa sorte*," Nora repeated.

With a wink, Blake hoisted the lobster trap and disappeared into the garage.

Clyde took her to Scribner's, a rustic, waterfront pub in Machiasport, popular among tourists. Long ago, Ed had played some gigs there with The Keepahs. The vibe had changed little in the decades since, though Nora's tolerance for noise and deep-fried foods had dwindled. Perched on a bench that shone with grease, nibbling at onion rings the size of bracelets, she felt sorely overdressed and a little cold. The breeze off the water had gained a nip as the sun went down. Clyde, however, appeared right in his element. The waiter was one of his students at the U, and they exchanged witty predictions on the state congressional election while Nora sipped beer from a plastic cup and pretended to follow the conversation. For much of dinner, Clyde regaled her with teaching stories, lamenting the continued decline in student enrollment (and *engagement*) at the regional high school, recounting one particularly alarming account of a run-in with a student who had been high on meth.

"Only one pregnant this year, though," he informed her. "A sophomore who thinks the Civil War took place in 1975. The baby's going to be the least of her problems."

Nora nodded and drained beer number two.

"And how's your newly legal kiddo? Fridge filled with PBR yet?"

"Oh, Morning Glory's not like that," Nora said. "Too focused on her work."

"What a party!" Clyde grinned at her. "You ought to throw one like that every year—presuming I'm invited, of course."

He touched her hand across the table, and her heart quickened. But at that moment, a band started up on the platform below. After that, they were forced to shout their words at one another over a din of classic rock—an effort Nora quickly found exhausting. Bass guitar reverberated in her stomach with the few bites of chicken sandwich she managed to force down. She lost track of the beers she had consumed. By the time they exited the restaurant, she discovered it was difficult to stand up straight. The earth tilted strangely beneath each of her steps, as though she were participating in one of the lobster car hopscotch races of her youth. She clung to Clyde's arm to keep from plunging.

"You're shivering," he observed as he helped her into the truck.

"It's nothing."

No sooner had he tucked his tweed sport coat over her shoulders than a fist of acid surged up her throat. Vomit gushed out over her dress, his coat, the dashboard. Clyde stared at her, open-mouthed, hand frozen on the key he had stuck halfway into the ignition. At her sob of humiliation, he recovered and scrambled for napkins as she doubled over in the passenger's seat.

"I'm sorry, I'm so sorry . . ."

"Don't worry about it, Nora. You poor thing. Let's get you home."

The fatherly kindness of his voice somehow made her feel worse.

"Your book talk . . ."

"Oh, that's not the end of the world. I'll catch up with Kit another time."

Had she not felt so physically miserable, the ride home might have proven even more excruciating. The nausea and dizziness helped to hold self-pity at bay. Never had she felt more thankful for darkness than during those thirty minutes in which she sat with her head pressed against the coolness of the passenger window, the smell of her own vomit rising up around her as Clyde attempted to make awkward conversation. And never had she felt more upset with her body. As she shifted in the seat, she realized quickly that her stomach was not the only organ that had staged a revolt. Part of her wished to wrench the door open and leap into the whirling darkness. The other part felt too drained to reach for the handle. She closed her eyes and thought of Ed, missing him more badly in that moment than she had missed him since he first vanished into the ocean. The missing was made worse by the recognition that it was not the husband of a year ago whom she missed, but rather the man she had married two decades earlier. The Ed Hayes who had promised to love her *in sickness and in health.*

Clyde's hand fumbled to her shoulder, where it sat like one more punishing weight leveled by the universe. "Poor thing," he murmured soothingly.

Nora feared that was all she had become, all she would ever be again.

Poor thing.

Alan wanted to FaceTime, so Morning Glory slipped on the new black lace corset ensemble she had purchased in Bangor with Kate and turned on the ancient kitchen stereo system to smooth jazz. Her mother would be in Machias with Mr. Mortensen until at least ten, so she and Alan had arranged a dinner date to celebrate their MCAT results. Both of them had earned scores high enough to make them contenders for Chapel Hill, Duke, and Hopkins, among other schools each had targeted. Setting up her iPad on the counter, she posed in her satin robe and sautéed vegetables, pausing every so often to give Alan a peek at what she wore beneath.

"Not fair," he grumbled.

They chatted about their respective Saturdays. Alan had spent the day at the Met with a high school friend; she had passed it reading and fishing off the breakwater at Wind Cove. When they first met, Glory had taken pains to conceal evidence of how vastly her upbringing had differed from Alan's, mortified by her inability to discuss Broadway shows or art exhibits or social justice figures, by her lack of a credit card and her preference for country music over the amalgam of eclectic genres that comprised his playlist. The first time he took her to New York City, she'd nearly had a panic attack—not in reaction to the crowds or noise or smell, but the realization of how much catching up she had to do in acquainting herself with his lifestyle. Not until Alan had attended her father's memorial service that October had Glory exposed him—by necessity—to the humbling realities of her own life. The fact he never balked at the smallness of her rough-edged town, her calloused, denim-clad relatives, or her deeply religious mother had further endeared him to her. Yet even now, fifteen months into their relationship, there were times she grimaced inwardly at the disparities between their lives—which was why, though she badly wanted to ask Alan his opinion about granting Gordon power of attorney, she refrained. Her mother's situation embarrassed her, but so did her lack of knowledge about how to help her. Glory did not wish to spoil the mood of the evening. So instead, she carried her plate and iPad to the table, where she shrugged the robe off her shoulders as she picked up the fork.

"This is cruel," Alan complained. "You understand I'm one step from jumping in my father's car right now and driving up there?"

"What would it take to push you to that last step?"

She was in the process of tugging loose the lace cord that harnessed her breasts when the door banged open, and her former history teacher guided her mother through it. For an instant, she was too stunned to move. Her mouth fell open at the sight of her mother, the front of her dress covered in vomit, her face pale as a death mask. The shock appeared mutual. Her mother's lips parted mutely as her eyes fell on Glory's corset, but she seemed too sick or else too astonished to summon words. Clyde Mortensen, on the other hand, began clearing his throat as if he had something stuck there. Her mother pulled away from him and stumbled down the hall as Glory scrambled to pull her robe back on.

"Oh, come on, babe!" Alan's voice protested from the iPad.

Glory slapped it shut. She sat clutching the robe closed at her throat as Clyde loitered uncertainly by the entrance, his big hand rubbing at the back of his neck like the scene had given him whiplash.

"Your, er, mother got a bit sick. Must've been something she ate."

Glory sat still, waiting for him to leave. "I'll take care of her. Thanks."

"Sure. I, uh, hope she feels better."

After he departed, it took Glory a moment to get a hold of

herself. Anger eclipsed embarrassment as she marched down the hallway to the bathroom. The door stood closed.

"Mom? What's going on? Did you get food poisoning?"

"I'm fine," came the faint, predictable response from within. "Go back to whatever you were doing, Morning Glory."

I was just trying to have a lousy date! she wanted to scream. *And thanks to you, I just gave my former teacher a frigging striptease!*

But she managed to wrestle down this frustration, just as she realized that her mother was crying. It started as a few muffled sniffling sounds, then slowly escalated into the kind of wrenching sobs Glory used to overhear through the floor of her bedroom after Benji died. The kind only her father's low, patient murmurs ever succeeded in subduing, and which chafed against Glory until they wore the edges of her heart raw.

She had not been able to help her mother then. The anguish of that had never left her. Now it rose inside her once again.

She dropped her forehead against the door and tried the knob, but it was locked. It still amazed Glory that the woman who refused to lock the exterior doors of the house was so ready to bar the interior ones.

"Mama," she whispered.

But her mother turned on the shower to mask the sounds of her grief. Sitting down against the door, Morning Glory pulled her knees to her chest and listened to the water run and run.

14.

Quinn lay back in the bed of the pickup, her belly full of ice cream and her head brimming with happy thoughts. Papa had taken her to the Big Dipper to celebrate her making it through the final weeks of third grade without incident. Ice cream nights with Papa were the best. He always said she had inherited his sweet tooth and liked to joke that maybe she would lose it the next time one of those little white nubs in her mouth came loose. So far, no luck. She could keep pace with him in devouring a pint of rocky road.

The *tourons*, as Papa called them, had hogged all the picnic benches, so they made their own campsite in the back of his truck. Papa sat with his back propped against the rear of the cab, his arms dangling over his knees as he pretended not to watch the pretty college girls scoop ice cream from big stainless vats inside the glowing shack.

"You oughta ask one of 'em out," Quinn said. "I like the blonde one with the nose ring. She always gives me extra sprinkles."

"Extra sprinkles are a plus," he agreed. "Never been big on blondes, though."

"Beggars can't be choosers."

He hoisted an eyebrow at her as he bent to wipe a smudge of hot fudge from her cheek with his thumb. "So I'm a beggar now?"

"You're lonely. Ain't that the same thing?" She propped herself up on one elbow. "You need a date."

"I got one, right here."

He raked his fingers through the tangles of her ponytail and dropped his head back to study the crescent pendant of the moon. Scooching up beside him, Quinn plucked a sprinkle from his shirt and popped it in her mouth.

"Blake's lonely," she remarked. "Maybe you could ask *her* on a date."

Papa suffered an outburst of coughing that gave way to chuckling.

"What's so damned funny?"

"*You*, Quinnie. And by the way, that'll be ten cents."

He held out his palm. She was in the process of deciding exactly what, besides a dime, she could slap into it, when something large and heavy struck the side of the truck. Before she could get a full look at the two bearded faces advancing in their direction, Papa shoved her to the floor of the bed and launched himself over the side of it.

"What the fuck?" he shouted, loud enough to draw the alarmed stares of the summer families at the picnic tables.

"You tell me, motherfucker." Quinn recognized the voice of Tim McDowell—father of Eric, the third grade terror. "You got sixteen hundred bucks to reimburse me for my gear?"

"The shitty way you set, you must be missin' a lot more than sixteen hundred bucks' worth."

Quinn bit her lip. She had seen the pile of McDowell buoys in the yard last Sunday, after Nicky brought her home from shopping. They had since been blasted to smithereens by Jonny's AR-15. Papa even let her take a few shots with his clunky old pistol. *Oh God*, she thought.

Tim and his big brute of a brother strolled right up to Papa and stuck their bearded chins so close that Quinn could smell their beer breath when she peeked up over the side of the bed.

"You got a death wish, Savard. No war hero brother to protect you no more, neither."

By now, even the pretty girls scooping ice cream were watching them. Quinn clutched the rim of the bed, frightened by the way Papa's shoulders had formed a hard ridge, his hands two tight, ready fists.

"Go away," she croaked over the side. "All we're doin's eatin' ice cream."

Both pairs of murky blue eyes shifted toward her. The look in them sent ice daggering straight down to her pelvis. Tim McDowell sneered, showing stained teeth.

"Won't be all you're doin' in a few years, girl."

As Papa lunged, Quinn caught him around the neck with her skinny arms. Still, his momentum nearly pulled her right out of the truck. She pressed her face to his cheek, murmured in his ear, "Don't, Papa. Please, don't."

"*Please don't, Papa*," mocked the brute with the brown teeth. "Yeah, that'll be about what it sounds like."

He gave her father a hard shove in the chest. "Sleep tight, asshole."

Quinn clung to her father until the men strode off across the parking lot. She could feel the tautness of his shoulder and chest muscles, the sticky heat of his anger. Gradually, the wide-eyed observers turned back to their bowls of melting mint chip and rainbow sherbet, and Papa pried her arms from his neck.

"Don't you *ever* do that again," he hissed. "*Jamais!*"

Startled tears stung her eyes. She dropped back in the bed, her ice cream now a bubbling swamp in her stomach. Somehow, she always managed to anger him, even when she tried to help him. Maybe she just needed to stop trying.

*   *   *

Blake slept late that Sunday. Most of the night, she had spent tossing in fitful dreams of the prison. In one, she paced the shabby rec yard, ankles shackled, wrists cuffed to a chain at her waist the same way they had been when officers led her into the Lowell courthouse for her arraignment. Rocks kept pelting her from the direction of the guard tower. When she raised her eyes toward it, she discovered posed there not the figures of the usual COs, but those of Leland and Quinn and Morning Glory. She tried calling to them, but they continued to reach into a bucket of rocks and hurl the missiles at her, laughing. Quinn's high, sweet voice chanted *Killer, killer, killer!* Blake awoke, curled in a tight ball, her skin smarting from the imaginary blows. When she saw that the sun already blazed high in the window, she tumbled from the tangled sheets and scrubbed her face clean of tears. Today, she would go to the farmhouse, she decided. She would open all the windows and let in the summer wind. She would mount the stairs to the second level and face whatever waited for her in that old bedroom.

Today would be the day she drove out the ghosts.

She packed her knapsack full of sandwiches and a few of the remaining chocolate chip cookies Quinn had made for her. The girl had yet to master the art of not charring the edges, but these, at least, would not break any teeth. Cigarettes in hand, she tromped down the stairs and out into the driveway to confront the sight of Nora's pickup still sitting by the house. She checked her watch and confirmed it was half-past ten, then raised her eyes at the sound of the screen door slapping shut. Morning Glory emerged in jogging clothes, earbuds already wedged into her ears. When Blake flagged her, she reluctantly tugged one out.

"Your mother isn't going to church?"

The girl placed her hands on her hips, bending her tanned, supple body one way, then the other. "She's sick."

"Can I see her?"

"She won't talk. Not to me, at least. Maybe you've got some magic I don't." Her eyes sparked in a way that called back Blake's unpleasant dream. But then a sheen of tears dampened their fierceness.

"I don't have any magic, Morning Glory."

The girl just sighed and stuck the earbud back in. Sweat already glistened at her temples. "There's nowhere on earth I feel more useless than here," she said.

Blake frowned. She watched Morning Glory lope off down the drive, feet kicking up little tornadoes of dust. Then she walked to the kitchen door and entered without knocking.

The house felt dark and cool, as always. Somehow, the dimness made Blake more conscious of the noise of her boots on the linoleum. She peered down the hallway and saw Nora's lavender dress hanging, soaked, from the shower rod in the bathroom. Something about the sight made her heart kick nervously.

"Nora?"

Blake rapped twice on the bedroom door and twisted the knob when she received no response. The lock was flimsy. Blake's urgent hand broke it loose. Inside, Nora lay atop the made bed with her back to the door. The fan that turned slowly above played with the limp pieces of her hair, the hem of her sateen nightgown. She lay so still that Blake thought she might truly be sleeping until, at last, with a soft moan, she turned her head in Blake's direction. Not even on the day they met had her face appeared so exhausted. Her eyes were swollen, and her skin stretched so tight against her bones that Blake had the brief impression she was gazing at a woman upon her deathbed.

"Nora? You okay?"

Nora let one thin arm drop vaguely in her direction, the palm of her small hand tilted up.

"You owe me ten bucks," she said hoarsely.

Blake stared at her before recalling her bet of the prior evening.

"Oh, Nora."

She looked about the room as though it would provide her a clue of how to console a heartbroken woman. All she saw were medicine bottles and stacks of laundry, and on the wall above the bed, a driftwood cross woven with dried flowers.

"It's hopeless," Nora whispered. "I'm broken, Blake. I tried so hard not to be—but I am."

Blake's teeth clicked. She wanted to tear down that cross above the bed—particularly because the way Nora was lying at that moment, her arms flung out limp at her sides, every ridge and slope of her frail body visible through the thin fabric of the gown, she too much resembled that worn-out martyr.

"Get up," Blake said. "Please, get up."

She did not recognize her own frayed voice, but she knew in that moment she had made a decision, one she would never be able to unmake.

"I want to take you somewhere, Nora. Do you think you could get dressed, let me show you something?"

Nora's face betrayed its first detectible flicker of life. "Show me what?"

"You have to see for yourself."

Without waiting for an answer, Blake turned and began rummaging through the drawers of the bureau. She pulled out underwear, socks, a pair of impossibly small capris, and a short-sleeved blouse. She laid these carefully on the corner of the bed.

"You decide," she murmured when Nora did not move. "I'll wait in the kitchen. Five minutes, Nora."

She walked out, clicked the door shut behind her. She needed a cigarette, but she remembered what Glory had said about smoke, and so she paced the faded linoleum, arms crossed over the freight train in her chest. She was frightened. Yet with each minute that ticked by, hope wove its way more stubbornly through the scrap pile of her other emotions. *Drive out the ghosts. Drive them out.*

Nora emerged seven minutes later, gripping the wall with her good hand. Blake realized how bad off she was when the space between the hall and the kitchen table proved an insurmountable obstacle. Without speaking, she guided her to the chair, where she knelt and worked Nora's feet into their white sneakers, tying the laces snugly.

"All right," she said. "Let's go."

They drove in silence over the country roads lit in summer's bold, ripe light. Nora sipped the bottle of water that Blake had packed for her and came slowly to life as the familiar scenes of Raker dropped behind them and they pulled onto a rougher county road that bumped southwest. After a while, she pressed down her window and let the warm breeze hit her face. Though Nora closed her eyes, Blake thought that it was not so much to block out the passing piney woods and fields of wildflowers but to better absorb them. She found it hard to refrain from glancing at her often. Nora's delicate face underwent so many changes in that brief trip, and Blake wished to catalog all of them—that gradual evolution from despair into soft contentment.

When they reached Harlow's Crossing and turned up the dirt road that led out to the farm, Nora finally spoke.

"Are you kidnapping me, Blake?"

"You got into this truck of your own free will."

A faint smile broke across Nora's lips. "I did, didn't I?"

Then, as Blake pulled up the hill to the farmhouse, Nora sat up straighter, confused.

"What're we doing? This is private property."

"Yep." Blake parked the truck carefully before the old house. "It's mine."

She pulled the keys from the ignition and drew a deep breath before turning to meet Nora's startled eyes.

"I own this place," she said slowly. "I'm a Teale, if that means anything. My mother was Margot Teale, and my grandfather, Jesse, left this farm to me."

Nora's brows knit as her eyes jumped back and forth between the house and Blake's face. "You . . . you've owned this the whole time? Why didn't you tell me? I thought you were from away."

"I am. My mother left this place when she was seventeen. My father was part of a migrant group that raked blueberries just south of here. They ran away together, ended up in Massachusetts . . ."

Blake waved away these facts, overwhelmed already by the prospect of having to explain them further. She saw the incredulity building in Nora's face, the tinge of fear.

"Come," she said quickly. "I told you I wanted to show you something."

She walked around to the passenger's side and helped Nora from the truck.

"Leave it," she said as Nora reached for her walking pole. "You can use me."

Side by side, they made slow progress across the front yard, which remained a tangle of weeds except in the places Blake had trampled down with her own feet and the wheelbarrow. Blake did not mind Nora's weight against her, nor the fact that she had to walk in half-steps to keep pace with her. She felt almost certain that Nora could hear the pounding of her heart, but her friend—her *friend*—remained preoccupied with trying to take in all that she saw around her. Before they came within view of the garden, Blake halted and lowered a hand over Nora's eyes.

"Wait," she instructed, smiling at the flutter of lashes against her palm. "Don't open your eyes until I tell you to."

Nora ventured one blind step after another through the trampled grass, staggering against Blake as she threw out her casted hand for balance.

"I've got you," Blake said, her fingers tight around her arm. "Just a little further, okay?"

Nora managed a nod, still reeling from Blake's earlier revelation. Now, every step, every breath, felt like a plunge into unchartered territory. She trembled slightly, as much from uncertainty as from the residual weakness of the night before. She did not trust her body, but she trusted Blake's, so she allowed herself to be guided across this land that smelled so similar to her own—a tangle of flowers and salt marsh and weathered wood. Briefly, she wondered if, in fact, Blake were somehow guiding her home.

Blake kept her calloused palm lowered over her eyes. "Watch your step here," she said as Nora's foot suddenly struck a new texture. Crushed stone.

"Just a little further. Good. Okay. Now, sit here. Keep your eyes closed."

Blake grasped both her shoulders and guided her onto a stone bench.

"Can I look now?"

"Okay. Yes. Now."

At first, all Nora saw was sunlight. Then she realized that she was looking through a great arbor of yellow roses. Her eyes traveled the arch to its base, then slowly took in the ocean of color that surrounded her—so much color, her eyes could not absorb it all. There were large, blue globes of hydrangea, explosions of violet lupine and golden coreopsis, stalks of amethyst liatris, orange poppies, white bearded iris, and delicate, pink astilbe. As she turned slowly on the bench, Nora saw that she was, indeed, engulfed by flowers on all sides. She lifted a hand to her mouth and sat in silence as she attempted to figure out what this place was, what it meant.

"What's the matter?" Blake asked. "Don't you like it?"

She stood beside the rose arbor, her long hands locked before her. Her face, for once, appeared completely naked, as if she had stripped off every taciturn layer while she had been shielding Nora's eyes and now stood before her a different woman, pensive, almost shy.

"I love it," Nora whispered. "This is where you've been going, isn't it? All those afternoons? Those Sundays?"

Blake nodded.

"Why didn't you tell me?"

A hummingbird darted across a patch of daylilies. Blake watched it, hands still locked tight before her.

"I liked having a place all my own. A secret place."

Nora tried to digest that. "Then, why did you take me here? To cheer me up?"

Slowly, Blake came to squat before the bench. Up close in the sunlight, Nora discovered, her dark eyes contained flecks of amber. Fine lines fanned from their corners.

"I don't want this to be a secret anymore. And yes, I wanted to cheer you up. I hate it when you're sad, when you don't feel good. I can't stand that."

Nora touched her hand to Blake's cheek, which was warm with sun and surprisingly soft.

"I never meant for you to get stuck in the mire of my life,

Blake. I'm sorry I ever tripped on that stupid step and tugged you in."

Blake covered Nora's hand with her own, holding it there against her cheek. "Please, don't ever say you're sorry for that."

She had intended to tell Nora everything in the garden. If ever there were a time or a place for peeling back the lid on the truth, that was it. But the instant Nora touched her, Blake knew she risked losing not just a friend, but the fragile light that had been lit in a place she had long ago written off to darkness—a flickering candle within the veritable tomb she had carried around inside herself. Now that she had glimpsed that slim glimmer of light, she longed to be lit up like a cathedral, for every shadow to be driven out and for all of her dark, slick walls to shine radiant as glass.

What to do with the past, then? To deny it all would be to deny the very ground she stood upon and the child who lay buried a hundred yards from where she knelt. It was not so easy, after all, to extricate the darkness from the light. In Blake, they were entwined tightly as a helix. Perhaps at no other moment in her life had she felt so keenly aware of this. Had it not been for Angel Salazar, she never would have come to this place at sixteen nor known the love, even for a little while, of a pair of old and gentle people or a child of her own blood. And had she not lost that child, she would not have lost herself for so long, taken a life and paid for it with two decades of her own. But the story did not end there, for, were it not for those two lost decades in prison, would she ever have stopped to appreciate the delicate beauty of an iris? Would she ever have bothered to get to know people like Leland or Quinn, or looked twice at meek little Nora Hayes and discovered the first true friend of her life?

Blake lacked the words to make Nora understand all of

this. Moreover, she knew too well that the human mind often snagged on the wrong facts and made of them one eclipsing picture. She feared which fact Nora's mind might snag upon—and it was a big fact, after all. A fact that might easily have defined Blake's whole life had it not been for Dawn Evers and her relentless wrecking ball of challenges to the idea that a person was either worth saving or was not. Dawn had cooled the fire of self-hatred in Blake, left it to her to stamp out the sparks and clear the ashes, kindle in its place a different kind of flame. Somehow, Blake had done it. Now she wished only to protect it—even if that meant forever shouldering the leaden weight of certain secrets.

So she abandoned words in that moment and pressed Nora's hand to her lips. She kissed the ridge of her small knuckles, watching Nora's face for the flinch, the shudder, the recoil. Instead, Nora pulled her closer. She lowered her mouth to Blake's and kissed her softly. When she drew back, her whiskey eyes grew wide and bright and searching.

"I—I don't know why I did that."

Blake saw her own surprise reflected in Nora's features. She closed Nora's fingers in her own, fearful they might flit away from her.

"You don't have to know why. You don't ever have to do it again if you don't want to."

"But I do want to. Is that . . . all right?"

In answer, Blake took Nora's face in her hands and let her explore the taste of her trembling smile. She had not been kissed in many years, and never like this, in a way that brought every cell of her body to warm and willing life. She drank in Nora's Ivory soap smell with the rest of the garden fragrance, then lifted her to her feet so that they stood much as they had in her kitchen the week before. For a long time, they held on to one another without speaking. When finally Nora tilted her head up to gaze at her, a timid smile pulled at her mouth.

"It's not just me, is it?" she asked.

Blake shook her head. She ran her fingers through the honey tangles of Nora's hair, touched the tiny scar on her forehead from her fall that spring.

"No, Flower Queen. It's not just you."

To hold Nora this way, and to be held, without the accident of alcohol or party music, seemed miraculous to Blake. She might have spent hours gazing down into Nora's flushed face, tracing her cheeks, her lips, the slope of her small chin, had she not detected her fatigue. So, gently, Blake picked her up and carried her to the knoll overlooking the garden. There, they sat together on the sunny grass and shared the sandwiches and cookies that Blake had packed in anticipation of a long day of physical labor on the house.

It was pleasant just to perch side by side, their shoulders touching as Nora told her about her disastrous date. She laughed sadly at the demise of the dress and the sport coat, at her own clumsiness. She also related how she had found Morning Glory when she returned home. It explained, at least in part, the girl's dismal state from earlier that morning. Blake listened, nodding, smiling, wishing to reach for the hand that rested in the space between them. Instead, she folded her arms around her knees, fearful of spoiling whatever magic had just transpired in the garden. *Magic.* She remembered Morning Glory's words now. Reconsidered them.

"What are you planning to do with this place?" Nora asked, peering back at the house.

"Save it," Blake said. "It'll take some time to fix up the house, make it like I want. I got to earn the money first. And it'll be a long time before I have my lobster fishing license."

"So you plan to stay, then?"

Blake caught the caution in her voice and felt uncertain how to interpret it.

"Yes, I plan to stay. This is home."

Home. The word felt foreign on her tongue. As an adult, she had never had a home—had all but given up on the idea. Even during the Sundays she had labored in this yard, she had not quite allowed herself to think of the place that way. Yet Nora's presence beside her, and Quinn's cookies in her lap, and the thought of returning to Leland's boat the following day— all of these things made the word *home* feel true. And when Nora lowered her head against Blake's shoulder, it was all the confirmation of that truth she needed.

The jog had not improved Glory's mood. No amount of pounding pavement succeeded in purging the troubled thoughts that crowded her brain or shaking off the sadness that had coiled around her like a stubborn vine. Upon her return, the discovery that Blake's truck was gone and her mother's room was empty left her further wounded. The prior evening, her mother had shut her out of her most recent personal catastrophe; now she had taken off with the strange, unsmiling woman who inhabited their garage. She was becoming more and more of a mystery to Glory.

And her life had no more room for mystery.

She found the spare key to the garage apartment easily enough. Her mother kept it on the same ring as her car keys, which she never removed from her truck. Mounting the plywood stairs, she did not bother keeping quiet. She wanted the whole garage to feel her agitation, her ownership, so she stomped up heavily and sent the loft door crashing open.

The first thing that struck her about the space was its austerity. Blake had made no effort to personalize it beyond stacking a collection of books on the pool table. No dishes sat in the drying rack. No laundry lay heaped on the floor. In making a preliminary sweep, Glory found that even the bathroom was scrubbed sterile as a hospital water closet. A single towel hung folded crisply from the chrome bar. A tube of mint paste sat upright beside a toothbrush in a small ceramic cup. Store brand shampoo and conditioner sat on the shelf inside the shower. Something about the strict tidiness of it all made Glory uneasy. What middle-aged woman wished to display no artifacts of her past in her living quarters? Did she keep *everything* in drawers? Or was she planning for a hasty exit?

Aware she was about to embark on a major violation of privacy, Glory justified it by telling herself that Blake Renato occupied *her* property. She had a right to investigate who exactly it was who shared their land, their porch—and sometimes, even their dinner table. Surely, she had a right at least to *look*.

Most of the drawers offered no help. Blake's indifference to fashion evinced itself in the scant collection of earth-toned tops and straight-leg jeans, flannel shirts, sports bras, and men's-size shoes. A single tube of lip gloss and a deodorant labeled *Summer Rose* struck Glory as feminine aberrations in a room that just as well could have belonged to a man for all its lack of accessories and décor. Just as she was about to give up and resign herself to the fact that Blake must keep her personal effects elsewhere, she thought to check the kitchen drawers.

Neatly stacked where she had expected to find cutlery, Glory instead uncovered a pile of mail collected from a Raker Harbor P.O. box. Most of it consisted of postcards sent by someone named Dawn—brief missives containing inspirational quotes from various spiritual and literary figures.

It was not the messages that caught Glory's attention, but the name of the addressee. *Blake Alvares.*

Tucked beneath these postcards, she discovered a hefty stack of paperwork. It contained a copy of Blake's application for a lobster fishing apprentice license, as well as her apprentice log sheet. Both documents listed the name *Alvares*. Carefully, Glory thumbed through the rest of the documents and found a county map, an application for a peninsula library card, a pamphlet on PTSD stamped with the Downeast Community Hospital logo. Then came a publication labeled *Massachusetts Department of Correction—Program Description Booklet.* Heart thumping, she flipped through pages describing educational and vocational programming for convicted felons, many of which bore small checkmarks and hand-scrawled notes beside them. By the time Glory reached a printout of a Substance Abuse Program certificate, stamped by an official from MCI-Framingham, her body had gone cold. She stuffed the paperwork back in the drawer, relocked the door, and descended into the safety of sunlight. There, she typed the words *Blake Alvares, Massachusetts* into an internet search on her phone.

The top hits were all social media profiles for young Hispanic men. Not until the bottom of the second search page did she discover the 1999 *Boston Globe* article: *Lowell Woman Sentenced in Slaying of Local Father.*

Her mouth went dry as she clicked on the link and confronted a mug shot of a young, sunken-eyed, dark-haired woman who was unmistakably Blake Renato. She scrolled down, skimming the text of the article.

Last week, a superior court jury found Blake Alvares, 24, of Lowell, guilty of voluntary manslaughter in the death of Angel Salazar. Alvares, who had been recently discharged from the Army, fatally stabbed Salazar

the night of August 2nd, 1998, during an altercation involving his twelve-year-old daughter in Armory Park. Judge David Borne today imposed the maximum sentence on Alvares, citing the defendant's lack of remorse among the reasons for his decision . . .

Glory never read the rest of the article. She copied the link into an email to Gordon, then ran for her car and took off burning rubber up the Post Road.

Allowing Quinn to wash his truck was the only way Leland could find to make up for what had happened at the Big Dipper the prior evening. Together, they listened to the ball game over the radio as they took turns soaping and hosing down the bug-spackled Silverado. While Quinn had not lost her love of blasting him with the sprayer, a heaviness crept between them when he finally switched off the water and handed her a towel. He tried consoling her by insisting that the McDowells were full of shit. But his daughter was too sharp to swallow that line. For the first time he could remember, she looked truly scared.

"I wish Jonny was here," she murmured in response to his feeble reassurances.

That made two of them.

As he groped for the next distraction, Morning Glory's Prius came tearing up the drive. She jumped out, copper ponytail flying, expression a cross between panic and fury.

"You could have told me I had a murderer living in my garage!"

Leland's heart dropped. He hooked the towel around his bare shoulders and braced himself for the whirlwind of her discovery.

"Mornin' Glory—"

"You son of a bitch! How could you keep something like

249

that from me?" Tears spilled unchecked down her face as she paraded through the puddle left by the hose. "Blake *Alvares* is a killer, and this very minute, she's out with my mother, who knows where—"

"Calm down!"

He snatched the phone she was waving at him and glanced at the headline of the article on the screen. He'd already read it, weeks back, after Blake had come clean with him. From the hood of his truck, he felt Quinn's jaw drop as she gripped the bucket of suds. *Great*, he thought. *One more way to brighten her day.*

"How'd you find this?" he asked.

"I looked inside her apartment, found a bunch of stuff from the *prison*." She spit the words through her furious sobs. "Her name isn't even Renato—but of course, *you knew that!*"

"You went through her things?"

"It's my house."

"Jesus." He clicked off the phone, groping for words that might calm her down. "Mornin' Glory, all this happened before you were even *born*. That's a hell of a long time ago."

She brought her hands to her face as though she wished to rip her skin off. "You had no problem hiring a murderer?"

"Stop it!" He seized her shoulders. "I trust her, all right!"

The barked words seemed to rattle Glory out of her hysterics. She stepped away from him and glanced at Quinn, who sat frozen on the truck, eyes wide with horror. Leland realized he would have a lot of explaining to do later with his daughter. For now, he focused on his unraveling friend.

"Listen to me!" His voice turned pleading. "You wanted to know more about Blake? Here it is: She's the best worker I've ever had on the boat. She saved Quinnie's life. And if she hadn't helped your mother that day she fell, who knows what would have happened? Tell me what else you need to know!"

"That man she killed—"

"He was a dealer. A child molester."

"Says who? *Her?* I didn't see anything about that in the article."

"*Ciboire!* Not everything in this world's laid out in print, Mornin' Glory. You ought to know that as well as anyone."

The color drained from her face. She looked back and forth between him and Quinn, swiping at her cheeks. Beyond them, the radio announcer's voice soared with excitement.

This one's way back! Way back! Gone! And the Sox are up four to three in the eighth!

"Mom has no idea who's living in her garage," she rasped. "When she finds out—"

"You really gonna make a woman suffer for a mistake she already spent twenty years answerin' for?"

Glory blinked. "That's a *big* fucking mistake, Lee!"

"Yeah, and to you, we're all big walkin' collections of mistakes."

She stared at him as though he had just sent his knuckles into her ribs. For the first time that summer, he felt like he had said something she actually heard. Maybe, he thought, the reason Glory could not understand how a person like Blake could change was because she had not yet been forced to pivot from some uglier version of herself. She had charted a steady course for her life from which even her father's death failed to derail her. Her own mistakes had been the featherweight kind that peeled off in the wind.

"So it wasn't her friend."

Quinn's quiet voice made both of them glance toward the truck. She had inched forward, her skinny, tanned legs dangling down over the dripping grille.

"Come again?" Leland said.

His daughter tossed out the soapy water and let the bucket clatter to the dirt.

"Blake told me she had a friend in prison. That I didn't want to end up like her friend because they do awful things to you in there."

Leland gaped at her. "When'd she tell you that?"

"A long time ago."

Suddenly, Quinn leapt off the truck. She threw herself at Morning Glory.

"She ain't bad! She looks big and scary, but she wouldn't even smush a caterpillar!"

Morning Glory looked stricken as she folded her arms awkwardly around his sodden little girl. She lifted her eyes to Leland, who wished he had put on a shirt and were not standing before her in sagging, soggy jeans. Jonny's dog tags clinked against his chest as he stepped forward and extricated Quinn from her waist.

"You got to use your heart on this. For godsake, Glory, just listen to your heart for once instead of your head."

Her lips parted, but he left her standing in the puddle by his truck. Had he lingered any longer, he knew he might take his own advice, end up with another bruised cheek.

From the box of childhood junk beneath her bed, Glory retrieved the folding knife her father had bought her for their first father-daughter camping trip. It was one of the cheesy, trading post souvenir ones with an abalone shell inlay, but at six inches, the blade had proven effective enough at most woodland tasks. At the time, she'd enjoyed pretending she was an outlaw toting it around on her hip. Now she touched a finger to its tarnished tip and pressed until she drew a pinpoint of blood. Could it really protect her? she wondered. Was she capable of thrusting it into another living being? That took power, precision, intention. The more she tried to envision it, the more it disturbed her. Only a monster could commit such an act.

She checked her email. No response yet from Gordon. Then it occurred to her that he had said something about a fishing trip up by Grand Lake Stream. Was there even reception up there? Perhaps some trick of the Maine woods would snarl her missive and suspend it forever in the netherworld of cyberspace. Suddenly, she did not know which she was hoping for: a rogue bar of 5G or a major glitch of the Internet?

What else you need to know?

She shrugged off the memory of Leland's hands on her shoulders, his pleading words, as she heard Blake's truck trundle up the drive. Folding the knife into her back jeans pocket, she made herself walk calmly down to the porch.

Not everythin's spelled out in print.

The woman who came up the path so little resembled her mother that Glory did a double-take. Nora's face was pink from sun, her hair windblown, her clothing grass-stained. Her eyes shone, but the biggest transformation of all was her smile. When she called out to Glory, she revealed all her teeth, even the crooked ones of which she felt self-conscious.

"Can you picture a more lovely afternoon, Morning Glory?"

She shook her head mutely, heart racing as Blake came into view. The tall woman, too, was barefooted and carried her mother's sneakers, along with a bouquet of slightly wilted lilies. Glory forced herself to meet the same dark eyes that she had seen only hours before, staring, unrepentant, from a booking photo. They appeared equally unrepentant now, though Blake's face was strikingly softer and bore a touch of the same sun-flush that her mother's did. Glory watched her guide her mother across the last flagstones.

"I thought you were sick," she said.

"Oh, I feel much better now, honey."

Even her mother's voice possessed new lightness. Nora halted at the base of the steps and shaded her eyes to peer up at her. "Something wrong, Morning Glory?"

Glory kept her eyes pinned on Blake and hooked her thumbs in her back jeans pockets. Her tongue turned to cotton.

"Just glad you feel better, Mom."

Her mother touched her shoulder as she climbed the steps. "Join us for dinner, Blake?"

Placing the sneakers and the bouquet upon the bottom step, Blake caught Glory's stare. She took a step backward, jaw hardening. "No, thanks," she said. "You both have a nice night."

That evening, Quinn lay in bed doodling in one of her old school notebooks with the sparkly gel pen she had stolen from Aunt Nicky. The window stood open on the sticky dusk. Across the yard, she could hear her aunt arguing with her latest boyfriend over which pirated movie they would watch on her laptop. After a while, the arguing turned to different sounds, and Quinn put on her headphones, listened to Carrie Underwood sing *somethin' bad about to happen*. She wondered why Carrie sounded so excited about that fact. There was nothing exciting about knowing something bad was headed your way.

Nothing at all.

Lip snagged in her bottom teeth, Quinn drew spiral after spiral, one for every worry cycling her head, until the page filled up and the pen tip snapped off and a flood of glittering purple ink gushed across her notebook. She shoved the mess to the floor and flopped on her back. Even if she managed not to think about the McDowells or what they might do to Papa, every other thought she had was mottled by shadows.

So the Amazon had killed a man—an evil man, according to Papa. Try as she might, Quinn couldn't fit the word *murderer* with the woman who had pulled her from the sea and breathed life back into her lungs. The woman who had dubbed her *amazona pequena*. If someone as smart as Morning Glory believed Blake was a bad person, then maybe the world was all mixed up.

Quinn threw a fist into her pillow, an old and confusing anger boiling up in her belly. She didn't know how to set the world straight. Sometimes, though, she wished like hell she could knock its teeth out.

The following day, Blake worked faster than ever. She had the traps re-baited nearly as quickly as Leland hauled them up onto the rail and made short work of banding the keepers in the sorting box. By midmorning, it had begun to irk him that he was having his ass handed to him once again by a middle-aged woman.

"Slow the hell down, huh?"

"Who pissed in your Cheerios?" she sang back to the tune on the radio, flying a jumbo-size lobster at him like a toy airplane. Her good mood confounded him, given that a storm front was pushing in. They were both getting beaten to hell by cold spray and shifting gear. On top of that, most of his traps had turned up light, like all the lobster had suddenly wised up and beaten feet. He paused finally to study her.

"Sure you ain't drunk? Never known you to show your teeth 'less you're preppin' to bite my head off."

"I haven't had a drink in twenty years." She even half sang these words.

He groaned. "Anyone ever told you, you can't hold a tune to save your life?"

She grinned wider and tossed the lobster overboard. "No singing clubs in prison."

"Well, you're the tone-deaf fuckin' proof!"

He found it hard to share in Blake's playfulness. A dozen more McDowell buoys bobbed along his southernmost string—an open challenge. He left them alone, silently brooding on what he would do when they finally set so close to his traps that the lines got entangled. The fact they had left his own buoys untouched disturbed him more. If they'd chosen not to take revenge here—then, where?

Blake watched him steer clear of the buoys and gave him an approving nod.

"Look at you, Captain, showing restraint!"

She only ever called him *Captain* in sarcasm, but the word bore a different ring that day. He wished he deserved the hint of respect that showed in her eyes before she turned away to start singing again.

That same Monday, the orthopedist removed Nora's cast. The X-ray showed the fracture had healed nicely, so he sent her home with an Ace bandage and a list of exercises she was supposed to work through four times a day until she regained strength in her wrist. It was strange to have use of both hands again. Nora kept glancing at her wrist in disbelief, startled by the sickly pale of the skin that had not seen sun in eight weeks. She wondered if all of her had looked so terribly pale back then and felt as though she had emerged from those two months a different species entirely. A better version of herself somehow.

Not everything about her had improved, though, as the second appointment of that day would confirm. Her MRI scan had, in fact, shown a number of new lesions on her brain. In conjunction with Nora's admission that her fatigue and poor coordination had proven relatively unremitting since her prior appointment, her neurologist projected that she had, indeed, entered the secondary progressive phase of her disease. Morning Glory, who had requested to accompany her to the appointment, sat quietly in the chair, watching as the doctor tested her strength and reflexes, her eyesight and her memory. Nora had difficulty repeating in proper order the list of words he rattled off to her. When it came to reading the lower levels of the eye chart, she failed miserably. At last, with prescriptions for two new medications and a referral to an ophthalmologist in hand, Nora made her escape into the summer afternoon on the arm of her daughter.

"I'm driving home," Glory announced. "Now that I know you're blind as a bat."

"I guess I really am," sighed Nora.

She sank into the sun-warmed passenger's seat, grateful for the opportunity to sit and watch the scenery pass. Gently, she worked her newly liberated wrist back and forth.

"Thank you for coming, Glory. You're much better company than Gordon."

Her daughter's eyes shifted between her phone and the road, the muscles of her face taut. The past few days, she had looked more tired and anxious than ever. Nora had hoped that receiving high MCAT scores would take a weight off her daughter. Instead, it seemed to have added on another.

"Are you worried about your applications?" she ventured. "You look so troubled."

"I'm fine, Mom."

"You can talk to me, you know. I'm capable of listening, at least."

Glory gave a short sigh, finally tucked the phone beneath her thigh. "There's just a lot going on. That's all."

Nora suspected she was part of the "lot," though she prayed daily not to be. Perhaps the new treatment would work, and her body could pause its nonsense. This was how she chose to pitch the outcome of her appointment to Blake later that evening, when she came over to sit on the porch. Her smoky presence helped to dispel some of the gloom of those doctors visits. Gradually, Nora found herself recalling the tingling joy she had felt that Sunday afternoon in Blake's garden. Since then, she had passed two sleepless evenings wondering if all the sunshine and flowers had caused her to hallucinate. Had she really kissed Blake on the mouth, and had Blake really kissed her back? And if so, what did that mean? Did it have to mean anything? The quandary did not so much distress as excite her. It was a welcome distraction indeed from the knowledge that her illness had launched a new offensive— one that would push her ever-closer to immobility.

"MS is bullshit," Blake remarked quietly, picking at a thread on her jeans. "The way you handle it, I think you're very brave."

"I'm not brave at all, Blake. Just about everything scares me."

"Do I scare you?"

Though she asked the question lightly, Nora sensed a deeper current to the inquiry that she could not quite decipher. She drew a careful breath.

"At first you did. A little. Now I think you're one of the best people I know."

Encroaching storms had chased away twilight early. Beyond the solar stakes that lined the front walk, darkness swaddled the porch. Nora could see only the profile of Blake's face, but she detected a strange tension in her body.

She remained silent for so long that Nora began to worry she had somehow offended her. Then Blake's hand landed atop her bare wrist. She encircled it easily with her thumb and forefinger, held it gently.

"Nora . . ." Her voice trailed off into the humid dusk.

Captivated by the tender bracelet of Blake's fingers, Nora never pressed her for the rest of the thought. It had not been just the sunshine and flowers, she knew then. Not the summer heat, either. It was this woman. God worked in mysterious ways—and this was the most mysterious yet.

Abruptly, Blake released her and unfolded herself from the step. "Rain's coming."

She stood still, staring out into the darkness, her long hair blowing loose, hands shoved away into her pockets. "Do you still pray for me, Nora?"

"Always."

"Don't stop, okay?"

A breeze swept the marsh like a wet sigh, carrying with it the heavy salt of the incoming tide. Nora nodded, but Blake had already disappeared down the path.

15.

The Fourth of July delivered a boom of chatty summer people to the restaurant. Nora spent the morning teetering about with coffeepots and dishes of jam, swept up in the festivity despite the fact her left leg was all tingles and stiffness and a migraine had begun to bloom in her temples. That evening, she, Glory, and Blake had plans to join Quinn and Leland on his lobster boat to watch the fireworks up by Jenksport. It was the first year they would not be watching from her husband's boat, and Nora was pleased by Leland's invitation—even more pleased that both Blake and her daughter had accepted it. The restaurant would shut down at three, which meant Nora could hurry home to prepare picnic bags for all of them and surprise Quinn with the Oreo cookie bars she had begged for all spring.

"Good night for fireworks," Bert Adler kept declaring as they bumped into one another behind the counter. "First real clear one we've had in years."

Nora nodded happily. A view of the stars from the water would be one more gift. She was in the process of changing out the coffee filter when her brother's Buick pulled up to the sunny curb. The sight of him shouldering his way through the tangle of waiting parties made her stop short in confusion.

"You not answering your phone anymore?" he demanded, swinging onto the only empty counter stool.

"I thought you were on your fishing trip," she stammered.

"I was. Seems like vacation isn't in the cards for me this year." Though he kept his voice quiet, Nora heard the agitation in it, the building of something unpleasant. "Grab me a black coffee to go, will you?" he said.

She prepared the beverage, burning her fingers in her haste to fill the cup as her mind cycled through possible motives for Gordon's visit. She had hoped to put off discussing her neurology appointment until after the holiday. Surely he hadn't driven back early just to talk about *that*.

When she set the coffee on the counter, he slapped a thick manila envelope beside it.

"I signed everything," she told him, frowning. "The lawyer has the papers . . ."

He flicked up his sunglasses and showed her his bloodshot eyes. The anger in them took her aback.

"This isn't about the goddamned lawyer. This is about the felon you've got living above your garage."

Nora blinked. The brunch crowd around her was too caught up in holiday exuberance to pay them any attention. Still, she felt as though Gordon had just shouted the words.

"Blake's not a felon."

"Oh, no?" Gordon frowned. "Her name's not even Renato. She's been lying about that, like she's probably been lying about a lot of other things." He tapped the envelope. "'Course, you might have known that had you ever bothered asking for her ID. Had you made any attempt to *protect yourself*, Honora."

She stared at the envelope. Her voice, when she found it, squeaked out small and hoarse.

"How do you—"

"Let's just be thankful your daughter did some overdue diligence."

261

Nora's left leg buckled. She caught herself on the counter, shaking her head as though she could prevent these words from lodging in her brain.

"Morning Glory . . . ? No, this is absurd, Gordy. Blake's not . . ."

Her brother pushed the envelope toward her, his face darkening.

"Of course you aren't going to believe *me*. You never do. Ed poisoned you against me a long time ago—even though we both found out how trustworthy *he* was, didn't we?" The words brought a rush of heat to Nora's face. "But it's going to be difficult not to believe the *Boston Globe*. And the *Boston Herald*. And the *Lowell Sun*. Not to mention the criminal background check I got my pal Jerry Spaltz to run. Hell, even he was impressed. You've got a bona fide killer sleeping twenty feet from your—"

"Stop!"

She seized the envelope, hands shaking so badly that she tore off a long strip. Even without her glasses, she had no difficulty recognizing the woman in the prison jumpsuit whose picture stared up at her from the stack of printouts. *Blake Marie Alvares.* Her heart clenched. She shoved the papers back inside the envelope and looked about frantically, as though some face in the room might offer conclusive evidence that this was all just some terrible mistake. But no one paid her any attention. The din of clacking silverware and laughter swelled to a dull, meaningless roar in her ears.

She found less satisfaction than pity in Gordon's face when her wild gaze finally returned to his. He caught her hand across the counter and pinned it beneath his hot palm. "This is the last thing you need, isn't it?" he said quietly. "The very last thing, my poor sister."

All at once, Nora's body went numb. The pain in her head ceased. She was no longer conscious of her troublesome leg.

"I'll take care of it," she whispered.

He gave her hand a pat before sliding his glasses back atop his bulbous nose.

"She gives you any trouble, you call me, understand? I've got some business over to Jenksport." He tossed several wrinkled bills on the counter as he plucked up the to-go cup. "Next time you take a tenant," he muttered, "I vet them first."

Back home, alone in the cool dimness of her kitchen, Nora spread the articles upon the table and forced her throbbing eyes over each line of text. The reading proved more excruciating than any Kit Sheldon novel. Even the headlines brought out gooseflesh on her arms.

Brutal Stabbing Leaves Lowell Father Dead
Female Vet Charged with Murder of Local Man
Girl, 12, to Serve as Key Witness in Sidewalk Slaying

Visceral as Nora's horror was her sense of betrayal. She had opened her whole life to Blake—every painful, humiliating detail—and meanwhile, the woman had kept silent about an atrocity that had shaped over twenty years of her life. It left Nora chilled, violated, empty. But anger swiftly took root in the void. Anger at Blake, for her secrecy and her deception. And even greater anger at herself, for proving the exact kind of fool Gordon and her daughter had always believed her to be.

Poor thing. Yes, she was. A poor, foolish thing.

Nora did not know what to do with her anger. Weeping offered no relief. Nor did hurling her vase of wildflowers against the counter, watching her mother's Irish crystal shatter across the scrubbed linoleum. She found herself staring disconsolately out the back slider. And then, all at once, she was moving outside, stumbling across the sun-washed yard to the vegetable garden they had planted that spring. In swift, vicious strokes, she tore up the peas, the beans, the lettuce, the cucumbers. She uprooted the tomatoes they had tucked in later, sent tender bushes flying and spraying dark earth. She ripped out the corn stalks, the vines of squash and pumpkin that had just begun to flourish. The violence of the effort left her breathless, her hands bloody, her face streaming sweat. She spared no plant, no living vein of green. When she had finished, she collapsed atop the empty earth. She brought her hands to her face and screamed.

After she and Leland made an early landing, Blake raced out to Harlow's Crossing. Some scarlet dahlia had come into bloom, and she wished to collect the prettiest ones, weave them with some daisies into a crown for Nora—a small holiday present to cheer her in the wake of the news from her neurologist. Today, the garden offered her a bounty. She whispered her thanks as she assembled the ring of flowers, then drove back to Raker, smiling too much to finish her cigarette. She tossed it out the open window and high-fived the wind. If she made it home before Morning Glory, she could find some way to surprise Nora, elicit that broad, unabashed smile that lit up the world. She envisioned lowering the crown upon her head as she kissed her. Blake had not been able to stop thinking about kissing her, about all the places she wished to place her mouth—her wrists, her ankles, the hollow of her throat. Nor had she succeeded in stifling the longing for Nora to reach for her again and touch her face in that curious way in which Blake had never been touched, never been wanted. There was no calm in her any longer. All was skips and jumps and frantic beats. And she did not care, could no longer cling to her glum, solitary peace.

The Prius was not in the driveway when Blake came

barreling up, so she leapt from the cab with her crown of blossoms and strode into the house, breathless, giddy.

"Nora? Where are you?"

Her feet crunched against broken glass. Halting sharply, she glanced down and saw the shattered vase, the pool of water in which the stems of wilted flowers floated. Then she noticed the open slider. The breeze that slithered through it had scattered a bunch of papers on the table, sent a few skittering over the floor. Blake stooped to collect one.

Lowell Woman Found Guilty of Manslaughter in Armory Park Slaying

Her breath died in her lungs. She looked about, discovered the other articles, then the printout of her booking photo. That horrid image. The crown of flowers slipped from her hands. She moved to the slider, spotted Nora on her knees in the garden beyond. The *ruined* garden.

"No," she whispered. "No, no, no."

She swallowed the wail building inside her, made it all the way to the entrance of their vegetable plot before Nora registered her footsteps. The face she raised from her hands had become a mask of blood and dirt and tears.

"Is your name Blake Alvares?" Her voice came like the growl of a frightened cat.

"Nor—"

"Answer me!"

Blake's shoulders fell, the demand like a blow to her sternum. In her mind, she watched a steel door slam. "Yes."

At this single, broken syllable, Nora inched backward atop the pile of wilted plants. Blake saw the fear in her eyes, but there was something else there, too. Something raw and wounded that made all the muscles in her abdomen clench at once.

She took a step forward and held out her hands. "Nora, please—"

"Get away from me!"

Nora tried to scramble to her feet, but something appeared to be wrong with her left leg. She could not get it to turn the way she needed it to, and she fell forward on her hands. Blake started toward her, but Nora lashed out and flung a clump of ruined tomatoes at her.

"Get out! I want you out of my garage! If you don't leave, I—I'll call the police."

Blake backed up, cornstalks snapping under her boots.

"At least let me help—"

"I don't want your help! I don't want anything to do with you."

Catching hold of one of the stakes at the corner of the garden plot, Nora used it to brace her weight as she hauled herself to her feet. Then she pulled it right up out of the ground, brandishing it like an awkward spear.

"I won't have a *liar* in my house. I won't have a *killer*. Goddamn you, Blake! Get out!"

The ground might as well have given way beneath Blake. She felt herself free-falling into a pitch-black abyss that must always have been waiting for her. Blindly, she turned and crossed the lawn to the garage. She mounted the steps and pushed into the apartment—four walls, but no refuge any longer. With numb hands, she commenced cramming her belongings into the duffel bags she pulled from beneath the bed, gathered her books, her clothes, her toothbrush, the pile of papers from the kitchen drawer. It took three minutes. She had, in the end, very little. Still dressed in her fishing clothes, she collected the bags and lugged them to the door, then wrenched the key from the ring.

She nearly forgot about the pistol. It had acquired a faint

film of dust inside the sponge box under the sink. She hefted it in her hand, stuck it in one of the duffels, and walked out.

Morning Glory pulled up the drive just as she slung her bags into the cab of the pickup. Warily, the girl climbed from her car while Blake walked toward her with the envelope of money she had pulled from the drawer. She counted out five hundred dollars in cash and extended it.

"Give that to your mother. It's for the rest of the month."

Morning Glory did not meet her eyes.

"You're leaving?"

"Yes. Take care of your mother. She loves you."

Her voice sounded as brittle as the rest of her felt. She climbed inside the truck, backed out along the long driveway lined with smiling daylilies, and sped away down the road with the rearview flipped up and all the sounds of the July evening sealed out.

"Quinnie, tie your shoes before you break your face."

Leland stood at the sink, scrubbing the pile of dishes he had let collect there over the past several days. Behind him, his daughter twirled around the kitchen in the latest ensemble she had rustled up from his sister's wardrobe. In her denim shorts and T-shirt that sparkled with sequin fireworks, hair tied up in an American flag bandanna, she looked like a beauty pageant contestant who had fallen off a hillbilly truck. He could hear the words out of Morning Glory's mouth now, foresaw years of arguments ahead over what qualified as appropriate attire. For now, he let it pass. Quinn was too excited about their evening outing on the boat to be bothered with changing her outfit. It was the first time all week he had seen her smile.

Meanwhile, he struggled to keep his own expectations of the evening in check. He had no idea where he stood with Morning Glory and wavered between a desire to patch up their friendship and a compulsion to press his luck. Quinn was probably right. He needed to find a girlfriend, and fast. Thankfully, the sun had begun to set, which meant they would soon depart for the wharf, and he would not be subjected to yet another round of Katy's Perry's "Firework," complete with Quinn's best imitation of an exploding rocket as she leapt off the sofa.

"Come help dry these," he told her when he caught sight of Blake's truck coming up the drive. "Looks like that kooky Amazon's early."

When she stepped into the kitchen a moment later, however, the expression on Blake's face stopped him in the middle of double-knotting Quinn's sneakers. She was still dressed for baiting traps. His daughter clocked him in the head with a plate as she spun around to greet her, but Blake's eyes, hot and wounded, never deviated from Leland's face.

"Why'd you do it?" she asked, her voice no more than a whisper.

He rose, taking in the long, muscular arms that hung limp at her sides, the broad lips that quivered strangely. For an instant, he had no idea what she was talking about. And then, as he watched her reach into her pocket and produce the printout of a newspaper article, he realized, with a kind of dull horror, what had happened. He shook his head slowly.

"I didn't. I would've taken that to my grave. I hope you know that."

Blake stared at him, weighing the words. She crushed the paper in one fist.

"Nora kicked me out. She doesn't want anything to do with me. She . . ."

Her voice faltered. Before he could think of something to say, Quinn let the plate drop on the counter.

"It was Morning Glory! She told your secret. She found it out on the internet!"

Confusion leeched into Blake's features. She stared at his daughter, brought one hand to her mouth and let it drop again. "*You* know ... about what I did?"

Quinn shrugged. "Big deal. My own grandpa killed someone."

Blake's stricken look made Leland drop his eyes to his feet.

"You're still comin' tonight, ain't ya?" begged his daughter.

"No," Blake whispered. "I'm not coming."

"All because of some stupid secret?" Quinn whipped the dish towel across the kitchen. "People are so fuckin' ridiculous!"

"Quinn!" Leland snapped, but she darted past them, sent the screen door shrieking on its hinges as she bolted into the twilight.

Blake looked as though she was about to collapse. Every vestige of stony composure had deserted her. She locked her hands together and stared at the floor, hair hanging in hopeless wisps from the sloppy braid that drooped across one slumped shoulder.

"Nora will come around," Leland muttered. "Sure she's just in shock."

Blake shook her head. She seemed incapable of speech.

"You can stay here," he offered. "That trailer out there just needs a little cleanin' up."

"I have a place."

"You still gonna stern for me? Christ, Blake, you ain't quittin' over this, are you?"

She lifted her eyes to his face and held them there a long minute. It made him remember the first time she had entered his kitchen, the day she had come to ask for work and caught him on a bender. He had loathed her back then. Now the thought of losing her jabbed him with panicked sorrow. He could not envision fishing without her. She was his luck—the first he'd had in ages.

"No," she said. "I'm not quitting. I'll be there to help you tomorrow."

Before he could acknowledge this, she plodded out through the open door, boots leaving behind two perfect muddy prints on his floor.

When Morning Glory caught sight of her mother standing in the ruined garden, she drew a tight breath and told herself she had braced for this—had been bracing three whole days. The Maine woods had worked no magic. That morning, Gordon had hit reception, and within an hour, he was calling her at the clinic. *Does your mother know? Unbelievable. I'm on my way now . . .*

At first, Glory had felt relieved. No more waiting. Her uncle would handle this problem. But something had clenched inside her when she hung up the phone, and by the time she slipped out of the clinic an hour early, she could scarcely breathe. Now she jogged out to where her mother leaned weeping against one of the garden stakes and enfolded her in her arms, alarmed by the way her body gave like a bundle of brittle twigs.

"It's all right, Mama," she whispered, the taste of this lie so strong, she could scarcely swallow it.

Her mother just sagged against her. In the end, Glory had to half carry her back to the house.

It took little time to confirm what had brought on her breakdown and Blake's speedy exit. The printed Boston news articles lay scattered about the kitchen, the violent disarray itself proof of their impact. After helping her mother into a chair, Glory scrambled to collect the articles and sweep up the shattered glass. Maybe if she could clear the mess fast enough, it would not seem so bad. Yet one glance at her mother slumped at the table, face in her filthy hands, spent from crying, obliterated that hope. Wetting a washcloth, Glory pried away one hand, then the other, and blotted gently at her mother's face in an attempt to sponge away the grief.

"You're all right now, Mama," she murmured, but the words opened a throbbing silence between them.

Her mother's lips trembled. She pulled away, cradling her newly healed wrist. Glory wondered if she had reinjured it doing whatever she had done to the garden. Lacked the nerve to ask.

"She left money for the rent," Glory whispered, placing the bills on the table.

"Keep it." The words came out like the scraping of dead leaves. "Put it toward your books."

Suddenly, Glory realized why the broken look on her mother's face was so familiar; it was the same one that had resided there for months after Benji's death. The same one she had worn that autumn when her husband vanished—a mask that hardened on for the long haul. Glory barely refrained from grabbing her shoulders and attempting to shake it off of her before the sorrow could set like a stain.

"Mama, I didn't know what to do. I was afraid."

Her mother acknowledged her with swollen eyes. "How long did you know?"

"A couple days. I thought Gordon—"

"Yes, Gordon." Her mother's voice came out flat as a horizon. "Gordon was right. You were right. I trusted her, and she lied to me."

She pushed to her feet with a grimace. Glory knew she was about to embark on a long retreat into her bedroom, so she caught one of her hands, felt her fingers cold as marble in her own.

"What can I do? Tell me how to help you, Mama. How to fix it. Please . . ."

Her mother just stepped away. "Forgive me," she whispered. "That's all. Just forgive me for being stupid."

Clutching her wrist once more, she receded into the gloom of the hallway.

Blake made it to the farmhouse without cracking apart, though she sensed the fissures—a thousand of them—snaking their way through her heart. She lit a cigarette and began the process of forcing her mind into a cold, blank space the way she had learned to do many long nights in prison, when she found herself reeling toward the edge of sanity. Parking the truck, she clutched the wheel and counted her breaths. When her thoughts snuck off toward the ruined vegetable garden or Nora's staggering attempt to drag herself from the dirt, she slapped herself so hard that her teeth clicked and her vision jumped.

Fool.

Her hand closed around the cool frame of the pistol she had tucked inside the duffel. She pulled it out and stuck it beneath the seat, did not want it inside the house with her— not until she gained a firmer grip on her thoughts. Bleakly, she shouldered the bags and staggered up the overgrown walk. *Home*, she told herself. *I am home.* But as she pushed inside, she could still smell death in the walls. The flaking plaster looked worse than she remembered, and when she let all the bags drop from her shoulders at once, the echo of their thump reverberated painfully in her chest.

In the gloom, she sank upon the living room cot. Resting her wrists in her lap, she hung her head. A towering wave of sorrow launched itself at her, and she let herself tumble, give way.

She shook with noisy tears, leaving the spiders and beetles and termites that skittered around her to wonder what ailed the strange wretch who had invaded their dark paradise. As she doubled upon the edge of the bed where her grandmother had died, she wept for her and for her grandfather and for the little baby who would have been a man now and old enough to take her in his arms and comfort her. She wept for her father, who had departed the world on a train track without a goodbye. She even wept for her mother, who had been too weak to protect her from Angel, too weak to love her despite her ugliness and her mistakes. Now she knew she truly had become a person unworthy of affection, a person whose past and imperfections were too unforgivable. The knowledge threatened to strangle her, and she dug her fingernails hard into the scar on her wrist, seeking a more bearable pain.

"I thought Amazons didn't cry."

Blake's head snapped up. She saw the girl standing in the shadow of the doorway, her flag bandanna askew in her wild hair, her eyes wide and luminous in her thin face. As she stepped into the room, the boards creaked softly beneath her sneakers, which trailed ragged laces.

"How did you—"

"Your truck bed ain't very comfortable. And you drive worse than Aunt Nicky."

Quinn came to stand before her, her breath sweet with grape candy. Very lightly, she laid her small hands upon Blake's wrists.

"This place another of your secrets, or did you break in?"

"It's mine," Blake whispered. "My grandpa left it to me."

Quinn looked about at the moldy paper peeling from the walls, the dismal shroud of the curtains, the darkening phantoms of the furniture. Blake held her breath as the girl's fingers ran across the scars on her wrists, reading them like Braille.

"I don't care if you killed a guy—especially a *bad* guy. I think that's brave."

More tears dripped from Blake's eyes. "It wasn't. It was terrible. But I can't change it, Quinnie."

"That why you're cryin'?"

"Partly." Blake wiped her cheek on one shoulder.

"It's 'cause of Ms. Nora, ain't it? She hurt your feelin's."

"No, Quinnie. I hurt hers."

Blake reached to fix Quinn's crooked bandanna, unable to shield herself from the girl's earnest gaze. She wished to tell Quinn that she did not belong here in this gloom with a woman who had screwed up her whole life, that she deserved only sunlight and happiness.

"Your papa's gonna be worried. You're supposed to be at the fireworks."

"I don't care about fireworks."

"Sure you do. You even got 'em on your shirt."

A scratching sound on the roof made Quinn start. She grabbed Blake's wrist again.

"That's just a squirrel."

"Or a ghost!"

Blake smiled sadly. "Ghosts are all in here." She touched a finger to the center of Quinn's chest. "That's why they're so hard to get rid of. My advice: Don't make any."

Wiping at her cheeks, she rose from the cot and peered down at the little girl whose skin had already taken on a certain dusty quality from the room. Her breath came more easily now, but the whole cavern of her body echoed with pain.

"I need to take you home. Before your papa shits a brick."

She winced and dug a coin for her pocket, pressed it into

Quinn's waiting hand. "Come on. We'll pick up some food on the way. Your choice."

Leland thrashed along the woodland trail, calling for his daughter. It was fully dark now, and he had to switch on the flashlight of his phone. Quinn had pulled disappearing acts before, but never after sunset. The dark still frightened her, even if little else did. Usually, she picked a hiding spot close to the house, somewhere in Jonny's trailer or inside one of the decaying vehicles collecting mice and rust by Nicky's hovel. He had checked all of these places, though, and now that he had shouted himself hoarse, he was beginning to worry.

When he came out at the creek, he saw the tide was peak, the plain of the marsh flooded with black water.

Dear God, Quinnie. Tell me you didn't.

His daughter had learned to swim several years ago, but the strong currents and frigid waters of eastern Maine rendered swimming skills almost irrelevant if the water caught you by surprise—and if you were as tiny as Quinn. He gave the marshland before him a frantic sweep, the mud sucking loudly at his boots, cordgrass sawing at his shins. In the distance, several firecrackers soared up and fizzled.

He cupped his hands. "Quinn! Quinnie! Are you out here?"

Images of his daughter lying face down in some snag up the creek began to bombard him. He pressed his fingers to his temples and wondered if fatherhood would ever cease to be one heart-stopping terror after another. He was getting nowhere. The grip of the mud proved so strong that he went plunging several times and had to dig his boot out by hand. At last, he found his way back to the woodland trail. He hoped that when he returned to the cabin, he would discover Quinn waiting for him on the porch, pouty but alive. He could deal with pouty all live-long year. All live-long *century*.

A sudden crash ahead brought him to a stand-still. He watched as a large doe lurched into the perimeter of his phone light. At her side staggered a fawn on spindly legs. The drunken way it moved made Leland think it was injured, but the doe kept it close, staring down Leland until her baby had blundered safely out of the circumference of his light. Once the forest had re-engulfed the fawn, she plunged onward through the maze of branches. He stood a moment, listening to her flight, the intensity of her iridescent stare blazed into his retinas.

His phone buzzed. A text message. Blake.

Quinn hitched a ride with me. Sorry. I'm bringing her home.

16.

After Quinn had convinced Blake that the Quik Mart on 189 had the best watermelon slushies, Blake agreed to make a detour there, even though the popular fill-up stood halfway to Swift Harbor. Her phone had died before she got any text response from Papa—a fact that led to the eventual delivery of two more dimes into Quinn's palm. By the time they reached the Quik Mart, Blake had jammed the *useless goddamned piece of fucking plastic* into her jeans pocket and switched on the radio. Apparently, she was not in the mood for talking. Not that Quinn minded. She had just discovered another of Blake's secrets: She owned a bona fide haunted house. She wondered what else the woman might be holding back. It was pretty hard to top the two most recent revelations on the *Jesus-fucking-Christ scale*, as Aunt Nicky called it.

Tonight, the convenience center was lit up like a carnival. The Quik Mart was enjoying its zenith of popularity for the season, thanks to the summer people—and a lot of thirsty folks from Swift Harbor. Quinn marched inside, pausing briefly to admire an impressive display of sparklers and tiki torches before proceeding to the slushie machine at the back wall. She wondered what moron had decided to locate the expansive coolers of beer adjacent to one of the biggest children's attractions in the joint. It meant she had to push her way through a tangle of sweaty and sunburnt bodies to reach the cup dispenser.

Behind her, Blake stood puzzling at the list of flavors.

"Ain't you ever had a slushie before?" Quinn asked.

"No."

Quinn supposed they did not have slush machines in prison. She pulled out a cup for Blake, who picked blue raspberry, then filled her own with watermelon before veering down the crunchy and salty aisle—the one Papa had renamed the Hangover Delights.

"You got to pick actual *food*," Blake grunted.

But at that moment, Tim McDowell rounded the corner with the bearded giant Quinn recognized as his brother. A third and even more frightening specimen of McDowell, short, emaciated, and inked from neck to ankle in blackish tattoos, trailed them, carting a 24-case of PBR. Quinn halted so abruptly that Blake crashed into her, slopping blue raspberry ooze onto her arm.

"Quinnie?"

The hair on her neck stood up when Tim's ice-blue eyes latched upon the two of them. Seizing Blake's hand, Quinn tugged her in the opposite direction, but not before she heard a sneering voice announce, "Look, Doug! It's Savard's entourage: the Mexican dyke and the tiny tramp."

Suddenly, it was Blake who was tugging *her*. They fell into line at the counter, gripping their overfilled cups. Blake kept her hand crushed around Quinn's until she had to let go to retrieve her wallet. Evidently, dinner was going to consist of slushies. At the last minute, Blake reached below the counter and tossed two Kit Kats beside the register. Normally, Quinn would have celebrated this decision, but she could see, out of the corner of her eye, the tattooed demon making kissy faces at her, and she lost her appetite. If Blake saw, she gave no sign of it. She collected her change and the candy bars and nudged Quinn toward the exit. Not until they were safely back inside the truck did Blake ask her about the men.

"The McDowells," Quinn said with a joyless sip of slushie. "They wanna hurt Papa."

Blake glanced at her sharply. "Why do you say that?"

"'Cuz he was an idiot and cut a bunch more of their gear. Like, a *whole* bunch. He used the buoys for target practice."

Blake looked like she wanted to hurl her cup at the windshield. Quinn felt bad for ratting out Papa, but few people scared her like the McDowells did. They idled a moment, punching at sugary ice with their straws. Blake seemed lost in thought as she stared at the steering wheel.

"Why does Papa have to get so angry and do dumb shit?" Quinn murmured.

Blake gave a weary sigh and started up the truck. "He's got ghosts."

The shortcut back toward Raker Harbor consisted of graded dirt and big dips that Blake made no effort to avoid. The two of them bumped around, their slushes sloshing over their hands. Quinn wondered if Blake was trying to cheer her up by simulating a roller coaster ride, or whether her mind was as far from the road as Quinn's was. The route wove across vacant farmland. No one even bothered to plow it in winter, but summer people sometimes took the "scenic cut" toward the beach. In the distance, now and then, Quinn saw fireworks soar and pop like flares. If Morning Glory had just kept her mouth shut, they would all be out on Papa's boat right then, huddled under blankets and watching the sky explode with color. Afterward, Papa would have let her hit the horn as many times as she liked, joining all the other boats in a honking chorus of applause. And Blake and Ms. Nora would have been happy like they had been the night of Glory's party, when Quinn peeked in the side door and spotted the two of them dancing. She wondered how a gentle, kind person like Ms. Nora could get so upset at Blake. Maybe she had ghosts, too. Maybe all grown-ups did—even the ones who went to church and did not cuss.

When the headlights first bounced into view in the side mirror, Quinn did not think much of them. She had managed to polish off most of her slushie and was busy stabbing at the last hard nuggets of ice at the bottom of the cup when she realized the lights had grown suddenly much closer. She glanced at Blake, who had wedged her cup in her lap in order to place both hands on the steering wheel. Her dark eyes flickered to the rearview, where the headlights soon pulled so close that they disappeared behind Blake's tailgate.

Through the open windows, Quinn could hear the challenging rev of the monster engine behind them. She grasped the seat with slick hands.

"Blake?"

"Hold on."

Blake stepped down on the accelerator and sent them rocketing forward over the pitted road. Quinn's teeth rattled in her skull. Her earlier, rocky experience as a stowaway in the bed paled in comparison to this shuddering journey. Blake pushed the speedometer to 70—an unthinkable speed on such a rough, winding road. They hurtled over a dip and came down with a crash that sent the rearview clattering down from the ceiling. It hit Quinn's knee.

They managed to pull a short distance ahead before the pursuing truck, a mammoth Ram quad cab with an elevated chassis, roared up beside them. Quinn caught a glimpse of one bearded profile before a glass bottle came hurdling through the window.

It struck Blake in the temple hard enough to knock her

head sideways. She managed to catch the brake, but the brief, involuntary jerk of her arm against the wheel sent their truck careening off into the drainage ditch. Quinn's scream never made it out of her throat. When the pickup finally rocked still in a thicket of alders, she found Blake's arm flung out across her chest like a kind of guardrail. Quinn grasped hold of it and let out a sob when she saw the bloody gash just above Blake's left eye, the broken bottle in her lap. Blake touched a finger to the blood. She squeezed her eye shut as she twisted toward Quinn.

"You okay?"

Quinn shook so hard, she could barely nod. "You're hurt."

"It's not so bad."

But at that moment, taillights flickered up on the road. The Ram was backing up along the shoulder, flattening wildflowers beneath its big wheels.

"Fuck!"

Blake dragged the truck into reverse, but the tires spun in the mire of the ditch, refusing to catch hold of anything that might propel them. Frantic, she tried shifting into drive, but they lacked the clearance to avoid a pair of spruce that loomed before them like twin sentries. Half blinded by the blood of her wound, she pulled her deck knife from its sheath on her hip. She punched Quinn's seatbelt loose and thrust the knife into her hand.

"Run!" she commanded. "Straight into those woods. Don't stop, understand me? No matter what, just keep running!"

"But—"

"Go!"

Quinn had never heard Blake's voice so fierce. She tugged the door handle and tumbled out into the thicket. The vegetation rose up dense beyond the ditch, and she scrambled through it, stifling cries as thorny twigs sliced into her bare skin and yanked at her fallen hair. She ran. Her heart became a thunderbird, hoisting its beating wings higher and higher until it seemed ready to lift right out of her chest and into the black trees above.

After a full minute of sprinting, she paused, winded, beside a giant oak. She threw her arms around it as though it were capable of embracing her back. Pressed against the tree, Blake's knife clutched in her fist, Quinn heard several shouts, the slam of a car door. She dropped her forehead to the rough bark and tried to pray the way Nora once taught her.

God, if you exist, protect the Amazon. Help her like she helped me. Please, please, please . . .

She shook so hard, she could barely feel her feet, but suddenly, they were carrying her back toward the pickup. Whispered words would not help Blake. If Amazons could cry, then they could be hurt by McDowells—even if they knew how to kill.

Moving at a crouch through the undergrowth of ferns and decayed leaves, Quinn took care where she placed her feet to avoid sudden snaps. The sound of male laughter carried through the trees and guided her back toward the thicket of alders. Through it, the grim glow of Blake's taillights illuminated her profile, which was backed against the rear bumper. Quinn's heart jumped when she saw that Blake held a revolver in a two-handed grip before her. Incredibly, this seemed only to encourage the three McDowell men. They continued their slow advance like a trio of scraggly-bearded wolves.

"Drop it," Tim growled at Blake, staring straight down the barrel of her gun.

Blake stood still, hands wrapped tight around the ivory grip.

"Step back."

Tim cocked his hairy head at her and jabbed his brother in the ribs. "The spic's givin' orders, Doug. You gonna take 'em?"

"Nope."

Quinn pressed her hands to her mouth. They tasted like the mossy bark of the oak. *Kill them, Blake. Kill them. They're going to hurt you.*

Tim advanced another step as his two brothers fanned to either side. In a moment, they would have her surrounded. It would be too late, even if Blake was an incredibly quick shot.

"Please, step back," she repeated, blinking the blood from her eye. "Please."

Quinn did not recognize Blake's voice. It splintered with desperation.

"Hear that, Doug? She said *please.*"

The big one named Doug snickered. The tattooed one just pitched his cigarette in the weeds. Then, as one, they surged forward. In disbelief, Quinn watched Blake let the gun fall from her hands. She did not see where it landed, for in that instant, the McDowells threw Blake so hard against the tailgate that Quinn thought she heard her spine break.

"Let's see if you got more balls than your captain, huh? My money's on you!"

On her knees in the brush, Quinn crushed her hands to her ears and squeezed her streaming eyes shut. *God, where are you? God!*

Something landed in the dirt so close that Quinn might have reached out and touched it. Through one slatted eyed, she made out the heap of Blake's jeans. A surge of watermelon sweetness pushed up her throat. She tucked her chin to her chest to try and hold it in. Male voices filtered in through her plugged ears. Then the repeated *whap* of a belt's strike.

She waited for Blake to cry out, to scream, but in the pulsing stretch of time that Quinn spent folded in the brush, the Amazon made no sound at all.

Beneath her shuttered lids, sparks flared and popped. She grew aware of the puke that had dribbled down her shirtfront, of her own, muffled breathing. Then Tim McDowell's words lifted from the din funneling through her palms.

"Give our regards to your captain, señora."

An engine thundered to life, followed by the growl of tires as they grabbed at the gravel and raced away into the night. Quinn remained on her knees, too frightened to open her eyes. But the blind silence proved more terrifying. She groped for the knife that had fallen in the leaves, then crawled, quaking, out of the brush. It took a moment for her eyes to adjust and find Blake.

She lay on her side several feet from the tailgate, bloody face pressed into the dirt, legs drawn up against her belly. Her hair had been sawed off above her shoulders. Her clothes were gone. Sniffling, Quinn touched her fingertips to the cool skin of her shoulder. At Blake's single, muffled sob, she began to cry harder, from both relief and fury.

"Blake!" She peeled a clump of black hair from her face. "Amazon. Get up. Please, get up."

But Blake just lay there with her eyes screwed shut, her hands balled in useless fists.

Each distant pop of fireworks made Quinn's heart lurch in fear that the McDowells were returning to finish off the job. She did not know what to do and worried that Blake might die there, naked in the dirt, before any kind of help showed up. And all of this was her fault. If she had not made Blake drive her to the Quik Mart, the McDowells would not have come after Papa's sternwoman.

She sank her teeth into her arm to stifle a scream. What

kind of revenge was this? How did a bunch of cut gear justify this cruelty? Why hadn't Blake cried for help?

Quinn feared she knew the answer to the last question. The knowledge turned her cold with shame. Blake had not screamed because she did not want Quinn to hear and come running back. For the second time that summer, Blake Alvares had tried to save her life.

Whimpering still, Quinn felt around in the weeds until she located Blake's clothes. The jeans were salvageable, but her T-shirt was torn right down the middle. Quinn had no idea where they had thrown her bra or her boots. As she searched, her knee mashed on something soft: Blake's hair, still bound in its braid. She stuck it in her pocket, then scrambled back to the Amazon.

"Blake? Can you hear me?"

Blake twisted her head up, lips peeling back over her bloody teeth. Her hand floated to Quinn's cheek.

"Sorry . . ." she whispered. "I'm sorry, Quinnie . . ."

Sorry for what? Quinn wondered. She pulled the bandanna from her hair and attempted to wipe some of the dirt and blood from Blake's face. *I'm the one who's sorry.*

With great effort, Blake pushed herself to a sitting position. She folded her arms over her chest in a weak attempt to conceal what Quinn had already seen—a sprinkling of round scars like the ones on Papa's back, and a series of mean welts that had begun to rise along her ribs.

"Here," Quinn said, holding open the jeans. "I'll help."

Blake blinked hard. She let Quinn help her work each leg into the pant holes and shimmy them up over her hips. Then, with evident agony, she pulled on the vestige of the ruined T-shirt like a vest. It gaped open on her chest, but it was better than nothing.

"I can't find your boots," sniffled Quinn. "Or your phone."

"Forget them . . ."

Resting a minute, Blake dragged air into her lungs in pant-like breaths. Blood continued to leak from the wound above her eye. She used the bandanna to try and stanch it. Then she reached for Quinn's hand. Between the two of them, they summoned enough strength to restore her to her feet.

Now, a scream of pain escaped Blake. She staggered so badly that Quinn feared she would topple right back into the dirt, so she pressed her body against her hip and let Blake use her as a kind of crutch. At the truck, Blake paused and braced herself against the tailgate, doubled at the waist. Quinn thought she was going to be sick. It took her a moment to realize that Blake was peering at the tires, attempting to discern a way out of the mire.

"I need you . . . to do something," she wheezed at Quinn through the dirty, chopped strands of her hair. "Get behind the . . . wheel and . . . put it in neutral . . . N."

Quinn knew what neutral was. She had some practice helping Papa free his own mud-logged truck from their yard. She did not know how, exactly, Blake was going to manage pushing a truck when she could barely walk, but she did not ask questions. Alive with adrenaline, she climbed behind the wheel and dragged the shifter into neutral. She could scarcely see above the dashboard as Blake maneuvered through the alders. When she reached the front of the pickup, she rested a moment before throwing her weight against the grill. All of her teeth were bared, and in the headlights' ghastly glare, Quinn saw the raw determination in her battered face. She rested and pushed, rested and pushed, until finally, Quinn felt the truck roll free of the rut.

When Blake dragged herself back into the driver's seat, she spent several moments with an arm thrown across the wheel, her forehead dropped to the leather as she tried to recover her breath. One hand clutched at her ribs. Quinn watched her with a mixture of awe and agony. It took all her courage not to cry again.

"I wish you'd killed them," she whispered.

Blake turned her head where it lay braced against the wheel. She met Quinn's devastated stare and held it. Quinn sensed that Blake was trying to tell her something with that look, though she did not fully understand what it was. Maybe it had to do with the past she had never talked about. Or maybe it was something simpler, about pain or fear or even love. For Quinn knew then that she loved Blake in a way she might have loved her mother if she were able to remember her—a fierce, steady, unflinching way that made her wish she had been bigger and braver and able to protect her.

"All right," Blake whispered finally, dropping her hand to the gearshift. "Let's go."

At the sound of Blake's truck, Leland tripped out into the yard, prepared to ground Quinn for eternity. But then she catapulted from the passenger's side and sprinted toward him, plastered in blood and dirt and pink stickiness. He tried to encircle her in his arms, but she dodged the effort. With wild eyes, she pulled him toward the truck, shivering and crying and shouting all at once.

"Help her, Papa! Help her!"

His alarmed brain scrambled in confusion. Then the driver's door cracked open and his sternwoman stumbled from the cab. He stared, speechless, at her battered, muddy face, the hair shorn off raggedly above her shoulders, the bloody rag of a T-shirt she held closed across her chest. As she took a step forward, her legs buckled. Leland just managed to catch her. Lifting her great weight into his arms, he carried her inside the cabin and laid her out on his bed. Her arm dropped, and the shirt fell open. A gruesome collage of swelling welts stood out beneath the shock of her scarred breasts. He drew up the sheet with a muffled sound of horror and tucked it about her shoulders.

"Who did this?" he asked, dropping a hand to her forehead.

She looked up at him through the glistening slats of her eyes and said nothing.

Quinn stood on the opposite side of the bed. Her filthy face still streamed tears. Leland's gaze swept over her clothing. Appalling thoughts flashed through his head before she lifted her eyes and read the trembling question in his features.

"They didn't hurt me, Papa. She saved me."

"Who's *they?*"

His daughter looked at Blake, who lay drawing labored breaths beneath the sheet.

"Quinnie."

But he knew already. His daughter's strange silence only confirmed it. He dragged his hands through his hair, grabbed the box of tissues from the dresser, and sank onto the edge of the mattress to blot gently at Blake's face. She had closed her eyes, against the pain or further questions, or maybe both.

"You need a doctor."

"No." She flinched as he examined the wound at her temple. "No doctor . . . just rest . . . and ice."

He strode to the kitchen, thankful for the mission, the excuse to look away from her. He dug through the freezer, dragging out every bag of frozen vegetables he could find. The intermittent crackle of fireworks from across the marsh ripped through his thoughts. He paused to glare toward their oblivious glitter, new pain burrowing into a part of him he had just managed to shore up. The impulse to drink, to mute the scream of anger and guilt and futility that pounded against his skull, grew almost unbearable. He wet a cloth with soap and water and carried the stack of makeshift icepacks back to the bedroom. There, in the soft glow of the nightstand lamp, he found Quinn seated on the bed beside Blake, tenderly working pine needles and other debris from her hair. He fetched the first aid kit, then pulled up a chair and lifted uncertain eyes toward his daughter.

"Start with her face," she whispered.

So he did.

In the course of her short life, four years of which she had spent motherless, Quinn had witnessed her father undertake a range of activities that men were not typically called upon to perform. He had attended elementary school picnics, helped her construct class valentines, taught her how to string beads and paint pictures, let her paint his nails. He had bandaged her cuts, sung her lullabies, and coached her on the electric slide. He was far from perfect. Yet as she watched him tend to Blake, Quinn thought Papa danced as close to that word as he had ever come.

His gestures carried a gentleness so far removed from the brutality of the McDowells that it did not seem possible Papa belonged to the same species of man. Patiently, he worked the layers of gore and grime from Blake's face, dabbing antiseptic on her wounds and murmuring apologies each time she winced or sucked in her breath. He held up her head so that she could swallow ibuprofen tablets with the glass of water Quinn carried in from the kitchen. He snipped off the bloody remains of her ruined T-shirt, peeled the sheet a discreet distance down her chest, and wiped away the spattered blood and dirt. Then he tugged the sheet free from the bottom of the bed and bathed each of her cut-up feet and ankles, taking care to extract the thorns and splinters. Leaving her jeans in place, he rolled the sheet carefully upward over her abdomen and blotted where he could, halting when she twisted away from the pain. Only once did she cry out, and that was when he tried to maneuver a bag of frozen broccoli beneath her back. After that, he set to work tending the scrapes on her arms.

Blake kept her eyes closed throughout this process. Sometimes, Quinn could not tell whether she had drifted into sleep or was simply trying to retreat from the pain. Only when her dark brows suddenly knit together did Quinn realize she was fully conscious. She worked her comb delicately through what remained of Blake's hair, trying to make it as pretty as possible. Eventually, she remembered the braid in her pocket and laid it on the pillow beside Blake. When Papa saw this, his eyes went glassy. He dipped his head toward Blake's hand, which he was in the process of bandaging. Afterward, he held it in his lap, and Quinn saw that Blake's fingers had curled around his.

None of them spoke. Only when Blake's breathing finally settled into a deeper, slower pattern did Papa signal Quinn to his lap. She crawled into it gratefully and let him cradle her to his chest, the way he did when she was very little. Her nerves still felt electric, though. Each time she closed her eyes, she saw Blake pinned to that tailgate and heard her swallowed sob as she'd lain in the dirt. Papa felt her muscles tensing every few minutes. He dropped his mouth to her ear.

"Tell me what happened, Quinnie. You don't have to tell me who. I know who. I just need to know how."

So, in whispers, Quinn told him what she could, which was really just a fraction of what had probably happened, what she might have seen had she found the courage to open her eyes and look. She told him about the truck that came out of nowhere, about the flung bottle and Blake ordering her to run, and then a little bit about what she had seen the men do. She did not mention the part about finding Blake curled naked in the dirt. Her mouth refused to form the words. But Papa seemed to get the idea without her saying anything, because, when she'd finished, he asked, in a strange, hoarse voice, "They do anythin' else . . . 'sides hit her?"

Quinn burrowed her fingers into his shirtfront and began to cry again, very quietly, a slow seep of grief at her own cowardice, her inability to repay Blake's kindness. Papa's arms closed around her so tight that it seemed he intended never to let go.

"Oh, Quinnie," he whispered.

And he rocked her until she fell asleep.

Blake lay adrift on an ocean of pain. Sometimes, it tugged her under completely, only to spit her out, gasping for breath, for life itself. Her physical agony was the deep red kind, so mixed up with other hurts that she ceased trying to decipher which was which. In her fitful half-dreams, she saw the men, faceless, bearded assailants laughing at her body, striking it, shoving it. Mostly, though, she saw Quinn hovering over her with those streaming green eyes that would never unsee. The thought of how close the girl had come to those evil hands made her shudder. It was only partial consolation to her that Quinn had evaded them—for now, the girl knew. She had looked into the black mouth of men's violent delights and would not forget.

Because no girl ever did.

In other dreams, she knelt with Nora in the garden, tasted her shy smile, caressed her sun-warmed skin. She woke just after midnight with a longing so fierce, it threatened to rip her battered body apart. Then she remembered that Nora had evicted her, in every way a person could be evicted, and a whole new assault of pain bombarded her. In that moment of brief, excruciating wakefulness, Blake knew she could not stay in Raker Harbor—not now that all the ugliness of her past had found her here and begun to repeat itself. She could not shed her darkness on Quinn any more than she already had. Nor could she ever live on the edge of the same tidal marsh that drained out past the Hayes home, past the woman she had hurt, the woman who had cast her out.

Goddamn you, Blake.

No need. She had been damned long ago.

And even as she thought this, she felt Quinn's sleeping breath against her shoulder, her bird's wing of a hand resting atop her chest. Blake held the small palm briefly against her heart, hoping it might absorb all that she wished to tell the girl and convey it to her in the sweetness of some dream. When she managed to peel open her good eye, she saw the young lobsterman asleep in the chair by her bed. His face, aged so far beyond its years, appeared softer, almost boyish in sleep.

If I had a son, she thought. *If my son had lived . . .*

She closed her eyes on these thoughts. Let them flicker out.

Leland woke to Blake's form towering over him, a pillow gripped to her chest. In the first gray light that cut through the blinds, her battered, bandaged face was nearly unrecognizable.

"Need to borrow one of your shirts," she said, her voice a croak.

He rose and saw Quinn curled asleep on the bed beside the dark braid. Blake waited, regarding him steadily out of the one eye that was not swollen halfway shut. Her chopped hair stuck out at strange angles. Beneath the bruises, her face held no color at all.

"Why?" he asked. "You're goin'? Where?"

"Away. I'm sorry. I can't stay here."

The words stuck him like knives. But he did not like the

idea of carrying on an argument with a half-naked woman, so he dug one of his flannel shirts from the drawer and handed it to her. Without comment, she turned from him and set the pillow on the bed. His mouth fell open at the sight of her back. It was plastered in black and blue from the shoulder blades to the base of her spine. Just above the band of her jeans, at the tapered small of her back, ran a scripted tattoo. *R.J.A. Amor eterno.* She tugged the flannel quickly across this tapestry of ink and bruises.

"Goddamn it, Blake." His voice broke. "You're beat to hell."

"I'll be all right."

"Will you?"

She kept her back to him as she worked the buttons.

"This has to end," she said. "This shit with the McDowells. It has to end for Quinn's sake."

"I'm supposed to forget about this? How can I forget about this? *Tell me how.*"

Blake turned and gestured at Quinn's small form in the sheets. "*That's* how. It ends with me. Swear it, Leland. Swear to me on your daughter's life that the bullshit ends. That's the only way—the only way I can stand this."

He met the pleading eyes that stared out from her ruined face. Tears beaded on her lashes. He forced himself to nod.

"What do I tell her? Won't you wait until she wakes up?"

"No."

She collected her keys from the nightstand where he had set them, every movement stiff with agony. Then she walked barefoot out of the room without looking again at his daughter or the braid of hair she had left behind on the pillow. Leland followed her out. He scraped for something to say but found himself as ill equipped to change her mind as he had been the day she first entered his kitchen and announced herself his new sternman. Outside, fog smothered the clearing. He saw that Nicky had made her way home sometime in the night and wondered what species of jailbait was currently sharing her bed.

Blake crossed the yard in slow, wooden strides, one hand clasped to her back.

"Can't I give you anythin'?" he blurted out as she climbed into her truck. "For fuck's sake, Blake, can't I do that?"

She found her pack of Merits and worked loose a cigarette. She held it toward him through the open window.

"A light," she muttered. "You can give me a light."

He dug the lighter from his pocket and touched the flame to her cigarette. Then she twisted the key in the ignition and trundled away through the fog, like something he had imagined a long time ago that was finally proving itself another of his hopeless fantasies.

17.

The next morning, Glory called in sick to the clinic. She tackled the laundry and cleaned the whole house, attempting to scrub out any vestige of Blake Alvares that might touch off another ripple of grief in her mother. True to prediction, she had failed to emerge from her bedroom. As Glory brooded over coffee, she wondered about the wilted crown of flowers on the table. Finally, she tossed it in the trash atop the news articles and hauled the bag out to the barrel beside the garage.

A wraithlike fog lurked over the marsh beyond. She paused to listen to the squawk of invisible birds, watched her mother's wind spinners turn sadly in the slight breeze. The flag she had hung from her father's boat hung slack in the damp. Glory struggled to believe just two weeks had passed since she sat on the gunwale with Leland and Blake, listening to Quinn perform her song. Just two weeks since the yard had been filled with music and happiness and she had caught her mother dancing barefoot with Blake Alvares.

With heavy feet, she climbed up to the garage apartment, hoping to find relief in the emptiness there. Instead, the space stared back at her in silent accusation, so immaculate it appeared as though no one had ever lived there. Feebly, Glory told herself that she had not betrayed Blake's secret; it was Gordon who'd completed the puzzle and took action. But she knew, ultimately, that the blame rested on her—that she had acted on fear, and maybe even on something worse. Was it Blake, the murderer, who had driven her to it? Or Blake, the woman, who had stepped into the void her father left in her mother's life and somehow filled it, at least in part?

Glory slumped into the oak rocker and pulled her hands to her face. Part of her had believed, until this morning, that she had acted in protection of her mother. That she had done right. Now, however, a different part acknowledged that she had been trying to protect herself from a thing she did not understand: the connection between her mother and a woman she had never even tried to get to know.

Recognition of her selfishness hit her like a cold wind. She recalled the Hippocratic oath. *Do no harm.* One day, she would need to pledge these words. And yet she had done harm here. Great harm. She knew it as she rose to walk the vacant apartment and discovered the single book Blake had left behind on the pool table: *All the Light We Cannot See.* A message? A gift?

Picking it up, she flipped through the pages, half expecting some cryptic message to fall out. Instead, a half-dozen dried, pressed flowers fluttered down to the felt. She ran her fingers over the fragile petals and watched them crumble. Clippings from her mother's garden, she guessed. She understood then that the only thoughts Blake had harbored toward her mother had been tender ones.

Glory left the flowers on the table and headed for Wind Cove. She needed to talk to her father and halt this violent unraveling that had begun inside her.

The fog on the point proved so dense that she could not make out any of the gated entrances to the summer homes. The weather would anchor the vacationers inside in front of their flat-screens and tablets, keep the speedboats docked and the kayaks grounded. In fog, in all foul summer weather, really, the peninsula once again belonged to those who had been born there. But the turnaround at the breakwater was not empty. Leland's truck sat alone, the bed filled with the usual assortment of junk he hauled around all fishing season. Glory parked beside it and took her time picking her way across the chain of boulders, her visibility limited to just a few feet in front of her. Off in the bay, the bell buoy clanged fiercely. The tide was up, lashing the rocks with angry spray. As she inched farther toward the white-capped cauldron, part of her could not help believing that the ocean's foul mood had something to do with her.

The end of the breakwater emerged suddenly, and with it, Leland. When she dropped down beside him, he made no sound, barely looked at her as he sat finishing his cigarette. In one hand, he held his brother's dog tags. He closed them in his fist when she joined him.

"I know you're angry," she began. "I'm sorry."

"No, you're not. She left. You got what you wanted." His voice was empty, cold. He flicked away his cigarette. "Never deserved her as a sternwoman anyway."

"What?"

"She *left*, Morning Glory. Not just to that run-down old farm she inherited. She's *gone.*"

He turned his head toward her, his hair wet with fog that had beaded along the shaggy curls of it. The look in his red-rimmed eyes cut her to the quick.

"Don't worry," he growled. "It's only part your fault. Other part's all mine."

"How—"

"Just shut up! Please. Stop talkin' to me. I don't want to talk. I want to burn the world down. And I promised her I wouldn't."

He opened his palm and ran his thumb across the stamped lettering of the dog tags. Then abruptly, he pitched them hard into the fog. Glory never heard them hit the water. The din of the surf was too loud. But their disappearance sent a chill through her. One more thing lost to the sea. She stared into the gloom as the wet breath of the morning collected on her face, newly chastened by the awareness that the thing she had done had cost Leland his sternwoman—and whatever else Blake Alvares had been to him.

"Sometimes I wonder if you got any heart left," he said.

She dropped her chin to her knees. "I came here to talk to Dad. Not you."

"That who you take advice from? A ghost?" He snorted. "Seems to me he fucked up pretty big, too, screwin' my sister behind your sick mother's back."

He shot to his feet, face twisted with anger.

"My daughter walked in on that, Mornin' Glory. Go on and talk to him about that!"

Nonplussed, she held her hands up as though to stop him. "I—I know what he did, Lee. Okay? I didn't know about Quinnie, but I knew . . . I can't help it. I miss him. I still miss . . ."

Leland's shoulders sagged. He shook his head. "Yeah, I know," he muttered. "I know all about missin.'"

He spun around then and started back down the line of boulders. In a moment, the fog had engulfed him, and she was alone, surrounded by the gnawing surf and the bell buoy that tolled the cold end of her peace.

By the sixth day, Nora made herself get dressed. She knew it was a Sunday, and while she possessed no desire to see or speak to anyone besides God, she dragged on a clean skirt and blouse and forced her leaden limbs through a neglected routine of self-care. Lack of food rendered her woozy. Gingerly, she felt her way down the hall and discovered her daughter seated in the kitchen wearing a solemn black dress with white petal buttons. It was a relic from high school, one which Glory had objected bitterly to wearing the day Nora finished stitching the hem. It still fit perfectly. Upon the table lay a spread of fruit and granola, a new vase filled with freshly cut geraniums. As Nora sat and unfolded her napkin across her lap, she did not inquire about the inspiration for this occasion. She recognized atonement when she saw it.

"All right if I join you today?" Morning Glory asked.

Nora just reached for her hand atop the table. They ate in silence.

Since they arrived at church late, Nora was spared the ordeal of having to greet Clyde or make small talk with the usual cluster of women with whom she helped to host church socials. The annual St. Cat's Summer Bean Supper was approaching, but Nora could no more imagine dishing out plates of food and rounding up small children for field games than she could running the Boston Marathon. She was grateful for the back pew, the smell of beach roses drifting through the propped door, her daughter's freshly scrubbed presence beside her. She let Morning Glory speak the words from the prayer book and remained seated during the hymns, waiting for the familiar tunes to wrap around her like a blanket. She wished to be pulled back into the safety of all these rituals and be healed of the wound Blake had torn inside her. How was it, she asked God, that she had come to care for two murderers in one lifetime? What did it say about her that she was drawn to people with violent hearts?

And yet she had felt so sure Blake's heart was gentle. From the first time she had lain her cheek against it, she had believed in its goodness. She had witnessed Blake's capacity for kindness. So how was it possible that she had taken a man's life in front of his own daughter? Plunged a knife into him not one but *three* times and left him to bleed out on a city sidewalk? Even if she thought she had been acting in defense of a child, as the newspapers alleged, whatever dark thing inside Blake that had possessed her to commit such an act would not have just turned to dust. The hands in which Blake had cradled her face—those *same hands*—had gutted a man.

"Mom?" Glory's anxious whisper reached her ear.

"Get me out of here," Nora pleaded.

They managed to draw only a few glances as they made a hasty exit mid-hymn. Once the cool breeze hit her, Nora revived. Arm in arm, she and her daughter walked out to the sea wall, where they stopped to gaze upon the restless waves. Nora thought of her husband but found, in that moment, that she could summon no clear picture of his face. By now, he would be only bones, and she was startled by her calm acceptance of this fact, the strange relief she felt that whatever remained of him would elude her recognition. It suggested that, despite her initial belief to the contrary, she had survived the loss of him. Perhaps, then, she could survive Blake's betrayal, which felt, at present, like a fatal wound.

On the drive home, Nora directed Glory to take a right toward Harlow's Crossing. She wished to look upon that old farm with fresh perspective, commence tearing away the illusion of the prior Sunday. If she found Blake there, she would at least apologize for swearing at her and state her disappointment more civilly. But also, now that she had recomposed herself, she wished to determine how her body would respond to Blake's presence, see if her prayer to be free of that involuntary magnetism had been answered.

"She's not here, Mom."

Morning Glory's voice came quietly across the ripple of

wind through the window. "Lee told me the other day that she quit him. She left."

Nora allowed this information to settle. "Left for where?"

"I don't know."

It could not be true. Blake had spoken with such passion about fixing up the property. Why had she gone to such lengths to cultivate that elaborate garden only to abandon it? More doubt pushed into Nora's heart. Maybe it all had been another deception. Maybe Blake had not owned the property at all. If she had kept them in the dark about two decades of her life, certainly she was capable of concocting a fable like the one she had told that day at the farm.

Before Nora could ask to abort their mission, they were pulling up the slope to the Teale property. Leland Savard's pickup sat out front—a sight so unexpected, she tried to blink it away. Then Quinn came bounding around the porch. From the way her face fell, Nora intuited that she had been hoping for a different visitor.

"What're *you* doing here?" the girl demanded, scowling as Morning Glory stepped from the truck.

Nora's daughter appeared chastened. "Mom wanted to come see."

"See *what*?" Oily tears streaked the girl's cheeks. "Blake ain't ever comin' back. They beat her up so bad, she left."

Nora, who had been struggling to navigate a patch of weeds with her pole, drew up sharply. "Who beat her up?" she cried, one beat behind her daughter.

Quinn slatted her eyes, as though she could not believe their ignorance.

"Bad men. They cut her hair and ripped her clothes off and left her in a ditch."

Nora felt herself sink to the grass, all earlier strength deserting her. "They . . . what?"

Quinn's small mouth trembled. "She could've killed them. She could've! And she didn't do it. She let them . . ."

Leland emerged from the door of the house then. Several days' worth of stubble darkened his face, which bore a vaguely haunted expression. When he saw Nora in the grass, he started forward, but Morning Glory sprang to intercept him, crouching by Nora with a sharp hiss of breath.

"It was the McDowells, wasn't it?" She hurled the words at Leland. "They went after your sternwoman because you're such a provocative, fucking idiot!"

"*You're* the one who told on Blake!" shouted Quinn, narrow shoulders tensing with rage. "And Ms. Nora kicked her out! You made her cry! You made the Amazon *cry!*"

Nora grasped her stomach, which threatened to revolt on her. "Oh, Quinnie. I didn't . . . I never meant . . ."

"Enough." Leland pulled his daughter against him. "I don't think she'd want us doin' this, barkin' at one another. It won't change nothin'."

"So, why are *you* here?" demanded Morning Glory.

"I asked him to take me." Empty of rancor, Quinn's voice sounded wrenchingly sad. "This was her place, and I like it here."

Nora gazed at her in quiet grief. "She took you here, too, Quinnie?"

The girl gave a sheepish shrug. "I hitched a ride once."

They regarded one another in silence. Insects droned menacingly from the high weeds. Suddenly, Nora grew conscious of the silvered structure looming before them, as though it had been listening to their squabble and now regarded them all with its dark windows like so many condemning eyes.

"I've never been in there," she said. "Just the garden."

A big brown grasshopper sprang from the step when Leland shifted his feet.

"She left the door wide open," he frowned. "There's some stuff upstairs. Maybe you should come look, Nora."

Nora knew she had no choice now, that she would have to face whatever new and terrible revelations this house might contain. Stiffly, she found her feet once more, and the four of them moved together, unspeaking, up the broken steps. Morning Glory looped her arm through Nora's, and Quinn slid her hand into her father's, as though even she experienced some trepidation of what awaited them inside.

Once through the crooked mouth of the doorway, Nora's first impression was of looking at an old movie set someone had forgotten to strike. At some point—likely many years before, given the layers of dust and insect nests and water damage—life had simply come to a halt here, and no one had made any particular effort to clear the evidence or salvage the artifacts of value. Blake seemed to have left it all undisturbed. Something about that touched Nora with new pain. It struck her that the woman had been trying to preserve something that was beyond preserving—but why?

Quinn's fingers left thin trails in the dust as she dragged them lightly across the furniture. Had Nora not been making so much effort to avoid tripping over her own feet, she, too, might have felt compelled to touch the walls, the mantle, the old stove. Perhaps they would speak to her, tell her things that Blake never had. It occurred to her how little, in fact, she knew of the woman's life beyond what the news clippings told her.

But as it turned out, she did not have to try and interpret the past from these disparate objects. When Leland led them upstairs to a small bedroom overlooking the back garden, so many details came colliding together at once that Nora found herself speechless. She saw the bed first, with its faded coverlet of pink and green stripes and its yellowed, lace-trimmed pillows. A matted bear with a rainbow stitched upon its belly sat propped between them. Beside the bed stood a crib, a quilt of sea stars folded over one rail, its mattress stripped bare. And on the wall above it hung a hand-stitched sign in a wooden frame: *Renato J. Alvares.*

The springs squeaked as Nora sat down hard on the bed. A small cloud of pollen and dust rose around her. Leland stood watching her from the doorway, his face drawn in the filtered light of the single window. Quinn tugged free of his grasp and joined Nora on the bed. She scooped up the bear and sat it gently in her lap, stroking its tattered ears. Meanwhile, Morning Glory's eyes remained fixed on the sign.

"Renato," she murmured. "So who was *Renato?*"

"Look in there." Leland gestured with a finger toward the rickety nightstand whose drawer lay partially ajar.

Hesitantly, Nora reached inside and lifted out a stack of photographs. They stuck together from the moisture that had seeped into everything in the house, but she saw at once that they contained images of a tiny swaddled baby with a shock of dark hair and two apple-red cheeks. The writing on the back was indisputably Blake's tight, neat hand: *My Love, 12.28.92.* If there were any doubt whose baby it was, the fifth photograph in the stack put it to rest. A teenage Blake smiled from the image, her face, rounder, softer, and dominated by a pair of sparkling dark eyes. She stood cradling the infant between a solemn old woman in a church dress. The caption on the back read: *Ren's first Christmas, '92.* She had drawn tiny hearts above the *i*'s.

"Oh, Blake," Nora whispered, touching her finger to the words.

Quinn and Morning Glory peered over her shoulder at the images, several more of which depicted a strikingly young

Blake sitting with her baby, who grew progressively fuller in the face and brighter in the eyes as the deck progressed. The caption on the last image read: *Three months! 3.21.93*, and showed Blake bundled for winter, her baby dressed in a wooly snowsuit whose hood featured puppy dog ears.

"So, what happened?" Morning Glory asked, her voice hushed.

Nora worried that she knew. There was something elegiac in the way the room had been left, with stacks of cloth diapers and infant clothes still folded inside the drawers of the scarred bureau, a package of unopened pacifiers stuck in the back of the nightstand drawer. Carefully, she replaced the photos, then made herself follow Leland down the hall.

A larger bedroom stood there, evidently the one that had belonged to Jesse and Edna Teale. A leak in the roof had worked patiently on the drywall of the ceiling until a whole chunk had given way, exposing dusty rafters and a brown ring of rot. The collapse had taken out the boxy television set, which lay smashed on the floor beside a dirty snow of plaster. But on the dresser sat several framed photographs of the Teales, including one of a thinner, unsmiling Blake in military fatigues, *Pvt. B. Alvares* stamped in black stitching across her breast pocket. Nora picked it up and noticed the change in her eyes, the shield that had come down over them. It was the same shield she had worn the day she had shown up to rent the garage apartment. Nora never registered when exactly it had lifted, knew only that the eyes she had looked into the prior Sunday in the garden had been different from these—more like those of the girl in the photographs from the other room. Eyes that let her in.

"I don't understand," she murmured. "Blake said her mother ran away from this place before she was born. What was she doing here? Why didn't I ever hear about a Blake Alvares?"

"Maybe these people were protectin' her from somethin'." Leland's words came muffled through the hand he dragged over his face. "She had all these . . . scars."

"What kind of scars?"

It was Quinn whose whisper floated from the doorway, where she stood hugging the matted bear to her chest. "Like Papa's. Only—worse."

Nora stared at the girl, whose forlorn face she wished to cup in her hands in assurance that this was all just some fiction they were attempting to stitch together. But Leland's daughter was beyond such comfort, already too exposed to the horrors of the world to believe in soft words. It broke Nora to think of the things this child had witnessed, just as it broke her to consider all the wounds Blake had carried in silence.

She replaced the photograph on the dresser, stroked the tarnished frame with her thumb. She wondered if the others could hear the sob trapped in her throat, grief for the olive-skinned teenager who had taken refuge here with her baby, then lost herself somewhere in the world beyond. In the end, she and Blake were not as different as she had always believed. They both had been mothers, and they had both buried a child. Had that pain been the invisible thread that bound them all along?

"Why keep so many secrets?" Glory asked, pale-faced, as they drove home. "She could have told us *something*."

Nora dropped her head in her hands. "I sent her away. I told her to leave, and those horrible men . . ."

The thought was unbearable. Blake had asked Nora to keep praying for her. And Nora had all but told her to go to hell. What kind of person had she become? While her discoveries that afternoon did not mute the horror of Blake's crime, they had extinguished the possibility of reducing her to a deceptive criminal. Without such reduction, her absence became a gulf posed to swallow Nora.

In the days that followed, she scrambled for a way to reach her former tenant. The number she dialed was out of service. Her emails went unanswered. She could only hope that Blake's ownership of the property at Harlow's Crossing would necessitate her return. But as weeks passed and the garden out back all but dried up, Nora's hope dried up with it.

Blake had taken Nora's cold instruction. She was really *gone*.

18.

Ellsworth stood at the gateway to Mount Desert Island, a tourist haven staffed by transients where a person could pose as nobody—at least, until the leaves turned. A full hour south of Raker Harbor, it happened to be the place where Blake's battered truck ran out of gas. She took a room in a rickety dive occupied by Slavic seasonal workers and spent the first week half-conscious on a stained mattress, riding out unremitting waves of physical and emotional pain that sometimes left her moaning, and always a bit emptier, a distance further removed from the woman she had been just one week earlier, hauling traps on Leland's boat and dreaming up surprises for Nora. The McDowells had stolen her gun. Her phone was lost somewhere to the dark brush of that country road, and her new room boasted no landline, no TV. Thus, cut off from the world, Blake's universe shrank once more to four walls and a locked door, and she made no effort to resist its shrinking. Surrendered to her new prison.

Something in her spine had popped when the men had thrown her against the truck. The pain kept her awake long nights, though the rest of her body gradually ceased to scream. By day nine, she could walk without groaning, so she scrubbed off the remaining filth of the ditch and cleaned up her hair the best she could, which meant cutting it nearly to chin length. Then she struggled into clean clothes, lit a cigarette, and wandered out to find food that did not derive from a foil package.

At the Walmart, she purchased a burner phone along with a new sports bra and work boots. She got a good look at herself under the fluorescent lights in the pharmacy section and realized she did not stand a chance of snagging a job while looking like Hillary Swank in *Million Dollar Baby* (a favorite film among the inmates in her block at Framingham). With certain resignation, she tromped down the cosmetics aisle in vain search of a foundation tailored to her skin tone. Even this simple task triggered sharp memories of Quinn's obsession with makeup and Nora's perfectly drawn features, and she wound up snatching at random packages, eager to flee.

An urgent billboard at the McDonald's advertised the need for help. Recalling that Dawn had said something about the fast-food chain hiring felons, Blake picked up an application with her value meal and hunched in a booth to fill it out. After pushing through these initial tasks, however, her brief spurt of momentum died out. The pain came boomeranging back. She picked up a liter of Tito's and fell so hard off the wagon that her head hurt for three days. The lack of relief the alcohol delivered left her baffled and desperate. She considered investigating who among the other occupants in her building might possess access to a more powerful antidote but stopped herself just short of venturing human contact. Instead, she drove east. *Water always finds a way back to the sea.* She knew of nowhere else to go.

She wound up in Acadia National Park. There, she spent hours wandering on narrow roads that wound around bald granite peaks overlooking the North Atlantic. The sweeping, salty beauty of the place helped tamp down some of her despair. For a while, she tried to play along with the tourists, stopping to read the signs about wildlife and park history and fill her head with something more than memory. It was difficult, however, to tune out the whirl of families around her, the couples posing for pictures, the children scrambling blithely over rocks. To avoid drowning in her own solitude among the hordes.

Late in the afternoon, she coaxed the pickup to the top of Cadillac Mountain. Perched alone on a great, granite boulder, she peered north across the ragged line of coast toward Raker Harbor. Her grandparents had taken her up here once, the October before her son was born. When they had parked at the peak, life began to kick so impatiently at her ribs that she had pulled the old woman's hand to her belly and asked, *Is it time?* Her grandmother's gentle smile a memory that floated back to Blake as she soaked in the open air, oblivious to the hikers who picked their way between the surrounding peaks. One group of teenagers made the mistake of approaching her to take their picture; a number of them struggled to muster natural-looking smiles when she grudgingly removed her cap and they got a full look at her face. Even as the bruises receded and the gash above her eye began to heal, she knew she frightened people. Her face, never beautiful, had at last become a reflection of what resided inside her. Let children stare, let adults make pitying assumptions. What did it matter?

She carried Dawn's number on a card in her wallet and came close to dialing it. Slapped the phone shut each time. Ashamed, she could imagine the conversation well enough—just another loop of the one they had shared all those years ago in the hospital.

I want to die. You want to help so much, Doc, tell me how to do it.

What's hurting you, baby? This is just hurt, you know. It's hurt that's messing with you bad. You've got to name it first. It's always got a name.

I'm the name. The hurt is me.

The hurt is never you. Hurt is the thing that tries to become you.

It's too late. I let it in. I wanted to kill those men, and I couldn't. I let them hurt me. I wanted to be hurt. I wanted to die.

Bullshit. You wanted to live. And you knew what would have happened if you had pulled that trigger. Everything about you would have died.

Blake dropped her head in her arms and listened to the wind whistle across the high rocks. A late fog swallowed her view of the cruise ship in Frenchman's Bay. Now the mist came curling up through the conifer-spiked gorge between Cadillac and Dorr Mountain, its spectral advance unchecked by the great granite shoulders carved by glaciers millennia before. If she found any comfort, then, it was in the knowledge of her insignificance within this landscape, the renewed recognition of nature's mighty, indifferent forces that could grind anyone to dust and scatter the infinitesimal specks to the edges of the world. Maybe that was when pain truly ceased to exist—when one's particles were reabsorbed into the collective mass of all things anchored to planet Earth. Now maybe she had simply to surrender herself to the ocean beyond this fog, just as the old man had done. Let it crush out this hurt and reclaim her as it did all its broken waves. Then she could become part of that heaving blue that reached all the way to Leland and Quinn and Nora. She could be close to them again, in a way that would not wound them.

I don't want your help. I don't want anything to do with you.

The echo of Nora's words splintered through her. She hugged her knees to her chest and gulped back a wail.

The hurt is losing her, she told Dawn. *That is the hurt. The hurt is losing my friend.*

Well, shit, Alvares. I think we're finally getting somewhere.

Quinn gave August's arrival the cold shoulder. On the north side of Papa's trap shed, she had chalked out a crude, human profile she envisioned to be Tim McDowell, or Douglas, or the other tattooed monster. Plastic quiver slung over her shoulder, face smeared with muddy war paint, she devoted hours each afternoon to sending missile after missile into the wall, not satisfied until she landed at least a dozen arrows in the silhouette's imaginary heart. Sometimes, she felt Papa watching her from the stoop of the cabin, where he would come out to smoke and fidget with his traps. She tuned out the world around her, wielding that bow as she imagined a real Amazon might, channeling all her energy into acquiring lethal precision. Perhaps, if she focused hard enough, the McDowells themselves would feel the impact of those arrows and seize their chests, go tumbling to the ground like cartoon villains. Could hope work like that?

Aunt Nicky must have complained about the racket—that, or Papa started to worry she was getting too good—for, by week's end, he announced that he had signed her up for the free Math Booster program at the regional school.

"Rather have you improvin' your brain than takin' down my shed," he said. "You wanna go to college someday, you got to get all the school you can."

Quinn was stunned by this decision. Since when had Papa decided she was going to college?

"I wanna be a fisherman!" she screamed at him. "And I hate fuckin' math!"

But no matter how much she raged or how many pencils she snapped in protest, he stayed firm.

"You ain't gettin' stuck here. You're gonna have choices, you hear me, Quinnie?"

She might have suspected Morning Glory were behind

this shift in Papa except for the fact the two were not quite on speaking terms. Neither Ms. Nora nor her daughter had come to visit since the day they met at the farmhouse. Only through rumors she'd overheard at the restaurant had Quinn learned that Ms. Nora was having another of her bad spells. Papa avoided talking about it the same way he avoided talking about Blake. So, finally, Quinn quit talking to *him* altogether. On the morning he packed her off to math camp, she refused even to look at him. Only a deranged human being signed his daughter up for number torture after she had lost her best friend.

Yet Papa had lost something, too. The new heaviness of his shoulders and the shadows under his eyes were impossible to ignore. Both of them were grieving, but their sadness and anger kept colliding like conflicting currents, carving out a strange space between them. Quinn didn't know how to fix it, and in place of knowing, she clung to her rage.

And it clung back.

On the first day of summer school, as she sat, stewing, among the rows of other unfortunate, underperforming students who'd shown up on the promise of free breakfast and lunch, in shuffled a tardy Eric McDowell. A crop of greasy blond hair concealed most of his anemic face, and he wore the same ill-fitting cargo pants he'd sported throughout most of the third grade. Quinn recognized the tar stains along the left pantleg. At the sight of him, she contemplated sprinting right out of the room and hitchhiking the eight miles back to Raker. But the impulse faded when she watched him slouch into a seat several rows away. There, he remained awkwardly hunched throughout the morning, sucking on hard candies and picking nervously at his calluses. Every time fat-armed Ms. Lowery called on him to answer a question, he practically jumped out of his skin. As she observed him twitch and dodge the eyes of his curious classmates, Quinn's revulsion simmered into malicious intrigue. She labored through three-columned subtraction problems, all the while contemplating the ways she might avenge Blake.

Midmorning recess finally arrived. Summoning all her Amazonian courage, Quinn waited for Eric just outside the door to the basketball courts. As he emerged, alone, she stepped into his path and made her voice low and vicious.

"Your dad's a sack of shit. He oughta be in jail."

Eric jerked his head to clear the hair from his face. Mottled vestiges of an old bruise decorated his right eye. "So should yours," he muttered, breath heavy with the sickly cinnamon of an Atomic FireBall.

"My papa don't beat women."

Something flickered in the boy's flat, sullen face. "Lucky you don't have no *mama* to beat."

Quinn glimpsed a fresh gap in his side teeth—a hole wide enough to stick two fingers through. She bristled as he shuffled around her, crunching over the shoelaces she had neglected to tie. Mortified by the tears that prickled in her eyes, she retreated to the far side of the playground, too heartsick to join the other girls chattering about TikTok videos on the swings. Their heroes were glittering pop stars and sassy socialites. Hers was a chain-smoking felon who had given back her breath, stared down three evil men, and pushed her own truck out of a ditch after she had been beaten up. Amid this playground of children, Quinn felt old.

And utterly alone.

Her big friend was gone. Blake had departed without a goodbye, and all Quinn had left of her was a dusty stuffed bear and a braid of dark hair she kept stashed in her nightstand—a braid she took out from time to time and pressed to her cheek in hopes some trace of Blake's smoky smell might return to her.

Amazona pequena. She whispered the words, eyes narrowing as they fastened once more upon Eric McDowell.

He was kicking around among a trio of boulders that stood at the perimeter of the ball field—ancient, craggy relics from a quarry that had abutted the campus. Slowly, Quinn lifted her arms and stretched the string of an invisible bow. She imagined the bite of rawhide against her index finger, the wink of the arrow's steel tip as it caught the sunlight through the tree limbs. Teeth clenched, she calculated the distance between herself and that shaggy figure wandering among the rocks. Then she exhaled and let her missile fly.

Her enemy struck the ground before the largest boulder. Blinking hard, Quinn dropped her arms and swiped the film of sweat from her eyes. Her heart thumped. Had it really happened? Had one of her imaginary arrows finally hit its mark?

She rose warily. Eric lay on the ground, clawing at his throat with one hand as the other beat his chest. He must have seen her take aim. Now he was playing along, mocking her.

She would show him how she played!

For Blake! she thought as she swooped across the field, wild, Amazon hair rippling behind her on the breeze. *Give my regards to your father!* she would cry, once her fists had left their bloody message on his face.

Yet within a few yards of the boulders, she stopped short. Eric's face had turned the color of an overripe tomato. He made a strange flailing gesture with both arms as he flopped among the pebbles and pine needles. Quinn's startled eyes swept his body for an arrow. Finding none, she realized suddenly what was happening.

The FireBall! The Atomic FireBall was beating her to revenge!

"Hey!" she shouted, springing across the rocks. "Hey!"

Neither of the teachers at the playground were paying any attention, consumed with trying to referee a pickup basketball game that had grown rowdy. Quinn uncurled her fingers and hauled Eric up by the back of his shirt, began pounding on his back. She did not realize she was screaming until shapes began moving toward them from across the playing field— Mrs. Lowery with her big bosom bouncing and her lanyard swinging; Mr. Paul in his wilted tie and foggy glasses. But they were too far away, moving in slow motion. And because all the pounding seemed to do no good, Quinn pivoted and slugged Eric as hard as she could in the stomach.

He lurched forward. The villain candy flew from his mouth with a sickening *pop*. It landed like a pink musket ball in the dirt, followed by a surge of cinnamon-tinged puke.

"What's wrong with you!" Quinn shrieked as he crumpled beside her, wheezing, alive.

She continued to bring her fists down on his back until Mr. Paul finally hauled her away and deposited her among a cluster of sweaty, staring math flunkees. There, she waited, dazed and trembling, as Mrs. Lowery bent over Eric.

"You beat the puke out of him!" someone whispered.

"No, she saved him," hissed somebody else.

Eric's streaming eyes met hers through a clump of fallen bangs. The raw terror in them brought a sob jerking from her throat. Hands crushed to her ears, she kicked away across the field, the imaginary bow tumbling, abandoned, in her wake.

After a week of staring at her half-packed suitcase, Morning Glory finally emptied it out and stuffed it back beneath the bed. Earlier, she had drafted an email to the dean, requesting a second leave of absence. She had stopped just short of sending it. Her paralysis shamed her. She had not hesitated to press send when it came to sharing the news article about Blake.

Now she struggled to summon the courage to do what was *right*—or, at least, what she believed was right.

The prior evening, when she'd reluctantly floated to Alan the idea of once again postponing school, his disapproval rang sharply across the line. "By postpone, you really mean *scrap*. Your mom isn't going to get *better*, MG."

The truth of that sat like a cold stone in her heart. But what kind of person left her own parent behind to self-destruct? Maybe the same kind who had managed to sabotage her mother's first chance at happiness in years. Silently, Glory resolved not to abandon the frail wisp of a woman who continued to drag herself to work each morning at the restaurant and, afterward, drive out to Harlow's Crossing to try and resuscitate the garden that Blake had abandoned. Perhaps her mother would stabilize, and then Glory could go back to school. Or transfer. There were plenty of Maine schools. Surely one of them would have her. After that—well, she could no longer afford to think so far ahead. Like her mother, she would have to learn to take the future day by day.

Nora moved as though she were pinned together with titanium screws. Even her smallest clothes had begun to bag on her. And yet she could not be persuaded to give up on Blake's garden. She returned home each evening with her hands stained with dirt, her hair full of pollen and leaves, too exhausted to eat. Glory knew it was useless to try and convince her to save her strength; she understood that, for her mother, tending the garden had become a sacred duty. Glory wondered if she herself possessed the capacity for such devotion. If it could be inherited, like a gene.

Gordon had taken to visiting weekly, laying out his own plans for the weeks and months ahead. They would sell the boat, he had decided. The garage apartment would be rented to a *qualified* tenant. And if Nora was to remain in her home, then she must consent to the installation of a ramp at the entry and to wearing a Life Alert button whenever she was alone.

"Fine, Gordy," her mother would say vacantly, as though he were discussing the management of someone else's life and not her own. "Whatever you think is best." And then, to Glory, with little more expression, "You see? You don't need to worry. Your uncle's worked it out. You should go right back to school."

But as Glory watched him depart one evening, the wheels of his Buick grinding over a bed of lilies at the end of the drive, she felt a cord inside her draw so tight that, were it plucked, it might snap with a shrieking note. In need of a purpose, she walked out and collected several days' worth of mail from the rusted box.

At the top of the pile sat an envelope that caused her heart to skip a beat. It was addressed in a tight, mechanical hand she recognized as Blake's, and it bore her mother's name, though no return address. She sprinted back to the house in her clumsy flip-flops.

When Glory handed her the letter, Nora looked afraid to open it. She lowered herself upon the faded couch and stared down at the envelope, tracing the postmark with a thin, soil-stained finger. Finally, she handed it back to Glory.

"Read it to me, please. My eyes . . ."

Her mother looked away at the ruffled curtains, which billowed out in the cool breeze pushing through the screen. Carefully, Glory broke the seal. Out slid a card whose cover bore a watercolor image of a single sunflower.

"*Dear Nora,*" she began, voice quiet with trepidation. "*I hope you can forgive me. I came north this spring to make a new life. You gave me the glimpse of one with your flowers and your kindness. I never got to thank you for that. I'm sorry.*"

Nora closed her eyes with a soft sound. Glory dropped beside her and grasped her hand before continuing.

"I never meant to cause you pain. I wanted anything but that. Be careful on your steps. Let people help you, and let them love you, too. You deserve that.

Sincerely,

Blake."

For a long time, her mother said nothing. She sank against the pilled cushions, shivering slightly, as the last afternoon sunlight slid down her lap and puddled on the floor. Glory reached for the afghan and tucked it around her.

"She's not coming back," Nora whispered. It was all she said.

Glory inspected the envelope once more. It bore an Ellsworth postmark. A cluster of remote communities down by Mount Desert Island had their mail funneled through Ellsworth. Blake easily could have dropped the card in the post there and moved on. Yet, as of two days earlier, she had been in Maine. Perhaps she was there still.

"I'll find her, Mama."

Nora looked at her. She shook her head slowly. "She's gone, Morning Glory."

"Maybe not."

A current of pain passed through her mother's features. At last, she said, "I found the grave. The baby's grave. There's an old apple tree out behind the garden at that farm. And there's a slate—this tiny slate with his initials. I found it several weeks ago . . ."

Glory thought of her own brother's grave with its little collection of Legos brought by her mother. A hard place to visit, even all these years later.

"Oh, Mama."

Nora lifted a hand to tuck a curl of Glory's unruly hair

behind her ear the way she'd often done when Glory was a child. Back then, the gesture had inspired Glory's fierce annoyance, a boiling impatience to break free. Now it filled her with sudden, wild love.

She knew what she had to do—a thing that would mean more than any words. Folding the letter gently in her mother's lap, she walked out into the fresh twilight to dial Leland.

"You butt-dial me?" came the grunted greeting when he picked up on the fifth ring.

"I need your help."

"Why not ask your dead dad?"

She bit her lip, realizing they would get nowhere over the phone. Her best chance at having a true conversation with her old friend was to catch him in his natural habitat.

"Do you think I could join you on the boat tomorrow? Sternman-for-a-day kind of thing?"

Such a long silence ensued that she wondered if they had lost their connection. At last, she heard a pan clatter, a cabinet slam.

"Five sharp," he muttered. "I ain't waitin' on you."

"Fair enough," she replied, and hung up.

In the blue pre-dawn, Morning Glory could pass as any other fisherman waiting on the wharf. Hunched on an overturned lobster crate and cradling a steaming thermos, she was dressed in the rubber overalls she used to wear while tending traps on her father's stern, bright hair tucked under a ball cap, feet sheathed in trawler boots. It had been a year since Leland had seen her geared up for a day on the boat. The image triggered memories of childhood summers spent on rivaling decks, of early morning ribbings and late afternoons sharing Cokes up at Moody's store, dreaming up adventures. He brushed those memories away and steeled himself for business, though he'd slept little the night before, uncertain how to interpret her phone call.

"Forgot your gloves," he observed, voice too rough, too obvious.

She gazed up at him, eyes catching the glow of the pier's single floodlight. "I thought you might have an extra pair."

Leland grabbed hold of her hand and ran his fingers over her smooth skin. "Better hope I do, Mornin' Glory."

They spoke little as they loaded his skiff and motored out to the mooring. Since Blake left, he had reacclimated himself to silence. Fortunately, Glory recalled enough from her sterning days to require minimal instruction. She prepared his deck while he switched on his electronics and brought the big diesel engine to rumbling life. Not until they were motoring out to his first sets did she approach the cockpit. She stood there sipping fragrant tea and watching the horizon.

"You still drop over by Sully's Island?"

"Few pair." He ignored her wrinkled nose as he lit a cigarette. "Ain't you s'posed to be back at school soon?"

"In two weeks. *If* I go back."

He shot her a glance, but she stared straight ahead through the salt-streaked windshield. "How's Quinnie?"

Leland shrugged. He had not planned on opening up to her, but her remark about school startled him out of his stoicism. Gradually, he explained the incident between Quinn and the McDowell boy earlier that week, still shocked and puzzled by the claim made by several teachers that his daughter had somehow saved the boy from choking. Quinn herself had flatly denied it. "Just a lucky punch," she had croaked. But Leland sensed she was holding back, the same way she had done the night Blake was attacked.

Glory listened in silence. Leland doubted he could make her understand how sick he felt about Quinn, how badly he wished to reach inside his daughter's troubled memory and scrub it clean as a plate of glass.

"I've ruined her," he confessed, knuckles white where he gripped the wheel. "Christ, Mornin' Glory, she's only nine, and I—"

"No, Lee. Don't you see? Quinnie did a good thing. She's a good kid, still—and she's *yours*."

She reached for the cigarette he held clamped in his teeth and stubbed in out on her boot. He did not bother resisting, too surprised by the earnest way her eyes searched his face.

"If there were any way to make things right with Blake, you'd do it, wouldn't you?" she said. "You wouldn't hesitate."

"There's no makin' it right. There's just fuckin' livin' with it."

Her head dipped. "I only see the worst in people. You were right."

"Well, hell just froze over, I guess." He reached inside the forward cuddy for a wad of paper towel, but she just took it and balled it in her hands.

They worked in silence through his first set of traps. Glory lacked Blake's strength and deft speed, but gradually, Leland accustomed himself to a new rhythm. Watching her, he found something almost mournful in the way she changed out the bait bags and discarded the critters who had caught a free ride in his traps. To Morning Glory, he realized, fishing had become an act of remembering—one inextricably woven with pain. The last of his bitterness softened then, and sloughed off him like an old, filthy skin. He was glad to be rid of it.

"I think I know where she is."

Glory's announcement made Leland pause at the winch. "What?"

"She sent Mom a letter. It had an Ellsworth postmark. I need your help to find her."

He frowned. "No return address? That means she don't wanna be found, Mornin' Glory."

"Or maybe she didn't think anyone would *want* to find her."

As he turned fully toward her, he made no effort to conceal the conflict in his eyes. He could no more help what he felt for Morning Glory than he could help his need to forge out onto this ocean morning after morning and wrangle a living from the murky deep. But Blake had taught him something, after all, about restraint.

"You got to do this yourself," he said. "I can't help you. Not with this one. I think it's on you. Okay?"

She looked back toward the shaggy coastline. Wind sent bright tendrils of her hair sailing loose from her cap. Her jaw twitched, but she nodded once. After a moment, she pulled away and turned to extract the final lobster from his trap.

"Three keepers," she called out.

"Copy that," he said.

The stretch of Route 1 from Machias to Ellsworth meandered past coastal villages and fallow farmland that unspooled a requiem to rural America. The route boasted plenty of million-dollar views but also an abundance of decaying trailers and abandoned roadside businesses. Morning Glory seldom drove this road. When she wished to seek a slice of the civilization that television and pop culture insisted she should want (namely chain restaurants, big box stores, and Cineplexes), she cut across to Route 9 and over to the interstate, where twenty more minutes of stomping on the gas delivered her to the glorified former lumber town that northern Maine passed off as a big city. While she preferred the scenery of old Route 1 to the endless tunnel of trees and asphalt she had traveled back and forth four times a year since she had entered college, in summer, she lost patience with tourists in big cars who slowed down to snap pictures or contemplate random turnoffs. On this particular trip, over-caffeinated and under-confident about the search she was about to undertake, every red wink of taillights left her cursing under her breath.

Looking for Blake Alvares in the sprawling coastal vicinity of Ellsworth was probably a fool's errand, but Glory knew she had more than earned the frustration. She started by scoping out the by-the-week motels that littered the town's perimeter. She lacked a clue where a recuperating felon might seek employment—somewhere off the books, she assumed—so she explored the smattering of small businesses and restaurants strung along the town's feeder roads of 1A and 180 and 184, then resorted to crawling down the choked and perpetually under construction Route 3, which trickled out toward Mount Desert Island. It was possible Blake had taken seasonal employment in Bar Harbor, but the sheer number of campy shops, B&Bs, and dining establishments that clogged the famous tourist destination so overwhelmed her that she swung a U-turn at the campus of the College of the Atlantic before she reached the snarl of downtown. She had a hunch Blake would find the crowds equally repulsive.

By noon, she had grown weary of pulling into random campgrounds and scanning parking lots for the battered beige pickup with a triangle dent in its hood. No one she consulted claimed to have any knowledge of a woman of Blake's description. She was wasting her time. Parked at a tourist trap that sold lobster buoy birdhouses alongside Native American lawn totems, Glory debated aborting her mission. Then her eye caught upon a display of hand-wrought wind spinners turning in the side lot of the souvenir shop. Thoughts of her mother's loyal toiling in Blake's garden and her discovery of the child's grave washed Glory clean of self-pity. Armed with a fried haddock sandwich and an iced tea she purchased from the adjacent roadside shack, she pressed on.

A salesclerk at the Walmart thought he remembered a woman like Blake making a purchase at his register. "Bad bruises?" he asked, touching the side of his face.

Glory nodded grimly.

"That was weeks ago," he said. "Haven't seen her since."

Another two hours of searching, and her renewed optimism fizzled. Exasperated by a clog of traffic created by a highway construction project, she veered onto a gravel road dressed up as a detour, and she wound up flying past the ill-marked turn, rattling down the snake of a fire route that devolved abruptly into rutted dirt. Her GPS indicated that this nothing-path ended at the bay, so, tired and desperate for a temporary refuge from tourists, she pushed the Prius farther, morbidly curious whether this haggard road might dump her out without warning into the sea. It bumped between wooded ridges threaded with hiking trails that revealed themselves sporadically through the dense growth of red spruce and ferns. Then, after a mile of teasing her with glimpses of blue, it simply quit at a stony scar of the coast—a shelf of jagged, granite ledges that fanned like talons toward the great, heaving rumple of the bay.

At higher speed, she might have careened Thelma-and-Louise-style into space. But at a cautious twenty miles per hour, Glory had time to catch the break and halt the car several feet shy of a beige pickup that sat half-concealed in a thicket of blueberries.

The chill that brushed her neck rendered her motionless behind the wheel. Even dented and mud-splattered, something felt very wrong about the pickup's presence here at the end of such a lonely road. No sign designated the place a scenic vista, though scenic it was, those stippled granite walls festooned with seabirds and battered by surf. When she finally climbed from her car, Glory was struck by the contrast of the still woods—as though all the trees were holding their breath—and the white-capped bay busy huffing and puffing and spewing spray below.

She knew the truck was Blake's long before she spotted the keys hanging in the ignition, the battered copy of *The Sun Also Rises* flung up on the dash. Clearing a tangle of brush, Glory located the dent in the hood, and her brain began to fill with anxious static. She pushed through a low screen of bushes onto a steep knife slash of a path that skirted the cliffs. In the bay beyond spread a confetti of lobster buoys, the glinting mirage of a cruise ship as it trundled toward open sea. Uneasiness eclipsed her appreciation of this beauty. The path led to the very edge of the earth.

And at the end of it, she found not Blake, but a pile of clothes.

They lay in a neat stack: black sneakers and slacks, a button-down shirt, and a visor stamped with the golden arches. Glory dropped beside them and discovered Blake's Merits and her wallet with its Massachusetts driver's license and unsmiling photo. She stilled. The thunder of surf below pervaded her bones. Slowly, she raised her head and forced herself to peer out over the ledge where she knelt. The wreck of a lobster trap lay snagged among the rocks there, and a great snake of warp lashed to and fro in the cauldron of froth and foam.

"Blake!"

Her voice struggled to gain traction over the noise of the ocean. Still, she called out until her lungs threatened to split apart and the corrosive tang of regret claimed her tongue.

She had come too late. Blake had vanished here at the edge of the world. She rocked forward and spread her fingers across the damp rock, groping for something solid amid the sense she was plummeting. Then a twitch of pale movement caught her eye. Peering east, she followed the craggy line of rocks out two hundred yards farther to a pebbled hangnail of shore so small, it hardly qualified as a beach. There, a figure came thrashing from the water, tall and naked, streaming seafoam.

Morning Glory shot to her feet. She watched Blake Alvares squint up at her in shivering bewilderment. Her black hair clung to her scalp, and a tangle of brown seaweed had snared itself around one of her ankles. For an instant, she seemed to contemplate bolting back into the sea. All her muscles were tensed for flight. Then Glory called out once more, and Blake began a cautious advance up the gnarled staircase of rock that divided them.

It took her several minutes to pick her way across the gauntlet of barnacles and seaweed. Glory's breath caught as the woman staggered and slipped. Then, all at once, Blake unfolded herself upon the ledge before her, dripping and gasping, one hand pressed to her back. She made no attempt to cover herself as she returned Glory's incredulous stare.

"Are you real?" Blake's voice rang hoarse with salt.

Words deserted Glory like slips of paper on a breeze. None of the ones she had prepared would have been right anyway. She knew this as she gazed, open-mouthed, at the puckered scar on Blake's temple, the fading slash marks that crisscrossed her abdomen and hips. A bouquet of yellowing bruises bloomed along her rib cage. Above them, her breasts hung, heavy and glistening, dappled with a dozen pale, round scars. She wanted to look away. Could not.

Blake rubbed her eyes, which were laced with gruesome red. Deep purple crescents stamped the skin beneath them. "How are you here, Morning Glory?" She appeared almost frightened, as though convinced she was hallucinating.

"I took a detour . . ." That sounded ridiculous. Glory tried again. "Your letter was postmarked Ellsworth—so I came to Ellsworth."

Even this explanation felt absurd. The odds of finding Blake on this isolated claw of rock were infinitesimal. And yet here she stood, staring at a woman who had all but disappeared from the face of the planet. A woman who, perhaps, she ought to fear. But she didn't. As she stood gazing at Blake Alvares, Morning Glory felt only astonishment twined with regret.

Blake's arms dropped to her sides. She gathered her fingers into fists, enduring Glory's stare but still making no effort to reach for her clothes. When she spoke again, her voice was empty of anger or surprise. Weariness alone weighted her words.

"Does your mother know you've come here?"

"She...I told her I would find you. I owed her that much."

Face reddening, she picked up the pile of clothes and offered them to Blake, who clutched them in a ball, as though she had no use for them.

"What are *you* doing here?" Glory asked.

"Swimming. I like to swim."

"Here?"

"No one bothers me here."

Only when her teeth began to clatter did Blake seem to remember the clothes. She pulled them on stiffly. Glory noted the plastic name badge pinned over the breast pocket of her shirt and recalled the photo from the farmhouse of a teenage Blake in Army fatigues, her prison photo in the jumpsuit. It saddened her to consider the disparate uniforms this woman had worn in a single lifetime.

"Lee told me what those men did to you," she said quietly. "If I could undo all of this, I would."

Blake shrugged these words off into the wind. "No one gets that chance, Morning Glory. Forward's all there is."

She forced her feet into their big sneakers and walked out to the cliff's edge. There, she lowered herself upon a shelf of haggard rock and lit a cigarette, staring out across the bay. Glory followed uncertainly, her thoughts now all broken shards that she tried to piece together into what she truly wished to say.

"Mom misses you terribly, Blake."

The woman turned her face away. "How's that possible?"

"She's trying to save your garden. Even on days she can barely walk, she's out there, working on it."

Blake's cigarette burned down, forgotten, between her fingers. A long column of ash collapsed and scattered in the wind.

"She found the grave," Glory ventured softly. "You had a son, didn't you? Renato?"

At this, Blake pulled her knees to her chest and dropped her head against them. Over the humped mountains to the west, the sun poured brilliant fire. It lit her hunched shoulders, the sodden, salt-stiff tufts of her hair. For a long time, she made no sound at all. Then a ragged sigh escaped her.

"Ren," she whispered. "I called him Ren." Lifting her head, she fastened raw eyes on Glory. "His father was the man I killed."

"You mean . . . Angel Salazar?"

Blake's jaw tensed at the name. She nodded once and looked back at the water, voice so muted, Glory barely caught the words over the din of the surf. "He'd hurt me since I was eleven—burned me, beat me. Worse. Then I got pregnant, and I came up here. I had nowhere else to go."

Glory reached for a nearby pebble of dirty quartz and squeezed it until it left an imprint in her palm. That sharp, tiny pain helped to steady her. "Did the jury know?"

"No one knew. I couldn't tell them. I wouldn't." The hard lines of Blake's face threatened to collapse. "Ren was mine. Just mine. He was never Angel's."

Glory nodded. But she could not imagine it, the love a woman could feel for a child that had been forced upon her. A love that would lead her to live entombed by secrets. She uncurled her fingers and let the pebble tumble down the rocks into the surf.

"What happened to Ren?"

Blake tightened her arms around her knees.

"Crib death, they called it." Her lips quivered. "I never understood how it just . . . happened. I still don't."

"I'm sorry, Blake."

Glory realized that *this*, really, was what she had come to say, what she needed Blake to know. But whether the words reached their target or simply floated down into the waves, she could not tell. Blake's gaze never broke from the sea. She just sat there, shivering quietly, until her watch gave a brisk chirp, startling them both.

"I have a shift," she said, unfolding her body from the rock with a faint grimace. "I have to go."

"But—"

Blake was already climbing toward the trail, sneakers scuffing hurriedly through the dirt. "Please tell your mother I'm all right. Tell Leland and Quinnie, too, okay?" She halted just long enough to catch Glory's eyes. "Will you do that?"

As she scrambled to her feet, Glory briefly contemplated a standoff, a stoic refusal to return to Raker without the woman for whom she'd come searching. Yet, even as a plea for her to come home rose in her throat, she sensed its futility, maybe even its selfishness. Blake was free, after all. She had spent half her life in prison, but now she did not owe anything to anyone. If she chose to live out her days plunging alone into a frigid sea, she had earned that right. But Glory struggled to believe there was truth in the message Blake had requested she deliver. Struggled, and nodded assent nonetheless, for it was a small favor and the only one she was able to grant this woman she had so egregiously misjudged.

Maybe Leland had been right; in the end, the only remedy for mistakes was just fucking living with them. Maybe that, in itself, was a kind of bravery. But it did not feel brave. It felt a bit like shrinking. Once Blake had left her there upon that windy ridge, Glory felt smaller. And the ocean surrounding her had never felt so massive.

Though she had spent the past three years attempting to distance herself from it, she was grateful now to go home— even if that home was a ramshackle house on a salt marsh, inhabited by a woman who had spent too much of her life resigned to sorrow. Glory realized that the anger she had been dragging around all these years was a child's anger. As she drove back home along the darkening coast, she knew what she must become, what it would require all of her patience and courage to become. A woman, in the end, was no single thing, but an amalgam of hurts and dreams, victories and secrets, beauty and ugliness. And if she found another kindred soul in the universe with whom to share the complication of her being, with whom to make of her past a canvas of colliding colors to wonder at, then she was lucky. *Blessed*, her mother might say. Glory hoped Blake would see that she had a chance to seize upon that luck. But perhaps it was impossible to expect a person to recognize such an opportunity. That was the grinding truth of it all: Sometimes, by the time you saw the luck clearly, like the glimmer of a shell in the surf, it was dragged out with the tide.

19.

Quinn found the bones of the fawn scattered at the edge of woods by the marsh. She had been plucking idly at blueberries, popping them into her mouth to crush their tart flesh between her molars. The litter of bones made her drop the collection she had gathered in the pouch of her T-shirt and squat to inspect the arcs of yellowed ivory that poked up from the rotting leaves. A small canvas of spotted hide still flapped from a portion of rib cage. She stroked it with one berry-stained finger, head bent in tender mourning. She thought of the mother who had guarded this doomed creature through its first wobbly days and wondered what had become of her. Did mother deer grieve their lost children? Or did they flee deep into the woods and forget them?

She left the fawn's bones for the sun to bleach and waded out through the gold-brushed cordgrass toward the creek. There, she perched on the embankment slick and stippled with clay and watched the tide meander out. The blueberries had left their gritty skins in her teeth. She picked at them absently, feeling as empty as that carved-out snake of creek before her. Maybe that was all growing up was, a slow, inevitable hollowing out.

The breeze carried to her the smoke of Papa's cigarette

before she heard his feet in the grass. As he came to sit beside her, he let out a soft sigh, which Quinn interpreted as an expression of relief. He had warned her not to wander off from the house without telling him, but Quinn did not like having to report every time she felt she needed a little distance from the cabin.

He nodded at her purple fingers. "You save any, or did you eat 'em all?"

She shrugged.

"Thought we could try makin' a pie. Get Nora's recipe. She makes 'em good."

Quinn just dipped her head.

Papa's gray eyes rested on her a long moment. Sometimes, he looked at her like that, like all the words he had planned to say got scrambled up at the last minute and stuck in his throat.

"Quinnie," he said at last. "I'm proud of you for savin' the McDowell boy. I should've said it sooner."

She glanced up at him, hands clenched between her knees. "I told you, I didn't. An Amazon doesn't save her *enemies*."

Papa frowned. "Seems to me that Amazons do the right thing. Without even thinking about it, *n'est-ce pas?*"

Quinn bit the insides of her cheeks. "You ain't mad?"

"*Marde*, no." He put out his cigarette and plucked a stray leaf from the tangles of her hair. "Blake didn't want us to have enemies, did she?"

Quinn swallowed. "Blake ain't here."

"No," Papa sighed. "And I have no sternlady. So I done some thinkin'. Maybe I ought to be trainin' a new one—once she's done with math camp."

The words took a moment to register. "Thought I was banned."

"Well, if you want to run a lobster boat, I s'pose you got to learn how." He lowered his hand to her knee. "But Quinnie, you can't ever take off your lifejacket. And you got to do everythin' I say. I can't lose you, *ma puce*. You're the one thing in the universe I just can't lose."

Leaning against him, Quinn welcomed the familiar loop of his hard, heavy arm around her shoulder. He was going to give her another chance. She had not disappointed him, after all.

Still, she heard the worry in his voice, the fear he was pushing down for her sake. There would be no Blake now to help if something went wrong. It was just the two of them, Papa and his *flea*, charting a new course for themselves.

"You ain't gonna lose me," she said. "Not ever."

A week before Morning Glory was scheduled to return to school, she took Nora to Machias to get her nails done. Nora was not the sort who wished to develop a habit of dropping forty dollars in a salon every few weeks when she could pick up a bottle of Sally Hansen at the drugstore, but she lacked the heart to turn down her daughter's rare invitation, aware that when she departed for Virginia, they would not see one another again until Christmas. The thought of living alone now felt even more unbearable than it had the prior autumn. She tried to banish the dread of it from her mind as she and Glory reclined in mammoth massage chairs, their feet floating in bubbling pools of mineral water while Enya chanted through hidden speakers.

"Feels good, doesn't it, Mama?"

"I'm afraid I'm going to be terribly spoiled after this."

Her daughter smiled at her, a tender smile whose warmth caressed an aching place inside Nora. "That should be part of your daily regimen, along with the meds and that awful exercise bike. *Spoilage.*"

"You're going to be a very popular doctor if that's part of *all* your treatment plans."

Morning Glory lifted the hand Nora offered her across the chair, examined her fingers gently. They had grown rough from all the impromptu garden work she had undertaken at the farm. Nora had ceased bothering with gloves, wishing to experience all the textures of the plant world while she still could. The slime, the prickles, the thorns, they were a repertoire of tiny miracles that she resolved to commit to memory.

"You've got a splinter," Glory said. "You can't feel that, can you?"

Nora shrugged. Just as well she had been spared life's most minute pains.

The technician lifted one of her feet from the pool and toweled it dry, then worked a gritty pink cream into places where she had not been touched in a long time—the arch of her foot, the shell of her ankle. Nora closed her eyes and wondered who else beyond a lover would ever wish to touch someone there. Then she thought of how Blake had guided her foot into her sneaker, gently as she might a child's, the day that she had brought her to the garden. Blake, who had shown Nora so many small, shy acts of kindness.

"Mama?" Glory's voice pressed quietly through the memory. "I don't know if I can go back."

"Back where?" Nora asked.

But she knew. Suddenly, she found herself sinking into the massage chair. She reclaimed her hand and grasped the armrests in a clumsy effort to make herself taller, more resolute.

"I thought we settled this. I forbid you from staying here, Morning Glory. *Forbid.*"

Her daughter frowned down at her bubbling feet. "I've thought about it—*prayed*, even. And I couldn't forgive myself if—"

"—if you denied me the chance to see my only daughter

walk across the stage in May?" Nora shook her head. "No. I'm not sure that *I* could forgive you for that, either."

Glory made no reply. Both of them knew too well the changes that a year—or even a single day—could bring. Like water on its inevitable course seaward, life moved sometimes in meandering trickles, at others, in forceful torrents. While Nora struggled not to live in fear of its fluctuations, she was determined that her daughter would not.

"I've already reserved the hotel room for your graduation," she said. "Nonrefundable. So, enough of this."

After they had been scrubbed and moisturized, buffed and polished, they took the long way back to Raker Harbor. Nora knew Glory would bring her by the farm. Since her trip to Ellsworth, her daughter had joined her in puttering about the property, trimming, plucking, and tidying. She had even recruited Leland's help to haul over the lawn tractor, and the two of them took turns carving out a lawn from the wilderness of tall grass. The place did not look so neglected now, though there could be no question when gazing upon those long, vacant windows veined with cracks that the house belonged to the past. Wind and rain and snow would continue their patient work on it until the bones gave and the shingles scattered. Whatever refuge it had once provided, it would not offer again.

Each time they drove up the gravel lane, Nora's breath hitched a little in the hope Blake's truck might materialize there beside the house, her jaunty form come striding around the thicket. But today, like every other, the yard lay empty. Morning Glory veered toward the front walkway to pluck at weeds while Nora pegged her way slowly out back to survey the garden. The roses had come into full glory on the arbor, and the black-eyed Susans had exploded in great bundles of tawny gold along the perimeter of the quadrants.

And everywhere, there were butterflies—red admirals and monarchs and painted ladies. Such was August in eastern Maine, Nora thought, a stretch of breathtaking beauty that left one just drunk enough to endure the bleakness of another winter.

Today, in more pain than she wished to admit, she elected to sit once more beneath the apple tree. She had cut back the undergrowth there and taken to leaving upon the little slate a single bloom of whatever plant proved most spectacular that afternoon. On this day, it was a butter-yellow rose clipped from the arch. She tossed away yesterday's wilted offering, a scarlet lily, and touched her fingertips to the initials carved in the slate. Closing her eyes upon the sun that spilled through the twisted branches, she listened a long time to the whisper of dragonflies, the stirring of leaves, the supplicant nod of seeded blossoms. To the soft crunch of approaching feet that halted several yards behind her.

"I'm all right," she told Morning Glory. "Just give me a moment."

But when the breeze came up, it carried to her a whiff of cigarettes and sea. She steadied herself. If this were a dream, she did not wish to open her eyes.

"Stay," she whispered. "Please, stay."

The surrounding grass quivered. Head bent, Nora envisioned Blake kneeling there beside her, flannel work shirt tucked into faded jeans, black hair scattering in the wind. She summoned a memory of the pale scar that skirted her jaw, the shy flecks of amber that swam in the darkness of her eyes. She drew a timid breath and let herself hope.

"I know why you kept all those secrets," she began softly. "I've tried to understand, at least. It hurt too much, didn't it? And maybe you were afraid . . ."

Shadows danced beneath her quivering lids. Her hand

found the tiny comfort of the necklace. "I was afraid, too. Maybe I still am, a little. I told you I wasn't brave. But I want to be. I won't ever stop trying. I promise."

The hushed sigh might have been the breeze, or the rustle of dying leaves. So Nora kept her eyes shut and pressed her other hand more firmly to the cooling slate. "Will you tell me about him someday?" she whispered. "About your son, Renato?"

No answer came but the call of distant marsh birds.

Nora's shoulders sagged. She let go of the necklace. And then, a calloused thumb brushed her own upon the slate. She raised her head and saw how the air around her had filled with the flutter of sunlit wings—the latest arrivals to the blooming world whose creator squatted, scarred and solemn, beside her.

Blake spread her hand across the stone and lifted her face to the swaying branches. Light tangled with shadow as it skipped across her softening features.

"He was born the first day of winter," she said. "It was my seventeenth birthday."

She arrived in town too late to catch the *All In.* As she passed the harbor, she glimpsed the boat tethered out on her mooring, jouncing stoically against the ruffled expanse of deep blue and the distant, bristled silhouettes of the pine isles. Home now, she took her time passing through the village, greeting its landmarks once more and wondering if the thing she felt unfurling inside her was joy or merely the tease of nerves. Too early to tell. Shades pushed up, she drove out along the pitted road northwest, past thick bursts of Queen Anne's lace and trees just beginning to sport their autumn fancywear. When she spotted the dented mailbox with the lime-green buoy nailed to its post, she hooked a left down the trail to the Savard cabin. Leland's truck sat in the clearing beside a heap of gear. Blake gripped the wheel and scanned the yard for Quinn. But it was the young lobsterman who stepped alone from the cabin, still in fishing clothes, his hair so long, it nearly touched his broad shoulders.

He jogged down the steps, eyes wide with boyish surprise, the hint of teeth flashing beneath his stubbled lip. As she stepped from the truck, she scarcely managed to clear the door before he engulfed her in arms so powerful, they elicited a throb from her still-healing spine.

"Amazon," he said. Greeting enough.

It took Blake a moment to recover from that hug. She flushed, stammered, reached for her cigarettes. Leland had his lighter ready. His eyes swept over her in a shy investigation. She did not forget the gentleness of his hands that throbbing night in July, the unexpectedness of that, of him. She took an unsteady drag and cleared her throat.

"You keep your word?" she asked.

His face darkened. "Not rainin' hell on those McDowell assholes is the hardest thing I ever done, Blake."

She rested a hand on his arm and squeezed it once. "There'll be harder things, Captain."

"Maybe. Maybe not."

A small pile of traps leaned against the old shed, awaiting repairs. Blake considered it as she exhaled a stream of cautious smoke. She felt jittery, her limbs all pins and needles. In her pocket, she touched the petals of the yellow rose Nora had given her—a rose she might press and keep, the first of a new collection, or perhaps surrender to the wind, where some things of fleeting beauty better belonged.

"I came by," she began, "to see if you might need a sternman."

Leland cocked his head, eyebrows knit. "Already got one, actually."

Her heart fell. Then she saw his mouth twitch, the roguish creases his smile made in his poorly shaven face. He pointed toward a gap in the trees that opened onto a narrow path.

"She's out by the marsh, pickin' heather. Maybe the two of you can work somethin' out."

Blake punched his shoulder and stamped out her smoke. She started down the trail of ferns and roots and blueberries, her feet noiseless, breath timorous. She could hear the girl's voice before the forest dropped away, the high lyrics of a new song floating across the vast sweep of cordgrass.

When Blake emerged at the edge of the marsh, she saw her, loose-haired and gangly limbed, twirling with her bundles of heather, her face tipped up to the pinkening clouds and kissed with all the simple, unstolen joy that Blake wished for her forever.

She advanced a short distance, reluctant to interrupt this ceremony. She knelt in the grass and waited. And when Quinn's eyes finally detached from the heavens and spotted her, when her waif's body ceased its twirling, there was no hesitation in her shout or the way she sent her fistfuls of flowers flying, her arms arcing wide. She ran at Blake, who barely managed to absorb the sunny, salty force of her.

"Quinnie!"

It was the only word she could manage—a declaration of love irrepressible. The girl had gotten hold of her. She did not let go.

Water Finds a Way

Acknowledgments

My eighth grade English teacher, MaryBeth Wing, dubbed me "a writer". Twenty-five years later, I'm grateful for this opportunity to thank her in print. She remains a mentor, friend, and inspiration.

My deepest gratitude extends to my agent, Felicia Eth, who believed in this book and never ceased fighting for it. Thank you, also, to the talented team at Delphinium Books: Jennifer Ankner-Edelstein, for her guidance and encouragement, and Joe Olshan, whose keen insight made *Water Finds a Way* a better novel.

To the earliest readers of this manuscript, particularly Ann Ratcliffe and Leigh Crank Perry, a heartfelt thanks for your uplifting words and insistence that this novel be brought into the greater world. An additional thank you to my extraordinary CLAS and WC team for their grounding humor and steadfast support. And to all the women of words who generously offered me their time and insight regarding the road to publication: I will not forget your kindness.

When I was a child, my father taught me his love of the ocean. I remain grateful to both my parents for introducing me to so many different passions and experiences. For my mother, who will never take any credit: you have brought more beauty into this world than I can ever hope to bring. Thank you.

Lastly, to Christopher, my Canadian goose: You helped make this dream come true. I could not ask for a better partner in life, love, and adventure.

About the Author

Meghan Perry grew up in New England and holds an MFA from Emerson College. Her work has appeared in *Sycamore Review*, *Cold Mountain Review*, and *The Fourth River*, among other publications. A lifelong educator, she currently directs the Writing Center at an independent secondary school on the North Shore of Massachusetts and devotes her free time to exploring wild and remote places with her family. *Water Finds a Way* is her first novel.